DEEP
DOWN

KAREN HARPER

DEEP DOWN

**Doubleday Large Print
Home Library Edition**

MIRA®

ISBN-13: 978-1-61523-028-0

DEEP DOWN

**This Large Print Book carries the
Seal of Approval of N.A.V.H.**

"The Cherokees speak of the ginseng plant as a sentient being. . .able to make itself invisible to those unworthy to gather its roots."
—William Bartram, naturalist, Philadelphia, 1791

"Ginseng is the child of lightning. It blends yin and yang, darkness and light."
—Chinese legend

"I'm not afraid of my ginseng garden being robbed anymore. . .my guns will hold their position with their eyes wide open day and night."
—L. J. Wilson, *Special Crops*, 1908 journal

"For the love of money is the root of all kinds of evil."
—*I Timothy* 6:10

1

Eastern Kentucky, Appalachia
September 4, 2007

Head down, her eyes skimming the ground, Mariah Lockwood walked the woods. She was looking for ginseng, not to dig and sell its roots as so many Appalachians did, but to count the plants that sprang from the precious roots. At this altitude, the herb was especially easy to spot right now with its yellowing leaves and clusters of red berries. The buried treasure of the ginseng root was worth millions to its buyers, especially in the massive Chinese market. Wild wood American ginseng, locally called sang, was getting so rare it was threatened, and that's where she came in.

Seven years ago, her daughter, Jessica, had gotten her the nice-paying job of ginseng counter in these parts. The human-body-shaped ginseng root was on the U.S. government's endangered species list. If Mariah's yearly count went down too far, exports would cease and lots of Appalachians, as well as the Chinese and other deep-pocket buyers, would be spitting mad.

Since the sun was sinking fast, this site would be Mariah's last stop of the day. Yet, feeling the pinch of hunger, she stopped to pluck some pawpaws. Most places, the little, banana-shaped fruits ripened later, but where the setting sun streamed past the peaks, they were ready early. Their sweet flavor was an acquired taste, but she and Jessie loved them baked and served with cream.

As she savored the soft pulp, Mariah wondered what her girl was eating in Hong Kong at that big conference on cultivating ginseng. Probably chop suey, rice and lots of tea. More than once, Jessie had wanted her mother to travel with her, but traveling to Lexington for her doctorate graduation was as far as Mariah wanted to stray from this area she knew and loved.

"This is the forest primeval," Jessie had quoted from some poem the last time the two of them had walked the woods. Ever since Mariah had agreed to let Dr. Elinor Gering take Jessie into her home near the Kentucky university campus in Lexington, she'd taken fast to book-learning, though the little town of Deep Down and its people still ran fierce in her blood. Although Jessie used to spend every August here, she'd been too busy this year, and Mariah couldn't help but wonder if Drew Webb's return had something to do with that.

Before she checked her last sang spot—one of her secret ones, far back in the smallest hardwood cove huddled up to the stony skirts of Snow Knob—she got her a notion to walk the rocks of Bear Creek, just like in the old days. She and Nate had courted here beside its rushing waters, jumping from rock to rock and sitting out on the biggest one to share corn bread and kisses. When they were both nineteen, smack-dab in the middle of that rock—their island, they'd called it—he'd asked her to marry up with him, and Jessie had been born the very next year. The precious, nearby sang patch had provided roots that paid for her gold wedding band, their marriage license and some blankets and dishes to set up housekeeping.

With her pack slung over her shoulder, she jumped to the first rock, then leapt from stone to stone, just as she and Nate had, holding hands. The year Jessie turned eight, she'd lost him in a freak accident when he was repairing a barn roof for extra cash. Though she was still young and could have used someone to support them, she'd never wanted to wed again. A one-woman man, that was her. And sometimes here, like right now, she felt her curly haired and sky-blue-eyed Nate was still with her, laughing, leaping. No way this place made her sad.

Finally, reluctantly, much farther down the creek, she stepped back on firm ground again. In the spring or after a rain, the creek rose high and covered some of these stones as if they weren't here at all—like folks you'd loved and lost but you knew were still there, just below the surface of your rushing thoughts.

From the slant of sun, Mariah reckoned it was after seven. Evening shadows stretched long and dark, 'specially here at the foot of Snow Knob. Hurrying now, she set off again. She was fixin' to get this last site counted before she went home. The familiar forest trail snaked through the fern-carpeted floor ever deeper into the bass-wood and walnut trees, the kinds sang liked for company. A ragged canopy over-head that threw mottled shade and sun—that was sang country.

Already she could hear Bear Falls, which fed the creek, crashing down its limestone stairs. She'd once joshed Seth Bearclaws, the only full-blooded Cherokee round here, by asking if the falls were named after him. But Seth didn't have a sense of hu-mor, 'specially about someone counting or digging sang in the old sacred places of his people.

As if the thought of diggers had sum-moned them, Mariah's practiced eye picked up signs they'd been through here, or at least someone had used the sharp edge of a shovel or hoe as a kind of cane as he walked this path. A few small limbs were snapped off too, as if to mark a way back out. She prayed they hadn't found her special spot, untouched all these twenty-eight years, maybe even longer. Folks not only poached sang off-season, but outright stole and even killed to get or protect the root. Right now was legal sang season, but diggers had to get a license and fill out all kinds of government forms when they sold it, and the local game was to get around all that. Her friend Cassie had said she thought picking sang was a rite of passage 'round here, and Drew Webb had opined it had something to do with testosterone, or whatever that male hormone was that made men feisty and daring.

Vern Tarver, who owned the sang store and historical museum in town, had argued that if George Washington knew the value of ginseng and Daniel Boone made money selling it, why should folks today have to change their ways? Appalachians over the centuries had considered hunting anything, anytime, their God-given right and couldn't abide the government telling them what to do. Not when sang money had brought many of their kin through the Depression or tided them over in other tough times.

Mariah figured it didn't take the likes of Vern Tarver to know sang roots were worth as much as one thousand dollars a pound in Asian markets. It was next to useless to try to tell Eastern Kentuckians to let the sang alone for a few years till it matured or to be sure to replant the precious berries when they dug up a site, no matter if the new sheriff said times and laws were different now.

The Chinese buyers who came into Vern Tarver's store, smooth as they were with their clean hands and hard cash, Mariah liked less than poachers or careless diggers. The big money market encouraged ripping out roots, legal season or not, and she knew Vern was only too happy to play middleman to get his cut. No use trying to talk sense to him, 'specially not since she'd told him to stop trying to sweetheart her. He'd near on had a fit when she'd told him no to his fancy marriage proposal, and if he couldn't accept that, just not to come 'round no more.

Yes, she saw the footsteps with the hoe marks heading toward her deep woods sang patch. If that fancy GPS thingamajig or the tiny cell phone the government had given her worked worth a darn in these hills and hollers, she'd use them right now to call Sheriff Drew Webb, tell him to watch in town for illegal sales of prime, old roots. She'd have him stake out another spot she knew. She could give him the location by the landmarks she always went by, never mind satellite coordinates that were no good, no how here. Why use things in outer space to find where you were, when you knew these woods like your own back forty?

Mariah hunkered down to examine the torn ground where someone had dug out the patch of sang—four-prongers, at least, if she rightly recalled her notes from last count. In all her forty-eight years, this was the weirdest-looking dig she'd seen. Odd hoe marks, strangely curved, pierced the ground in a pattern. A big hoe, a sharp one, but not carelessly used. No, the slashes in the earth were exact, deep and powerfully placed.

She couldn't picture anyone from Deep Down doing this so precisely, then stuffing their prizes in the usual pillowcase or back-pack and just hightailing it back to town.

Strangest of all, the lopped-off yellowing plants and their red berries were laid out in designs around the edge, like some foreign work of art.

Then, even through the muted roar of the falls and the rustling leaves, she heard a sound she couldn't place.

What in creation? A footstep? Someone snapping a branch? She'd been a wildcrafter almost all her life, picking wild herbs, mushrooms and moss to sell to outsiders as far away as Highboro or even Lexington. She knew the normal forest sounds and scents, but some new, heavy smell—fetid and yeasty, or was it moth balls?—came to her on the breeze.

Slowly, in the middle of the ravaged, rearranged sang patch, she stood. Turning her head, she tried to pierce the narrow shafts of sun stabbing almost horizontal between the tree trunks. For once, this vast, deep woods seemed to press in on her. Mariah had never claimed to have the sixth sense of some mountain women, including her own mother, but she sensed danger now. Someone else was out here close, something waiting for the shadows to deepen, maybe for her to leave. It could be a bear, but she didn't think so. They liked to make themselves real scarce, and they didn't smell like that. It wasn't skunk, she thought, as her nostrils flared.

Hair prickled on the nape of her neck. Maybe she'd surprised a digger who'd rubbed some sort of homemade liniment or bug juice on his skin, and he was watching, waiting. Maybe he knew she'd recognize him and didn't want to get caught without a license, afraid she'd tell Drew Webb.

For the first time in her life, alone in the woods, Mariah Lockwood tasted bitter, raw fear. She'd surprised poachers and diggers before, and they could be as dangerous as those who grew the stuff and guarded it with shotguns and no shut-eye. But she'd always just made a quick retreat or told them she'd keep quiet. When a mountain person made a vow, that was that. So why did this feel different?

Hefting her pack with her precious records and lists of landmarks, Mariah edged back toward the path she'd taken coming in. She wouldn't walk the rocks of the creek this time, but hightail it back to the old logging road.

Then, about thirty feet away, she saw something blocking her path.

She let out a half grunt, half scream. The sun-streaks behind the large, dark thing blinded her. *Was* it a bear? This was not some sort of prank or joke. Pure menace reeked from it, along with that smell.

She threw her trembling arms over her head to make herself look larger and shouted in a loud voice, "Bear, go! Go!" Not only did it not run, but it took a step forward and lifted something in its paw or hand.

Not a bear, no, it held itself more erect. And bears didn't use tools. Bulky, maybe human, but grotesque with that fur—that obscured face and strange-shaped head. Despite all the legends of forest creatures, none told of an Appalachian yeti or big ape. It had something shiny and sharp in its paw or hand. Hellfire, had that thing been digging sang?

Though it would take hours in the dark to get back down to town another way, she turned and fled. Her pulse pounded in her ears; her innards nearly let loose. The things in her pack bounced; the shoulder strap slipped down her arm so the pack almost tripped her. She hadn't run dead out in years . . . dead out.

Her breath rasped in her throat. Was this a nightmare, and she'd wake up? Was that thing a haint like folks said appeared from the dead? A shape-changing monster from one of Seth's Cherokee myths?

She took a tumble over a tree root and lost her pack. She scrambled up again, on hands and knees at first, then stumbling, staggering. It was coming after her in wide strides at a jogging pace, breaking tree limbs, hitting something against tree trunks. With stark fear in her soul, she was sweating, shaking. She did not look back at the thing, but looked into her heart. Jessie, she thought, so far away, so smart. Proud of her, she was, though sometimes she regretted giving her away, sending her away . . .

Away . . . She had to get away . . .

Despite the heat and humidity hitting her like a hammer, Dr. Jessica Lockwood was excited to get out of the plush, air-conditioned lobby of her Hong Kong hotel. Most people at the conference spoke decent English, but for this foray outside she'd hired one of the translators, Sunny Chan, to accompany her to nearby Ko Shing Street, also called Ginseng Street.

It was only a little after seven in the morning—that would make it just after 7 p.m. of the previous day at home, she thought—and she was astounded by the impact of the oppressive weather and the push of people, both in business suits and traditional clothing. Cursing her naturally curly, flyaway tresses, sprung loose by the instant steam bath of humidity, she shoved her chin-length hair back behind her ears and headed out.

The crowds seemed as oppressive as the heat. However much she had travelled for research or relaxation, she never quite seemed to shake the habit of judging everything against quiet, little Deep Down, the tiny Appalachian town with a population of 127 where she was reared—raised up, as her mother would put it. Sometimes in her head, the slow, flat drawl of her mother's voice battled with the undulating speech of Elinor, the Lexington professor who had been her guardian from the time she'd turned sixteen.

"I can't believe how busy it is already," Jessie told the petite, pretty translator as people rushed past. "I was hoping to talk to a few ginseng sellers before the masses hit."

"Masses hit?" Sunny echoed in her clipped, British accent as she arched her winged eyebrows. "Oh, you mean before it gets crowded. Believe me, the shop owners would be very honored to speak with you."

Although Jessie's presentation on how ginsenosides from the ginseng herb significantly slowed the growth of breast cancer cells in test tubes had been well-received, she realized Sunny meant that the reputation of wild Appalachian ginseng was strong in Asia. As they managed to avoid darting workers with cloths coiled around their heads for elaborate sweatbands, the first shop they came to proved the power of U.S. sang.

She couldn't read the handwritten calligraphy on the sign, but the U.S. flag was elaborately drawn and colored in on a poster next to a picture of a hairy, two-legged, two-armed ginseng root and an arrow beckoning buyers to step inside. Yes, wild forest Appalachian sang had a strong reputation here and was increasingly trendy at home. If it proved useful in the battle against endocrine-driven cancers, its demand and value would escalate even more.

But suddenly, strangely, this place was getting to her.

Jessie had loved the lofty view from her quiet room in the almost futuristic glass-and-steel skyscraper hotel, with the freighters and junks in the harbor and the mountain-studded monster of mainland China looming beyond. But she felt enclosed, trapped here. This cluttered, crowded shop was a far cry from Vern Tarver's Fur and Sang Trader at home. Amidst all these unique, jumbled herbs, a strange smell slammed her square in the stomach, fetid, rich, yeasty. The familiar ginseng, yes, but something else, something forbidding, even dangerous.

Jessie glanced around for the source of the smell. Displayed on wooden trays in the long, narrow shop, which seemed like something out of a medieval time capsule, were some things she could recognize and some she could not.

"Bird nests and shark fins—very expensive—for health-giving soups," Sunny was explaining in a singsong voice as she translated the cards sticking out of each box. "Dandelion for gallbladder cleansing, deer tail for back pain, dried lizard to improve weak kidneys, dried sea horse for asthma and, oh, for sexual problems, too."

Sexual problems, Jessie thought. The only problem she had was the lack of a man in her life. In fact, her past with guys was as gnarled and twisted as the sang roots she spotted heaped up farther back in the store, where a Chinese woman with a face webbed with wrinkles was pawing through a pile with a calculator in one hand.

Sunny rattled off some Chinese to the old woman, though the only word Jessie could pick out was *jen-shen.* The Chinese word for the herb meant "root of life." The woman's wizened face lifted; she eyed Jessie as if she were going to price her to sell. Though Jessie had longed to see the inside of a ginseng shop in the land where much of the $52 million-a-year market was based, she had to keep herself from fleeing. The woman was not frightening, so what was wrong with her? Was she coming down with some exotic sickness, or were the smells and heat just getting to her? All this seemed so far away from her mother and Kentucky. And from the strange yearnings she'd had for Drew Webb, whom she knew was back in Deep Down.

"She's saying," Sunny told her, "last year she had a root she displayed on velvet cloth go for six figures in American money. Came from Kentucky. She wants to know, you have any to sell?"

"She must know it's all regulated," Jessie protested. "Did she get that root from the black market?"

"She says she know nothing of black market."

Jessie's head was beginning to pound. She had to get out of here. Her heartbeat sped up, as if she'd run miles.

"Now with Americans putting *jen-shen* in power drinks and health foods," Sunny was translating again, "costs going up . . ."

Jessie squinted back into the dim reaches of the shop where women of all ages bent over rows of cardboard boxes on long wooden tables, sorting ginseng. When the shop owner saw where she was looking, she spoke to Sunny, who said, "She say her sorters, even if they are old, have soft, young hands from touching the *jen-shen* all day. She say the herb preserve *yin,* the life force, and good for aphrodisiac and keep people young."

If her head had not been pounding and her stomach roiling, Jessie would have laughed. If ginseng was a fountain of youth, why did this old woman look like some ancient sorceress who had stepped from the pages of a book on primordial myths? She had to get back into the calm of the hotel. She felt a stab of longing for her mother, for the cool, leafy coves in the skirts of the mountains.

"I feel a bit faint," Jessie told Sunny and managed a polite nod to the old woman. "Please thank her for speaking with me. I'm going to head back to the hotel."

She walked as steadily as she could, though she felt the urge to run. Had the other-side-of-the-world time zone difference given her delayed jet lag? At least her headache wasn't caused by staring too long into a microscope at floating ginsenosides attacking tiny cancer cells and tumors in the test tubes. Hours of research sometimes made her eyes cross and her brain blank out. She felt like that now and, worse, as if something in the midst of these towering skyscrapers in old-new Hong Kong were chasing her.

The shrill ring-ring, ring-ring dragged Jessie from deep, dream-haunted sleep. It took her a moment to recall she was in her Hong Kong hotel room. Exhausted, she'd collapsed in bed after her visit to Ko Shing St., almost as if that strange smell in the herb shop had drugged her. Her bedside table clock read 7:17 p.m. She'd missed the afternoon lectures and the tour of the city she'd signed up for. Maybe it was some conference attenders on the phone, wondering if she could meet them for dinner or why she'd missed the tour bus.

She grabbed the receiver. "Dr. Jessica Lockwood."

"Jess? Sheriff Webb in Deep Down—Drew."

Her heartbeat kicked up even more. No one has ever called her Jess but Drew. Despite the coolness of the room, she shoved the duvet and covers off. She began to sweat. She'd know that voice anywhere, deep, husky. It was a voice she'd known since her earliest memories, one that haunted her. Something must be wrong at home, very wrong.

"Drew, what is it?"

"You were hard to trace. Cassie gave me your Lexington apartment and your lab number, but then I found this Hong Kong hotel number with a note in your mother's kitchen. Jess, I know you're thousands of miles away, but can you come home right away? I'm sorry to inform you that your mother's missing."

She gasped. "Missing? What happened? Missing how?"

"As best I can tell she went out counting sang and just didn't come back. Vern Tarver dropped by her house after dinner yesterday evening but couldn't find her, though her truck was there. He checked all around, called people, but she wasn't at Cassie's—nowhere—so he called me. I rechecked her neighbors and friends but no leads. I've had a search party out since daybreak—they're still out, some even with hounds. But she covers a wide area, and I don't know her sang counting spots. Do you?"

She raked her fingers through her hair. "Some. I—I'm not supposed to head home until tomorrow. Maybe she twisted her ankle or something like that. Please keep looking. She knows those woods like the back of her hand."

"Yeah, but some of those spots are secret and deep in. I'm really sorry to have to call you like this. Be assured we'll keep looking, all of us. You—you did know I'm sheriff here now?"

"She told me. Be a good one, Drew. Please, please find her safe and sound. I'll make arrangements to fly back as soon as I can, and I'll call you. Here's my cell number if you need it." She recited it to him, and he gave her his.

"But you know it's better to use the land-lines around here," he reminded her. "Even now, the mountains make a difference. Jess, take care and see you soon."

The line went dead. For one moment, she stared at the sleek receiver in her hand, seeing Drew that last night, furious, hurt—naked. She'd just been told the last thing in the world she could bear to hear. And from the last and only man she had ever really loved.

2

"You want me to call in more guys with their hounds tomorrow?" Sheriff Chuck Akers asked Drew over the two-way radio. His former boss and mentor, sheriff of the Lowe County seat in Highboro, was out in the woods with one of the search parties for Mariah Lockwood.

Drew was running the rescue effort—he hoped to hell it wasn't a recovery operation—out of the old house that was now his police station: an apartment where he lived upstairs; downstairs, a reception desk and phone center behind a counter, both run by Emmy Enloe; his office; a supply room and two holding cells. He had no deputy, so Emmy was his entire staff. Today he'd moved her onto the front porch to keep track of volunteer searchers. Usually as quiet as the grave, his office and the whole town were in chaos today.

Drew had just come in from using a search warrant to go through Mariah's unlocked front door, which he'd secured and put police tape across when he left. Two days ago, he hadn't gone farther than the kitchen when he went in, looking for Jess's contact information when the numbers her friend Cassie had given him turned out to be dead ends. Mariah's place looked neat enough. He'd need Jess to tell him if anything was really disturbed or missing, other than two pairs of old shoes he'd taken to scent the hounds with.

"Drew, you read me?" came Akers's scratchy voice.

"I read, Sheriff. You're breaking up, but go ahead."

"I got me two more groups I can send out tomorrow."

"I'll let you know first thing in the morning. We need to call it a night now before it gets pitch-dark. Besides, I don't trust some of the volunteers to just look for signs of her instead of shooting at anything that moves, like the Shelton kid did. Said he saw a huge buck. I've got the woods full of search parties, and I don't need someone killed," he said and signed off.

Someone killed. The words echoed in his head. He'd been praying that something terrible hadn't happened to Mariah. If it had, he didn't know how he could tell Jess. But then, he wasn't sure how he could face her, anyway, after all this time. Water way over the dam, sure, but it still ate at him. She was twenty-eight now and he was thirty-four, so that meant they hadn't spoken for nearly twelve years before that brief international phone call. What happened between them was so long ago—almost in another life. So why did it still haunt him?

He startled when someone spoke close behind him. He prided himself on being aware of people sneaking up, but then Cassie Keenan had always moved as silently as a wraith.

"She's just nowhere I knew to look," Cassie called out as she poked her red head in the front door.

"Thanks for searching, anyway," Drew told her.

Once Jess's best friend, Cassie was the local beauty, if you could look past the vacant stares, when she sometimes seemed to drift off to somewhere else. For once she didn't have her darling little four-year-old, Pearl, with her. A wildcrafter like Mariah, Cassie had no husband, never had.

Though an illegitimate child was fairly common around here, she'd never told anyone who Pearl's father was, and she was such a loner no one yet had managed a good guess. Just the other day, Drew had told Vern Tarver to shut his yap when he'd joked about Pearl being the second child ever born by immaculate conception.

If Cassie wanted to keep that secret, it was fine with Drew, except she was barely making it financially on her own. More than once he'd bought her groceries, using the excuse he appreciated her cooking a meal for him. That was a big lie since she always put strange plants and herbs in about everything she made, and Drew had always favored meat and potatoes—or since his years in Italy, pasta.

"I been to lots of spots with Mariah to

gather moss and herbs," Cassie went on, "but can't find hide nor hair of her in any of them, nor the sang spots I know. Guess she had to keep her counting spots real quiet, so they didn't get poached or dug up. I can 'preciate that—her keeping something to herself. But if she was counting sang at her secret sites, Jessie's the only one might know all of them."

"That's what I figured, too. She'll be home—here—in a couple of hours. She called when her plane landed in Cincinnati before she caught a commuter to Lexington."

"Poor thing, driving in the dark to all this. Too bad Dr. Gering died last year, or she would've come with her sure. I'm praying she's not lost her blood mother, well as her foster one. You just let me know when she's here now, 'cause maybe I can help her some." With a flutter of one delicate hand, she was gone.

Cassie's comments made Drew realize how much of Jess's life he had missed. He'd never met the woman who had been a second mother to her. After the big blowup here over Jess and him, Mariah had sent her to live with a UK professor who specialized in Appalachian dialect. Jess had come home every August, so he'd heard, but, except for a couple of month-long leaves, he'd been away for years, first overseas with the marines and then as a deputy in Highboro, around the other side of Big Blue.

He thought he'd made a good life for himself, but so had Jess. Though some in town resented her "fancy book-learning," as far as he was concerned, she was Deep Down's big success story. He thought Jessica Lockwood made a mockery of the stale, old joke that the only good thing that ever came out of Deep Down was an empty bus.

"Sheriff, how 'bout I fetch you some more coffee or apple pie? Or you in dire need of a good back rub?"

Audrey Doyle, who ran the only restaurant in town, the Soup to Pie, draped herself in his doorway. He had to admit she'd been helping with things today, offering free coffee to search parties. Unfortunately, ever since he'd been back in town, she'd been offering him a lot more than that and she didn't like to take no for an answer. With her long, platinum hair and too tight jeans holding in a voluptuous figure, Audrey was cruising for a third husband. He was not interested in more than food and local information from her.

"No, thanks. I'm fine."

"You sure are. You're doing a great job."

"I'm not doing a great job, because we haven't found her," he said, as he brushed past her onto the porch where Emmy and two other girls were sitting at a card table, manning the lists and locations of searchers. He saw several groups coming back into town, some walking, some in their pickups with yapping hounds in the back. He wondered if anyone had taken sang from Mariah's precious sites, so carefully counted.

Audrey sidled up behind him, close enough that he could feel her breath on the nape of his neck. "I know some folks resent having a sheriff here, but I think it's long overdue," she whispered.

"Thanks for the vote of confidence," he said and bent over Emmy's shoulder to skim the lists. Audrey took the hint and sashayed back toward the Soup to Pie three doors down.

Despite Audrey's soft-soap compliments,

Sheriff Drew Webb knew he had a lot to prove to Deep Downers and those in the surrounding rural areas of his jurisdiction. He had things to prove to himself, too. And now to Jess Lockwood.

Despite the fact he'd been hell on wheels in his younger days, Drew had been sent from Highboro to his old stomping grounds as their first sheriff for three reasons: first, he'd earned a good reputation both in the marines and in Highboro; second, Sheriff Akers was getting too old to leave Highboro and police this area every time something went wrong; and third, because the town, despite its sleepy demeanor and rural charm, was smack in the center of this area's lucrative ginseng trade, and the state was really cracking down on sang as an endangered herb.

Strange that a plant, a root, had got him his job. But it meant he made enemies, too, every time he enforced the Lacey Act antipoaching laws against those who illegally took or bought sang in these hills. Worse, Deep Downers thought that gathering sang, even in the cultivated forest patches planted by others, was their right. Drew knew he had to watch his back—and he was starting to fear Mariah Lockwood should have watched hers, too.

Jessie Lockwood ached all over from holding herself tense, waiting to hear news about her mother on the cell phone she kept on the car seat beside her—not that cells worked well more than half the time in the eastern part of the "Great Commonwealth of Kentucky," as she'd so often heard the state called. She felt stiff from the endless flight back to the U.S., mentally fogged from the jet lag and now from this three-and-a-half-hour, twisting drive from Lexington to Deep Down. On a short straightaway, she snatched another swig from her now-cold coffee container.

Darkness had descended like a steel trap about halfway home—if Deep Down was really home anymore—but she knew the roads well. Over and over, she agonized about what could have happened to her mother: a sprained or broken ankle in a groundhog hole; tripping on a tree root; a slip on a mossy stone in a creek, so that she fell and knocked herself out. Maybe she'd run into illegal diggers who had been more than she could handle and had tied or beat her up. But then, why didn't the searchers find her?

Familiar landmarks swept by as Jessie fought to keep her mind on her driving, her bloodshot eyes on the corkscrew road between Big Blue and Sunrise Mountains. Despite her visit during the Christmas holidays last year, she should have come home in August as usual. She should have visited more often, not let the breakthrough in her lab work and her nerves about facing Drew Webb keep her away. As much as she was grateful for her life outside the hills, she didn't need a shrink to tell her she still had a deep-seated anger issue at her mother for giving her away. Nevertheless, she should have phoned her from Hong Kong, whatever it cost, to say she was all right and to check how her mother was.

What if she never saw her again? What if she could never tell her that she was grateful for the sacrifice she had made to let her live with Elinor and get an education and—

Deep Down, 3 miles. The sign leapt into her headlights from the darkness.

Three miles and a lifetime back. She

was twenty-eight, but it suddenly seemed only yesterday she'd left with Elinor . . .

"You can call your mother and speak to her anytime you want, you know, Jessica." She heard Elinor's voice now as clearly as she had in that big sedan twelve years ago, heading the other way on this road. "My work brings me back into this area often, and I'll bring you for visits, of course."

"I still don't want to leave. What'd you mean when you said on the phone that I was your lies and do little? I don't lie and I been a hard worker, both me and Mommy, ever since Daddy died."

A little smile peeked at the corners of Elinor's mouth. "Of course you're truthful and a hard worker. Mariah is, too. I've been impressed by both of you ever since you first helped me with the vocabulary and the definitions. You see, I didn't say 'your lies' and 'do little.' Eliza Doolittle is a character in a play—in a Broadway musical, too. A man named Professor Henry Higgins took her into his home to study the way she spoke and to help her to speak more properly, and I'm hoping that's one of the gifts I can give you. A bright girl like you doesn't need to spend her whole life looking for herbs and moss in the woods like Mariah and your friend Cassandra."

"I was fixin' to be a wildcrafter, too. It takes lots of know-how in the woods."

"Of course it does. But there's an entire world outside places like Highboro and Deep Down. Jessica, as I told your mother, I don't have a child, and I will give you that wide world—my world—as best I can. Besides, that Webb boy who accosted you is a no-account. He'd ruin you and never look back . . ."

But Jess was looking back now.

Deep Down, 2 miles

Drew had not accosted her. She wasn't sure back then what that even meant, but she knew what they'd been caught doing had been powerful and mutual, despite the fact they weren't even sweethearting and he had another girl. She guessed that was mostly why her mother decided she should go live with Elinor. "I don't want you breeding Webb young-uns, living in some trailer in a holler!" she'd screeched at her that night. Later, Jessie heard Drew had left, too, joining the marines and living overseas.

But now she was going back to where

she and Drew might have to work together to find her mother, going back to where she needed him in a whole new way from how she used to . . .

Drew Webb had been the most handsome, exciting—if hellfire raised—boy she'd ever known. Sure, he was six years older than her sixteen when everything blew up, but that was real exciting. He'd seemed so experienced compared to her. Why, back then, he'd been to far places like Frankfort and even Ohio, visiting kin. Of course, from the time she fell for him at age twelve till that only night he'd touched her, he hadn't known she was alive, at least not the way she'd wanted him to. "Skinny and bug-bit," Cassie said he'd called her once.

That night, Drew had beat up his own father because he was roughing up Drew's mother. Jessie had seen it all. She'd been taking Gaynell Webb salve for her bruises, from supposedly falling down some steps. When Jessie saw the fight, then Drew take off, she followed him down to Skitter Run, past Fancy Gap Hollow where Cassie still lived today.

He hadn't gone to see Cassie or her

folks, though. He'd gone to wash his wounds and be alone. But Jessie had seen the beating he'd taken and given, seen how Lem Webb treated his wife and kids, though about everybody knew it. So when Drew stalked off, limping and bleeding, she'd followed, to help or comfort him. Fran MacCrimmon was his girl, but Jessie couldn't help herself. She'd loved him from afar, with his black Irish looks of rakish, raven hair, his don't-give-a-damn slouch, even his frown below those steel-blue eyes. Writing about him in the diary Elinor had given her the first time she'd visited them, putting herself in his path just to say hi, even following him and Fran one time into the woods to see what they done there . . .

Deep Down, 1 mile

What they *did* there, she corrected her thoughts. For years Elinor had teased that she could take the girl out of the mountains, but not take the mountains out of the girl. But Elinor had given her a whole new world. Though it had been a painful transition, Jessie had come to love Lexington and the University of Kentucky campus where Dr. Gering spent so much of her time teaching and researching. They had lived nearby; Jessie could even walk to campus. Since Elinor taught graduate courses in sociology and linguistics, Jessie had come to know many of her academic colleagues and students—people whose interests were a far cry from those of her little hometown. Elinor's research had taken them to the British Isles, especially to Scotland and Northern Ireland, where the Appalachian dialect had originated.

Jessie's expanding mind had soaked it all in; soon she'd seen huge gaps between where she'd been and where she wanted to go. How hard it had been to be a curiosity to Elinor's associates at first. But Elinor had not only studied her but taught and loved her and, slowly, life in Lexington—or visiting New York or London—had become part of her, the new Jessica, a different woman from Jessie of Deep Down.

And when she'd made her own life, attending college at UK, majoring in biology and then choosing to go to grad school and pursue research of her own in the lab, she had finally found a way to meld her old life with her new. Who would have thought that the ginseng that had supported her mother and Deep Down for years might be able to slow the growth of certain cancer cells?

Still, her adolescent years in two different worlds had been difficult. Was she really Jessie or Jessica, or could she manage to be both? When she had come home to visit, she'd tried not to sound uppity as Vern Tarver had called her once. During her first visits, she'd gone back to talking the talk, but a little voice in her head had often corrected Deep Downers, even her mother. She'd been pulled one way and then the other when she moved between her two worlds.

Just northwest of town, her headlights illuminated the entries of three old logging lanes, now mostly derelict and moss-covered. Such roads ran like veins in this area, which had not been mined and had barely been logged. Could her mother have taken one of those roads back into the forested hills to her counting sites? Why hadn't someone seen which way she went? Why hadn't she given Cassie some hint about where she was heading?

Deep Down, Welcome, the town limits sign read.

Despite Jessie's utter exhaustion, she sat up straighter. The tires of her car made a hollow sound over the Deep Creek Bridge. She'd expected to see lots of people in the short, single street, klieg lights set up, police cars, but that was only her memories of city search scenes on the eleven o'clock news. Still, a light shone from Audrey Doyle's B and B, where she took in boarders she fed down at her restaurant. Where the few commercial buildings clustered together, lights were out except for the old MacCrimmon house, which her mother had said now housed the sheriff's office. It was lit up, throwing a big block of yellow light into the dark street where she pulled in.

Emotions overwhelmed her. Tears blinded her eyes as she saw Drew, tall, wide-shouldered and ramrod-straight—no slouch now—come out to greet her. She still had the car door locked when he tried to open it. Every muscle in her body, every buried memory in her brain seemed to scream as she turned off the engine and fumbled to unlock the door.

"No news?" she asked as he opened the door, then reached in to help her out. His hand was warm through the elbow of her shirt, his grip strong.

He shook his head. He wasn't in uniform, but he wore a utility belt with a flashlight and prominent pistol on one hip. Shadows etched deep into his frown. His body was filled out now, mature, solid. But he was still the Drew she'd carried and buried in her mind and heart.

"The news is you're here safe," he said, "and we'll find her together."

She had to lock her knees to stand; she was shaking all over. His arm, like an iron band, went around her shoulders as he led her inside.

3

Jessie felt as if she floated; her feet were hardly under her, and her right leg trembled from alternating between the accelerator and brake for hours. No using cruise control in these hills—no control in her life at all right now.

Drew led her past a waist-high divider, through a small reception area with a single desk, then into a separate room with the open door labeled Sheriff. Inside, he sat her in a carved wooden chair near the door, but did not go around the desk to sit in his leather chair. He lowered his muscular frame into the wooden one next to hers.

"Coffee or water, Jess?"

"No, thanks. I'm too full of coffee."

"The bathroom's at the back of the hall. Help yourself."

"Later. No news at all?"

"Nothing." His face serious, even sad, he bit the corner of his lower lip, then the words tumbled from him as if they'd been dammed up. "We've had six different search parties out for two days. I scented three packs of hunt hounds on shoes I took from her place. Hunt hounds aren't as good as a K-9 crew—they get distracted by game trails. But the state police can't get one here until day after tomorrow because there's a couple of Boy Scouts lost in Boone National Forest. Two of the hounds evidently briefly picked up her scent on the old logging trail under Snow Knob but nothing panned out.

"Besides, it rained heavy the first night, enough to wash off her scent. Tomorrow, we'll start where her trail vanished, but it's like *she* vanished. She didn't take her truck, but she was—is—" he corrected "—such a strong walker we have a big area to cover. I'm hoping you can help me find some of her off-path or secret haunts."

Haunts. The word snagged in Jessie's exhausted brain. *Haunts,* as if Mariah had come back from the dead to walk the woods as they said some spirits had over the years, folks from long-ago pioneer and Indians days who'd gone out hunting game or sang and had never returned . . . never been found.

"At first light, we'll start again," he went on, his deep, resonant voice both reassuring and disturbing. His mere physical presence, handsome yet rugged, unsettled her. His black hair was clipped fairly close, but not a military buzz cut as she'd expected. Under bronze skin, a light beard stubble peppered his square jaw. A small scar she'd never seen slanted into his taut lower lip; his nose still had that slightly crooked look from one of his boyhood fights. Tiny, white crow's-feet perched at the corner of his eyes fringed with black-as-night lashes, so thick for a man's. The cleft in his chin and the angular slant of his cheekbones were more pronounced than she recalled, despite the weight and muscle he'd put on over the years.

"We'll find her," he was saying, "probably with a broken ankle or some such in one of her sang counting spots, living off late berries and gourmet mushrooms, eating pawpaws for dessert and drinking mountain spring water most folks would pay a bundle for. She's a survivor, Jess. She could probably outlast a corps of marines on a survival bivouac in those woods."

Grateful for his trying to comfort her, she gripped the arms of her chair and managed to murmur, "I really appreciate all you've done so far."

"Cassie says you've gone sang counting with Mariah the last couple of years. That so?"

"Yes, off and on, but she used landmarks to find some of her sang counting spots. She's only supposed to count them once a year. She took lots of notes for her annual report, so maybe I can turn up something in the house. I can probably find a few of the places from memory, but I'm not sure about one near Snow Knob. So you've called off the mass search?"

"You don't mind going out just with me, do you?"

Their gazes met and held. She wondered if he was hearing echoes of Vern Tarver and her mother yelling at him that night. She'd tried to explain to them that Drew hadn't hurt her, that she'd let him hold her and take her, but no one was listening and everyone was blaming him.

"If you think that's best, that's fine with me," she said, trying to keep her eyes from wavering the way her voice did. When this was all over, when they had found her mother, maybe they could talk of that other time. Just to clear the air. What happened had been as much her fault as his. In the meantime, yes, it would be difficult being with Drew. They'd never had a real relationship in the first place, though she'd built one in her mind and heart during the four years leading up to that night. She wondered, after all was said and done back then, if he thought she was cheap or crazy.

"This was Fran MacCrimmon's home," she said, glancing around at what had once been his girlfriend's house.

"Right." Eyes narrowed, he was studying her intently, even as she had him. But he was a police officer, trained to analyze people. She mustn't read in more than that. He might be afraid she'd get hysterical. She'd done that the last night they'd been together. Why did that seem as if it was really just last night?

He took a phone call, evidently from Sheriff Akers in Highboro. She strained to listen, at least until it turned out to be just a check on progress. Then her gaze darted around the room.

Drew's office was spartan, neater than any place she'd ever seen in Deep Down, as if he could control this eccentric town by being tidy here. A big, old oak desk held stacked metal baskets of papers and supplies; he had a mobile phone, desktop computer and peripherals. Four tall filing cabinets, two on each side of a window, lined the wall behind him. A flag of the commonwealth of Kentucky, a marine flag and an American flag stood against the wall facing his desk. On one side wall, large maps of the local area were marked with colored lines and pins stuck in, but didn't seem related to this search.

What really captured her attention on the side wall with the other window—both windows were covered by neat, dark-blue vertical blinds—were two chrome-framed photos. One was of Drew with two other marines—oh, his younger brothers, Josh and Gabe—in sharp uniforms under a banner that read *Semper Fi.* The other picture was of him with Highboro's long-time sheriff, Akers, pinning a badge on Drew's chest. In the marine photo he wore a shiny dress sword at his side; in the police one, a sidearm. She tried not to gape, but to see Drew Webb standing so stunningly, stiffly at attention in crisp uniforms—a man who's family had never heeded rules and regs—shook her to her very core.

Jessie sensed a full blush coming, just the way it had when he'd so much as glanced her way years ago. How foolish, childish and inappropriate, she scolded herself. Despite her exhaustion, she had to get control. She felt she was still rushing forward, in a plane, in a car. She needed a bed and soon, but she dreaded going home without her mother there.

"I will use your facilities," she told him when he hung up. "I've been sleepless since Cincinnati and feel like a zombie. I hope I can sleep tonight without her there."

She started to stand, but, dizzy, sat back hard. Drew rose and took her hands, pulling her up beside him, almost propping her up. She was five-eight, but she had forgotten he was so tall, maybe six-one or -two. In all those years she'd had her secret crush on him, she'd seldom been this close.

"You've got to be exhausted as well as strung out," he said, keeping his hands under her elbows. "But I can't let you back in Mariah's house until we can take a careful survey of her property tomorrow. I used a search warrant to go through briefly today, then crime-taped the place."

"Crime tape? It's a crime scene? Is that agent from the big Chinese buyer still coming in here to buy sang at Tarver's? What about the guys from the pharms and the ginseng-laced power drinks companies? I can't see anyone around here hurting her, but those outsiders might do something to keep her sang count up so that—"

"Let's go over all that tomorrow. The crime tape's just a formality. Now, listen," he added, his voice darkening as he gave her the slightest shake, as if to force her fears back down. "I'm going to phone Cassie, because I'm sure you can stay there tonight. Then, after we check out the house for any sort of clues—"

"For clues? You *do* think something awful has happened to her, don't you?"

"Let's not assume the worst for a woman who knew the woods so well. I'm sorry I can't let you go home tonight, but we can keep your car here, and I'll take you out to Cassie's, then pick you up just after dawn. I'll transfer your things to my vehicle now. You want to give me your keys, then I'll help you to the bathroom before I call her?"

"I'll be all right. But she has to be all right, too!"

Damn, she was going to cry. Her mother was missing, and she couldn't go home. But neither could she have a meltdown. She had to focus on finding her mother, and that meant going along with Drew, in more ways than one.

"I'll be all right," she repeated, blinking back tears as she pulled away from him and fished her keys out of her purse. When she handed them to him, their fingertips touched; a jolt of lightning might as well have leapt between them. She thought he felt it, too, but his words came calm and steady.

"Stay strong, Jess. We'll work through this together."

Not trusting her voice, she nodded and went out of his office and down the hall, with both hands on the walls to stop the place from spinning. Neither of them was saying it, but they knew a lot was at stake in Mariah's sang count and, therefore, in her disappearance. It was all tied in with mountain pride and worse—big money both here and abroad.

Jessie knew she had to deal with a new Drew, but then, she was a new person, too. One with a missing mother who might be as endangered as wild wood sang.

Drew had to fight the urge to pull Jess against him and hold her. It was an insane thought, considering the last night they'd been together and now this nightmare. Despite her obvious exhaustion and frustration, he was astounded at how beautiful she'd become, delicate and edgy, yet sturdy and strong. Tall, slender with tousled, curly blond hair and blue-gray eyes that bored right into you. Yeah, just as he'd remembered her and yet not the same at all. Filled out, at ease in what had once been a string bean of a body, self-assured despite her dilemma . . .

"Here, let me open the Jeep door for you," he said as she stepped outside to join him on the porch.

"It looks more like a truck. Is this Deep Down's version of a cop car?"

"It's a Jeep Cherokee with a wired-off backseat in case I have a prisoner to transport. I've only got two small holding cells here."

"A Cherokee? I'll bet Seth Bearclaws likes that."

"I tried to give him a lift the other day, but he won't ride in it. Says it's just another thing ripping off his people's heritage."

He went back to the office, turned out the lights and locked the door before he got in the driver's side of the front seat. He was proud of this silver, four-wheel SUV he'd been issued when he'd taken the job. It had made his measly salary sound a lot better. It was a sturdy vehicle for the mountain roads. It didn't have a light bar, just a single red light he put on the roof if he had a pursuit or an emergency. Traffic jams were nonexistent here. He'd been tempted to have *Sheriff* stenciled on both front doors, but realized it might make some folks in his jurisdiction nervous or even trigger-happy. Still, with some characters in the outlying areas, he felt as if he had a bull's-eye on his doors and on his back. Could Mariah have run afoul of any of them?

"One of my little causes around here," he told her, "is reminding people to lock their doors. The times, they are a changin' 'round here." She seemed very far away, not just across the console; she looked as if she was glued to the outside door. "Seat belt," he reminded her, then had to help her click it in the unfamiliar lock.

"Lots of locks. So big-time crime's coming in here?"

"I wouldn't go that far. In the four months I've been on the job, it's hardly been cops and robbers," he admitted, as he turned on the headlights, pulled out and headed toward Cassie's. "I broke up a fight between the Talbots and the Enloes so that feud wouldn't restart."

"As I recall, that feud went back to the Civil War. If the truth were known, probably to the old clan wars of Scotland. So that was a good day's work. What else?"

He was touched that, despite her own problems, she seemed genuinely interested. About half the local population insisted there was no need for law enforcement here. He almost confessed to her how hard it had been to see the sneers and overhear the snide comments about Drew Webb, of all folks, from all families, coming back to uphold what the government said was right.

"I arrested a guy from Frankfort for letting his six-year-old son chase deer on a noisy ATV. The dad was hopping mad, said he'd sue—he was a lawyer, no less, who should have had some brains. The kid could have been killed with the ridges and rills around here. I deal with a lot of pranks from kids who are just plain bored," he told her. "I think we can both sympathize with that."

A moment's silence stretched between them.

"Yes."

"I do a lot of knock-and-talks, playing

counselor as well as enforcer. The things I thought would cause me the most problems, drinking and policing illegal patches of marijuana, haven't taken much time. Hardly anyone makes their own moonshine anymore, and when I find pot patches, I destroy them. But I don't make an arrest or apply to have the land legally confiscated if I'm not sure who planted it."

"Unless you catch them in the act, you're never sure."

"Right. Besides, like sang spots, a lot of it is planted far outside of town."

"I'm sure sang is even harder to police," she told him, slanting her body slightly in his direction as he turned off onto the side road toward Cassie's. "I mean," she went on as they began to bounce down the long, rutted lane, "sang's more of a heritage here, a God-given medicine and money-maker."

"That's exactly it. Local diggers and foreign buyers alike don't give a damn what the endangered species laws say."

"And your knock-and-talks?" she asked. Again, it really got to him that, as whipped and upset as she was, she was focusing on what he'd said. He hadn't realized he'd been so lonely, coming home to Deep Down.

"I've arrested two guys and driven them into jail in Highboro for domestic violence. I owe my mother that much. Above all else, I took this job because I can't stand guys who rough up their women and kids, and there's still a lot of it in these patriarchal parts. I—I almost lose control—again—when I see that. Sometimes I think life was easier in sunny Naples, Italy, when I was MP—military police. I was in charge of the brig for drunken sailors and marines. They didn't expect favors from a one-time bad boy from a hellfire family."

He realized he sounded angry. He hadn't really let loose with anyone since he'd been here, not even with Chuck Akers. He'd been walking a fine line between building bridges and enforcing the law.

Cassie's house came in sight, pouring light into the darkness of Fancy Gap Hollow where she'd been raised. Her form appeared at the window, then disappeared before her front door opened. In a long, ghostly white nightgown, with a shawl around her thin shoulders, she came out on the porch as they pulled up. Jess opened the door before he could get out.

"Jessie!" he heard Cassie cry as she embraced her friend. "Despite the troubles, welcome home!"

4

Cassie Keenan had known Jessica Lock-wood her whole life. Both only children, a rarity in the area, they had clung together like sisters, however different their person-alities. Cassandra and Jessica—Cassie and Jessie—their lives had seemed to rhyme like their names, until Mariah sent Jessie away. If folks thought Mariah did that just because of Drew Webb, Cassie knew they were wrong, 'cause Mariah had always wanted a different life for her child.

Still, however distant their lives had be-come, Cassie treasured how they could pick up where they'd left off, just like they hadn't been apart a long time. Though Jessie hadn't visited Deep Down this August as usual, she'd been here last Christmas with all sorts of gifts for her and Pearl. But things might be different now with Mariah missing. Desperate to help her friend get through this, whatever befell, Cassie hugged Jessie hard, then led her inside while Drew followed with her suitcase and matching smaller bag.

"I hope we won't wake Pearl," he said as Cassie sat Jessie down at the plank table, shoving potted herbs aside to make a spot for her. She'd meant to straighten up the little house a bit when she heard Jessie would spend the night, but there was nowhere to put her precious plants unless she carried them outside with the others. Herbs, both live and dried, covered the floor, walls and ceiling. It was like a grotto in here, Elinor Gering had said, when she'd come to record Cassie talking about life here in Deep Down.

"Now don't you all fret about making noise," she told Drew. "Once that little angel's out, she sleeps like the dead."

Cassie saw Jessie wince at that. She

scolded herself for not thinking ahead of her mouth. "This here's ginseng tea with a touch of chamomile," she told her friend as she set a cup before her. "Gives you energy and yet makes you sleep. Drew, you want some coffee? Won't take a minute."

"No, thanks. I'm coffeed out for the day and need to hit the sack myself for a couple of hours."

Looking beyond exhausted, Jessie wrapped her hands around the hot cup, then lifted it to her lips.

"I'll be going," Drew said. "Jess, I'll be here at eight sharp, though I know you need the sleep."

"What I need is my mother back," she said, turning to face him. Then she added, "Sorry about the heavy bag. I didn't repack at home, just got my car and headed out."

Cassie watched the two of them talk, both tipping their heads in the same direction and leaning slightly toward each other as if they were straining against a fence. She recognized the wild wind between them, the kind you couldn't hold back. She'd figured both of them still had feelings for each other, and now she knew it. Tarnation, she understood that sort of pull, that turning toward the sun as if it were the source of life itself.

"'Night and thanks, Cassie," Drew said as he started for the door.

"Come a few minutes early for pancakes," she told him. "I'm gonna put a good, hot meal in Jessie first thing tomorrow, so you come, too. Thanks for that bag of groceries you brought me back from Highboro the other day," she added, hurrying after him to the door. "Me and Pearl's beholden to you, 'specially for standing up for my right to keep silent. I heard what you told Vern Tarver."

"You're only beholden for a pancake breakfast," he said. He stood at the door as if he hated to leave, then looked past her to Jessie again. "We'll find her, Jess," he said and went out into the night.

"Whew-ee," Cassie said as she went to sit across the narrow table from her friend. "I know you two will find Mariah. But for now, least you found each other."

"Except for the fact I need his professional help—" Jessie's voice came real sharp "—our past has nothing to do with the present situation."

"Listen, my Deep Down sister, don't you go lecturing 'bout things of the heart, even if you are way smarter'n me," Cassie scolded, shaking her finger at Jessie like she did at Pearl. "My girl's daddy may be out of my life and hers, but she was a love child." Afraid she'd say more, she pinched her lips tight.

"Of course she is. I never said otherwise."

"So I know it when I see it, even if I don't have it no more." Cassie made herself sit back and calm down. No way did she want someone clever as Jessie catching on to who Pearl's daddy was or what she had planned.

"I don't know which way's up, that's all," her friend said, taking another big swig of the tea. "What you're seeing and hearing is sheer exhaustion. I just feel so weak—helpless."

"I got some mushroom soup and corn bread, if you're hungry for that kind of food 'fore you go to bed."

"My system's so screwed up from time zone changes and I have stomach cramps from being afraid and grieved—"

"And on edge back with Drew again.

Like most men, he may be dense as a wall on that, but you're not. Anybody like you who can look in a microscope and find a way to stop killer cells can—"

"Can find a killer?" Jessie blurted and, to Cassie's dismay, burst into tears. She banged the cup down and covered her face with both hands. Her shoulders shook and the curly blond hair Cassie had always thought was way better than her own straight red hair bounced against her hands. "It's just," Jessie got out between big, choking sobs, "I think something awful—might have happened—to her. She knows the woods, she's always safe in the woods . . ."

Cassie jumped up and went around the table to hug her from behind. "Sorry," she said. "I didn't mean to set you off, and I shouldn't bring up Drew like that. I promise, I won't say no more about it till you're ready to admit it."

"You're so damned annoying and stubborn, Cassandra Keenan."

"That's me," she said and went back to her place across the table as Jessie reached in her purse, looking kind of surprised to find it still over her shoulder, and took out a tissue. "'Member how Elinor told us that Cassandra in some old Greek stories was a woman who always told the truth, even predicted the future, but no one believed her?" Cassie asked.

"Elinor said a lot of things," Jessie muttered and blew her nose. "She once made me read a book she loved called *You Can't Go Home Again,* and here I am. And I hated the book."

"Jessie, anything I can do to help, I will."

Jessie reached across the table, past the plants, to put one hand on hers. "I'd better get to sleep. Morning and Drew will be here early."

"I'm gonna sleep with Pearl, and you take my bed. Want to wash up?"

"In the morning. Right now, I just need a couple of things out of my carry-on bag and a bed."

Cassie rolled Jessie's big suitcase into her bedroom, the one that had been her grandparents' and parents' room before it was hers. In truth, she was glad to give it up, 'cause after watching the smothered desire between Jessie and Drew, she might be too het up and not sleep well in there tonight. Too often she didn't, remembering her own sweeping passion in that bed and then how the midwife had helped her birth the result of that there.

She'd buried that love and lust now, put it away and closed up all her wounds, though they still festered under the surface. Sure as rain, she was laying plans to make him pay for his betrayal of her and Pearl. She knew people whispered that she never spoke his name nor hinted who he was because she was too shattered over the desertion, still so much in love that she was giving him a pass, protecting him.

Well, they were all dead wrong. As soon as she got her herbal potions mixed, no matter how important a man he was, he was the one who was gonna wish he was dead.

Something woke Jessie instantly. A shifting sound. Movement. Shadows huddled in the room. As out-of-it as she was, she became instantly alert with her pulse pounding in her ears.

Was that noise inside or out? Yes, another sound, but from where? Someone sneaking in through the door she'd left ajar? Had Cassie locked the outside doors? What if someone who wanted to stop her mother from handing in her ginseng count had heard Jessie was back and thought she knew more than she did? What if . . .

She didn't move, didn't breathe, concentrating, straining to listen. Yes, something outside. Maybe a branch scraping or tapping against the glass. She wished Cassie had a clock in the room.

With a groan, she got out of bed and shuffled to the window, shifting the left edge of the homemade drapes slightly aside. Black as it was outside, a half moon etched the bizarre backyard in faintest silver.

The usual clutter stretched across the back of the house between two herb gardens. Jessie saw the solid, black silhouettes of the old iron kettles where her friend boiled the natural dyes she used to make wild plant mordants, which weavers used to set colors in cloth. Above that, lines of barbed wire dangled from tall post to post, not to keep people out but to dry moss

Cassie sold to florists and craft stores for about five dollars a sack. Humps of moss were draped there now, looking like the tops of furry heads peering over the wire at the house.

Then one of them on the top wire moved. It rose, turned away, then disappeared.

No. No, she could not have seen that. It was just the breeze moving the moss, the slant of moonlight or even her tired eyes playing tricks on her.

She squeezed her eyelids tight, then opened them to look again. The moss-heavy barbed wire shifted in the breeze, gilded by moonlight, that was all. Surely, she had not heard something scratching on the window or seen a big, hairy head move. She was getting back in bed at least until dawn or until Cassie, ever an early riser, woke her up. Even now, her stomach did a little roll and plunge to think that Drew was coming for her, even if it was to find out what dreadful thing must have happened to her mother.

Back in bed, she tossed and turned. She didn't think she slept again, but she must have because she saw strange shapes of huge, hairy ginseng roots come to life and chase her, through the trees, through the Hong Kong market . . .

"Aunt Jessie?" came the tiny voice and then the little face peered up over the side of the bed in the graying room. "I heard you was coming. But why isn't Mommy here in this bed 'stead of you?"

"Pearl, sweetie, how are you? But your mommy's in with you. She let me sleep here for the night." As her head cleared, she helped the child climb up beside her. "You mean she's not in bed?" she asked.

Pearl shook her head, making her reddish-blond hair swing. "Maybe she's in the bad part of the garden. Even in the dark, she's there."

Jessie frowned at the child's babble, but covered her up with the blanket, then got out of bed to be sure that Cassie was around somewhere. Surely, those nearest and dearest to her weren't just disappearing.

She glanced out her window first at the drying moss and iron kettles. Yes, that's what she'd seen last night, nothing else.

"Stay here," she whispered to Pearl. "I'll be right back."

She checked the bathroom—empty—then peered out a side window. In the first dusting of dawn, Cassie was in her eastern garden, gone to riot in late-summer growth. She was cutting herbs with a long, curved knife, hacking away as if she were angry at them. Jessie knocked on the window and waved. Startled, Cassie looked up and held up a finger to indicate "just a minute," then bent back to her work.

Her friend had always been a hard worker, but then she'd had to be, especially lately to eke out a living for herself and Pearl. Cassie would not take donated money. But why work out there in the dark and chill of morning? Maybe she'd gotten behind, since, like so many Deep Downers, she'd spent time looking for Mariah.

Jessie padded back to the bedroom, checking her watch as she went by the dresser. Seven. She had to get moving to take a bath—no shower here, just a big, old claw-footed tub you could almost swim laps in—and get ready for a grueling day before Drew arrived.

"She's outside, just like you said," she told Pearl, who looked like a little elf in the middle of the big double bed. The child had a pert, freckled face; her pale complexion and reddish hair were a clear heritage from her mother. No hints of who might have sired her in the child herself. If Mariah didn't have a clue who might have made Cassie pregnant—or so she'd said—no one but Pearl's parents must know.

Mariah and Cassie had also been close for years. Sometimes, Jessie thought with a pang, it was as if, after Cassie's mother died and her father left the area, Cassie took Jessie's place. Besides digging some sang, both Mariah and Cassie made their livings from wildcrafting for seasonal moss, ferns, morel mushrooms and herbs to sell to craft and floral shops, health stores and dyers in Kentucky towns. But Cassie had said, just before they went to bed, that she had not been to most of Mariah's sang sites with her and she couldn't find a trace of her in their usual wildcrafting areas. Jessie could only pray she'd find some of her mother's notes in the house or that she'd recall the sang counting sites once she was out in the woods with Drew.

She snapped open her big suitcase and pulled out two of the silk scarves she'd bought in Hong Kong as gifts for friends and coworkers—and for her mother, as strange as it would be to see her in silk. The jade-hued one she tied around Pearl's cotton nightgown like a sash while the child was all big eyes, so excited at the gift. The scarlet one she kept out for Cassie, since that was her favorite color.

"Now you just stay snug as a bug in a rug in that bed until I take a bath, and, after I get dressed, you can help me set the table for breakfast," she told Pearl.

She bent back down to her tightly packed suitcase and dug past her two business suits and the array of blouses she'd taken until she found the single pair of clean jeans and a long-sleeved sweatshirt that, unfortunately, was emblazoned with a Phi Beta Kappa key. Not that most Deep Downers would know or care what that was, but what had seemed so right for the conference was all wrong here. She decided she'd just wear it inside out and find something of her mother's to wear later—if Drew let her touch anything in her house.

"You from the *Highboro Herald* or another paper?" Drew asked the blond guy with the expensive camera equipment. The stranger was leaning against Jessie's car, in front of the police office, to steady himself while he took a picture down the street toward the bridge. He looked almost Nordic—like a Viking—with light blue eyes and white-blond hair.

Drew had been wondering if Mariah's disappearance would attract any media. Unless he could find out she'd been abducted and taken out of the area, he didn't want them involved, but it was hard to keep the search low-key with so many people helping.

"Newspaper? Not me," the man said almost defensively as he lowered the camera and turned to face Drew. "Officer, I plead not guilty to being part or parcel of the American media today." Unlike most civilians, he did not hesitate to step forward and shake hands. "Tyler Finch," he said. "I was just in the area, that's all. I'm doing a photo book on Appalachia."

"Sheriff Drew Webb. You just drive in this morning?"

"I stayed in Highboro last night at a B and B—my cousin's place, actually—so I do know the basic area. My bread-and-butter job is as a site analyst for the advertising firm Bailey and Keller, in New York City."

Drew observed he had a video camera as well, hanging behind his back on a shoulder sling. A notebook and pen stuck out of his denim jacket. Drew didn't put it past a reporter to try to sneak in around here, but for some reason, he believed this man.

"We've got a missing person case ongoing here, Mr. Finch. That's why I thought you might be media."

"Sure, no problem. Besides my own stuff, my paying assignment is to shoot some possible scenes for future magazine and TV ads, but I'll be sure to stay out of your way. Actually, I'm going to photograph what my boss calls the mecca of ginseng. Bailey and Keller's going to do some ads for G-Men and G-Women new caffeine and ginseng drinks. Their company rep, Beth Brazzo, has already scouted some places, but I'm not very good at directions, even with notes."

Drew thought of Mariah's notes on her sang sites. He hoped they weren't missing. But he could hardly force this guy to stay out of the woods around here.

"I've met Ms. Brazzo," he told Finch. "Tall, brunette."

"That's her. Look, I know you're busy, but could you suggest someone who'd like to be my assistant—point out spots for shots?—I'd pay them."

"I do have someone in mind. How about I meet you right here around eight-thirty and bring her along? Cassandra Keenan's her name, and she's what they call a wildcrafter, knows the hills well from gathering herbs and such."

"That would be great. Let me know if I can do anything for you."

After he drove away, Drew did think of something Tyler Finch might be able to do for him, besides providing Cassie and Pearl with some income to get them through the winter. If Drew and Jess found any evidence of foul play in Mariah's disappearance, he might need a photographer faster than it would take Sheriff Akers or the highway patrol to get one in here. He had an old camera in the Cherokee, but he was lousy with it.

As he turned down Cassie's bumpy

lane, he shook his head as if to rid himself of the growing fear that something really bad had happened to Mariah. More than once, he'd wanted a case to prove himself around here, but not this one.

5

Through the front window, Jessie watched Cassie arguing with Drew outside. She wore her new scarf, tied around her like a thin shawl, and it fluttered in the breeze, snapping itself into an S shape.

The scarlet letter, Jessie thought. An edge-of-the-forest unwed mother who wouldn't identify the father and an elfin child named Pearl, no less. Elinor would surely see some sort of portent or symbol in all that. In Hawthorne's novel, the heroine was keeping the man who had fathered her child a secret because he was respected in the community. He turned out to be a Puritan minister, who had his reputation at stake.

Jessie studied Drew, then Cassie. Why had Cassie asked him to step outside when he'd told her he'd met a man who would pay her for advice about sites to shoot photos? Drew seemed very protective of Cassie and Pearl, but Jessie admired him for that. Maybe he knew who Pearl's father was; it could be some friend of his. When, exactly, had his younger brothers left town to join the marines? Surely, Drew himself hadn't been anywhere around Deep Down when Cassie fell in love with someone who left her pregnant.

She scolded herself silently as she moved away from the window. It was just that she was so on edge that everything looked dark to her, everyone looked guilty.

As Jessie returned to listening to Pearl read aloud from a book of fairy tales—interspersed with her own babblings about buried treasure and magical spells—Cassie stormed in, untying her scarf. "We're going into town, Pearl, to meet a man about a job."

"In Drew's big car?" the child asked.

"No, in the truck. Run and get ready now. Wear your jacket."

They had all shared a peaceful breakfast until Drew had mentioned that he'd suggested Cassie's name to Tyler Finch. Cassie had about choked on the next bite of pawpaw pancakes, so rich with huckleberries and walnuts it was almost like eating Christmas fruitcake.

"Not a job you like the sound of?" Jessie asked Cassie now as she grabbed her purse. Drew had already loaded Jessie's bags back into his Cherokee.

"Grateful for the money, but don't like Drew fixin' me up with a stranger."

"Oh. But it's only a business deal."

"Never you mind. We got to get going so you can go through Mariah's house. Thought maybe I could help today if you're not sure 'bout something there, but now I'll be busy. I been in there more than you have since January. Pearl, shake a leg now!"

Jessie went out and climbed into the front seat. Drew started the engine but waited until Cassie and Pearl got in their old Ford truck and roared by.

"I ought to get her for speeding," he muttered and followed them down the rut- ted lane toward the highway. "And ingrati- tude."

Jessie was tempted to ask him when his leaves from the marines had been. She knew he'd been back to this area briefly off and on. But if he had secretly made love to Cassie, he would certainly have stepped forward to claim Pearl and her. Wouldn't he?

Cassie couldn't help it that she was fix- ing to have a conniption. Drew had more or less told a strange man she'd work with him—maybe go off in the woods with him. Did Drew guess she'd done that before, so reckoned she would again? Yes, she needed the money, but that's how the other had got started. But this man would be business—only business. Everyone, in- cluding Sheriff Webb and Mr. Tyler Finch, would see that clear enough.

Was that the man, standing there out- side the sheriff's office? Tall and straight as an oak, hair like sunlight and with blue eyes?

"You just keep quiet now, Pearl, you understand? Your ma's got to talk money with that man."

She got out and pulled Pearl after her. Icicle-blue, that's what his eyes were. Laws, she hadn't thought a man had looked that good for—for nigh on about five years. She even felt those dangerous little butterflies fluttering in her belly.

"Cassandra Keenan, this is Tyler Finch, a professional photographer," Drew introduced them. Jessie had stayed in Drew's SUV. Pearl kept hold of a back pocket of Cassie's jeans. She wasn't shy back at the holler but about everywhere else.

"The sheriff says you know the area well," Tyler said with a little nod as they shook hands and she sized him up. "I'd really appreciate some local expertise picking unique but typical sites." Wouldn't you just know, the masculine pine scent of him reminded her of high, pretty places up on Big Blue, and his smile was dazzling as sunshine on the stream.

"I could do that," she said, realizing this man was good with words and she was sounding like she couldn't string more than two of them together. She cleared her throat. "If you need pictures or movies of meadows, trees, hollers—hollows—mountains, you name it."

"Then you can name your price, Ms. Keenan. That is, if you wouldn't mind doing a little modeling, too—just a distant shot or two with the wilds behind you, maybe with you walking away down a path."

Cassie stared up into his eyes, ready to say no to that, money or not. Her gaze darted a moment as Drew said his good-byes and started away. Vern Tarver was leaning in the window of Drew's SUV, talking to Jessie. No way she wanted to work in that smelly fur and sang trading shop for him again this winter. Why, he'd made her dust all that old, dead stuff in his so-called museum upstairs and do that Chinaman's laundry, too, when she'd always heard they were the ones with laundries.

"I'd need to cart Pearl along with me," she told the eager-eyed Tyler Finch, "least most of the time."

"I'd pay extra for a picture or two of her, maybe the two of you together, not a close-up but a shot with the scenery in the distance."

"Then let's talk turkey."

"I'm so very, very sorry about Mariah—her going missing," Vern Tarver told Jessie, as Drew came back and got in the driver's seat again. Vern patted her arm on the ledge of her rolled-down window.

"Thanks, Vern. I know you two were keeping company off and on."

He nodded solemnly, looking sad but nervous, too. "We were getting serious. Of course, we didn't see everything eye-to-eye, but opposites attract. Listen, Jessie, I know you and Drew have a lot to do today, but just let me know if I can help in any way. I—I'm glad I realized she had gone missing so I could get folks looking for her."

Vern Tarver was the closest thing Deep Down had to a mayor. He owned the V & T General Store, Tarver's Fur and Sang Trader, and the so-called two-room historical museum above it. Vern seemed to make most decisions for the town, just as his father had before him. He ran the elementary school committee—children older than that went to the consolidated school between here and Highboro—and oversaw the tiny town park and the cemetery next to the Baptist Church, where he was an elder. Though most visitors roomed at Audrey Doyle's, Vern took in an occasional guest in his big brick house on the edge of town. Peter Sung, the agent for the Chinese Kulong family that bought most of the ginseng exported from this area, had stayed in an apartment above Vern's store for years.

In short, Vernon Tarver was Deep Down's answer to Donald Trump. Jessie supposed that Vern even resembled "The Donald," with his big build, pompadour of sandy hair and business suits, except they were old ones with wide lapels. Vern was probably the only man within a hundred miles of here whose uniform wasn't jeans.

As he stepped away and she rolled up her window, Jessie told Drew, "If we need to make a list of someone who could have—have spirited my mother away, Vern could be a lot of help. Sooner or later, locals and outsiders pass through his stores."

"Good observation. And good observations are what we're both going to need in your mother's house this morning."

"So, like I said yesterday, is Peter Sung in town? If my mother's sang counts were low and the government stopped exports for a while, he and that Kulong family in New York he represents would stand to lose a fortune."

"So he'd have to stop her somehow? Anything's a possibility, but he hasn't been around for over a week. Let's not think the worst. We'll case her place, look for clues to where to search the forests. If we find no help that way, I'm just praying you can recall some of her sites that were deep in."

"I'm ready to do anything I can to find her." Then she blurted out something she had admitted to no one—not Elinor, not Cassie, and, sadly, not her own mother. "I'm feeling guilty that I'm still upset she sent me away to live."

He bit his lower lip, then nodded. "My fault."

"No, it wasn't—really. Mother and Elinor had been talking about my going to live with her when it came time for college— the impossible dream for a Deep Down girl. It just—it just happened earlier, that's all."

"It's hell both loving and hating parents. I know that," he said, almost in a raspy whisper. He reached over to touch her hand, then quickly put his hand back on the steering wheel as they turned into the hollow where Jessie had been raised.

The next statement hung between them, but neither of them voiced it: It was also hell both loving and hating what had happened to them in Deep Down twelve years ago. If he insisted, she'd find some way to talk about that later, but she wasn't prepared to face all that today.

Neither was she prepared to see Seth Bearclaws sitting on her mother's front porch, right under the yellow-and-black police tape.

As Seth stood to greet them, Jessie saw he'd brought one of his big carvings, unless it had been put there since New Year's. A Cherokee, Seth was one of only a thousand tribal purebloods left, her mother had told her once. For years, besides hunting and trapping, Seth had made his living carving two- to three-foot tree trunks into local animals with chain saw, chisel and knives. At first, she couldn't tell what was carved from this one, though. Not the usual bear or deer head.

"Sad to hear your mother's missing," Seth spoke first to her, then turned to Drew. "Any news of Mariah?"

"No, but with Jessie home we'll have a better shot at finding her. That wasn't here yesterday, Seth," Drew added, gesturing at the carved tree trunk. "Did Mariah order that?"

"A surprise for her. I bring it now so when she comes home, she will have it."

Tears in her eyes, Jessie bent toward it, but a shiver snaked up her spine when she saw what it portrayed. In the fragrant, reddish cedar wood were roughly hewn two hands above a ginseng plant, as if the hands were protecting it. "That's really lovely, Seth," she told him.

"Mariah and me used to argue over ginseng, her counting it, allowing it to be taken from the woods for money. It should be for cures right here, not in other countries, not for power drinks for runners," he said with a sneer, eyes narrowing as he crossed his arms over his chest.

Seth Bearclaws was about seventy, though with his wrinkled, wizened face, he seemed either much older or ageless. For some strange reason, looking at him, Jessie thought of the old woman in the ginseng shop in Hong Kong, but she shook off that foolish thought. Seth had tattoos all over his arms and even one on his chin, most of them of bear paws and claws, similar to the leather thong necklace dangling long, curved claws he always wore around his neck. Mariah had said the tattoos were not done with a needle but by pricking gunpowder under his skin, a Cherokee tradition from way back. Seth had lived here from way back, too, first with his wife until she died and then alone with his memories and tribal causes. In a way, Seth Bearclaws was the original eco-warrior around here.

Since he'd protested sang being sold for other things but the herbal cures his people valued, Jessie almost told him about her breakthrough in the lab. It looked as if the ginsenosides from ginseng roots might delay or halt the growth of cancer cells, even tumors, and that could benefit all mankind. But she kept quiet, hoping he might say something more about her mother.

"But," Drew said, "this gift means you're not angry with Mariah over her ginseng counts? That you've forgiven her now?"

Seth shrugged. "When she returns, she will know what this means. That she must be strong to tell everyone the plant count is too low. For years, I was telling her the old Cherokee saying that a person who deserves life must pass by three sang plants before taking the fourth one. Now she understands that, so I bring her this."

"A person who deserves life?" Drew repeated. "Meaning what?"

"He means all plant life is sacred, don't you?" Jessie put in. "My mother believed that, too, but that doesn't mean there can't be good uses for sang or herbs."

"But some bad uses, too," Seth said, walking past them as if the conversation had suddenly ended. He lived not far away, down the creek. Had he walked all the way here with this heavy wooden piece? He surely hadn't carved it on site. And why had he been camped out on the porch, when he knew Mariah was missing?

"How could he have brought that heavy trunk here?" she asked Drew.

"I've seen him rolling them, but that

would be too far for this. I'm sure not buying the superstitions about Seth around here, that he can call up mythical creatures to do his bidding. I'll worry about him later. We've got to search the house, then get out to some of the sang spots others might have missed."

Jessie took a last, long look at the rough carving of the two hands and the sang plant. She should have thanked Seth for her mother. Later, when there was time, she would go to see him and take care of that.

"First of all," Drew said, "does anything look out of place—not just moved, but really disturbed?"

From where they were standing in the front door, Jessie surveyed the place that was once her home. A white, wood-sided house with a shingled roof, it had hardly changed over the years, while she had changed so much. This front entry opened onto a living area, with a big hooked rug and a flagstone fireplace. Six worn, dark wood chairs surrounded a long wooden table that served as the dining area; a store-bought sofa and two hand-crafted rockers faced each other before the long front window looking out over the porch. A short hall led to a kitchen at the back left and two bedrooms on the right with a small bathroom between. Her mother had put modern plumbing in after Daddy died. A long, glassed-in sunporch stretched along the back of the house, a place for storage but a lot of living, too. That was still Jessie's favorite room.

It was so strange to be here without her mother's presence. The place seemed too silent—haunted. "I don't think anything's out of place," she said, going in to look around the main room and kitchen. She peered into the back rooms. "It's as if she just stepped outside for something. But her denim jacket is gone from its peg by the back door and her favorite old, scuffed hiking boots aren't here." She heard a scratching sound and saw that Drew was taking notes.

"Do you know where she kept her sang records?" he asked.

"Some in her desk, some in a tin box in the closet—her idea of a filing cabinet." She sat down at her mother's pine desk in the front room, one her father had crafted with his own hands, jack-of-all trades that he was. Sliding different drawers open and gently rifling through things, she said, "Believe me, it took some convincing, from both me and Professor Gering—Elinor, to get Mother the sang counting job in this area. I made her take all the modern devices like a GPS and cell phone they offered, but she refused to e-mail her findings in on spreadsheets and snail-mailed them instead. Still, they knew she was the best person to find sang around here."

"As I said, we're going to have to find her sang spots," Drew said, hovering over her. "Anything about her counts there at all?"

"No, though I can go through everything more thoroughly later. Let's go check her lockbox."

"Will you need a key?" he asked, following her into the larger of the two small bedrooms. Mariah had made her bed; the familiar wedding ring heirloom quilt looked untouched, slumping into the shape of two human forms in the double bed her mother had once shared with her father and refused to replace.

"Believe it or not, she seldom locks it," Jessie said.

She opened the closet door and the earthy, fresh aroma of the forest hit her with stunning impact. Jessie closed her eyes for a moment, breathing in the scent she most associated with her mother, wishing this were a magic entry into the forest, to the spot where Mariah must have met with some accident. You're being foolish, she scolded herself. Too many childhood readings of *Alice in Wonderland* or *The Chronicles of Narnia* from Elinor.

Her mother's closet looked small but roomy, compared to her own walk-in closet at home that was stuffed with clothes, but that made it easy to see what was on the floor. Hiking boots, walking shoes, only one pair of nice-looking flats, one extra purse. In the back right corner of the closet Jessie spotted the black metal tin box, despite the fact it was covered by a still new-looking Lands' End backpack she'd bought her mother last year. Stubborn as ever, Mariah must still prefer her own, old, shoulder-sling pack.

Jessie knelt and slid the box out into the room. Drew squatted down to help her. It was about two-feet square and a foot deep and as old as the hills. Sitting cross-legged, Jessie lifted the lid—yes, unlocked.

"You mentioned about urging people to use locks," she told Drew, "but you can't teach an old dog new tricks." To her surprise, the papers in the box looked in great disarray, as if someone had pawed through the contents.

"Is it always that messy?" Drew asked, his shoulder bumping hers as he sat down cross-legged next to her.

"I haven't looked in it for years, but it's not like her. This looks like it's been stirred."

"Or ransacked. Let me carry it into the kitchen so you can go over it better. Don't touch the lid again, in case we need to dust it for prints."

Jessie watched, wide-eyed, as Drew took a pair of latex gloves out of a packet from inside his jacket and pulled them on. That bright yellow police tape he'd had across the front door—now this.

Her insides churned as a memory hit her hard. "Drew, when I was in Hong Kong visiting a ginseng shop, I had a panic attack."

Frowning, he snapped the gloves onto his big hands. "Tell me about it."

"I—I got suddenly claustrophobic, even though I'd been really looking forward to visiting such a shop. I couldn't breathe, the smells got to me and I almost threw up. I've never had anything like that happen before," she said as he hefted the box and bounced it once to get a better grasp.

"And?" he prompted. "Tell me the rest."

"I thought—felt—someone was chasing me, when that was ridiculous. I ran back to the hotel and collapsed for hours—then your call woke me. The time zones are hard to figure, but I'm thinking that would have been around sunset here, the night she went missing."

She walked ahead of him into the kitchen where he put the box on the table. He straightened, turned and put his gloved hands on her shoulders. Grateful, needful, she lifted her hands to grip his wrists, encased in the thin latex.

"So you're thinking it was some kind of ESP from Mariah?" he asked. "Like she was in some kind of trouble right then? You've never had the mountain woman sixth sense, have you?"

"Never. I don't really believe in it, even though my mother said her mother had that gift. I didn't mean to sound crazy—I know we need hard facts."

"I'm glad you told me," he said, letting her go and pulling out a ladder-backed chair at the table for her. "If there's anything else like that, let me know. But right now, let's see if we can find something to really go on. I'd like us to check some of her deepest forest spots in a couple of hours, but I think it's worth it to go through this stuff first. If you come across anything that seems even vaguely useful, tell me and I'll write it down. Go ahead, Jess, okay?" he added when he saw her hesitate.

Why did she feel so afraid? She felt almost closed in again, as if a big, black box were shutting around her. Or a coffin with the thud, thud of soil hitting its lid. With a shudder, she dug into the jumble of papers and photos.

6

"I never would have found this back road," Tyler Finch told Cassie as they bounced along a rutted track in her old Ford truck.

"No offense, Mr. Finch, but even if you would have found it, that compact rental car wouldn't get you back in where we're going."

"I'd like it if you'd call me Tyler."

Pearl, squeezed in between them, piped up, "Finch is better 'cause it's a real pretty bird. It crunches seeds in its pow-ful beak."

"Pearl's getting to be quite a reader," Cassie said. "All right, I'll call you Tyler and you call me Cassie, but Pearl has to mind her manners and call you Mr. Finch."

"And I promise I won't crunch any seeds," he said.

Pearl found that funny. Her girl was warming up to this stranger fast, a good reminder for her mother to keep her distance. Poor Pearl, with no daddy—not one she knew, anyway. Shy as she was, she took to most men once she knew them. Pearl's loss was even greater than her own, and another reason a certain man deserved to die.

"What's this mountain ahead of us called?" Tyler asked.

"Big Blue, but the place we're going for your first shots is right by Shrieking Peak."

"Sounds haunted. Does a story go with that?"

"Not that I know of. When the wind blows, which is most of the time, it sounds like a woman screaming."

"Your friend's mother you were telling me about—"

"Mariah Lockwood."

"Yes. Could she have wandered up into this area?"

"That's one of the good things about

working for you, Mr.—Tyler. We're going to keep a good eye out for signs of her, as well as for pretty places for your photos. Mariah Lockwood wandered far and wide, that's why it's been so hellfire hard to find her. Oh, sorry for the cussing. Pearl, you just forget you heard that now."

She parked the truck where the thick stands of oak and basswood began, and they hiked up toward the place she knew would not only suit Tyler Finch but awe him. Their pace was slow, because he didn't seem used to the rough terrain and Pearl's legs were still so short. Besides, might as well treasure their time together—the extra money, that is, 'cause he said he'd pay her each and every day.

"So," she said, trying not to stare at him, "tell me more about your work."

"There's hard work and then there is joy work. Not that I don't like my job, but I often have to go into the city—New York. It's a bit too crowded and noisy for me, and I'm always fenced in by someone else's ideas. For example, my assignment here is to get some photos of sites where TV ads for a power drink could be shot later—with live people."

"Better'n dead ones. Ginseng power drinks?"

"Right. I'd like some really winsome ads, but we'll probably have pro athletes hiking or rafting around here."

Cassie wasn't sure what *winsome* meant, but it must have something to do with winning. She nodded to encourage him.

"Our client puts caffeine and ginseng in their liquid sports aids," he explained. "G-Man and G-Woman Drinks. Bailey and Keller, my advertising firm, helps a client build a brand name and tell their story."

"Tell their story," she repeated. "That's important, I reckon, even for things, let alone for people."

"Someday, Cassie," he said, stopping and turning to face her, "will you tell me your story?"

She shrugged but smiled. "Not much to tell. Will you tell me yours then?"

"Yeah," Pearl said with an impish grin. "Like you have to go first!"

He smiled at both of them, then got serious again. "On paper, my story is not important. I plead guilty to being an artistic workaholic unhappily wedded to the corporate world. Divorced, no kids, not much family left but some cousins—one who lives in Highboro, so I know the general area and love it. I make a good salary, but that doesn't fulfill me. The joy work I mentioned is my own project, a book about Appalachia, mostly pictures, some text."

"So these photos you want are for both your hard work and joy work?"

Their gazes snagged and held. The wind ruffled his short, sun-struck hair. He looked so wholesome—winsome—kind of like he belonged here and yet was some sort of alien invader. Don't do this, Cassie told herself. Don't go feeling all shaky about this man just 'cause he looks like that and talks to you real heartfeltlike.

"Exactly," he said when she'd forgotten what she'd asked and Pearl tugged at her hand. "Are we almost there? I think I hear the shrieking woman and something else—a roar."

"It's not a monster, so don't worry!" Pearl put in.

Cassie thought of Mariah again, lost or hurt in these parts somewhere. Had Mariah called for help but there was no one to hear? Or had someone hurt her—or worse? Tyler was staring at her again, and Pearl was yanking her along.

"That roar's Indian Falls," Cassie said, as the world seemed to rotate back into place again. She had to keep shoving strands of her long red hair out of her eyes. "By the way, there's a Cherokee man lives 'round here you might like to meet if you want good stories for your book. He says his people believe waterfalls and large trees can capture your soul, and that the woods are a sacred but scary place."

Even when they climbed to the crest of the open hillside and Cassie pointed toward Big Blue's massive gray-and-purple shoulders shrugging off the crashing waters of the falls, Tyler Finch kept looking at her for a long moment.

"This takes my breath away," he said as he finally turned to see the sights stretched out before them.

"I feel like we didn't find a darned thing," Jessie told Drew as they headed for Mariah's door. She'd added one of her mother's jackets and a pair of hiking boots to her jeans and sweatshirt. They had found no clue about where to start looking for a needle in this massive haystack of trees and hollows and hills.

Jessie's feet and spirits were dragging now. Earlier, she'd been on a roller-coaster ride of emotions as she'd searched through her mother's things in her metal box. The deed to this land, records of income tax returns. A large, dried ginseng plant—a five-pronger—pressed between pieces of wax paper had somehow gotten stuck in the big envelope with her parent's marriage license. There had been old school photos of herself, skinny and gawky. "Man, you have changed!" Drew had said, looking over her shoulder. They had also found faded pictures of her parents in their courting days, a few of her father she'd never seen.

Also, copies of past ginseng counts, which had been pulled from another large envelope, then half-stuffed back in. But to their dismay, nothing hinted at particular sang counting sites, past or present. In haste, had her mother pulled what she needed from this envelope, then thrust the rest back in?

Jessie could tell Drew was upset, too, though he promised they'd spend days looking for signs of Mariah if they had to.

His words echoed in Jessie's head and heart. Signs, as if her mother had left a message behind, but wasn't around herself anymore . . .

"What's this behind the door?" Drew asked as he opened it for her to go outside ahead of him. He reached down to pick up a calendar that was wedged on its side, standing upright against the wall.

"Oh, a calendar I gave her for Christmas," she told him as he handed it to her. "I thought she'd like all the photos of the flowers for each month. It must have been tacked on the wall behind the door and got bumped off."

"Check it to see if she listed places she was going to count sang."

She flipped back a page to Mariah's major counting month of August and skimmed the entries. Vern Tarver's name was listed about twice a week with the name of restaurants in Highboro. Mariah's scrawling handwriting recorded a church covered-dish supper to raise money for Widow Winchester. "Look," she said, pointing at a Wednesday in August. "This doesn't say *Sang* but *Sung*—Peter Sung's name!"

"Your hunch about talking to him sounds

right on. I'll have to check if he was in town then. Anything under the first few September dates?"

She flipped to the current month. Since her mother had disappeared on the fourth, not much was filled in but for Vern's name— this time crossed off heavily, jaggedly, on the third. On the fourth, scribbled in light pencil, was *Semples OK.*

"Does that say *samples?*" Drew asked, reading it upside-down. "Maybe Peter Sung wanted some samples of wild ginseng to know the quality he could expect to buy this year."

"No, see—the *S* is capitalized. *Semples.*"

"Junior and Charity Semple? They're the only Semples in the area, and he grows raised sang up in the woods above his place. But would she count sang that's not wild but cultivated?"

"I'm pretty sure she always kept an eye on his crop—technical name, virtually wild sang. The crop's health is a valid indicator since, once he plants the seeds, Mother Nature takes over. He used to have a couple acres of sang, scattered throughout the woods above his house."

"It's worth a try, a place to start. And that notation is on the day she disappeared."

"You're sure she got that far—that is, left the house that day and wasn't somehow taken from here?" she asked.

"A couple of people spotted her walking along the highway that morning—come to think of it, in the direction of the Semples'. I'll go check on this at their place."

"You?" she challenged, stepping ahead and turning to face him as he tried to pass her to head out the door. She raised her chin to look him in the eye. "I thought we were working together on this."

"Jess, you remember Junior Semple. Believe me, he's gotten more cantankerous and off-the-wall over the years."

"Is he the one who tied copperhead snakes around his sang patch?"

"No, but he's paranoid about poachers. He's been in trouble before for his belief that the best defense is a good offense. I'll take you with me whenever I need help finding a sang site, but not out to the Semples'."

They faced each other squarely in the doorway, half in, half out. She didn't budge. "I realize the man used to be trigger-happy," she conceded, "but he might tell you more if I were there. It would be like a daughter just looking for her mother with your help, not some official investigation. You'd probably spook him, now that you're sheriff here."

"I don't want you getting hurt. You should be here, in case word comes about Mariah's whereabouts."

"You mean I'm allowed to stay here now?"

"Yes, but don't make this—"

"Difficult? It is, Drew! I'm going with you. Please, or else you can just lock me up in your jail cell!"

He opened his mouth to say something else, then just shook his head and raked his fingers through his hair. "All right. You just might be of help. But if Junior pulls anything, you do exactly what I say."

"Sir, yes, sir!"

He cocked his big head and squinted down at her. "You been around marines, ma'am? Then you know the chain of command is not something to mock or ignore. Let me have that calendar," he said, taking it from her and glaring down at it instead of her. "It may just be our first piece of evidence, not only because of Semples being listed here. Her crossing out of Vern Tarver's name, after this long string of dates, looks really angry. And if she was upset, maybe he was, too."

No one answered Drew's "Hello!" or knock at the Semples' one-story clapboard house back in Crooked Creek Hollow. Jessie hadn't been here for years, but the place boasted a typical scattering of buildings—not as ramshackle as she recalled—with deep forests hunkered above. Actually, the house looked newly painted, so maybe raised sang had paid for that. Her eyes took in the chicken coop with no chickens, the old rundown, roofless barn, sturdy smokehouse, and a work shed, all strung up a narrowing valley. Tombstones like broken teeth guarded a small family graveyard, the kind not allowed anymore. She couldn't read the dates on the mossy limestone markers, but the pioneers buried here had probably known Daniel Boone and Seth Bearclaws's ancestors, when all of this territory was their hunting ground.

"You got any memories about where Junior's sang patches are?" Drew asked her in a low voice. He kept shifting his narrowed stare, especially up into the deep shadows under the trees where a ragged dirt path zigzagged upward.

"No, but the patches will be on the northern exposure side of a gully, steep hillside or cove. Ginseng loves its privacy and leaf litter intact. Maybe in a woodlot with a beech or maple canopy overhead and maidenhair ferns and goldenseal to tip us off. I'll spot it if we walk up in there a ways. See, you do need me."

He turned and gave her a look that made her knees go weak. She hadn't meant to goad him. Was he just ticked off, or was that fierce look something else? He put a finger to his lips to signal silence as they went on.

After about a five-minute walk, they heard something before they saw anyone. A thud, crunch, thud, crunch. Someone digging. Maybe digging sang. Though Jessie had been leading, Drew seized her wrist and pulled her back behind him.

"Me first, now," he whispered as he

unsnapped the holster on his belt and pulled out his gun.

Drew noticed a couple of .22 caliber casings on the ground, the choice of rifle shells around here. Junior was one of the few men in the area who didn't keep coonhounds, so he was grateful they didn't have to fend those off.

Up ahead, on the breeze, he heard the digging sounds again. Ever since they'd opened that old, black box of Mariah's, stashed in her closet, he'd had a foreboding feeling that they hadn't found her because someone had buried her. Talk about Jess maybe having a sixth sense on this! The only capital case he'd worked over in Highboro was when a man killed, cut up and buried his wife in cardboard boxes in about ten different places. That whole investigation still haunted him.

Drew realized whoever was making the noise would hear them soon. Too many dried leaves on the forest floor and this path now, even though the trees hadn't shed this year's bounty yet. He'd love to get the drop on whoever it was, but it was probably Junior. He didn't want any trouble with Jess in tow, so he decided to sing out.

"Junior? You here'bouts? Drew Webb with Jessie Lockwood. Need a word with you!"

All was silent. Then Junior appeared to their side, not where the sounds had been. But Drew had seen many a mountain man move through the woods softer than a panther.

"Hey, now," Junior said. He had a rifle in his arms, at ease, not cocked. "Don't you know better'n sneaking up on someone like that?"

"That's why I yelled for you, like we did down below."

"Jessie," Junior said with a nod of his worn, backward baseball cap as he shuffled out from behind the tree. "Any word on Mariah?"

"That's why we're here, Junior," Drew said before she could answer. At least she seemed to be letting him take the lead. "Mariah had a notation on her daily calendar that she was coming up here the day she disappeared. So, did she get here—Tuesday, that is?"

Junior narrowed his eyes under his thatch of thick, gray eyebrows as if he had to consider his answer. Though he was probably about forty-five, his shaggy, salt-and-pepper hair made him look at least a decade older. He was tall and wiry but with big shoulders. He had a pronounced lazy eye, which always made it seem he was looking two places at once, both at you and past you, as if someone else might be sneaking up behind. Years ago, Drew and his brothers used to laugh about that cross-eyed look, but now it just made him nervous.

"Yeah, Mariah stopped by that day," Junior finally said after he made both of them swear not to talk about his sang patches to others. "She always does a count of a patch of my raised-up sang. To compare almost wild to the real wild, she says."

"So," Drew said, holstering his gun slowly, but leaving its cover unsnapped, "where and when on Tuesday, the fourth?"

"Right after dinnertime, 'bout one o'clock. Set a piece with Charity and me, had some Arizona iced tea Charity bought 'cause it has sang in it that could be our'n. Then

Charity went to see her mother in High-boro, so Mariah counted the spot where I was ready to dig."

"Would you mind showing us that spot?"

"But I'm telling you, not to breathe no word of any of this layout. Got me a friend other side of Big Blue guarded his forest sang spot like the dickens, but the one weekend he went away all summer, poachers hit and cleared him out of a $200,000 plus harvest. Don't trust no one," he said and turned away to hack and spit behind him. "Still, I know you got to look for Mariah."

Jess said, "We're really grateful for your help, Mr. Semple. Did she say anything about where she was going next when she left?"

Looking uncomfortable again, Junior shrugged, then said, "Up by Sunrise, I think, but that's a lot of land. Come on then, and walk behind me, right in my footsteps from here on up. Don't want no one trampling a sang plant down."

Drew knew enough about sang to see that there were no plants in this immediate area, so he wasn't sure why Junior was so touchy. Likely it was just his nature. Drew had had a fair-warning talk with him the first week he'd gotten here because Junior had gone far beyond leaving scarecrows around to frighten off possible poachers. He'd put out word of haints—spottings of spirits or ghosts—and even hung ghost-like sheets in the trees to scare off teenagers who had done some poaching. What Drew really feared, though, was how quick with the trigger-finger Junior could be. Sheriff Akers had said he'd been in jail for a month a couple of years ago for rigging shotguns to go off if anyone crossed a trip wire near his sang patches. He'd been a terrible prisoner, went berserk in his jail cell and was always yelling to get out.

"So how has your crop been this year?" Jess asked him.

"So-so," he said, though Drew could tell the patch they were approaching had three- and four-prongers, which were mature, valuable plants. But Junior had brought them to a very small, ragged patch, and he wondered if this really was the one Mariah had visited. What if Junior still had a shotgun or two rigged around here, and she'd gotten off the path and one discharged?

Would he just bury her to avoid trouble—
and a long stay in a prison cell?

"We heard you digging away," Drew
said. "Mind showing us exactly where?"

Junior turned and frowned. Drew had the
urge to pull Jess behind him again, but he
could get to his .45 as fast as Junior could
raise that rifle. "Tell you what," Junior said,
drawling his words more than ever. "I'll give
you the same demo I give Mariah."

In the same place? Drew wondered, but
he decided not to press his luck. Junior led
them around a large basswood tree and
pointed to a sang patch atop a sharp,
wooded hill with northern exposure. The
creek ran through a rocky bed about twenty
feet below. Sang plants, looking autumn-
yellow with their small clusters of red berries, nodded in the breeze along the whole
crest of the hill.

"I was digging somewheres right about
here while she counted," he told them and
pulled a homemade sang hoe out of the
leafy ground. It sported a sharp, needle-
nosed blade he must have cut and ham-
mered out from a shovel. Actually, Drew
thought, it made one hell of a makeshift
weapon.

"Damn poachers," Junior went on. "They done cut a lot out of this site last month, then slid down the hill over yonder and hiked out by the creek bed." He lifted the hoe, then stabbed it into the ground.

Drew could see he had already started to cut around a sang plant. Diggers always gave the root plenty of room to avoid cutting off the little root hairs. You never knew how big the so-called limbs of the taproot itself would be.

"Is this exactly where my mother did her count, just to get an idea of the rest of your patches scattered around here?" Jess asked, God bless her. He was right to bring her along. She knew when to keep her mouth shut and when to step in with a woman's softer approach to a key question.

"Right," Junior muttered, not looking up.

But Drew didn't believe him. Why would he show Mariah a spot that had been poached—unless he was just complaining to her so he could continue to justify his illegal attempts to attack poachers? Junior might have planted this sang and kept an eye on it, but the forest floor, even this close to his property, was open land. Unless Junior caught them, or unless they tried to sell stolen sang and didn't have a government license, poachers could get away with a fortune here. In the wilds like this, even if Junior slung the seeds and covered them up, the risk was all his.

"Ever think of starting a real big cultivation of sang, like they grow in farms in Wisconsin or Korea?" Jess was asking.

"Naw," Junior told her with a shake of his shaggy head. "Everybody knows sang's the most valuable nontimber plant you can grow in the woods. Even if the cultivated kind is easier to protect, wild sang's worth more, Miss Jessie, you know that. Still, gotta admit, high fences would cut down on varmints like deer—human varmints, too. That's the thing, and you both know it. When you're raising a crop worth five hundred dollars a pound that'll grow only in deep forest, you gotta do what you can to protect it. You understand that, don't you now, boy—Sheriff?"

Drew decided not to take the bait of another snide comment about his past. He knew Junior and others had no use for him, but he needed Junior now. But damn this old geezer for not volunteering the information about Mariah heading for

Sunrise Mountain three days ago. Knowing that could have kept search parties from wasting time around Big Blue. But was Junior even telling the truth now, or was this just a way to give them a quick show-and-tell and then get them out of here?

"This one's prob'ly four, five years old," Junior said. His voice had taken on a quickness; his hands on the hoe were actually shaking, and he'd put his rifle down on the ground, which made Drew feel a lot better. Maybe he was just overreacting to the scent of danger and duplicity here.

The ball of soil Junior was cutting out was about a foot around, six inches out from the stem on all sides. Cautiously, he tipped the root-ball out, then knelt and started to break the soil away with his fingers, careful not to harm the side roots or even their tiny hairs.

"I'll count the growth scars to see how old it really is," he told them. "Now lookie at this, good size! Dried, this root'll go for twenty dollars or more at Vern Tarver's, then end up with Peter Sung or that tall woman who buys for that power drinks company. Just think of that!"

He held it up toward them with the red

Appalachian soil still clinging to it. The root looked as if it was carved from old ivory, Drew thought, as Junior shook it cleaner. It had the shape of a twisted, crouching, many-legged beast. Seeing the sudden transformation in this man, from edgy and hesitant to eager and awed, Drew grasped the power of this valuable, strange plant people had lied and died for.

"That's it now," Junior told them, putting the root carefully on the ground. "That's what I did for Mariah—that's all I know. Go on back down now, by the same path you come up on."

Drew not only smelled the rich, earthy scent of the sang but a rat. Junior Semple was hiding something, but no way he could force him to tell what or run him in for questioning, though he'd like to get a crack at him without Jess around.

"Thanks for your time and the tip about Sunrise," Drew told Junior, and took hold of Jess's upper arm and firmly propelled her away.

"All right now," Junior called after them, all-too-obviously relieved they were going. "Just you watch your step on the path, 'cause it got some steep points."

"He's nervous about something," Jess said out of the side of her mouth. "He doesn't want us off this path." They started down until they were out of sight.

"Stay here one sec and let me just glance down the other side of this rise," he told her and put her on the far side of a big maple tree. "We'll never find footprints in this leaf litter, but I just want to see if I can spot a bigger patch nearby where he might really have taken Mariah for a count."

He moved quickly away and looked down at the crooked stream rattling along below. Someone could have taken a tumble along this jagged path through broken foliage, ferns and saplings. This was where Junior had said poachers slid down a hill. Yet he felt something was wrong here.

He walked back toward where he'd left Jess and saw her also looking over the edge of the rise. Maybe she'd found a clue, because she stooped and reached out for something protruding from the ground. At first he thought it might be a scrap of cloth. No, it was shaped more like a property line stake, though Semple's property was nowhere near this high up.

She heard him coming and turned his way, still reaching out toward the stake. "Drew," she said, "this looks like a half-buried marker stake, kind of shaped like a firecracker or something like th—"

Then he knew what it was, but the knowledge might have come too late.

"No—don't!" he shouted and threw himself at her, just as the thing went off.

7

As Jessie reached her hand out to examine the short, strange-looking stake, it hissed. She heard Drew cry, "Hold your breath!" but his big body knocked the air from her. He rolled them both away as the stake sprayed something into the air. They tumbled over the edge of the hill above the creek, clutching each other, bumping, hitting.

He did not try to brace them from going over; Jessie realized he wanted them away from the spray at any cost. At first, she thought they were in free fall, but they bounced downward against bushes that slowed them momentarily, then bent under their combined weight to release them again. Drew grabbed for branches; she tried to help.

His strong thighs clamped her legs between his so he took the brunt of each roll. Still, they cracked into saplings, spraying leaves, tasting dirt.

Dizzy. Would they roll clear down the hill to the creek bed? She banged her head against the ground, once, twice. Like so long ago, she was in his arms, spinning, wild.

Partway down the embankment, they slammed into a sapling that held them. Her head whipped back; his forehead hit her chin, but they stayed put.

"Wha—what was that?" she asked, clinging to him. His body felt as hard as the ground beneath them.

"Varmint stick—poison gas," he gasped out. "I'll have that bastard's head. Did you breathe any of it?"

"I don't think so. I heard it hiss, but then—then you—"

"Yeah. Thank God."

He struggled to sit up, balancing their weight against the sapling and the slant of ground. Wet leaves made them slip together; the sapling shuddered and bent, but held. Her legs were spread on either side of his hips, while his back pressed against the tree. Jessie tasted blood; she'd bitten the inside of her lip, but if that was the least that had happened, she was grateful. They must both be bruised and cut. He tugged her jacket and sweatshirt down in back where it had ridden up above her bra.

"You think Junior heard us?" she asked, clamping his shoulder with one hand and his bare waist with the other. His shirttail had come out; she touched skin over solid muscle. His back was wet, maybe cut. "Could he try to pick us off down here?" she asked and flinched instinctively. Both of them spoke with broken breath.

He looked beyond her, back up the hill. "If so, we'd be target practice by now. He obviously didn't want us to find that stake— or any others he must have planted to protect his sang patches."

"How poisonous is that stuff?" she asked to keep her sanity when she realized all this might imply. What if her mother had accidentally set off poison gas from a stake like that? And had not gotten away in time?

"It's deadly. The stuff's used to kill wolves and coyotes that threaten livestock, but it can kill a person. Cyanide and something else in there. I'm gonna get him on assault with a deadly weapon, I swear I am. You're sure nothing's broken?" he asked. His free hand skimmed and squeezed her arms and legs, as if to assure himself she was in one piece. She hurt all over, but the jolt of his touch muted anything else.

"If so, it beats breathing cyanide. You saved me, Drew. I should have known not to touch something like that, but I thought—"

"It's all right," he said, squinting up past her again, then twisting to look below. "Either he didn't hear us or did and hightailed it out of here."

"He said he wanted us to stay on the path. He said it was to avoid sang plants, but there wasn't one in sight then. Drew, I'm so scared about my mother. What if she . . ."

He hugged her hard, then said, "Damn, my gun's gone somewhere in our roll in the leaves. I didn't have the holster snapped shut. Gotta find it. When I do, I want you to stay put in my vehicle, then I'll take a rifle to arrest him. If he runs, I might need the longer range."

Pulling away from her while she held to the tree, he climbed up a ways, clawing through leaves, balancing himself on other saplings until he spotted his pistol and reached for it. "I'm starting to think we'd do better to go down instead of up, then follow the creek back out to the hollow," he told her, keeping it in his hand as he slid back to her. "You game?"

"You bet I am. From thinking we didn't have a lead, now we've got a couple. Junior Semple, Peter Sung and maybe Vern Tarver."

"Remember, Jess, you're next of kin, not deputy sheriff."

"You think she's dead!" she cried, seizing handfuls of his jacket and shirt as if she could shake something out of him. The sapling bent and shuddered under their weight.

"I didn't say that. Now sit down on your bottom, and we'll scoot from tree to tree to the creek bed. I've got to go get Junior."

She blinked back tears and nodded. As

crazy as it was, she would have stayed here longer with him, feeling safer than she had since she heard her mother was missing.

Jessie waited in Drew's locked Cherokee while he went back into the woods to arrest Junior Semple. He was obviously angry with himself as well as with Junior. Probably furious at her, too, but if she hadn't seen and set off the exploding stake, Drew would not have had an excuse to arrest and question Junior further.

While agonizing something awful had happened to her mother up in those woods and that something dire would happen to Drew, she used his first aid kit to doctor up the scratches on her face and arms. Looking in the rearview mirror, she picked leaves out of her hair, praying Drew would be safe and that Junior Semple would come clean about her mother. Or had he only been nervous that the sheriff would discover he had deadly devices—one at least and probably more—buried in public forest land around his sang patches?

She kept glancing up the path beyond

the holler, past the house and distant buildings. No Drew so far. Her stomach clenched. Had Junior resisted arrest? Laid a trap for him? Had Drew literally stumbled on another of those poison sticks?

Someone rapped on the back of the vehicle. Twisting around, she gasped. It was not Drew but Junior.

"Open up now!" he shouted, coming closer and knocking his knuckles on the front door. He bent down to look in the window and pulled at the locked door handle. "The sheriff's been hurt, Miss Jessie. I need some help to cart him down here. The wife's got our truck, so open up now!"

Her pulse pounded. Was he lying? What if he was telling the truth? She shook her head and reached for Drew's radio, though she wasn't sure how to work it. She bent over it, pretending to talk into the mouthpiece.

He lifted his rifle. For one moment, she was afraid he'd break the glass with the stock or shoot her right through the window, but he took off, loping toward his house. Dear God, she thought, what if Drew was really hurt and she didn't help?

As she kept an eye on Junior and des-

perately tried to turn the radio on, Drew
jumped out from behind the corner of the
house. When Junior lifted his rifle, Drew
tackled him; they went down, flailing, swinging fists, but Drew managed to get on top
of him, shove him facedown, yank his
hands behind him and cuff him. At least
she hadn't opened the door for Junior. He
must have wanted either the vehicle for escape or her for a hostage.

Though her first instinct was to get out
to help, she'd promised Drew she would
stay put. She watched as he dragged the
still-struggling man to his feet and hauled
him toward the Cherokee. Considering
Drew's rock-hard muscles, his agility astounded her.

Jessie unlocked the vehicle's doors for
them. "Watch your head, Mr. Semple," Drew
said, sounding amazingly in control, and
put him in the caged-off backseat of the
truck. "Jess, I've got to retrieve his weapon
and mine," Drew told her, matter-of-factly,
then got something else out of the back
storage area. Only slightly limping, he
stalked back to the Semple house and
stretched bright yellow crime tape across
the front door. He returned, carrying both

rifles and stowed them in the back of the vehicle.

"Did Mr. Semple have anything to say just now?" he asked her as he got in.

"Not a thing, though he'd earlier told me I had to open the door because you'd been hurt and needed help."

"Mr. Semple," Drew said as he started the engine, "I didn't know you were a fortune-teller. You must have meant *you* were about to be hurt and would soon need lots of help to avoid spending several years in jail."

Junior started ranting, but Drew ignored him for a moment and turned to her. He looked the worse for wear; she wanted to smooth his hair down and straighten his jacket and shirt, but just stared back at him. "I could use some patch-up work, too," he told her, evidently noting she'd used antiseptic on her cuts. But whatever he said next was drowned out by Junior's increasing tirade from the backseat.

"Man's got a right and a duty to protect his crop, Sheriff. The U.S. gov'ment's the one gives those sticks out for protection. Agriculture department through the Wildlife Services, you can just check on that."

"Oh, I will. And exactly who was it who sold or gave you those?"

"I said enough."

Jessie knew she should keep quiet, but she just couldn't. It was bad enough to kill an animal with poison gas, but if her mother had triggered one of those, it would be manslaughter. Though her back and rib muscles ached, she twisted around to glare at Semple through the wire mesh. He suddenly reminded her of a caged animal.

"You just about got us killed by that poison gas," she accused. "So what about my mother?"

"What about her? Left my place just fine, so don't you go trying to pin nothing on me. Went on up to Sunrise Mountain, she said. That's where she must of gone."

"I want the name of the man who sold you those poison sticks, Junior," Drew demanded as Jessie turned back in her seat and snapped on her safety belt. "If someone misled you, was a bad influence on you, I need to know. Spit it out fast, because once word gets out you're in the Deep Down jail—or the one in Highboro— some real bad boys are going to be looking for your sang."

"Anything happens to that, it's on your head—both of yourn."

Jessie got goose bumps, but Drew seemed to ignore that threat. "And I want a map of where you pounded in each and every one of those varmint sticks," he told Junior.

"Varmint sticks, that's what they are. Not for human animals, no sir, not on my watch and land."

"Here's a news flash, Junior," Drew said as he drove out of Semple's lane onto the highway. "The forests of Appalachia, however close they are to your house, are not your land. Besides Mariah Lockwood, if anyone got hurt up there—even if it was a poacher—you'd be looking at big prison time, not just a few days in a town or county jail!"

Jessie drove her car home from where it had been parked in front of the sheriff's office. Drew would not let her stay while he questioned Junior, who had gone as silent as a stone. He was going to drive him into Sheriff Akers's jurisdiction in Highboro after he completed the paperwork and initial interrogation.

Again, it felt so strange to Jessie to be coming home without her mother here to greet her. No Seth Bearclaws on the porch this time. She felt as if someone were watching her, though she figured it was just the funny feeling Seth's carved tree trunk gave her. It sat solidly by the porch, like a squat totem pole with its message to be read by passersby, though there were few enough of them back in the hollow. But in the shifting sunlight through the trees, the carving seemed to move with a life of its own, the sang swaying, the hands slightly moving. With a shudder, she wondered if his tree trunks, with deer and bear heads, seemed to come to life, too. She shook her head to clear it. This gift should just make her recall that she had wanted to thank Seth for it, that was all.

Jessie soaked her aching, bruised body in the bathtub, then unpacked her laptop and plugged it into the phone line. The dial-up connection was slow as molasses, but, of course, she'd been lucky to talk her mother into a modem so she could work here when she was home. She used Google to find the term *varmint sticks* and learned it was also called an M-44. The sticks

sprayed two poisons, M-44 and sodium flu-
oroacetate, more commonly known as
Compound 1080. She shuddered, then began to shiver. Several people had been injured or died when they got a direct blast of
the poisons, and at least twenty thousand
coyotes, foxes and wolves had been "relatively humanely eliminated" by the exploding, spewing cloud. Hundreds of dogs and
other pets had been "unfortunately killed
when they stumbled on the sticks."

Jessie hugged herself hard. *Had* her
mother stumbled on one of those and was
Junior burying more than sang seeds in
that rich, forest soil?

She shut down her laptop and phoned
Drew to tell him what she'd learned about
the varmint sticks. He said Junior wasn't
giving up his source, but was still ranting
about his rights to protect his sang. Drew
was going to drive him into the bigger jail
at Highboro and fill out papers to keep him
there, so they could pursue other leads
about Mariah. He was sending back a
couple of officers from Highboro to use
Junior's hand-drawn map to carefully dig
up the other sticks. He was also going to
talk to Charity Semple, who was visiting

her mother in Highboro, to corroborate Junior's story that Mariah had visited them the morning she went missing. He had already phoned the judge there for a search warrant and contacted a forensics tech to examine the Semple home for possible traces to show Mariah had been there, especially since they hadn't come forward with that key information in timely fashion on their own.

"The men looking for the other poison sticks will look for signs of my mother in the forest, too?" she asked Drew.

"Absolutely. Both officers were on the earlier search teams. First thing tomorrow morning, you and I will head up toward Sunrise to see if you can recall any sang spots Mariah might have counted there. Meanwhile, I don't want you talking further to the other persons of interest. Now that we've got Junior in custody, that's Vern Tarver and Peter Sung."

"Is Sung in town now?"

"Not that I know of. I'm gonna check with Vern soon. Did you hear me about not questioning people on your own?"

"Yes. All right."

"I'll call you and come out to be sure

you're okay when I get back from Highboro. Besides, I need some patching up, Doctor."

"You know I'm not an M.D."

"Look, Jess, we both need patching up deep down, and I don't mean that as a pun. See you later."

She hung up the phone. She had to do something, so she wouldn't go crazy just sitting here waiting and agonizing. And Drew had not said one word about staying away from Seth Bearclaws.

It would do her good to exercise her sore muscles, Jessie told herself as she walked down the creek toward Seth Bearclaws's place. She wore a pair of her mother's jeans, though they were baggy on her, with a checkered blouse and denim jacket. She tried to keep herself from scratching her back, just below her waistline. Poison ivy from the tumble down the hill, she figured. She had twisted herself around to look in a mirror, then awkwardly covered the red rash with Neosporin and calamine lotion from her mother's medicine cabinet. At least her mother had that; at Cassie's, she would have found only healing herbs.

The old, familiar rattling of Slate Creek calmed her some. The clear water looked almost tinted orange with the combination of red Appalachian soil and golden sunlight. Its flow was perpetual, and the surrounding hills and trees seemed eternal, as if there was, indeed, nothing new under the sun. But everything had changed now. She was back in Deep Down, back with Drew. But what had happened to her mother?

She heard Seth, or at least his chain saw, from a distance. The buzzing, drilling sound seemed to echo through the trees. Yes, she saw him outside his one-story log house, bent over a tree stump, hefting the noisy saw to cut into the wood. Numerous tree trunks littered his front yard, some already cut, some intact, some upright, some on their sides. She realized she should be careful not to sneak up on him, though that hadn't done her and Drew much good approaching Junior Semple.

Jessie stopped to watch him, but, as she did, he turned and looked her way as if she'd screamed his name. He shut the saw off and put it down. He gestured for her to come closer, even as he picked up a long knife from the ground, then buried it in the stump where it quivered, darting off reflections from a shaft of sun.

"I wanted to thank you for the gift for my mother," she called to him as she walked closer.

He nodded and gestured she should sit on another half-carved stump, this one with a bear's head emerging from the rough wood. She was glad he didn't ask her inside. Despite what had happened to her and Drew in the open forest today, Seth's place had always made her nervous. His now-deceased wife, Anna, had made the place livable, but Jessie had been bothered by the strange things on the walls there. Cassie's place might be festooned with green or drying herbs, but Seth's walls displayed things he claimed were sacred to his tribe, things she thought were creepy as a kid: rattlesnake and copperhead skins, all dry and twisty; a ball of spiderwebs wound like thin yarn; old hornets' nests, turtle shells, deer antlers and all sorts of animal skulls he'd found in the forests that peered at her with empty eyes.

"Any more news of Mariah?" he asked,

making her memories vanish into the here and now.

"Nothing for sure. We do know she stopped at Charity and Junior Semple's, then maybe headed for the Sunrise area. Can you think of any ginseng spot there she might have wanted to count?"

He frowned and shrugged. He'd sat down on the stump beside the long knife he'd stuck there. It bounced sunlight onto his pant leg as he said, "It was under Snow Knob at Sunrise Mountain that my people were herded years ago, like cattle, to be driven westward on what was called the Trail of Tears."

"Oh. When their land was taken from them."

He nodded. "Nothing has changed. It is still taken from us one way or the other. Sacred sang, coal from the mines on the other side of the peaks, the very bones of the land—the trees."

"At least this area hasn't been logged for years."

"It's still scarred with all those old logging roads from when it was. And they will try again."

"The government?"

Looking down at the blade, he shook his head. "Men with dollar signs in their eyes like in a cartoon I saw once. Men like Ryan Buford."

"Who is Ryan Buford?"

"If you don't know, a blessing. A snake in the grass. Supposedly a surveyor, but he looks at the trees with hungry eyes and uses words like weapons. I asked him once about a curve in the road and he said, 'You mean an asymmetrical horizontal alignment?' and laughed. He is the worst of those who pretend to walk the forest as a friend but would like to kill it."

"Did he try to buy your land?"

Seth shook his head. "He doesn't want my land, just the trees."

"I've heard some do sell their trees off their properties—and some are taken, rustled by timber thieves. But not around here, not that I've heard about. You don't mean that he has been here to try to—"

"I should not have mentioned his name, because I vowed I would not. He just came to my mind when I thought of those who stole my people from this land in the Trail of Tears. I hope, Jessie Lockwood, that you find your mother safe and soon, and there will be no more tears for you."

She was deeply touched. "Seth, if you think of anyplace she might have been, especially up near Sunrise, please let me know. Or if you know anything about anyone who would want to hurt her—stop her," she said as she rose. Her voice snagged. Her view of him blurred to make two Seths, two tree stumps, two shining silver knives.

Raising a hand to him in farewell, she turned away and started home.

8

It was almost dark when Drew phoned to say he was back in Deep Down. "If it's okay, I'll come out to debrief you on today," he told her. "Besides, I have a bribe. After I got Junior a nice, snug jail cell, I got carryout Chinese from King Wah in Highboro, Peter Sung's favorite place there. Since your trip to Hong Kong was cut short, I thought you might like some Szechuan."

Jessie recalled that King Wah was one of the restaurants—the last one—her mother had listed on her calendar next to Vern Tarver's name, so Drew might have an ulterior motive for stopping there.

"If you have half the cuts and scrapes I do," she said, "as you said before, I can patch you up. Where are you now?"

"Turning onto your road. You'll see my headlights in a minute. If you didn't want a friend dropping by with dinner, I was just going to be the sheriff."

"I'll take both—and the Chinese," she told him, before realizing she sounded almost as eager as he did. Or was that over-eager?

She met him at the front door. "You clean up well," he told her. "Sorry I'm still a mess. I just hope we didn't roll through a poison ivy patch or a chigger hangout because my back is itching like crazy."

"Chigger bites take longer to show up, so I'm betting on P.I. Well, misery loves company."

"You, too?"

She nodded. "Drew, did you stop at King Wah's to check whether my mother and Vern Tarver went there on what may have been their last date?"

"You got it," he said, looking impressed. "If I ever get the funds to hire a deputy, I'll keep you in mind. Yeah, that was part of my motive, and to ask nonchalantly if Peter

Sung had been around lately. It just so happens he was in Highboro off and on last week, but—supposedly—didn't set foot in Deep Down."

"Strange—so close and yet so far. Then, my mother could have seen him, or vice versa."

"Yep. As for Mariah and Vern, the waitress I talked with recalled them because she knows Vern."

"I guess everybody knows Vern."

"You'd better sit down for the rest of this."

They stood looking at each other as he handed her the warm sack of food. "Go ahead," she said, not budging. "Tell me."

"The waitress says they came in all lovey-dovey but had some sort of argument and were barely speaking when they went out."

"Vern told me they didn't see eye-to-eye on everything."

"But the waitress thinks it was supposed to be a special night. He had flowers for her—store-bought ones—and took out a little box that maybe had a ring."

"An engagement ring? I can't believe

that. She would have said something about it to me if they were getting that serious."

"Maybe he was, she wasn't."

"Her thinking of marriage would shock me. Nothing against Vern, big man about town that he is, but she just never showed the slightest inclination to get close to a man after my father died."

"At any rate, though I'm still just grasping at straws, more than one lovers' quarrel has turned ugly. And if he harmed her, it wouldn't be unusual for him to then be the one who reports her missing as he did."

She set the sack of food on the dining room table, then slumped in a chair, before looking back up at him. "I can't thank you enough," she said, "for all you're doing to help find her. I know as time passes, it gets harder, beyond the golden window of twenty-four hours or whatever they call that."

"In most places, law enforcement won't even look for a missing adult for a week, maybe longer. But there's no way she left Deep Down on her own. Jess, thank you for hanging in emotionally, so you can help. And for making it easy for us to work together after—after all this time. So," he said, clapping his hands once, "I got the Kung Pao Deluxe and the waitress's name in case we need her later."

"To testify at a murder trial?" she blurted and jumped up to go out into the kitchen. "No, I'm not going to get hysterical. You can wash up out here, if you want, or use the bathroom." Forcing herself to keep busy, she got plates and utensils out while he washed his hands at the sink. "Peter Sung's favorite place around there, huh?" she asked, terrified to stop talking and moving, because she might collapse. She got out tall glasses and poured herbal tea over ice cubes. "I've only met him once. He seemed a very happy, clever man, very much in charge."

"Personable and generous," he said as he carried the iced tea to the table and seated himself. "But then, he ought to be. By working through Vern, I figure he's legally hauling hundreds of thousands of dollars' worth of sang out of here every year for the New York-based Kulong family to export to China. So if he glad-hands locals with whiskey or gives out those lucky ginseng roots on a chain as if they were rabbit's feet, it's a small price for him to pay."

"He hasn't tried to get you on his side with gifts?"

"Yeah, can you imagine? I didn't take the cut crystal decanter of whiskey—Scottish whiskey, no less. The guy has very diverse interests, most of them expensive. Vern says Sung's hobby is raising Plott hunting hounds, the kind bred specifically to hunt bears. The dogs are worth thousands apiece, so he puts an expensive electronic collar on every one of the dogs when he hunts. But I suppose," he added with a sigh, "Sung's learned not to typecast me, either. When I turned down his offer of Scotch, I told him I drink only wine since my long stint in Italy."

"If so, you're the only nonbeer, nonrotgut drinking guy around. So, did he accept a turndown from you?"

"No way. He came back on the next trip with a bottle of *Montepulciano d'Abruzzo,* which I also refused. I told him to give it to Vern Tarver. He stays in an apartment above Vern's sang store when he's not in Highboro or home in Lexington."

"Is Audrey Doyle and her pretty little B and B place too fussy for him?"

She watched Drew shift in his chair; he frowned, though she wasn't sure what she'd said wrong. He was actually squirming. "What about him—or her?" she asked.

"Nothing. My poison ivy, that's all. Let's eat. Actually, I would have liked to keep that wine because, when I don't eat at the Soup to Pie, I like to cook Italian. Love the stuff, loved Italy."

"I've never been but would like to go. So how often did you get home when you were stationed there? Do the marines get regular leaves? When have your brothers been back?"

She realized she'd asked for too much information at once, but she'd been dying to know if one of the Webb boys could have fathered Pearl. When he recited the times Josh and Gabe had been around, the dates didn't fit when Cassie must have conceived. Jessie did not miss it that he hadn't mentioned the times he'd been back in the area, but she didn't want to raise his suspicions by asking again right now. After all, a sheriff and a former Marine MP must have interrogated enough people that he'd recognize when he was on the receiving end of pointed questions.

But if she thought being too nosy made her feel uncomfortable, it was nothing next to his hiking up his shirt after dinner to show her his poison ivy rash on his muscle-rippled back. "Poison ivy's better than poison gas, but it's driving me nuts," he told her. "How about some relief, Doc? The part of it on my backside's the worst."

His backside?

"Mine's right above my waistband," she said. "Isn't yours?"

"A little lower, too. Here, I'll just slide my jeans down in back a bit. You sure it's not chiggers? I remember once my mom used nail polish on those when Josh and me and a couple of friends got them in the Baptist cemetery."

She tried to steady her hand as she stroked on the calamine lotion with a cotton ball. Facing away from her, the man had unsnapped his jeans and lowered them about three inches to uncover firm, white flesh just above the swell of his trim buttocks. Yes, he had a redder rash there. What was the matter with her, that she felt all hot yet shivery? She was acting like a moony, silly kid again.

"Feels weird," he told her as she dabbed it on.

"Just hold still. If we had Cassie here, she'd be insisting on the old-time cure of buttermilk and gunpowder. Actually, this pink lotion is a lovely shade on you."

He snorted. She had to keep talking. "So how did you and some other guys get chiggers in the Baptist cemetery, of all places?"

"That was the time we got in trouble from sticking lightning bug bodies on our chests and faces so we almost glowed. Then we'd jump out from behind the tombstones as cars drove by and caught us in their headlights. Pastor Snell was so startled he drove into the iron fence, and then there was hell to pay—if you know what I mean."

"There. Done. But you'd better stand still a second to make sure it's all dry." Her instinct was to bend down and blow on it, but no way was she doing that. She moved back to the table and screwed the top back on the lotion, then threw the cotton balls in the empty fried rice container.

"Jess." He said her name so softly, then cleared his throat. "Thanks for the help here—with the P.I. and with finding Mariah. Maybe when this is all over—when we've found her and know what happened to her—we can clear the air about what happened to us."

"Right. A good idea," she said, starting to clear the plates. No way could she bear to get into that minefield of emotions right now. Her legs suddenly weak, she sat down at the table.

"One reason I really admire your mother," he said, his voice raspy now, still facing the wall, "is that when I came back as sheriff, she was one of the few who really meant it when she welcomed me back. She could have actually had me arrested years ago. Granted, she sent you away, and I got in all kinds of trouble for making love to you, but her not bringing charges gave me a second chance. And so now," he added as he hiked up and snapped his jeans before he turned to face her, "I want to find her for you, but for me, too."

It was all too much. *Making love to you,* he'd said. She knew it wasn't that, then, for him, even if it was for her. But having him here, so close, so kind, terrified her almost as much as her feeling something awful—fatal—had happened to her mother. She put her elbows on the table on their unused chopsticks and, though she tried to stem the coming torrent, burst into tears.

Drew came over, evidently unsure whether to touch her or not.

"Sorry," she choked out, swiping her palms down her slick cheeks. "I'm not a weeper—honestly, because I know it doesn't do any good. Well, maybe it lets some of the pain out. I'll be all right."

He knelt by her chair, then muttered something under his breath. He stood, picked her up, then sat back down with her sideways on his lap. She held to him and sobbed, soaking his shirt, shaking as he held her tight. Here she'd broken down in front of Cassie and now Drew.

"Sorry," she repeated when her sobs quieted to mere hiccups. "It's just so hard not knowing."

"Know this," he whispered into the mussed curls along her temple, his breath heating her already flushed cheek. "I will not give up, on finding her or on—or on our search."

Jessie nodded and forced herself to sit up straighter, then to slide off his lap and stand. She was absolutely certain he had almost said, "I will not give up, on finding her—or on us."

After Cassie got Pearl into bed—that child was so excited because she'd given her a dollar from the hundred Tyler had paid her for four hours of work today—she called Jessie to tell her friend about her day. Jessie filled her in on what had happened at Junior Semple's, then blurted out, "Drew just left a while ago."

"And either you caught a cold today, 'long with that poison ivy, or you been crying," she told Jessie.

"I did kind of lose it again, this time in front of Drew instead of you."

"You want to come on over here tonight, too? Love to have you."

"Thanks, Cassie, but I need to stay here. I *want* to stay here. I feel closer to her."

A pause. Cassie almost asked her if she meant something strange by that, like she was feeling that Mariah had passed on from this earth, but she just gave her a minute rather than pouncing on her like she had about her feelings for Drew.

"So," Jessie said, "it worked out well with Tyler Finch?"

"Oh, yeah. A real talented gentleman, a rare and endangered breed around here."

"You told me once Pearl's father was real polite and bright."

"But he's not around here. Well, now you wormed that much out of me! Besides, he turned out to be a jerk, and I don't want to talk about him."

"Okay, try this. When I was sleeping in your room last night, I heard some strange, scratching sound outside and peeked out toward the wires where you hang the moss."

Cassie gasped. Was Jessie making some connection between Pearl's father and the strange sounds outside? "And saw what?" she asked.

"Not sure. I actually thought I saw someone tall looking at the house over the top wire—"

"How tall?"

"I don't know. However tall someone would have to be to look over the top wire, unless he was standing on something out there. Then he—or she—turned away. But since Pearl says you go out a lot in the dark, I figure it was you out there, working, maybe standing on something to pick moss or whatever."

"Pearl says I go out a lot in the dark? That child's mixing reality up with some funny dream she had," Cassie insisted, but the hair on the nape of her neck prickled. Not only because Pearl knew she'd gone out a lot, but because Jessie, as upset and exhausted as she'd been, might have seen someone watching the place. More'n once, Cassie'd had the feeling the house was being watched, although not when she'd been out there in the early morning herself, working on her poisonous herbs. Yet what if someone was spying on what she was doing? What if *he* was back?

"I finally figured out," Jessie was saying, still sounding as if she was talking from a rain barrel, "that the breeze was just blowing the pieces of moss on the wires."

"Yeah, that was probably it. Not to change the subject, but I just wanted you to know that Pearl and I are taking Tyler up by Bear Falls tomorrow. He loved Indian Falls and took a lot of pictures, but he wanted a waterfall he could get closer to. And now, since you said Junior Semple gave you that hint that Mariah might have gone up that way, I'll keep a special eye out for—for anything."

"We won't get in your way, but I think Drew and I are going up that way tomorrow, too. I know some patches Mother counted in that general area, but I'll bet she had some secret ones there, too. She never mentioned or even hinted at a few spots like that to you, did she? It's a big falls and a big area, the forest and valley southwest of Sunrise."

"Not that I can think of offhand, but I'll sleep on it." Cassie thanked her again for the scarves she'd brought her and Pearl. When they said their goodbyes and hung up, Cassie peeked in to be sure Pearl was asleep in her own little bed. Then she pulled her old shawl around her shoulders and stepped outside into the blowing dark. Barefoot despite the chill in the air, she padded around to the side of the house. There lay her special herb garden, the spot she'd fenced off with wire so Pearl could not get near these plants.

She unhooked and went through the makeshift wire gate, then fastened it behind her. Jessie had to be wrong about someone being outside. And if it was him, she'd know it. But to calm herself, in the light from the sliver of moon and the dim window, she surveyed her poison garden.

This late in the growing season, only two kinds of these herbs were in bloom. The poison parsley most folks called hemlock had lacy leaves and delicate white flowers that looked like ghost moths in the dark. Though ground-cherry was a low, spreading plant, she'd trained it to climb a wire trellis, and its bell-shaped, greenish-yellow blooms stood out against its elongated, heart-shaped leaves. Like the nightshade plant, its leaves were highly toxic. Loss of balance, a sense of suffocation, dilated pupils, then heart problems before impending death . . .

Cassie collapsed as if her legs were water, right where her mayapple plants had been. All these plants had flourished here in the four years plus since her lover— her one and only lover—had mocked her and left her. It was a story older than time, but she'd fallen for it, for him.

"What do you mean, you're pregnant?" he had shouted, turning from man to monster in that moment. "I know a lot of Deep Downers are a few cards short of a full deck, but you're smarter than that, Cassandra. You think you can trap me into marriage or child support this way? How do I even know the baby's mine?"

She had gaped at him, unable to catch her breath. "I didn't mean . . . I thought we loved each other . . ."

"In this world, there are plenty of definitions of love and making love. I don't intend to stay around here, and you sure as hell can't play wife in my life, so—"

"So get out of here then! I just thought it was right and honest for the father of my baby to know, but I'll—we'll be fine, just fine . . ."

"You don't have to turn toxic on me."

Toxic. Nothing toxic could have brought forth that little angel sleeping inside. He was the poisoner. Even now, he made her terrified to trust or care about Tyler, the most tempting man she'd laid eyes on since he'd deserted her. But she'd show him toxic. The day he'd stormed out for the last time, he'd given her one last stab, just like driving a knife into her heart.

"If you really intend to rear a child here, Cassandra," he'd said with a harsh glare, "you should get rid of all these hanging weeds. A toddler could make himself sick."

Sick. Very sick, that's what he was. She was going to make that fancy-talking, lying and deserting seducer even sicker, whether he came back to see his child or whether she had to go looking for him herself.

Like last night, with a start, Jessie awoke from a deep, exhausted sleep. Had she heard something? Had a bad dream woken her?

Her heart thudding, she sat up in her mother's bed. Oh, yes, she'd been dreaming about lab work, about looking through the microscope to find the ginseng breast cancer cure. But instead, through the lens, she'd seen her mother tumbling down a hill, then running, running from poison— poison gas shooting from a sharp knife, poison ivy closing in with its tendrils in a death trap.

What a screwed-up dream! Was it just

poison ivy and a varmint stick spewing gas that had inspired the nightmare? She put her face in her hands. Surely, it had just been a dream and not some sort of vision like the one she'd had in Hong Kong about being trapped and feeling desperate to flee. Her mother had said that Jessie's maternal grandmother, whom she had not known, only had the mountain sixth sense when another woman was in trouble. Her grand-mother had been a granny woman, or mid-wife. When her patients went into labor, they didn't even have to send someone to her for help, because she knew when their time had come and went to them. That sort of story had gone in one ear and out the other when Jessie was young, but it sud-denly seemed of utmost importance to re-call things her mother told her years ago.

She thought again of the carved stump with the ginseng plant Seth Bearclaws had done for her mother. The two protective hands above the plant—were they praying hands? Praying for mercy, for help? Jessie decided that tomorrow she would roll it in-side and put it by the hearth, a memorial to her mother until they found her.

"Mother, where are you? Where are you?"

Throwing the covers off, she got up. She decided to go through her mother's treasure box for the third time, or at least its contents, since Drew had taken the box itself to dust for prints. He'd taken Jessie's fingerprints, too, so he could eliminate them. But since the items in Mariah's box had been disturbed, it had to mean something of import had been taken or still lay within the box or the house, didn't it? Before she went to bed last night, Jessie had searched the drawers, closets and cupboards. She'd even looked inside Mariah's shoes, under and behind every piece of furniture, under the heavy crocks in the back sunroom. She fanned through the pages of the family Bible and other books, looking for what, she didn't know.

Now she pulled on her mother's familiar flannel robe and turned on more lights, though it was still pretty dim in here. The old place made strange sounds at night, as if its bones were creaking. But she was not going to jump at each noise. The place was securely locked, and Drew had said she could phone him anytime and he could be here in ten minutes.

She soon became engrossed in the pile of her mother's things she dumped on the bed. At first, she laid the old photos aside, but then studied them. Her parents had looked so happy together. What a tragedy her father had died so young. She used to call him Daddy, when she was her Deep Down self. That part of her past seemed separate from the woman she had become in Lexington and in her studies, work and travels. So was she really Jessie of Deep Down or Dr. Jessica Lockwood of Lexington?

She stroked the stiff, wax paper-entombed ginseng plant her mother had saved for some reason, maybe because it was such an excellent specimen. It had originally been stuck in the envelope that held their marriage license, probably just because it got thrust in there when her mother pulled something out in a hurry and messed things up—or when someone rifled through the box, searching for something. Maybe the sang sites, just as she and Drew had.

But then it hit her: the preserved sang

plant was not just saved because it was a prime plant. It was in the marriage license envelope for a reason.

She remembered something. Years ago, her mother had said that a secret sang spot up on Sunrise had provided enough roots for her parents to buy not only a marriage license, but that thin gold wedding band she still always wore and some items "so they could go to housekeeping." Bed linens, kitchen ware or some such.

Jessie bent forward on the sagging bed and scrabbled through the other photos. She'd seen one here she needed, one that might be a piece of the puzzle. "Yes!" she said and leaned to the side of the bed so she could better study the small, faded color photo under the lamp.

It had evidently been taken up along Bear Creek with Snow Knob, a part of Sunrise Mountain, in the background. Her father was standing out on a big rock with the creek rushing all around him. Her mother had said once that's where they'd decided to "get hitched up." A far different place, she thought, from a Chinese restaurant in Highboro, if Vern had actually proposed to Mariah there. So did this giant, precious sang plant and its long-gone root come from near the site in this picture? Could it be where Mariah had one of her secret, almost sacred spots to count?

Jessie grabbed her wristwatch off the beside table. Five-thirty in the morning, too early to phone Drew. It might be a shot in the dark, but if they could just match this photo with a specific place along Bear Creek, maybe they could find the nearby site her mother went to count that last day and never came back.

9

The minute Jessie heard Drew's voice on the phone the next morning, she blurted, "I have a general idea where we can look up near Sunrise, under Snow Knob. It may be a long shot, but . . ."

"Great. That's the general area where a couple of hounds seemed to pick up Mariah's scent but then lost it along the creek, so you may be on to something. But can you drive into town instead of me picking you up? Vern just dropped in to see how the search is coming along, so I'm going to question him now. You can wait in the outer office. I don't want you going to Sunrise without me along."

"Sure, I can drive in. But I also wanted to tell you that I got a call from Mother's contact in Frankfort at the U.S. Fish and Wildlife Service, Frank Redmond, the man she sends the sang counts to. He wanted to know if he could pull some strings to send people here to look for her, but I told him that had been done and he should call you."

"Did he have any clue about whether her counts would be high, normal or low?"

"I didn't ask directly, but I think he was worried about it being low."

"He took his time calling back, since I notified him the day after she went missing. He probably thought she'd just wander back in. The big bad city folk think us hillbillies just wander the hills and hollers all the time. I'll call him again and tell him we'll keep him apprised. See you soon."

Jessie managed to tip Seth Bearclaws's carving, then roll and shove it in through the front door to the hearth, though she couldn't get it upright again on her own. Even here, in lesser light, the carved sang plant and the hands seemed to move. She had to give Seth credit: for a fairly crude work of art, it was awesome, almost eerie.

After locking up the house, Jessie drove into town and parked in front of the sheriff's office. A tall, muscular but wiry woman was stretching her hamstrings, leaning over her raised legs, which she propped one at a time on the fender of a new-looking truck. She wore dark-green sweats and black running shoes. Even though traffic was relatively sparse around here, Jessie wondered why she'd want to blend in with the forests instead of standing out from them.

"Hi, Dr. Lockwood." She greeted Jessie so quickly that Jessie wondered if the woman had been waiting for her. "Sorry to hear about your mother's disappearance. I'm Beth Brazzo, publicity rep for G-Men and G-Woman health and power drinks," she said and thrust out her hand, which Jessie shook. Brazzo's grip was so strong she almost flinched.

"Thanks for your concern about my mother. So, what does the *G* stand for?" Jessie asked.

"Our initial ad campaign had a customer contest to decide that," she said. Her voice was deep, almost mannish. "The top three winners came up with great, grand and glorious—not much of a stretch, but exactly what we wanted. My colleague is the photographer Tyler Finch, who's shooting some demo sites for ads," she added.

"I haven't met Tyler, but my friend, Cassie Keenan, is helping him scout the sites."

"So I hear," she said, now reaching back over one shoulder at a time to pull up her bent leg by the toes of her running shoes. She had a ring of keys on a chain around her neck. They jingled when she moved a certain way.

Beth Brazzo was a real physical specimen. Olive-skinned to begin with, she sported a deep tan. She looked as if she should be on that cable TV network where buff women bounced around on exercise mats to encourage the couch potatoes watching that they, too, could have bods like that. She had coal-black hair, lots of it, yanked into a high ponytail. Ms. Brazzo wasn't beautiful, but striking, almost overpowering with her size and vitality. In comparison, Jessie felt exhausted and drained.

"Tyler told me he hired her," Brazzo said.

"He's always working on his pie-in-the-sky book, too, so I'm sure he's getting shots for that. But he'd better stick to business because I want to get a film crew and actors in here ASAP."

"You can't just use real people—locals, I mean?"

"Unions, actors' guild and all that. But Tyler says your friend is a natural beauty, like she stepped out of a Botticelli painting."

"She is a beauty, but I don't think that comparison would mean much to her. Nice to meet you, but if you'll excuse me . . ."

"I just wondered," Beth said, falling into lockstep with Jessie as she headed toward Drew's office, "if there's any word on how your mother's ginseng count was going. That is, if it was low enough that the government might step in and halt the harvesting for a while. My company is really hot to have some of the local Deep Down ginseng for our products, since we believe in truth in advertising. We might even go with a 'deep down satisfaction' ad campaign."

Jessie turned to look up into the woman's mahogany-dark eyes. "I really can't answer questions about her ginseng count, Ms. Brazzo."

"Can't or won't? Hey, didn't mean it that way," she said with a playful punch at Jessie's shoulder. "I'm just concerned for your mother, as well as for the ginseng, that's all. Well, got to get my four miles in. I'm meeting Tyler and Cassie at her place before I head for the hills for a while."

"Do you know where her place is? I don't think Tyler's been there."

"I know most of the hollers and trails around here from my daily runs. Love this area to jog in. Please call me Beth—and call me if I can do anything to help."

With a wave, she headed down the side of the highway toward Cassie's, her keys jingling around her neck. Jessie thought Beth Brazzo was a bit abrasive, but then, she really didn't know her yet.

She went inside the sheriff's office. Emmy Enloe, whom Jessie remembered as a gawky child from the time she left Deep Down, sat in front of a computer screen with an earphone in one ear; this was obviously the sheriff's 911 or call-in desk. But Emmy was not alone. A young man—well, maybe he was midthirties—swung around from talking with her, then stood. Emmy popped up, too, as if Jessie were a visiting VIP—or as if they'd been caught at something.

"Dr. Lockwood," Emmy said. "Please come on back and sit down. The sheriff said he'd be out in a bit. I was just fixin' to run down to the Soup to Pie during my break, so could I bring you something back? And, oh, this here is Ryan Buford, a surveyor who works in these parts off and on."

So this, Jessie thought, was the man Seth Bearclaws hated for his big vocabulary and the so-called dollar signs in his eyes for timber. After they exchanged greetings all around, Jessie took the third chair, she asked him, "You're a surveyor for a timber company?"

His smile flickered but held. "Actually, I work for the Department of Transportation. Ever since the sixties when President Lyndon Johnson took an interest in poverty in Appalachia, we've been improving the roads. You know what they used to say about roads around here? They aren't passable, not even jackassable."

Emmy giggled as if he'd made the most

clever joke. Jessie could see why the girl looked agog over this guy. Good-looking—if you liked the preppy, no-hair-out-of-place kind of guy—a sort of Ken doll. Then she silently scolded herself for judging him as quickly as she had Beth Brazzo. Just because Seth didn't like the man didn't mean he was the devil incarnate.

"I'll be glad to sit here and wait for the sheriff, if you want a break, Emmy—both of you," Jessie told them.

"Oh, thanks, Dr. Lock—"

"Jessie's fine," she told the girl. "Just Jessie."

With a bat of Emmy's eyelashes toward Ryan and a toss of her hair—body language from an interested female, if Jessie'd ever seen it—the two of them headed out, and Jessie moved into Emmy's chair in case an important phone call came in. When the door closed and things got quiet, she realized that Vern's and Drew's voices could be heard out here. It was obvious that Emmy and Ken doll had been interested in each other, rather than the conversation. Still, she'd have to tell Drew that he could be overheard.

"Yes, yes, all right!" Vern was saying. "I

asked her to marry me and she said no. So what? You don't think I had something to do with her disappearance, do you? Is that what you been circling 'round all this time?"

"I'm sure you understand I need to cover all the bases."

"But I'm already at home plate, Sheriff. With my reputation, you've got no right to— Oh, hell, okay. I was shocked she turned me down, that's all. Of course, I was upset—hurt, not angry. But I'll tell you one thing. I'll never set foot in a restaurant again where the staff is eavesdropping . . . spying . . ."

"So where were you the day Mariah went missing, say, after 10:00 a.m., when she was spotted walking along the highway?"

"You're serious about my being under suspicion for something? Are you nuts? I don't have to sit here and answer these questions from the likes of—"

"Then get a lawyer. Either level with me or get a lawyer, and we'll go from there."

"In this town? I get a lawyer and the rumor mill will be up and running. Okay, okay. All day I was either weighing and buying sang or in the museum above the store, starting to put things away for the cold season. Never get any visitors after Labor Day."

"Did you get it all done?"

"Naw, Peter Sung called and we talked business."

"Called from where?"

"From his home in Lexington, of course. If he was in this area, he'd drop in."

"Are you sure he was in Lexington? Did he say so?"

"You got him in your lineup, too? I know he was in Lexington 'cause I could hear those fancy-bred hunt hounds in the background, all right? He never travels with them unless he's going bear running with that club of his. Those crazy Chinese. You know he believes that bear gall and bile will reduce pain and cure a lot of ailments? Now, I'm convinced ginseng's a panacea, but bear bile?"

Vern was trying everything to change the subject, Jessie thought. She was starting to feel the cold undertow of his tone toward Drew. Defensive, yes, but disdainful, too. She grasped more fully now what Drew had to face around here to be the embodiment of law enforcement with his rebel background. Like her, he, too, was dealing with the split between his past and present. It made her feel even closer to him.

She'd always liked and looked up to Vern Tarver, but she saw other chinks in his big-man-about-town armor now. As close as he claimed to be to Peter Sung, he seemed to look down on the Chinese, too. Maybe Vern was prejudiced against those with different ethnic backgrounds, because he'd never gotten along with Seth Bearclaws, either.

"So," Drew's calm voice drifted to her, "you were in the Fur and Sang Trader, either upstairs or down, the entire day Mariah went missing?"

"Hell," Vern exploded, "where were you? Where was anybody who had a stake in her ginseng count staying high enough, so that we could all still benefit from the tradition of great wild sang around here? If there's been foul play, you'd better interrogate everyone in the hinterlands around here, especially the ones who could be poachers she stumbled on. I hear you arrested Junior Semple. I don't care if he grows his own sang, ask him where he was all that day!"

"I have, but now I'm talking to you. Besides being romantically rejected, you're the middleman for most of the sang that changes hands around here. A low sang count would mean a huge financial hit for you, to put it mildly."

"Now you listen up, Sheriff Drew Webb," Vern said. Jessie could picture him leaning forward over the desk toward him, maybe pointing. "You want cooperation in searching for Mariah, you got it. You want a blow-by-blow of what I did that day, including sitting on the toilet, so be it. But you'd better find her first, or what happened to her. I love that woman and am convinced I could have brought her around to seeing things my way."

"To marry you or pad the ginseng count?"

"That's it! I'm outta here. I'll have a complete schedule of where I was when, with corroborating witnesses, by supper time. Right now, I got me things to do."

Jessie was convinced she might get more out of Vern than Drew's frontal attack had. Just to be sure neither of them knew how much she'd heard, she got up and opened the front door, then pretended to be coming in as Vern stalked out of Drew's office.

"Jessie," Vern said only as he pushed past her and went out.

Drew's expression was somewhere between frustrated and angry. "Give me a sec, and we'll head out," he said and went down the back hall. His words floated back to her. "I'm not going out there without some hardware."

Bear Falls thundered down massive slabs of bedrock as if in giant steps. "Ooh," Cassie cried, lifting her face to the cooling spray and holding tight to Pearl on the damp, mossy rocks beside the torrent. It had been a sunny, warm climb up here, so this felt mighty good.

"Hold that position, will you?" Tyler called to her from one level down. "Let me get a shot of you tilting your face up into the mist. Profile, just a bit to the left. Yes, good!"

"You taking Pearl, too?"

"I will in a minute. Don't talk. Just great," he called up to her, but his voice was almost drowned by the roar. "It's like you're fading into the mist—fabulous."

Cassie had allowed Tyler to take pictures of her and Pearl today on their hike through the woods, then along Bear Creek where Pearl had skipped rocks, and now this. He'd told her he'd pay her extra for every shot of them he used for the book, but he was already paying her twenty-five dollars an hour—an hour!—for just taking him around. He was such a joy to be with that she didn't think she'd take extra for the personal pictures. Besides, he promised he'd give her color five-by-seven copies of any ones she wanted, even get them framed for her walls, as if there was room with all her drying herbs. Though she'd been trying to keep her defenses up against the flood of her feelings for him, she couldn't help liking and trusting Tyler Finch. At least Pearl's father hadn't ruined her outlook toward men in general.

All three of them holding hands, they clambered down to the grassy edge of the pool where the crashing waters made waves before twisting into two separate streams, one that went in a series of smaller falls down the west side of Sunrise Peak and one that became Bear Creek.

"So," Tyler said as she took out the picnic flask and poured cider for all three of them, then produced huge oatmeal cookies she'd put dried fruit in, "are there bears around Bear Falls and Bear Creek?"

"Used to be. Hunts drove them higher on the peaks, least most of them. Black bears in Kentucky got so rare they put a stop to hunting for now, though if you get special permission, your hounds can run and tree them. It's s'posed to scare them so they don't come 'round humans, though that's hardly fair. I mean, just like the Cherokees, it was their land first. You want to shoot a bear legally these days, you got to go to West Virginia or Tennessee. Why? You'd like to shoot one for your book?"

"I wouldn't mind some pics of endangered wildlife, and some of deep forest ginseng, come to think of it. Yeah, that would all fit."

"Is it a book about saving the environment—staying green?"

He didn't answer for a moment, and she turned her head to look at him. "Well, spit it out," she said, then silently cursed herself for not having said that better. But he knew by now she was no refined lady, and she figured that might be her appeal to him.

"Cassie, my book is about things being lost—a way of life passing away around here. It's called *Fading Appalachia.*"

"So my way of life—my life—is history. Our ways are over and dead."

"I didn't say that. I'm trying to make you understand—"

"Tyler Finch, haven't you heard that us li'l old hillbillies are a few cards short of a full deck?" she shrilled. She hadn't meant to react so strongly, but he'd misled her. He was fixing to put her and Pearl in a book about a faded, colorless, dead-as-a-doornail—

"Cassie," he said, reaching for her wrist when she stood abruptly and pulled Pearl to her feet, who squawked until Cassie gave her arm a little jerk. "I wanted you to know and trust me before I explained all that," he said, "so you wouldn't take the title and my intent the wrong way."

"Trust you? My mistake. Yes, I need the money, but I'm not selling out to a man who waltzes in here with the idea of putting me and Pearl on display in a book that says we're all fading away around here!"

"Cassie, wait!" he protested as he scrambled to pick up his gear and follow her. "Let me just show you some of the photos, how achingly beautiful they are, how they speak for the beauty and the loss of a lovely way of life—"

"It's not lost, but you can just get lost, far's I'm concerned. I'll drive you back to town and you can pay fading-away me for the day, but that's it!" she threw back over her shoulder.

At least Pearl knew to keep her mouth shut. Maybe 'cause she could see her ma was crying.

10

Jessie was surprised they didn't see Cassie's truck parked on the old logging road, but she could have parked somewhere else to hike up toward the base of Sunrise. She didn't mention it to Drew; they were still getting caught up with each other's news, though he had told her next to nothing about his talk with Vern, so she told him absolutely nothing about overhearing some of it. She did, however, give him her impressions of Beth Brazzo and Ryan Buford.

"I've never spoken with the man," Drew said as they got their gear out of the Cherokee. Drew not only had his pistol on his belt but held a rifle diagonally across his upper torso. "Buford must have come in after I took Vern into my office," he went on, "maybe to see Emmy and not me. I hear he comes and goes, but he hasn't been around for a while. I'm sorry to hear he's sniffing around Emmy."

"You make him sound like a dog. Hope not, because she seemed pretty smitten."

At that, they fell silent. Jessie wondered if Drew was thinking of them, instead of naive, young Emmy and an older man, who no doubt had at least one other woman on his string—his leash.

As they approached the fringe of forest, high above them, clots of clouds devoured the sun while the jagged peaks of Sunrise Mountain seemed to rip the bottoms right out of those clouds. Slightly off to the west, bald, bulbous Snow Knob, which they would use as a guide, glared down at them over the tops of the trees. Shadows lengthened; the sweep of wind stilled as if holding its breath. But Jessie had learned long ago that the forest itself was never really silent. As they plunged into its blue-green depths, leaves rattled, limbs creaked, twigs snapped. Their booted feet crunched along the leaf-littered path.

She jumped when Drew, walking behind her, spoke. "The site in your photo looks familiar, but I'm afraid it's because so many places along Bear Creek look that way. Even with Snow Knob above, we might have to search a large area."

"I know," she said with a sigh. "But it's a clear enough picture of the rocks in the water that we should be able to find the spot, then look in the general area for sang—maybe even in a cove. She always said coves were the best."

"Coves along the creek or the lake up by the falls?"

"No, country boy. A forest cove. You know, deltas of rich soil near the foot of a mountain slope. Loam gets deposited there by streams coming down toward the hollows. Lots of hardwood trees with the overhead shady canopy that ginseng loves—I'm sounding like my mother."

It helped to talk, she thought. Drew kept her inner darkness and fears a bit at bay. It was only because their mission was so desperate and solemn that she felt the trees had eyes. She tried to buck herself up, but for once the familiar forests seemed not friend but foe. Was her mother here somewhere? If so, Jessie had to face the fact she might not only be injured but— but gone.

"Yeah, I've seen spots like that, hidden, some untouched," Drew was saying. "I remember one cove over on Big Blue where we used to hide out in an old drift mine shaft. You know, I never thought about the possibility that Mariah took refuge from the rain that night in an old pioneer mine shaft. Maybe she hurt her ankle and crawled in there for cover."

"But if she didn't have the strength to come back out, we might never find her."

He had nothing to say to that as the path got steeper. Now and then the clouds parted and the smothered sun shot shafts of light through the ragged canopy of old trees. Finally, they emerged in the long clearing that followed Bear Creek down from the falls above.

"Deer tracks," she told him. "I'll bet a lot of animals come to drink here."

"Even a coyote," he said, pointing. "Unlike dogs, they walk in a straight line. But with the heavy rain that first night Mariah went missing, I don't think we'll find her tracks."

They walked the south side of the creek, looking for the large rock Jessie's father was standing on in the picture.

"You inherited your father's curly hair," Drew said.

"I wish I could remember more about him."

"I wish I could forget more about my dad."

Witch hazel bushes grew along the creek bottom, their tight buds almost ready to burst in their autumn show of gold and yellow blooms. Jessie worried that years of plant growth might make the spot they sought look completely different from the picture, but she didn't say so. She didn't want Drew to give up on this stab-in-the-dark idea.

"Look, early pawpaws," she told him. "Mother and I love those."

"I always thought they were too small and mushy to fool with."

"You just never had someone fix them right for you, with cream, like custard. When we—when this is all over, I'll show you."

They could hear the distant thunder of

Bear Falls. Jessie recalled what Seth Bearclaws had said about his Cherokee people being herded together like animals to be driven westward on the Trail of Tears. Then she saw the big rock.

"Drew—there!"

He nodded, looking out at it, then took the picture from her trembling hand to study it again. They shifted their position slightly, so the rocks were aligned just right. "It sure looks like it. There are enough flat rocks along here that someone could easily get out to it—walk on top of the water, so to speak."

"Even if there was rain that first night, you said the hounds picked up her scent, then lost it. Maybe she walked along the creek for a while, then walked the rocks, and that's where they lost the scent."

"That could also mean she crossed the creek—that the sang site she sought was not necessarily on this side."

"If it is in a cove, it probably would be on the other side. I hope the daylight and weather holds, so we can really look around."

She put the picture in her backpack. Then, with Drew right behind her, their arms outstretched for balance, they went from rock to rock until they stood on the large one. "This is where he proposed to her, I'm pretty sure," she told him as he craned his neck to look all around. "She told me once it was like their own little island."

"So you think the spot they got the sang for money to get married is close to here?"

"I think we should look starting at the foot of the mountain where we might find a hardwood cove full of sang."

Standing on her parents' little island in a sudden slap of sun, their eyes met and held. He reached for her hand and squeezed it. Being with Drew gave her courage, but it was still what they hadn't said that scared her.

Cassie couldn't believe that Tyler had the nerve to return, after she'd told him to stay away. But here he came in that rental car of his, bouncing down the lane, driving right up and parking on the other side of the split rail fence where she was picking her early bittersweet crop she'd sell to craft stores. And what she hated most of all about his daring to come back, after just a couple of hours, was that she was glad to see him.

"Cassie, I know you're still upset, but don't run away," he said as he got out of the car, hauling a camera with him. He didn't even stop to close his car door.

"If you think I'm posing for more of your dead-way-of-life Appalachia pictures, you got another think coming!" she shouted.

"Just listen to me for a minute. I have to show you something in one of the photos."

"You did show me the photos," she told him, still madly snapping off the twigs of red-orange berries. "Real modern, how that digital camera can pop up all the pictures on its little screen. Why, it makes the old cameras we folks who are fading away use look like they—and we—are in the dark ages. How about a title like *Dark Ages Appalachia?*"

"Cassie, I'm sorry you took offense, but I'm serious about this. Look, please," he said and thrust the camera at her over the fence.

"It isn't something about Mariah, is it?" she asked, finally looking up at him.

"I don't know. I can't tell what it is."

His brow was crumpled into a deep frown. As mad as she was at him, she wanted to reach out and smooth it. She put her ragged bouquet of bittersweet on the ground. Her fingers were dirty, but she wiped them on her jeans.

"All right, let me see it."

"I thought you might know what it is," he went on as he handed her the camera. "I can't recall exactly where this was taken—before we got to Bear Creek and hiked on up?"

He was really distressed, but that was fine with her, she tried to tell herself, as she looked at the small photo on the screen. It was a picture of her and Pearl, holding hands, walking along Bear Creek before they went on up toward the falls. Tyler had taken the picture from the mountain side of the creek. The edge of forest was only about thirty feet behind them and full of shadows, but there was one really strange shadow, or tree trunk or . . .

"You mean that big, dark thing back in the trees?" she asked.

"Yeah. You said the bears are higher up."

"Maybe it's just a trick of the light. A

large tree trunk mixed in with the others. The sun kept popping in and out."

"I know, and the forest canopy made things look mottled, but . . ."

"It is really funny, isn't it? I mean, not 'ha-ha,' but weird. Can't be a person—too tall, with a strange-shaped head. What in tarnation?" she muttered as she continued to squint at it. She turned away, shaded the screen with her hand to see it better. "Black bears don't stand that tall," she told him. "This would be more like a Kodiak or grizzly, and we don't have them around here. I—I guess it could be a really tall person, but wearing what—and why? Can you make this bigger?"

"I've already tried, but it gets too fuzzy to make out. It needs more resolution with the zoom—to be clearer, I mean."

"Don't talk down to me, New York City photographer. What about printing it out then?"

"Yes, yes, I will, but my laptop and printer are back in Highboro at my cousin's place, and I might even need more enhancement equipment than that. You said the sheriff and Jessie were going toward Bear Creek today. Maybe they'll see it."

"Yeah, but if it is something weird, what if it sees them first?"

In the first hardwood cove, when Jessie saw the bony bundle on the ground, she screamed. Drew racked his shotgun with a loud *clack-clack* and rushed to her. She stood with her hands pressed to her mouth, staring at the thing sprawled in the leaves.

"A deer carcass, that's all," he said, throwing an arm around her shoulders and pulling her against his side. Her shoulder bounced his shotgun. His weapons had bothered her before. Now they made her feel a bit better.

She nodded but could not stop shaking. Yes, she saw what it was now, the deer skull and spine with tattered gray hide clinging to it. It made her sick to see that scavengers had scattered the leg bones. Predators had no doubt been gnawing at it . . . Her mind would go no further.

"Come on," Drew coaxed and pulled her away. "Don't let that get to you. Let's keep looking. One cove down and more to go."

"Seth would love to find something like that," she told him as they walked away. "He loves to collect skulls from the forest."

"I know. That cove had hardly any sang but the next one might."

He was right. The next cove under Snow Knob had more sang than she could have imagined, nodding its stems and bounteous yellowing leaves at them, sheltered by the cool rock and the embrace of tall poplar, beeches and maples. Rich loam, leaf litter, water runoff—the perfect place for ginseng to flourish.

"Amazing," she said. "I'll bet this is what ginseng patches used to look like before everyone learned the value of it, medicinal and fiscal. If only there were places like this where I could get some roots—maybe leaves too—to test in my lab," she said, walking through the nearly knee-high plants. "Either no one has found it for years, or it's one of the places mother counted and told no one about. Drew, look. Over here! Someone's dug out a part of the patch, and in a really strange way."

He came over quickly. "It looks like some sort of pattern—a design," he said.

A curved spade or hoe had slashed the earth where sang roots must have been dug out. A hoe like Junior Semple had been using?

"Mariah didn't mark her sites in any way, did she?" Drew asked.

"Not the few times I was with her, not that I recall. But look at the sang berries, too, carefully arranged. What is that pattern supposed to be?"

"Not sure," he said, squatting down to examine the bloodred berries closer. "Spears? Long claws? Fangs?"

Jessie shuddered. The sight of that ravaged deer carcass jumped into her mind again. "I wish we had Tyler Finch with us," she said. "If we had a photo of this design, maybe we could figure out something later."

"You're sure it couldn't be related to your mother's count? I mean, like she put the berries there to mark the number or the site. Or when she saw someone had dug here, she replanted?"

"Not like that. To replant, you just sling them, imitating the way the plants drop them." She moved outside of the edges of the patch to view the berries from the opposite direction. Were they in the pattern of fence posts, meaning keep out? No, Drew was right. It did look more like teeth or fangs. But then she caught sight of something bright yellow on the ground beneath the yellowing sang and moved to it.

"Drew—a pencil," she said, picking it up carefully by its eraser, a big one fitted on the end over the smaller one.

"Could it be hers?"

"It's what she used—the extra eraser, too."

He walked with her shoulder-to-shoulder as they searched the rest of the area, looking around and under the sang. "Jess, this area over here looks trampled," he said, moving toward the other edge of the patch. It was on the far side, back toward the path they'd walked in on but in the other direction.

Jessie looked down where he pointed. "Could someone kneeling have made this?" she asked.

"Or someone fell here, or—I don't know."

"Let's look both ways along the path from here."

"You'd think, as late in the day as she must have been way up here," he reasoned aloud, "she would not have gone farther into the forest. She must have been heading back the other way at this point."

"Unless, when she was here, she thought

she'd look around to see if there were more strange hoe marks or berries at another sang patch farther in—if these designs were made before she got here. I'm still praying she didn't surprise poachers and run into trouble with them."

Clutching the pencil as if it were a lifeline, keeping Drew in sight, Jessie started down the deeper forest path just behind him. He held his shotgun up as if he expected trouble. Her pulse pounded. Yes, there was another small patch of sang ahead, its autumnal leaves beckoning. Spotting it before he did, she started for it at a good clip.

"Drew, look, over there!" she called, pointing and cutting through the fringe of goldenseal that so often grew near sang. Again the deep, curved hoe marks, some dug sang and berries, this time arranged in a primitive bear head. And, radiating from that head were the strange lines again, but all pointing in the same direction.

"Are we looking at more of Sam Bearclaws's art?" she asked. "Bear's teeth, like he wears around his neck? Could the design be a warning?"

"I don't know," he muttered, frowning as they walked farther into the patch. He kept looking ahead, all around, instead of down. "I realize he didn't like her counting the sang, but if the count was low, he should have wanted her to report it, so the government would protect it. You don't think that carved tree trunk was some sort of atonement for his harming her?"

"You mean the hands protecting the ginseng could actually be his?" A shiver snaked up her spine. Just this morning, Jessie had brought that carved piece into the very heart and hearth of her mother's home. What if Sam had actually meant it to be a sort of tombstone or memorial to her because he knew she was dead?

"He did tell me," she said, "there's a Cherokee saying that only one in four ginseng roots should be harvested, and I'm sure he'd want to replant."

"When did he tell you that?"

"When I went to thank him for carving the tree trunk for my mother." Drew shot her a stern look. "Well, you didn't tell me he was a suspect. I can't help it if he is now, maybe the number one suspect."

"The sang does look ceremoniously harvested, but who knows what the Chinese customs are—or who would like to blame something on Seth," Drew said. "Let's not jump to conclusions."

"Drew, her pack!" she cried when she spotted the big, old denim bag. On shaking legs, she rushed to it. "I bought her a new backpack this winter, but she must have still preferred this one. She's been here! Yes, this is hers!" she cried and fell to her knees to hug it to her.

Lifting the shotgun, Drew went down on one knee beside her as he scanned the area. "Check what's in it. See if her counts and notes are there."

"It doesn't feel like anything is inside," she told him, still holding it to her before she slowly opened it. "See, nothing."

"Then someone emptied it, and it wasn't some forest creature. Bring it. Let's keep looking."

"Should I call for her?"

"If you want, but . . ."

"But what? Drew, she could be out here hurt. However this looks, we can't give up on that possibility, can't give up on her.

Mother! Mariah Lockwood! Mother!" she cried, but her voice broke on a sob.

"Mariah!" Drew took up the call. "Mar-i-ah!"

They strained to listen. As the wind picked up and shifted directions, they heard only rustling leaves and their own footsteps. The third cove they came to was also partly stripped of its sang and marked with the red berries. But this time, they could both tell what the patterns showed.

"Claws or teeth, maybe," Drew said, "but I'm betting on arrows, pointing the way."

She could barely breathe. "The way to what?" she whispered.

They went different directions around a massive, hollow red cedar, the kind the Indians and early settlers used to take shelter in during storms or snow, the kind of tree that was sacred to Sam's people.

Nothing but more trees lay ahead, thicker in the deeper woods. Had they missed the meaning of the arrows? But now, with the change in wind direction, Jessie smelled something. Not skunk. Dear God, not something dead?

They circled back. Then, within the hollow shelter of the cedar, mostly hidden under slashed and dying sang piled inside the trunk, there she was—or what had been Mariah Lockwood.

11

The awful scent of death reached for them as they gaped at the half-obscured body, mostly shrouded by the dying plants. Mariah was curled up with one arm thrown across her head as if to protect her face. The thin band of her wedding ring glinted on her stark white, waxy finger.

Jessie heard a woman scream, "Mother! Mother—noooo!" Another scream rang in her ears as she pushed past Drew to run to the tree. The woman screaming—it was her.

Drew's iron arm hit hard around her middle, knocking the breath from her.

When she fought him, he picked her up, draped over one arm while he dropped his shotgun with the other. Her rear and the backs of her legs pressed into his hips as he bent over to stop her thrashing.

"Jess, no, she's gone! You can't touch her, go to her. We have to stay away!"

"I have to see—"

"No closer. Crime scene!"

His words pierced her panic. Crime scene—crime. She sucked in a huge sob. Drew, steady as a rock, held her to him, wrapped in his arms. Finally, the trees stopped spinning. She almost regretted that her brain cleared. Shock and horror had been easier than this smothering devastation.

Had her mother huddled there and died? Of an injury? Hiding from an animal attack? A human animal? *Had* she been murdered by a poacher?

"If someone killed her, I'll kill them!" she cried so bitterly she didn't know her own voice. She tried to wrench free of Drew again.

"Stop fighting me!" He sat her down tight against him, pulling his shotgun into his reach. At first she sobbed so hard she couldn't breathe, couldn't talk. Then, holding to him, she quieted. Drew still wasn't looking at her, but, with his hand on the gun, scanned the area. "We don't know for sure it's murder," he said, his voice raspy as if he, too, would cry. "She might have hurt herself somehow, then left those arrows to show a rescuer where she was and cut sang to hide under and keep warm at night. Stay here a minute," he ordered and pulled away to stand and go closer to the tree.

"I'm not leaving her," Jessie choked out, swiping at her slick cheeks with the sleeves of her jacket. "I'm not leaving her here alone any longer."

Still looking around, then down at Mariah's body, Drew held his breath and peered closer, then hurried back. "We need help, but cell phones and even my two-way won't work from here. We're going to have to hike back out, then get help to return for her body."

"I said, no! We can't leave her!" she said, scrambling to her feet. "I'm staying with her if you have to go for help."

"Jess, this area and the other three sang sites have to be preserved the way they are, and I'm responsible for that. For more than one reason, I can't leave you here."

"I won't touch her. I don't think she got there on her own. Someone did this, and we've got to find out who."

"Which means we'll have to find out why."

"Fear of a low sang count."

"It may be more. But I repeat, I can't leave you here. I'm going to have to be the one who secures the site. Can you handle a handgun, a repeat fire Beretta?"

She hated guns; she'd never fired any kind of gun, but she swiped at her tears again and told him, "I can handle anything I have to, to find who did this. I got us here, I can get out, then back again with help— if you'll take care of her."

Without a word, they hugged hard. She pressed her face against his shoulder.

"Jess, Jess, I'm so sorry. About what we've found, and that it took this long to find her. Yes, I'll guard her. Still, in case someone's hanging around here, I don't want you walking out alone. But I don't see another way."

"I'm not scared," she vowed as she stepped back from him. She glanced again at her mother's hiding place while Drew took out the handgun and his car keys. "I'm just," she told him, struggling for thoughts and words, "desolate but determined. If you can't find who's behind this, Drew, somehow, I will."

Cassie met Tyler just beyond her front porch, where he'd driven his car around while she'd checked on Pearl. "I'd go back toward Bear Creek with you," she told him, "but Pearl's really tuckered out and says she has a stomachache. Got to get some mint tea in her."

"It's all right. Can I leave my camera gear with you, though? If I'm not weighed down, I can retrace our steps up toward Sunrise faster. I'll feel naked without it, but if I see the place where that thing was again, I'll just mark the site and return later. It's going to be too dark soon for taking more shots of the site anyway. I'd rather not leave things in the car."

"Sure. 'Course, I can keep your stuff," she promised, realizing that her anger at him was gone with the wind. She took the camera and bag of equipment he handed her, pulling the strap of the heavy bag up over her shoulder. But she worried about him going back into the woods without her. "You sure you remember the way?" she asked as she went out toward his car with him. "It's easy to get lost if you're not used to the area. Now, if you don't see the sheriff's SUV or Jessie's car—a blue Miata—don't you go traipsing into that forest, you hear?" she demanded, realizing she was starting to sound as if she was talking to Pearl. "The sheriff's armed, I'll bet, so—oh, what's all this?" she asked as she bent down to poke her head in the passenger side of the front seat of his car and saw a pile of dark clothes on the floor.

"I didn't mean to leave that there. A couple of costumes I thought someone could wear for a photo."

"Like who? Me and Pearl? Old-fashioned outfits, right?" she asked, touching a black bonnet and stroking the big, furry coonskin cap.

"I thought a sort of Daniel and Rebecca Boone photo in one of the little graveyards around here might be good. I gotta go, Cassie. I just hope the sheriff doesn't think I'm nuts. I guess the photo could be of some strange-looking tree or even a black bear standing on a stump to reach something, which made it look taller. Maybe, if I can find the exact spot, we can figure it out, Sheriff Webb and me."

"I didn't mean it, about not working for you anymore. I guess Appalachia *is* fading away."

"But with you," he said, bending forward to glance out at her as she moved away from the car, "it's never seemed so real and vital to me. Don't worry about me. I think I remember the path and, if I don't see their vehicle, I won't hike in."

He pulled out so fast his wheels spit dirt. She watched his rental car bounce down the bumpy lane and disappear. It had touched her heart how concerned he'd seemed about her friends, how anxious he was to tell them something strange might be in the woods. Besides, Mr. Tyler Finch of New York City had called Miss Cassandra Keenan of Deep Down, Kentucky, *real* and *vital.* Somehow, those were the two prettiest, sexiest, soft-soap words she'd ever heard.

Left alone with Mariah's corpse, Drew said an awkward prayer for Jess's safety and for his own strength to solve this case. It was only since he'd felt so alone, in the midst of his old hometown, that he had started to pray again like his mother had taught her sons. Then, taking advantage of the sinking sunlight, he carefully examined the area for any clues they might have missed.

Considering the position of the body, he figured it was pretty much in the center of the three sites with the sang berries pointing like arrows this way. He had to face it, the evidence so far suggested Seth Bearclaws. But he couldn't fathom the man doing this, not unless he'd snapped. Seth had always seemed odd but nonviolent, and Drew was certain he had admired Mariah. But then, she was one who took living things from the forest, and Seth deeply resented that. If that was a motive, could Cassie be in danger, too?

Although Sam was his number one person of interest, that didn't clear Vern. Besides, Vern evidently liked the old Cherokee just a little less than he liked the new sheriff, and was clever enough to set something up to shift the blame. All that aside, it was still possible that Mariah'd had a heart attack or seizure. She could have left signposts so someone would find her, then crawled into this huge tree trunk for shelter where she died. Without moving the ginseng plants, he couldn't be sure, but he thought there was blood on her skin. He was tempted to uncover the corpse, but he'd need corroboration from others—damn, he hoped Sheriff Akers brought a camera—before any of the evidence was moved. Then he'd have to wait for the coroner's report.

"Sorry I didn't find you sooner, Mariah," he whispered. "I'll try to help Jess, but she's probably going back to the other life you gave her."

For once, the woods kind of spooked him. He kept his hands on the shotgun as he paced the perimeter of the area, unsure what he was looking for, especially since rain and blowing leaves had evidently obliterated any footprints from the day Mariah disappeared.

His foot snagged something on the ground; he jumped back, thinking it might be a snake. Damn, Junior Semple's varmint sticks had made him edgy. But it was a short belt or piece of black leather, lost or hidden under the leaves about fifty feet from the hollow tree that had been Mariah's forest coffin these last four days.

He lifted it with the shotgun muzzle. Had it come from a weapon or even a camera? Some kind of a restraint? A dog's collar? The kind with a computer chip or homing device embedded in it? Maybe one like Vern told him Peter Sung's special hunt hounds wore, so he could follow them when they chased bears.

Jessie alternated between fast walking and loping, at least until she got a stitch in her side and had to slow down. Light bled away under the heavy canopy of trees. By the time she got Sheriff Akers and some others out here, they would need lanterns. But she'd still find the way to lead them to the scene. She would not leave Drew or her mother out in the black depths of the forest all night.

Though she kept putting one foot before the other, she was shaking all over. If she had to shoot Drew's gun, which she carried out rather than in her backpack, she'd never hit her target. But surely, whoever had hurt—murdered—her mother must have fled long ago. Fled, like her thoughts . . . Her mind wandered, taunting her with long-ing and regrets.

"Please never forget or doubt how much I love you, honey," her mother had said when it was time for her to leave with Elinor that first time, the morning after she'd been caught with Drew. It had been *coitus inter-ruptus,* she'd heard Elinor whisper to a friend later and then had to look that up in a dictionary. Actually, Jessie realized now, as her thoughts came all jumbled and jag-ged, it was *lifus interruptus.* Her entire early life had been shattered when she was forced to become someone else. Af-ter that, even on visits to Deep Down, whether with Elinor or alone, nothing was quite the same. Nothing was right here ever again, maybe because, once she was through the rough patches with Elinor, she felt guilty about loving her new life.

And now this. This final, brutal, horrible parting. Why hadn't she told her mother how much she loved her, too?

Suddenly exhausted, thinking she might become sick, Jessie stopped and leaned against a tree. She could hear Bear Falls rushing over rocks, rushing on, like her life. She got hold of herself and pushed on.

Deeper, darker, the forest closed in around her. Childhood fears came back to her. She was Little Red Riding Hood hoping no wolf was stalking her, and the setting reminded her of the Grimm Brothers' tales of giants and ogres and beasts. But now the stories seemed real.

She saw she'd wandered slightly off the path, but got back on, checking for the tenth time to be sure she had the key to Drew's Cherokee. Drew. Drew Webb was back in her life. Was that only because they were forced to work together on this? When they found how her mother had died, who was at fault, would they be parted again? Her childhood home and the land in Slate Creek Hollow was hers now, but her life was in Lexington and in her lab. All those wilting ginseng leaves and plants heaped over her mother, as if for a funeral pyre. She had been wondering for weeks if she should test sang leaves to see if they could produce ginsenosides, just like the roots did. Leaves would be easier . . . cheaper and—

She heard the loud crack of a limb.

Where? What did that? It took something with great weight.

She glanced quickly behind, around. Shifting shadows, shuddering limbs and leaves. Quickening her pace again, she pressed her hand with Drew's key against her side and put her finger gingerly on the trigger of the gun. He'd given her hurried directions, though she still hadn't told him she'd never shot a gun. He'd said a round was in the chamber and that it wouldn't misfire. That she wouldn't have to cock it—just pull the trigger. That she had fifteen shots. What else had he said?

The wind picked up as if the woods were breathing; the breeze lifted her hair and dried her tears. The once familiar forest seemed to close in around her; the tree trunks rushing at her. Her footsteps through the leaves sounded incredibly loud.

Did she hear footsteps besides her own? Surely, nothing echoed in here like that. Footfalls, only in her fears. Folks said that certain places were haunted. She'd never heard tales of ghosts in these woods, but Seth had said many of his people had died marching through here on their brutal Trail of Tears. Had Sam chosen the place his people had faced death to kill a white person in revenge? No, too far-fetched. Too—demented. But was he? If someone had harmed her mother, he had to be deranged.

Dusk suddenly descended as if a lid had been closed on a box. Now, maybe she heard a deer shuffling through the leaves. She glanced back and gasped. In the last shreds of thin, setting sun through a pass in the mountains, dark, demon eyes glowed at her. A shrill cry escaped her, and she saw a raccoon skitter away. Like cat's eyes in the dark, those of coons and deer reflected light, that was all, that was all.

She broke into a run, but skidded on acorns down a slanted part of the path. That sent six feeding grouse into the air with flapping wings. Trying to break her fall with both hands, she went down hard. Her trigger finger jerked; the pistol discharged, a sharp sound that shook her arm and soul.

She prayed Drew hadn't heard that gunshot, or he'd be panicked. But he was surely too far away. Too far away . . . Her mother was so far away and never coming back and . . .

Scrambling to her feet, she retrieved the gun and hurried on. Limping slightly, she checked again to be sure she hadn't lost the key. It was still here. She was doing well, she tried to tell herself. She must be almost to the place they'd left Drew's Cherokee. Yet the woods seemed endless.

Then she was sure she heard someone, something, panting, running hard in this direction, coming closer, faster.

Should she make a stand and get ready to fire the gun again? As if her life depended on it, Jessie ran.

12

Frenzied . . . out of breath . . . trying to hold the pistol, Jessie sprinted for the edge of the trees where she'd find the road back to safety, to sanity. Except . . . except . . . if someone had killed her mother, would they want to kill her daughter, thinking she knew something, thinking she would just take over the sang counts? Precious sang. She needed it for her cancer work, so maybe she should stay here and fight for it, fight whoever did this . . .

Footsteps somewhere in the trees, coming closer, chasing her. Should she hide behind a tree? Had her mother hidden in that tree?

She stepped partly behind a tree trunk, turned and raised the gun, holding it with both hands to steady it. Her finger trembled on the trigger as she tried to stiffen her arms, and—

Tyler Finch ran out into the clearing. Had he been stalking her? Why hadn't she seen him on the path? She'd almost fired at him, but lowered the gun and hid it behind her hip as she stepped out in view.

"Ms. Lockwood," he said, out of breath. "I was trying to find you and the sheriff when I heard a shot. I think I got off the path—I must have passed you. I wanted to warn you that I got a shot—you know, a photo—of something strange in the woods today. I think it was watching Cassie, Pearl and me."

She was still so terrified that she had trouble grasping his words. "The sheriff and I found my mother's body," she blurted. "I'm going for help."

Saying that, especially to a stranger, made it suddenly real. It was as if the whole forest, all of shadow-shrouded Snow Knob and Sunrise, fell on her.

"I can go for help," he said, but it seemed his words came from a great distance. She locked her knees to stand.

"No. I'll need to lead them to the sheriff and to—to her."

She started walking again and motioned for him to come along. As he fell in beside her, they were both sweating and panting. "What about the photo?" she asked him. "Who's in it? We'll need every clue we can get about who was in the woods."

"Not sure about the who, because it's more like a what," he explained, gesturing as if something were tall with a large head. "It may be nothing. I'm not sure, but it looks like a big bear. Cassie's got the camera for safekeeping."

Safekeeping, Jessie thought with a sigh of relief as Drew's Cherokee and Tyler's car came in view. But would these woods and mountains ever feel safe to her again?

Jessie was running on pure adrenaline as she led Sheriff Akers, a two-man paramedic team with a stretcher and the county coroner back into the woods after dark. As in many small towns or rural areas, Lowe County's elected coroner was not a pathologist or even a medical man, but, in this case, the owner of the largest funeral home in Highboro. Tyler Finch was permitted to accompany them, too, with his camera this time, because the Highboro Police Department photographer was not in town. High-powered flashlights and battery-powered lanterns lit their way into the forest. Only once did Jessie get them off the trail, but then right back on.

"You're amazing," Tyler told her. The gear in his backpack bounced rhythmically as he walked fast to keep up with them. "I wandered off this path right away, even in the light."

Tyler dropped back to tell the sheriff about the strange "creature" in his photo. While he was waiting for the search party to form, he'd downloaded it to his laptop in Highboro and had cleared his camera, so he didn't have it here. The sheriff kept shaking his head, whether in disbelief or amazement, she wasn't sure.

All they needed to bring more chaos to little Deep Down, Jessie thought, was a bunch of thrill seekers trampling the woods, not only looking at a possible murder site but searching for some sort of monster, Appalachia's answer to Bigfoot or the Abominable Snowman. The media could get hold of it and turn this entire area into a believe-it-or-not circus. Once Tyler got his photo enlarged, she was certain it would turn out to be just some strange juxtaposition of tree limbs. Or a large bear had wandered down from the heights for food. When they stretched to claw a tree, establishing territory, they could look much taller than they were. But in a crazy world where a potato chip that looked like the Virgin Mary could go for hundreds of dollars on eBay, who knows what Tyler would do with that photo.

"I'll take a look-see of that when you get it blown up," Sheriff Akers told Tyler.

Blown up—that's how she felt. Her mother's life had been obliterated, along with her own chance to say how much she had loved her. She wanted to thank her for giving her the best of Deep Down and of the outside world.

It wasn't that she hadn't loved her early days here—she had. Long wildcrafting walks with her mother, impromptu picnics in the woods. Lots of fun times running around with Cassie, too, church socials and school dances and hayrides when the harvest moon was full and her heart was, too. It wasn't a wide world like Elinor had given her outside Deep Down, but it was a precious one to treasure always.

"I hear the creek," she turned around to tell the men. "We'll cross at a spot where there are some big rocks to walk. It won't be far then."

She prayed that Drew would be safe. Would he have lit a fire for warmth and to mark the site? What if whatever Tyler claimed was in that photo sneaked up on Drew in the dark?

Jessie was pleased she seemed to be thinking straight, recalling things, reasoning this out. If the coroner ruled it was a homicide, she had to convince Drew that she was stable enough to help him find whoever had murdered her mother. Of course, these men must look into the possibility that Mariah had hurt herself, but Jessie knew better. Her mother was sure-footed, and her health had always been good. So that meant someone— some human monster—had robbed her of the rest of her life and robbed Jessie of so much, too.

They carefully illuminated the rocks across the creek with all their lights, and everyone made it over the water. Talking was harder now because of the distant roar of the falls. With her big flashlight beam probing the night, Jessie strode a bit ahead, past the first sang site they'd found.

"Drew?" she called. "Drew! We're here!"

He materialized from the night. Her light caught his rugged features from below, making it seem he wore a Halloween fright mask. Everything seemed unreal now, different in the darkness. She didn't care what anyone thought, she ran to him and hugged him hard.

"Thank God, you're safe," he said, then set her back slightly to shake Sheriff Akers's hand.

"Got us a paramedic team and the coroner, Drew."

"Thanks for coming, men, and Mr. Merriman," Drew said, nodding at each in turn. The coroner, Clayton Merriman, had a trimmed beard and mustache. Jessie had not met him before this evening, but he looked the part of an old-time undertaker, solemn, stiff and stern, as if he'd stepped out of an old Civil War tintype.

"I haven't touched anything in the immediate area," Drew went on. "It's a bizarre scene, to say the least. We'll need photos of three other nearby sites, too."

The men moved toward the hollow tree. Jessie was sweating but shivering, too. At first she stayed put, hugging herself for warmth, then went slowly closer, keeping her flashlight beam pointed at the ground, while the men had theirs trained into the hollow trunk. She saw the coroner pull out a jar of Vicks and put some in his nostrils, then pass the jar to the other men. The scent of the scene staggered her; she took some, too. Then, for a moment, she just stared into the outer darkness, until the strobe from Tyler's camera jolted her back to reality.

Longing to flee—to hide from this nightmare—she shuffled closer, listening to the crackle and swish of sang leaves as they carefully uncovered her mother's body. As the glare of lights and Tyler's flashes illumined the scene, she peered between the two sheriffs' shoulders.

She gasped. Long, red-black cuts or

scratches, like the patterns of the berries, marred her mother's cheeks and forehead. Her long hair, streaked and matted with blood, had come loose, but that didn't hide the fact her head was twisted at a terrible angle. Only that one arm, stretched out with her marriage band on the finger, seemed at all normal.

"It's not an accident!" Jessie cried, louder than she meant to, louder than the whine of wind or rumble of the falls. "It's murder!"

When Jessie woke, she wasn't sure where she was. Oh, yeah, Cassie's bed again. After the coroner had taken her mother's body to Highboro for an autopsy, Drew would not let Jessie go home again. He wanted to question Seth first thing in the morning. Seth lived too close to her place for her to spend the night there alone.

Cassie's bedroom was as black as the forest had been, and the wind moaned outside almost as bad as it did up on Shrieking Peak. A ghost floated into the room—Cassie in her long, white nightgown. Pearl had been sick to her stomach, but Cassie didn't want to leave Jessie alone, so she slept here but kept getting up to check on Pearl.

"You awake, Jessie?" she whispered.

"I think the wind woke me. What time is it?"

"Somewheres around three."

"How's Pearl's tummy?"

"Not much better, though I dosed her with feverfew and pennyroyal tea."

"Not good, old sang?"

"Would you believe, she doesn't like the taste of that?"

"Maybe she ate something from the gardens that made her sick."

"I got anything toxic fenced off out there." Her voice sounded contentious but then softened. "You want to talk? You 'bout collapsed when Drew got you here."

"There's not much to say until he tells us what the coroner learns from the autopsy. I've got to plan a funeral, and you can sure help with that."

"I'd be honored. I loved her, too."

"I know you did. We both had two mothers, didn't we?"

Cassie got back under the covers on her side of the bed and reached over on top of the quilt to squeeze Jessie's shoulder. "And sharing Mariah makes us at least half sisters, so anything I can do to help, I will."

Jessie clasped Cassie's hand before she pulled back. "I just can't fathom anyone hating or fearing my mother enough to commit murder. Can you? Why would anyone want to take another life, ever?"

Cassie shifted so hard away that the bed bounced.

"Cassie, do you know someone who had it in for her?"

"No, 'course not."

"Someone's going to pay. I know Drew will work hard at it, but I will, too. I'm going to take a leave of absence from my work, or maybe bring some of it here with me. I want to try using sang leaves instead of the rare roots to slow the growth of cancer tumors."

"It's a good thing you're doing—the lab work," Cassie told her, but her voice came muffled now that she was turned away.

"I want to ask you about something, to see if you think it's weird."

"Tyler's photo?"

"No. I'm thinking of using those ginseng plants that covered her body for lab work.

Then something that was with her at the end could be put to good use with the research. You don't think that's morbid, do you?"

"No. Waste not, want not. Mariah and I believed in putting things from the woods to good uses. 'Sides, lots of mountain women die from breast cancer, and it's near impossible to convince them to get mammograms. Your research might help them. And something else. You want to help Drew find out who hurt Mariah, I got a suggestion."

As Jessie leaned up on one elbow, she felt her poison ivy start itching again. Like her fears, it seemed worse at night. "Tell me," she said.

"Try catching flies with honey and not vinegar. You know, 'stead of taking someone like Vern Tarver on, like you said Drew did, pretend to lean on him. Vern, I mean. 'Sides, I'm not going to work for him this fall like I did last, so maybe he'll give you the job in the trade store, 'cause everyone who wants sang passes through there sooner or later. Peter Sung, that Brazzo woman, you name it."

"I had thought of that—being nice to

Vern, not working for him. But that's a good idea. I could put out the word I'm buying the sang plants while he's buying the roots. The leaves will just die back by winter anyway."

Again, Jessie was pleased that she was thinking straight, because she felt so twisted inside. This was all real, this living nightmare.

"Cassie, one more thing, then I'll shut up and let you sleep, because I know you've been up and down with Pearl all night. What did the thing in Tyler's photo look like to you? He said you saw it, but I haven't had a chance yet."

"Looks like a cross between a black bear too tall for these parts and an old mountain man. 'Member those stories some of the old miners used to tell about dead, trapped coal miners in those long-lost pioneer drift mines who emerged to take captives down below for company? They always wore some strange head covering and their skin and clothes hung real loose. I know, I know, just ghost stories, old haint tales. Emmy Enloe—works for Drew—was always one of the worst, telling those crazy yarns. She'll take to this one big-time."

"She's got another kind of critter on her mind big-time lately, and it's no monster. Some good-looking government surveyor named Ryan Buford's back in town, and Emmy looks ready to sign up for an up close and personal survey. Cassie, what is it?" she asked when her friend threw the covers off and got out of bed. "Sorry for yakking on, but it just helps to—"

"Pay me no mind. I just heard Pearl fussing, that's all," she said and hurried out.

Jessie dropped back on her pillow, blinking back tears that speckled her face and tracked down into her hairline and ears. She shouldn't have been carrying on so when Cassie, too, needed her sleep, but she was sure Pearl hadn't been fussing. Still, that was the thing about mothers: they could tell when their kids needed them before they even called.

She rolled onto her side and curled up in a fetal position. She needed her mother so bad now, so bad, but she was on her own.

Drew was surprised Jess looked as good as she did—she emanated an angry calm—when he picked her up the next morning at Cassie's. He told Cassie they knew nothing yet, and they waved to her as they pulled away. But when he looked at Jess this close, he saw her eyes were bloodshot from crying or lack of sleep. He hadn't been to bed last night, but she said she had.

"Really? Nothing yet from the coroner?" she asked as she fastened her seatbelt.

"The autopsy itself will be done this morning, but Clayton Merriman did some photos of the external cuts on her."

"But—those cuts didn't cause all that blood in her hair, did they? I was hoping—praying, she was already dead of a broken neck when she was cut. But dead people don't bleed."

Her knowledge surprised him. Most people who had seen TV or the movies or even Italian operas thought corpses bled dramatically all over the place. He turned to look at her, then immediately back to his driving.

"It looked like her neck was broken," he said, "but that wouldn't cause the bleeding either. On first examination, Merriman said she'd evidently been struck hard on the back of the head, some sort of skull fracture."

Jessie sucked in a quick breath and gripped her hands tightly together.

"Are you okay?" he asked. "You wanted the truth, so—"

"It isn't that. For one second, it was as if I saw and felt it—but not from afar. It was as if, as if . . . I don't know. As if I were going to relive that hallucination I had in Hong Kong I told you about. That feeling I had to run, run, because someone's chasing me. But I think I was just reliving the terror I felt last night when I thought someone was chasing me in the woods and it turned out to be Tyler Finch."

"Jess, I don't go much for the ESP, psychic stuff, but I know some pretty smart people do. Maybe when you get this flashback feeling, you should go with it, not fight it. Maybe it's as simple as something you've buried in your relationship with your mother that might give us some insight into who would hurt her."

She turned to face him. "What do you mean?"

"I'm not even sure. Maybe she said something about Vern or Seth or someone else in passing to you that will give us a clue about a motive. Hell, I don't know."

To his dismay she reached for the brown envelope he had stuck between his seat and the central console. "Are they here?" she asked. "The initial coroner's photos? The scratches on her are etched in my brain, but a closer look—"

"Jess, other than examining your own memories, you are not on this case!" he insisted, seizing her wrist with his right hand to stop her from seeing the photos. "Besides, they're hard to look at."

"They can't be worse than finding her like that, or was she cut places other than her face?"

"No."

"Was she assaulted—raped?"

He was shocked she sounded so matter-of-fact and that she was thinking clearly and like a police officer or investigator. "They don't think so," he told her, "but today's autopsy will tell."

"I'm going to see her body later anyway, Drew. I can do this. I'm a trained scientist, which is more than I can say for our Lowe

County coroner, I don't care how many dead bodies he's seen. I can look at facts and be objective. And I *am* on this case—not officially, I know. But don't think I won't be looking at everyone at the wake and the funeral. Don't think I don't mean to keep an eye on Vern Tarver. And I'm not putting the house up for sale—not yet, anyway. I'm going to bring some lab work here and ask Vern if he'll hire me at the Fur and Sang Trader."

He heaved a huge sigh and loosed her wrist so she could look at the photos. It surprised him how happy he was that she intended to stay for a while, despite the fact he was afraid she'd get in the way of the investigation. Worse, that she'd get hurt. He wouldn't mind her uncovering some inside information on Vern, but no way was he going to let her be bait to flush out whatever human animal had killed her mother.

And then, of course, there was the wild card possibility that this was a random slaying by some lunatic, who had just stumbled on a lone woman in the woods.

The envelope crinkled loudly as Jess pulled the photos out. "Did Tyler take these?" she asked.

"No, the coroner at the morgue. You okay?" he asked, glancing away from the road at her. She had gone pale and bit her lower lip. "Do I need to stop the car?"

"Neither of us is stopping until we find out who did this," she said, her voice strong and color coming back into her cheeks. "Maybe the killer wants us to think these claw marks are from a bear. You know that necklace Seth wears around his neck? What if those claws match this?"

"I've thought of that, and, no, you're not coming with me to question him. You stay put at home."

"I'm going to phone the funeral home in Highboro and then drive in to meet with them and choose a casket. I'd ask Cassie to go with me but Pearl's still feeling nauseous. Are you going to show Seth these?" she asked, evidently unwilling to be distracted by anything. She tapped a finger on the top photo, then shuffled through them a second time. "The cuts look like the exact pattern of the sang berries laid out at the three sites."

"If I have to show them to Seth, I will. I'm not sure how that will go."

"This all points to him so far, but I don't think he'd hurt her."

"I agree, because he'd so obviously be pointing at himself if he left all those clues, especially that bear face at the last sang site. But I have to start with him, then maybe move on to persons of interest who might want to blame him."

"People who hated Seth, not necessarily my mother? Who set him up and she was just the means to that end? And what about that photo Tyler and Cassie have seen? If that turns out to be a real bear, surely she wasn't killed by the animal? The slash marks are too perfect. Then to have her laid out and unmauled like that, when bears usually go for the soft belly parts—"

Looking as if she'd puke again, she amazed him by sliding the pictures back in the envelope. Tears trembled on her lashes, but she sat erect, looking, as she'd said last night, devastated but determined. He'd seen his mother react like that with strength and courage when his dad had beaten her. She'd stayed with the bastard for his and his brothers' sakes, because the whole area was poor and she had nowhere to go. Beaten down, yet never bowed or even bent—that's why Drew had dared to fight his father for her. Now, though he desperately wanted to protect Jess, his feelings for her had nothing to do with the way he'd loved his mother.

13

"Now you just come on in anytime after one this afternoon," Etta Merriman, the coroner's wife, told Jessie on the phone when she called the Merriman Funeral Home in Highboro to see when the autopsy would be completed. "I'm so very sorry for your loss, my dear, but we'll take good care of her and you can pick out a lovely casket here. Such a tragedy."

"A traditional casket," Jessie told her. "All wood, quite plain."

"Why, that sounds lovely. I'm sure that will suit her. I must tell you, Miss Lockwood, the newspaper people have been calling, but we always tell them no comment and, in this case, to contact Sheriff Akers or Sheriff Webb. I surely hope that will spare you some troubles."

Spare her some troubles, Jessie thought. On top of everything else, now outsiders would be asking questions and getting in the way. Mrs. Merriman assured her that, yes, she could talk to Mr. Merriman when she came in.

Jessie showered and dressed, putting on one of her mother's long denim skirts and jackets. She paced the house, seeing her everywhere, hearing her voice. Strange how she pictured her, not as she had looked in these later years, not as she looked all huddled up in that hollow tree smothered with sang, but younger. Somehow, Mariah had never aged for her. Those memories of when they lived here together haunted Jessie with bittersweet longing.

But she had things to do. She'd promised Drew she'd check Tyler Finch out online, so she got out her laptop and searched for him. A bio related to a professional organization he belonged to came up. That linked to some of his photographs— beautiful, evocative—mostly ones on the

Web site of his New York City employers, Bailey and Keller. *We will help you build your brand . . . We will help you tell your story,* the Web site promised future clients. That sounded great, but at what price, she wondered.

"What's the real story of what happened to you?" she asked aloud, as if her mother were in the house with her. She stared at the tree trunk Seth had carved for her, which Drew had helped her tip upright at the corner of the hearth. Then she added, "I'm going to find out, Mother. With or without Drew, I'm going to find out."

She had a lot of e-mail to read, but she merely skimmed it. Almost all were professional messages or newsletters to download. It would have to wait. Everything would have to wait now.

She planned to stay in Deep Down after the funeral to help Drew; she would bring some of her work here. She put her laptop away, then paced the house again, trying to decide where to put a temporary, makeshift lab. She'd need countertop space for her microscopes, test tubes and centrifuge, good light and a refrigerator to keep the cancer cells and isolated ginsenosides stored properly. She'd need room for bins to store the ginseng plants. Drew and Sheriff Akers had said, after they'd combed through it all, she could have the sang that had covered her mother in her forest grave. The next time he went back to the hollow tree, Drew had said he'd be bringing the plants out, and she planned to harvest more from the nearby sang sites. The great hope for her research was that she could use the leaves without harming the precious, protected roots.

Jessie decided the back sunporch where her mother had always dried or processed her herbs and other forest treasures would work best. The eight-by-twelve room had counters and storage, though it would need a good scrubbing, and she'd have to buy a space heater for the coming cold weather. The porch was entirely glassed in so the light would be good, though she'd put up some kind of better ceiling lights and install vertical blinds so she could work at night and not feel someone outside in the dark was watching her—watching her . . .

Jessie stood for a moment in the center

of the sunporch and stared out through the hollow toward the forest, then looked toward Slate Creek that connected her mother's—now her—land to Seth Bearclaws's. Could there have been some relationship between Seth and her mother, besides being neighbors or longtime friends? When her mother went out with Vern, could Seth have been angry or jealous?

"Damn, Jessie," she scolded herself aloud, "you're not writing a soap opera script. Get real."

But *everything* seemed unreal. To clear her head, she stepped out the back door to see how the sun porch looked from the outside. Windows might need caulking, cracks, too, from the autumn and winter winds.

"Dr. Lockwood," came a smooth voice behind her that made her jump. She gasped and turned. She had not heard a car, but one sat in front of the house. The black Cadillac must have arrived before she stepped outside. Much closer to her, as if he'd approached on silent feet, stood the Chinese ginseng agent, Peter Sung,

with a huge bouquet of white chrysanthe-
mums in his hands.

The roughly hewn tree trunk chair he sat
in hurt Drew's butt and back, though Seth
Bearclaws seemed quite at ease in an
identical one. They faced each other across
a plank table that had carved faces of deer
and bear staring up at him from under a
thick slab of glass. Jess was right; this
place gave him the creeps with its snake-
skins and array of skulls displayed on plank
shelves or nailed to the walls. Worse, on
the wall behind him, Seth displayed his
various knives, chisels and hatchets, which,
depending on how the conversation continued, Drew intended to have confiscated
and checked for blood and DNA.

"Say it, then, Sheriff," the old man told
him, frowning so his bronze forehead wrinkled in sharp furrows. "I told you, I was
carving that whole day she disappeared—
carving the tree trunk for Mariah you have
seen. Yet you keep asking me questions. I
am cut deep for her loss, but I did not
cause that loss. But if you do not believe
me, say so."

Drew shifted uneasily. It was strange

that he said he was "cut deep," but that just sounded like Seth. He would hardly have worded it that way if he'd been the one who cut her, would he? Drew wished he didn't admire this man. He hadn't hesitated to go for Vern Tarver's jugular in an interrogation, but he was wavering on this. Seth—who had seemed as ancient as the hills, even when he was growing up—had been a fascinating character to him and his brothers. Never once had they pulled a prank on Seth or Anna Bearclaws.

"Mr. Bearclaws, in three patches surrounding Mariah's body, sang berries were laid out in the shape of arrows, pointing toward where we found her."

"And the arrows link to me because I am Indian? I used to hunt with bow and arrow, but not for years."

"No, it's not the arrows that point to you, Mr. Bearcl—"

"Call me Seth. You are not a bad boy anymore but a good man. So you will believe what I tell you."

Their eyes met and held. The old man's were deepest mahogany, as if carved from that hardwood and polished to a high sheen.

"I want to," Drew said, "but sang berries outlining a bear head were found at one of the sites. That's not all. I'm going to show you photos of Mariah's face after someone left his marks on her."

As he'd told Jess, he wasn't sure he'd share these, but he'd talked himself into a corner. Despite how nervous the guy made him feel, for the past fifteen minutes he'd been here, Drew had the gut feeling he *was* telling the truth.

He pulled the four photos out and slid them silently across the table. Seth stared at them, picked them up to look closer, frowning and shaking his head. Below, where he'd rolled up his flannel shirt, the muscles in his lower arms seemed to contract and bulge, making the bear tattoos there move. The stoic old man blinked back tears, before lifting his gaze to stare at Drew again.

"I did not do this, would not. You think these are bear claw marks I put on her?"

Drew shrugged. Wouldn't Seth have pretended he didn't get the connection if he had anything to do with this?

"Take me out to the forest where some-one killed her," Seth said. "Let my eyes look with yours to see what we can find from who did this. And," he said, rising and pulling his bear claw necklace over his head and tossing it on the table where it clattered to a stop, almost touching Drew's hands, "tell the coroner to try to match these to her marks, because they will not fit."

"But other bear claws could have been used, not necessarily that neckl—"

"No," he said, dropping the pictures on the table, then thumping them with his index finger. "Those are claw marks of a badger, not a bear. I will prove it to you," he said, walking toward the wall where his knives glistened, even in the dim light.

Drew put his hand to his pistol, but Seth reached for a leather thong of claws hanging over a nail and tossed them on the table, too. "Badger claws from a dead body in the woods—a badger body." As Drew slid the bear claw necklace and the badger claws into the envelope without handling them, he watched closely as the man started back toward his weapons.

"Hold it, Seth," Drew said, standing with his hand on his pistol. "Here's the deal. I take you out in the woods with me, but not with your knives."

"Weapons, Sheriff?" he challenged, turning to stare at Drew.

"I'll level with you. I may need to confiscate those, but let's leave them where they are right now. Just from looking at the pictures you can tell it was done with badger claws? But a badger attack—or someone running around with its claws, other than you—doesn't make sense."

"Nor does blaming me for killing a fine woman I would never harm, even if she counts the sang for a government that thinks it can control everything." His voice was bitter, but it was not news to Drew that Seth, maybe more than most around here, hated any sort of government control.

As if he had accepted the bargain, Seth moved into his open kitchen area and, evidently, prepared for their excursion. Drew moved closer to be sure he wasn't pocketing a kitchen knife. Though it was risky to go with Seth into the woods, Drew planned to be heavily armed. He could use the old man's sharp eyes and woods wisdom out there. Besides, the cunning Cherokee could help him with one other thing.

"Seth, a photographer friend of Cassie Keenan's took a picture of what may be some sort of strange creature in the woods yesterday, not far from where we found Mariah. I'm going to have him send the photo to my laptop, and I'll enlarge it as best I can. Maybe we can find that spot and look around there while we're in the area."

Seth nodded. Drew was surprised he did not react further, but then the man had always been stoic. Maybe the old Indian just figured Drew was too ignorant to recognize a particular animal from a distance. He watched Seth carefully as he took from his refrigerator what appeared to be beef jerky; he filled a canteen with tap water. "Got sick drinking from Bear Creek last year," he muttered as if to himself. "Used to be pure as the land, but now it's polluted, just like everything else."

"I'll drive us up to where we can hike in, but I've got to phone the photographer first, then my office and Jessie. You haven't asked how she is."

"I know how she is. Strong, like her mother. And not going to sit still for this outrage."

Here Jessie was wondering, Drew thought, if she'd inherited the mountain women's sixth sense, when Seth seemed to have it in spades. Drew called Cassie on Seth's phone to see if she knew where Tyler was. She did—and handed the phone to him, so Drew asked if he could e-mail the photo.

"I've got my laptop with me today," Tyler said. "I've enhanced the photo a bit, but it's still not definitive."

"I'm taking Seth Bearclaws into the woods to find the spot and look around, so I need it ASAP."

"Cassie told me about him. How about if I bring you the one I've printed out? It's a lot clearer. Then I can go along with you. The three of us can surely locate the spot, and I'll take photos again if you find anything."

When Drew hesitated, he added, "I'll just consider that payment for the photos I took last night."

"If I take you along, I'll expect that any crime scene area photos—last night or today—become my property, not yours, in writing. I don't need those falling into the hands of the newspapers, which have been calling."

"Sure. I understand and agree."

"And, Tyler," he added, speaking low so the waiting Seth wouldn't hear, "I appreciated your help, but don't even point a camera in Seth's direction, at least not now."

"I think we understand each other. When will you be at the old logging road?"

"As soon as I make two more phone calls."

He called Emmy at the office to tell her where he was going, then called Jessie's number. She didn't answer, but then she'd said she was going into Highboro. Just as well. If he had driven by, he might have ended up with her along, too, and he didn't want that. He'd been nuts to let her walk out of the woods last night, but he'd seen no other way.

As Seth got in the Cherokee—which he'd refused to ride in before—Drew wondered if he'd made a mess of this interrogation. New information, at least, but no confession, no arrest. Rather, two new deputies of sorts, the one sitting next to him, whom he wasn't certain he could trust, and then Jess, who he was getting emotionally involved with, which was not only tricky but taboo on such a case. Now he'd have Tyler tagging along with a photo that might just as well be of an alien from Mars. But what he couldn't get out of his head was that his boyhood buddies used to claim that Seth Bearclaws, a full-blooded Cherokee, could call up huge, half human, half animal beings to do his bidding.

Peter Sung's arrival surprised and scared Jessie. He was one of Drew's so-called persons of interest. He'd told her not to talk to him, but she was caught now—besides, she didn't intend to pass up this chance to find out where he'd been lately. She recalled Cassie's suggestion, *You can catch more flies with honey than with vinegar.*

"These flowers are to honor the memory of your mother," Peter said, extending the large bouquet to her with a stiff, quick nod. "In my culture, white is not the color for brides, but for the dead."

"Thank you. That's very thoughtful. I hope they last so I can use them at the funeral."

"I believe you will find them quite hardy. When will the funeral be, if I may ask?"

"When the coroner releases the body—soon. My mother had a sitting up—a kind of wake—for my father. I'll have one for her, the night before the funeral at the Baptist church."

"If I am welcome at the funeral, I would be honored to attend."

Peter Sung was the most serious she had ever seen him, though she'd only talked to him once in the four years he'd been representing the Kulong family, which bought so much Deep Down ginseng. She noted again his slight accent, British, like those she'd heard in Hong Kong, she thought. He was tall for an Asian, with sleekly arched eyebrows, sharply slanted cheeks and thin lips, which were often smiling. But he looked genuinely grieved, almost pained. As usual, he was dressed impeccably, today in dove-gray slacks and a matching long-sleeved knit pullover sweater. He was thin and moved gracefully. His good humor—her mother had said he joked about buying "Sung's Sang"—and generosity always surprised people who expected him to be quiet and even shy.

She knew she should ask him in, but she hesitated to. She wasn't sure whom to trust anymore, and the man was on Drew's "hit list." But now, she wondered how to get something useful out of him.

"I was just taking a little stroll," she said, gesturing toward the creek with one hand. "If you wouldn't mind . . ."

"Of course not. I can always use the exercise. It's been a while since I've been out running with my hounds. Dr. Lockwood, I deeply admired your mother, and she provided an invaluable service in this area and for my clients. Will you be taking her place with the ginseng counts?"

She was going to deny that possibility, but perhaps being noncommittal would get her some admission from him. "I'm not sure," she told him.

"I realize this is too early for you to make such decisions, but please be assured that I and the concerned clients I represent will do all we can to help you in any way, whether you remain in Deep Down or not."

"When did you last see my mother? I understand you are only here from time to time."

"Ah, I think it was last June, mid-June. I'd actually have to consult my daybook. I stayed with Vern Tarver, and I sometimes saw Mariah with him, so he might recall, if you must know specifics. Yes, I believe it was when Mariah was in and out of the Fur and Sang Trader in mid-June."

So Vern and her mother had probably been more than friends for at least most of the summer, Jessie thought. Why hadn't she known? Surely, her mother didn't think that, after being true to Jessie's father for all these years, she would resent a romance? Or had it only been a friendship to Mariah and that had caused the friction with Vern—and perhaps more?

"So you weren't around since June," she said, hoping that sounded like a comment and not a challenge. "If you'd only been here when she went missing—and if you'd had some of your tracker dogs with you."

"Yes, that would have been of help. I've run them in this area before, so that might have given them a head start over the usual breed of hounds around here," he said, with a hint of scorn creeping into his voice. "But I regret I was called away from Lexington. I also represent the Kulong family interests in Wisconsin, where we buy cultivated ginseng—hardly of the quality of the wild roots here, of course."

So did that mean he had been in Wisconsin, or he merely wanted her to make that connection? He was lying, wasn't he? He'd been in Highboro at least during the time he claimed to have been "called away." Or could his timeline fit with his claim? She had to talk to Drew and let him pursue it.

"I do understand and sympathize with the grief you must feel," he was saying, perhaps a ploy to shift the subject. "Losing a parent—an elder—that is serious indeed."

"You sound as if you have been through this," she said as they walked slowly along the creek. Like a bride walking down the aisle, she held the flowers before her; he walked with his hands clasped behind his back.

"My father, just last year," he told her. "Though I am sure our funeral customs would seem, well, foreign to you. Now, for example," he said, "this little stream. Should a Chinese funeral procession cross water, the procession must be halted, for the soul of the dead cannot cross water unless the deceased is informed."

Strange, but what came to her mind was that the recovery team last night had carried her mother's body across Bear Creek. So to the Chinese, would that mean her soul remained on the other side, near where she had been killed?

"What else is different?" she asked. "What about the burial? After the funeral, my mother will be buried next to my father up on Cemetery Hill."

"Ah, a hill is good," he told her with a nod. "The higher up, the better *feng shui.* People today think that means arranging their furniture for best effect, but it is so much more. Then," he went on, stopping and turning back to look at the clapboard house, "the deceased elders will be worshipped by the family at their home, once the spirit of the deceased returns."

"Returns to the home?" she asked, turning also and clasping the fragrant flowers to her.

"Our custom and belief," he said with a slight shrug as if to dismiss his words. She sensed he was sharing the belief of others, not himself. Or were these subtle words of warning for her? She would definitely have Drew question this man. Had he really come to comfort and console, or was he trying to frustrate and frighten her?

"Seven days after the death," he continued, gesturing toward her house, "the departed returns to the home. The family remain in their rooms that day so as not to interfere, but they often sprinkle flour or talcum powder at the front door, so they know."

"Know what?"

"The footsteps of the souls of the dead blur the flour or powder on their way inside to the altar where they will reside."

"To be worshipped?"

"Yes. A far cry from Baptist beliefs, of course, but my condolences are sincere. If you need anything I might be able to provide, do not hesitate to call me, Dr. Lockwood."

He did that stiff little nod again, extended a calling card to her, backed a few steps away, and left her standing by the creek. She glanced at it: his address, cell phone number, fax, e-mail and the Kulong Imports Company Web site. So he certainly wasn't avoiding being contacted by her or by Drew. He had offered unlimited help and support, so why had he unsettled her so much? Just because he was sharing the Chinese customs of death?

When she went inside and put the flowers in a vase on top of Seth's carved tree trunk, she realized she'd made a sort of ancestors' shrine. This might be the heart of Appalachia, but the monument to her mother was now part Cherokee and part Chinese.

14

Drew swore under his breath. Not only was Tyler standing outside his vehicle on the old logging road, but another man with a truck was there, hauling out some kind of gear. If Tyler had brought someone else, that was it—he wasn't going with them. On the seat next to him, Seth squinted through the truck windshield and grunted.

"I can tell which one is your photographer," he muttered. "The other one is Ryan Buford, a surveyor of roads. I said good riddance when he left a couple years ago, but I see he's back. Now, there's a killer—of trees."

"Don't make waves just because he's with the government, okay? Besides, my office manager Emmy Enloe's evidently sweet on him."

"Buford is not to be trusted near virgin forests *or* virgins."

Drew almost choked at that. "So, when was he around these parts before?"

"I've said enough."

Drew didn't press Seth since he seemed to be cooperating. Could he be implying that when Buford was through here before, he was womanizing? His thoughts circled back to Cassie, but that was the least of his worries right now. He bit his lower lip and forced himself to deal with the here and now.

It looked like Tyler Finch already had his gear in a big backpack, except for a camera he held in one hand; he had a manila folder in the other, which Drew assumed held the photo he'd asked to see. He hoped he didn't flash it in front of Buford. Rumors of some strange creature loose in the woods, near a cut or clawed corpse, would turn the area into chaos, even around here where most folks were content to mind their own business.

Drew got out and walked over toward the two men while the stubborn Seth stayed in the Cherokee. If the old man went back on his word to help in the forest, he would arrest him. If he stayed put right now, so much the better, so he didn't have a shouting match or worse on his hands. Still, it would be just like Seth to disappear into the trees—or thin air.

"Tyler," Drew said and shook his hand. He took the folder and without looking at it, put it under his left arm, tight against his ribs, though he was anxious to see the picture. Buford ambled over. Strapped on his back was a tripod and a distance measuring wheel, like police officers used to calibrate tire skid marks at the scene of accidents. Other surveying tools were laid out near his truck with a pack he was evidently filling.

"Ryan Buford, surveyor for the Department of Transportation," the man introduced himself, extending his free hand.

Drew shook his hand, trying to size up both the man and his surveying equipment. "A lot of things to carry with you," Drew observed, taking a few steps closer. Laid out on the mossy track of what had once been a road lay a can of red spray paint, a level, a couple of plumb bobs, a bright orange safety vest that resembled a life preserver, a compass and a gas-powered, steel-bladed chain saw with a red handle.

"That's a brush ax, for clearing bushes and small trees, government issue," Buford said when he saw Drew staring at it. Gesturing at the other things, he added, "All tricks of the trade."

"Which is surveying roads for what reason?"

"Although this timber was never heavily cut, some of these roads from the old logging days may need to be widened or, eventually, paved."

"For modern logging equipment? Decades ago, selective, minor logging was done around here. If this area's going to be logged again, the locals will be up in arms."

"Like most of us, I just follow orders," Buford said with a shrug. "I'd guess the roads might be paved for retirement homes, bring a lot of business besides the ginseng into Deep Down. I know that would please Vern Tarver for his general store and museum and make Audrey Doyle pretty happy about new customers at the Soup to Pie and her B and B. I'm staying at her place."

"Is that right?" Drew said, knowing full well that man-eating Audrey would consider this guy a tasty piece of raw meat. No wonder she hadn't put herself in his path the past couple of days. "I heard you were into the sheriff's office, but not to see me," Drew told him.

"I've been hoping to meet you, but I know you've been busy," Buford countered. They were like wrestlers, Drew thought, circling each other without managing a hold yet. He could see why Emmy had fallen for Ryan Buford. Unlike guys around here, he was smooth and self-confident without being cocky. He wasn't quite six feet, but was compactly built and just plain looked like Prince Charming.

"Emmy said you've got quite an investigation on your hands," Buford went on when Drew just studied him. "Real sorry to hear about the reason for that. I hear Mrs. Lockwood was a lovely lady."

"She was. Emmy is, too, though maybe a bit young and naive. But then, that's what you get with a backwoods girl who has a protective family of a father and four older brothers. Gun-happy, every last one of them."

Buford cleared his throat. He glanced at Tyler, but he was fooling around with his light meter. Buford looked toward Drew's truck; whether he could see Seth in there, Drew wasn't sure. "Emmy's a great girl," Buford finally said. "Well, I'd better get going. Just because I'm out here on my own doesn't mean I don't punch a clock."

The manila folder was burning right through Drew's jacket to be opened, but he couldn't let Buford go yet. "So when did you get here?" he asked as the man started away.

He turned back. "Just two days ago, on the sixth, right when everyone was out searching for Mrs. Lockwood—that's when I met Emmy."

So Emmy could vouch for his arrival, Drew thought. He'd assigned her to man the office and coordinate the search teams out in the forest, which is where he should be right now.

"Ever been through here before?" he asked Buford, knowing full well he had.

"Yeah, couple of years ago. Been down in Florida since then, laying out roads in the Everglades. It's so different from here, but both beautiful places. See you around town, then," he said and bent over his supplies.

At least the guy had not lied about having been here before, but he probably knew he'd get caught on that. With Tyler hovering, this was no place to ask Buford if he knew Cassie Keenan. Besides, she had always given Drew the impression that Pearl's father was someone local. She'd probably kill him if he asked her outright about Buford.

"If we don't get back by the time the retirement homes go up for sale," Drew called to Buford, "send someone after us. You're sticking around here, I take it?"

"For now, until I hear different," Buford told him as he quickly bent back over his equipment.

Drew went over to the truck where Seth sat as if carved from wood. Turning his back on Tyler and Buford, Drew opened the folder. Tyler had blown the photo up to an eight-by-ten, but it was grainy. Still, he immediately saw what had set everyone off: a broad-shouldered, big-headed form back in the dim, mottled forest. It reminded him of the silhouette of King Kong more than anything else. He passed the photo thruough the window to Seth.

"Sure not a badger," Seth muttered. "Not a bear, either."

"A play of light—a freak alignment of tree limbs?"

"No. It's something. Maybe we can find the spot. Let's go."

Jessie was actually relieved Cassie hadn't come with her to choose a casket, because she intended to question Clayton Merriman about his coroner's report. Her friend had enough to worry about with a sick daughter. Probably something Pearl had eaten, Cassie'd said, but she was taking her into the new walk-in clinic between Deep Down and Highboro today.

Merriman's Funeral Home, the wooden, hand-painted sign in front of the old mansion on the east side of Highboro read. Why did they call them "homes," Jessie wondered as she got out of her car and started up the walk. And Merriman seemed the wrong name for what most Appalachians still called an undertaker; this funeral director was also the coroner and seemed to be such a serious, solemn man. But in this case, it all suited Jessie just fine. At least she didn't have to go pounding on the door of the county morgue for answers.

With fluttering expressions of sympathy, Etta Merriman let her in and led her into a carpeted office where Clayton Merriman rose from behind his oak desk.

"A very brave young woman," he complimented Jessie, or perhaps he was addressing his wife. Jessie had noticed the other night that he seemed to talk in broken sentences. "Led all of us to where her mother was found."

He came around to sit in a maroon leather chair facing Jessie's, while Mrs. Merriman perched on the edge of the matching settee in the conference area of the office. Jessie didn't mean to pounce on the man, but she had to know.

"I'd like to hear the official cause of death. I realize you'll need to discuss all that with Sheriff Webb, but I want to know."

"Yes. Understandable. Blunt force trauma to the head. The death certificate—a copy of it, your property, of course."

"She was indeed murdered?" she asked with a shiver she tried to hide.

"At first, I thought she might have fallen backward onto a rock, but body lividity—the settling of blood—indicates she lay for a while where she fell facedown. Didn't crawl into that hollow, old tree and cover herself up with the plants."

"So—just to be completely clear, you haven't ruled an accidental death? It is a homicide?"

"Regret to say, but true."

Etta Merriman leaned over to place her hand on Jessie's. She let her, though her first instinct was to brush her off. "Blunt force trauma to the head," Jessie repeated his earlier words. "Would she have died right away or blacked out? I'm hoping that fiend didn't cut her face while she was alive."

"No, no, or the lacerations would have bled instead of just showed a hairline of dried blood."

"That's what I told Drew," she blurted, before she realized she'd said too much.

But he only nodded. "The initial, crushing blow means she didn't suffer, wasn't conscious," he said as Etta patted Jessie's hand again. "Worded in my notes this way, if I remember—'Deceased received nonsurvivable injuries and died very shortly after the injury, if not immediately.'" Jessie withdrew her hand from Etta's and gripped her other hand in her lap. She must have made a face, because he went on, "So, no suffering, after the impact of the weapon."

"Which might have been what?"

"Not sure. Something with some length or a handle to provide velocity when it was swung."

"May I see your notes or even your photos or sketches?"

"Only the death certificate until Sheriff Webb gives permission," he said. "In his jurisdiction, you see." He rose stiffly from his chair, took a piece of paper from his desk and extended it to her. She skimmed it, then reread it more slowly.

CAUSE OF DEATH: . . . depression fracture of the occipital region of the skull with epidural hemorrhaging and ruptured artery from a blow of blunt force . . . Estimated time of death uncertain because the body was not found for several days— unable to employ readings of rigor mortis or temperature. Legal time of death, 8:17 a.m., September 7, 2007.

"You put the time of death as last night," she protested, looking up.

"The *legal* time—when the deceased is pronounced by the medical examiner," he said, somewhat defensively. "First time I saw her body in the woods."

She looked down at the paper again. Her gaze snagged on the words, *a blow of blunt force.* Someone had forcibly taken her mother from her. Elinor had died of a heart attack last year and now this. A blow of blunt force . . .

A woman's voice pierced Jessie's silent agonizing as a hand extended a glass of water to her. "The best we can do for those we have lost is to honor them by seeing they are properly buried," Etta said.

"If they died naturally," Jessie replied as

she took the glass. "If not, there's much more to do."

"It's a good thing you took evidence photos of the sang berry art," Drew told Tyler when they reached the sang cove site. He stated the obvious: the berries were moved or missing.

"I dropped the photos off with your secretary just before I met you," Tyler told Drew. "I figured you didn't want to drag them around in the woods—except that one," he said, gesturing toward Drew's backpack where he'd put the photo of what he was coming to think of as The Thing.

"Seth," Drew said, "I'll have to show you the other photos when we get back to town. Let's take a look at the tree where we found her."

As they approached it, Seth stopped dead in his tracks. Looking up at it, he almost fell backward.

"What?" Drew demanded. "You know this place?"

"A grandfather tree," he whispered, his eyes narrowed, his head down now as if he could not even gaze on it again. "Old. Sacred."

"She was huddled up inside it, covered with sang," Drew told him.

"Atalikuli," he whispered.

"What?"

"Ginseng—*atalikuli,* it climbs the hills. To be buried with it is—good. It helps to take you—upward, into the sky above the hills."

Behind Seth's back, Tyler looked entranced; he leaned closer to hear, as Drew asked the old man, "So, do you know this place?"

Seth finally looked at him. "Yes. By tradition of my people. It was also the place where some hid under leaves—not ginseng, but dried leaves—to escape the soldiers who had come to take their homes, force them away."

"On the Trail of Tears?" Tyler spoke up, startling Drew.

Seth nodded. "And now we have another trail of tears. Now, because I know this place, because of what I said about *atalikuli* taking the dead onward, upward, you think I killed her and put her there, but I did not."

Drew put his hand on Seth's shaking shoulder, but he couldn't help picturing that unknown beast from the woods again. A buried memory stabbed at him. When he was really young, his father had told him a ghost story around a campfire. He'd said that, "Indians like Cherokee Seth could make monsters out of nothing, big, furry ones that like to eat kids like you."

Back then, brave and cocky, Drew had shaken his head and laughed it off, but he wasn't laughing now.

"I intend to hold a sitting up for her—a wake," Jessie told the Merrimans as they led her into a large back room with caskets arrayed on the carpeted floor and on deep shelves.

"Why, sure," Etta said. "My mother used to call that a settin' up with the dead. Used to be better attended than weddings, if I rightly remember. Haven't been to one of those for years, but then, we do encourage people to visit the deceased here where we can keep the casket proper."

"She had one for my father years ago, so I couldn't do anything less," Jessie went on as if Etta hadn't spoken. "I'll have a closed casket because of those claw marks on her face, though," Jessie added.

"You'll be pleased how she'll look,"

Clayton said. "But under the circumstances—well, always the family's choice.
No other kin then?"

"None, but most of Deep Down will
come by."

Jessie surveyed the choices of caskets
and immediately went to a plain-cut but
highly polished curly maple one with the
traditional flat top, wide at the shoulders
and narrow at the feet with handles on
the sides for the pallbearers.

She put both hands on its smooth surface. "I intend to bury her with ginseng
plants instead of flowers in her hands,"
she said.

"I just read the article about her work in
the paper today. That will be right fine and
proper," Etta encouraged her. "We'll have
you fill out her information for a formal obituary before you leave today, and we'll
phone it into the paper."

Jessie felt the formality of the rituals of
death now, wrapping around her like a tight,
heavy cloak. Just talking about the wake,
seeing the coffin—it hurt but it helped.

"I'd like to see her now, please."

"Suggest you'd wait till she's ready to
be laid to rest," Clayton said with a slow

gesture toward the coffin. "She'll look more like herself then."

"Yes, my dear," Etta said. "I promise you, I'll have her fixed up really lovely. How about you come early tomorrow and escort her back home in a little procession with the hearse. You can take all the time you want alone with her then, all laid out nice and proper."

Nice and proper? Nothing was nice and proper about any of this, Jessie wanted to shout, but perhaps they were right. Besides, she should be home when Drew came back from the forest with Seth and Tyler. Emmy Enloe had phoned after Peter Sung had left to say that Drew had tried to call her. If she'd talked to him, she'd have insisted her take her, too.

"All right," she told the Merrimans. "I'll be back tomorrow midmorning and plan to accompany her back home. I've arranged for the funeral to be at the Baptist church in Deep Down the day after that."

Would her mother's killer be at the wake or funeral, she wondered as she left the silent room and went back into the office to help write her mother's obituary. If so—

or if not—she and Drew were going to find him.

"Look! Look, that's the general place, I'm sure of it. I recall Cassie, Pearl and I walked here, along the creek!" Tyler said as the three of them bent their heads close over the photo, then looked up at the tree line again. "See, the trunks align, and that one boulder on the ground."

"Looks like it," Drew agreed and started toward the trees.

Seth came on silent feet behind him. Tyler, off to the side, made a lot of noise and new tracks, but what did that matter now? With the rain and falling leaves shifting around, finding tracks would be a long shot.

"About here, I think," Drew said. "Tyler, you've got the eye for this. Go on back out where you must have shot the photo—here, take it with you—and yell at us when we seem to be at the right place where this thing—this anomaly—must have been."

Tyler looked as if he'd argue, but he nodded and tramped back out with the photo.

Seth, who had been silent since they'd left the hollow tree, said, "Good that you sent him out. He doesn't want to take living things from the forest, but he wants pictures of it all—same thing."

"I didn't just send him out to get rid of him."

"But I see the place already."

"You do? I'm not sure from here, so—"

He thrust out his arm to keep Drew back. "Right here," Seth whispered, pointing.

"How can you be sure? I thought we could triangulate the place from Tyler's position and—"

"Because," Seth said, as he bent close to the rough bark of a huge oak, "the bark has snagged pieces of fur here, high up, but I see no claw marks."

Drew bent to view the bark at the same angle, his chin almost on Seth's shoulder. "Yeah, I see it. So it was a big bear rubbing up against it to mark territory?"

Seth shook his head. "Like I told you, badger," he muttered, plucking at pieces of gray and reddish fur, then sniffing at them. "Yes, a musky smell. But how can that be when they don't climb but dig underground when they are endangered or chased?"

"As you said, that tall, furry-headed thing in the photo is sure as hell no badger and not a bear, either. Maybe there's no connection to Mariah's death, because the animal she was killed by was definitely human."

15

A knock on the front door jerked Jessie awake. The room lay in the grip of deep shadows. Where was she? Oh, that's right. She was on the sagging sofa in her mother's—her own—living room. Besides being emotionally bereft, she'd exhausted herself cleaning the house for the wake and then arranging the chairs and unpacking baskets of food two church deacons and their wives had dropped off. She'd merely sat down to rest but had fallen into a heavy sleep. She snapped on a light; her watch read 7:15 p.m.

She went to the front door, but, on second thought, peeked out through the porch window first. Drew. Thank God, it was Drew. She unlocked and opened the door.

"Pizza delivery, extra-large, pepperoni, peppers and mushrooms," he said, flourishing a flat, white box. He had a big, brown envelope under his other arm.

"Are you planning to feed everyone at the wake tomorrow?"

"I'm starved from tramping through the woods," he said as she let him in, "and you have to eat. I picked it up in Highboro after I talked to Clayton Merriman. I hear you did your own interrogation of the Lowe County coroner."

Side by side at the big table, they ate pizza and drank cider by candlelight, telling each other about what they'd learned during the day. Drew told her nothing else from the coroner she didn't already know. He was not pleased to hear that Peter Sung had been here, but listened avidly as she recounted everything he'd said, especially the unsettling customs of Chinese funerals. Jessie glanced nervously over at the carved tree trunk on the hearth; Mr. Sung's flowers were still there, ghostlike in the dim room.

Drew told her he'd check into the nebulous timeline of Sung's arrival in the area and that he'd question him as soon as possible. Then he gave her a basic rundown of his time with Seth—more than he'd told her about his interview with Vern Tarver. He described how Seth had claimed the claw marks on her mother's face were made not by a bear but a badger.

"That's crazy," she cried. "Or could that crude drawing done with sang berries we saw in the woods have been a badger? None of this fits together. There's something we're missing."

Drew held up his hand and went on. "Just before I dropped Seth back at his place, he admitted that the day before your mother disappeared he'd had an argument with her he felt guilty over—unlike Vern. He wanted her to come up with a low count of the 'slow-growing, sacred sang' so the government would halt its harvesting and it could replenish itself."

"A mere government ruling would not stop poaching around here."

"True, but it would stop Peter Sung from buying and exporting so much. Seth also admitted he had an argument with Beth

Brazzo. He told her ginseng should not be dishonored by use in power drinks for healthy athletes, but hoarded for medicines for those who were ill."

Jessie heaved a huge sigh. "At least Seth would probably approve of my research. But I still don't think he'd hurt my mother."

"He said they'd argued on her front porch, but what if their quarrel actually happened out in the woods and got out of hand? Say that he accidentally hit her, shoved her—I don't know—and the back of her head hit a rock. Then, regretful, grief-stricken, he tried to honor her with some sort of Cherokee custom, including claw marks and a ginseng burial."

"And in the process intentionally made it look like *he* did it?" she challenged.

"I know, I know," he said, raking his fingers through his hair. "I'm just using you for a sounding board. Besides, if Seth was angry enough to kill your mother, whom I think he admired, why not knock off big, bad Beth Brazzo, too?"

Jessie shook her head. "Probably because even Seth couldn't catch her. She's a walking—running—ad for her product.

The woman said she jogs four miles a day, and she's built like an Amazon. It would take a tough, fast man to even get a hand on her."

Then, as if he'd been working up to it, Drew explained what he, Tyler and Seth had found in the woods where the weird photo was taken.

"Badger fur?" she cried. "So you now have evidence of badger fur *and* claws?"

He nodded and took a big swig of cider. "Of course, I guess badgers *could* climb a tree with their long claws. I'll show you some Seth gave me in a minute. But they *don't* climb with them, they burrow. And no way that was a badger or even a bear in the background of Tyler's photo—I've got that to show you, too."

"Why didn't you say so?" she asked, getting up. "Is it in the envelope? You don't think it's something Tyler Finch doctored up for his own reasons, do you? I don't know the man."

"I don't think so, but I'm not sure I really know him, either. He seems to really care about Cassie, though. Which reminds me," he continued as she came back to the table and handed the envelope to him, "have

you ever heard her talk about a government surveyor named Ryan Buford?"

"You mean Emmy's guy? Never. Why?
You don't think . . ."

"It's probably nothing," he muttered, so
she knew darn well it was something. He
shrugged and shook his head as he tipped
the envelope so that two claw necklaces
slid out onto the table. The moment she
saw the photograph, concern for Cassie
flew out of her head.

"Look at that!" she murmured, turning the
picture toward the candlelight, then snapping on a lamp to see better. Fear shim-
mered through her. "Even bringing up a
badger is laughable. It looks like a huge,
furry man maybe wearing a coonskin cap!"

"I hadn't thought of that. In other words,
the ghost of ole Daniel Boone or his cronies might haunt these hills? All I know is,
there's something or someone out there,
and Boone's ghost makes as much sense
as anything else right now."

Straining to listen in case Pearl called
for her again, Cassie sorted and tied her
newly picked bittersweet into bunches at
the table. As soon as Pearl got over what

the nurse practitioner at the walk-in clinic had called a "virus bug," she'd have to take to the woods to harvest more, 'cause she had a big order for it this year. The child had a fever of one hundred and two, so she'd given her a cool bath before she put her to bed. So far the Tylenol had not brought the fever down, so first thing in the morning, she was planning to start her on the antibiotics they'd picked up at the High-boro drugstore.

She nearly jumped out of her skin when Pearl spoke right beside her.

"Ma, I saw Big Bear out the window."

Cassie dropped the bittersweet and turned to her. Her nightgown was soaked again, and she held by one paw the tat-tered teddy bear Jessie had bought her ages ago. But Big Bear was the child's name for an heirloom bear rug that Cassie kept in a trunk.

"Honey, we got to get you back in bed. And you didn't see Big Bear out the win-dow or anywhere. That's just like a dream— the fever talking."

"No, I saw him. A hundred times bigger than Teddy, looking in! I pulled the curtain back. He saw me and he waved."

Cassie took her by her hot hand and led her back into her room. First Jessie'd said that someone tall was looking at the house, now this. Not to mention that crazy picture of Tyler's. All coincidence, had to be. That moss drying on those breeze-blown lines looked like a big animal's head out there, bobbing, swaying. That was all.

"Out there!" Pearl said, tugging her hand away and pointing at the back window when they got into her room. "Out by the moss. It was Big Bear, looking at me! It was!" she insisted and broke into tears.

Cassie sat on the side of her low bed and rocked the little body in her lap, then when she quieted, took off her sopped nightgown and sponged her off with cool water again before pulling another cotton nightgown over her tousled head. She was going to have to start her girl on those antibiotics, though she didn't trust fancy medicines like that. But her initial dosings of herbs and tonics hadn't helped. At least Pearl was no longer vomiting.

"Don't let him come back or get in," the child pleaded, her eyes bright with fever and fear.

"It's not Big Bear, and I'm going to prove it," Cassie told her. "If you just let me take your temperature one more time, I'm going to show you that Big Bear is still where you and I put it away, since it used to scare you when it was on the floor."

"Mr. Tarver has one, in his store, too," Pearl said, rubbing her eyes with her fists, as if she could erase what she'd seen. "Maybe that's his bear outside."

"Come on now, Miss Pearl Keenan. You just let me check your temperature, and don't you go biting down on this old thermometer."

Cassie washed it with alcohol, then dipped it in water and put it carefully under Pearl's tongue. She'd have to get one of the modern kind that you put in a child's ear. This one was old as the hills, but it worked fine. Still, she was careful with it since mercury was poison, and in Cassie's book, poison was only for people who deserved it for the deception and desertion of women and children. That's why she intended to stay up late tonight, not just to keep an eye on Pearl or tie up bittersweet, but to get her mayapple leaves, ground-cherry and nightshade all chopped up and put into a couple of special tea bags. She might need them right soon.

"Still one-hundred-and-two degrees, honey, too hot, so I'm going to get you a real nice fruit drink." It was the way the nurse had told her to give Pearl the dose of medicine.

"I want to see Big Bear's in the box first," she insisted, crossing her thin arms over her chest. "If he's still there and still dead, then he can't be outside."

"Now, that's right. You just wait there a second. He's gonna smell though. You 'member how he smells from being stored away where the moths won't get him."

Regretfully, Cassie went into her cluttered back storage room and took mesh bags of drying sang roots off the old humpback, metal trunk. When she lifted the lid, the reeking smell of mothballs hit her right away. On top, wrapped in a sheet of plastic to separate it from the other items she had stored, was the bearskin rug from a huge black bear her granddaddy had killed—"kilt," as he'd put it—in the woods not far from here. It had been on the floor before the hearth for years, but it was too moth-bit and smelly to be there now.

It was heavy as she hauled it out and rested its old paws over her shoulders to drag it in on her back to Pearl with its fang-barred jaws atop her head. Then, on second thought, because she didn't want it to resemble the thing in Tyler's photo, she shifted the weight of it so it rested over her arms and its feet dragged on the floor, its back claws scraping.

She knew more than one house around here had a moth-eaten bearskin in a trunk or even on the floor. Maybe Tyler would like a picture of one for his *Fading Appalachia* book. But, no, once she calmed Pearl down and got that dose of medicine in her, this was going back in its trunk, unless she needed it again.

"See, honey?" she asked Pearl as she hauled it into the room. Cassie exploded in a sharp sneeze at the dust from it. "It was still in that trunk and whew-ee does it smell bad! After touching it, I'm gonna have to go take a bath, too!"

Pearl, still holding her teddy bear in one arm, reached out to pat the dark, matted fur. "I'm glad you showed me Big Bear's still locked up," she said. "I'm glad he's still dead."

They sat on the old sofa with its sagging, crooked pillows, talking. The wind howled outside, but Jessie felt safer than she had in days. Drew had volunteered to drive her into Highboro tomorrow, then back, following the hearse with her mother's body.

"And I'll be keeping close during the wake, funeral and burial, in my official capacity," he assured her, resting his arm behind her on the back of the sofa, so that any time she turned her head her hair pulled along his shirtsleeve. "I think not only the way Mariah was admired, but also the circumstances of her death will bring out a lot of people."

She turned to face him more fully with her legs drawn up on the cushions. "Including, maybe, her killer."

"It's been known to happen. Either the person feels guilty and responsible and tries to make up for the crime by attending and maybe mourning or—"

"Or he revels and gloats in what he's done. Drew, with everything going on, I haven't told you something else I decided for sure. I'm going to convert the sunporch to a makeshift lab and continue my work here, at least for a while. I've phoned a couple of friends who are going to bring some of my research supplies with them when they come to the funeral. And the woman who waters my plants while I'm away is bringing more of my clothes and books. I'm going to stay here, at least until I get some answers about my mother's death. That's what I wanted the ginseng leaves for—my lab work. I've got to find out if the ginsenosides in the leaves will work as well as those in the rarer, expensive roots."

"I'm glad you're staying for a while, and not just because I can use your help. We need more time together when we're not upset or grief-stricken or mad as hell."

She nodded; their gazes snagged and held. They leaned closer together. He was so near she could see herself reflected in the pupils of his blue eyes.

"I brought as much of the ginseng from the hollow tree as Tyler and I could carry," he said, his voice suddenly gone raspy. "Seth said it should stay where it is, so he didn't carry any. I think the fact I allowed that without a comment went a long way with him for honoring his beliefs, even if I still defied him to bring the sang back."

"I'll put the leaves to good use in her honor."

"Jess—" he said fervently, then bit his lower lip.

Feeling suspended, she hung on that single, whispered word. Of all her names and titles, that one from him thrilled her. When he said no more, she asked, "Why have you always called me Jess? No one else does."

He frowned. "I don't know. Maybe it's a way to show you're special. Years ago, it was probably a desperate attempt to just pass you off as one of the guys, so I didn't have to notice you."

"How could you notice skinny, little, bug-bit me with a hottie like Fran MacCrimmon wrapped around you most of the time?"

"Hey, that makes it sound like you were stalking me."

"In a way, I guess I was."

"Jess, what was between us that last night just happened, but what we did— even then, I felt it was a happening."

"That sounds like a greeting card," she said, her voice breathy, "one I would have saved pressed in a book of memories or a diary forever. I used to write things about you in a diary that Elinor gave me. Oh, sorry, too much information. You're going to think I was nuts. Drew, I've been wanting to say that what happened that night—when we were found and . . . and separated— was my fault as much as it was yours."

"No, it was mine. If you're to blame, it was only because that was the first night I took a good look at you—your warmth and concern for me as well as your beauty, the woman you had almost turned into. I was so broken, so down, and you reached out to comfort me . . ."

He stopped talking and cocked his head as if listening to something in the distance. Except for the wind, knocking a tree limb against the porch roof, silence stretched between them. Had they said too much? Jessie wondered. Once again, had they gone too far, too fast?

"And now," she said, when he didn't go on, "you are a comfort to me."

"There's a lot I could say, but—"

"But now's not the time."

"Your deciding to stay will give us some time."

"I don't mind waiting. First, we have to find who hurt my mother."

"Absolutely. If you're willing, I'll bring the two sacks of sang leaves in from the Cherokee now, and we can go through them together before you use them. We've got to be sure there's no kind of clue mixed in."

"Yes, let's. We'll be so busy tomorrow and the next day."

He rose and gave her his hand to help her up. But he pulled her right into his arms in a hard hug.

She clung to him, pressing her face against his shoulder, her hands clamped to the small of his back. He felt so solid, so strong. He brushed his lips against her tousled hair, dipped his head, and they were kissing. Moving together, tipping heads to miss noses and meld mouths. Breathing together.

She slid her hands heavily up his back to caress the nape of his neck. The short, crisp hairs there tickled her palms. His hands on her waist, he pinned her hard against him, from thighs and knees to breast and chest. She felt his unbroken kiss clear down into the pit of her belly. The world was going to spin out of control again, she thought, trying to snatch at sanity. Why had this man—the first man she'd ever wanted, the man who had haunted her for years even when she was with others—why had he remained the only one who could make her feel her inner power and yet lose herself?

Their breathing quieted; she was sure he forced himself to let her go. "I actually just grabbed you, hoping that you'd scratch my back," he said with a taut smile. "That poison ivy's still bugging me. I'll go out and get the sang. My mother used to say, 'Idle hands are the devil's workshop.'"

"As if you used to listen to her," she said, just to fill the awkward moment between them as he walked to the front door, shifted the curtain aside and looked out. She peered out over his shoulder. Pale moonlight sifted silver over the windy scene.

"But I did hear her, even though I seemed to never be listening to her," he said as he opened the front door and went out, digging his keys out of his jeans pocket.

Leaving the door open behind her, Jessie followed across the porch and down the steps to his vehicle. Then both of them stopped and stared.

She gasped; Drew swore.

"I can't believe it," he cried, smacking his hands on his thighs. "Some bastard keyed my car out here!"

"Keyed?" she said, staring at the long scratch marks that marred the entire driver's side of the vehicle.

"It's usually done with a fist of car keys," he said, not looking at her, but showing her what he meant with his own keys.

Gooseflesh, not from the chill, peppered her arms and made the hair on the back of her neck prickle. She was certain someone—something—was watching from the darkness.

"But this," he whispered, his voice now more awed than angry, "looks like some giant beast has clawed it."

16

Drew shook with rage. The scratches on the Cherokee were so similar to those on Mariah's face that he almost didn't need to try to make a match. Jessie stepped closer to him, but he put out an arm to keep her away.

"Stay back. There might be fresh footprints."

"You won't be going out there—after whoever did this?" she asked, still keeping close as he went around to the passenger side to unlock the doors and get a flashlight.

"It would be useless and stupid. Go inside, bring out our jackets and both of the claw necklaces. And another flashlight, if you have one."

When she went in, he trained the flashlight on the long scratches. They were deep, not ones that could easily be buffed out and repainted. He went all around the vehicle, but the marks were only on the side he'd parked toward the house, the driver's side. A double-edged message? A defiant threat to him or to Jess, since it was done here?

Damn, he'd been so proud of this Jeep Cherokee and had tried to keep it clean and shined. If it weren't for the familiar pattern of the marks, he'd think it wasn't even necessarily related to Mariah's death. Several locals had admired the vehicle; Seth had been the only one who had disliked the use of the Cherokee name, refusing to ride in it, at least before today. Surely Seth hadn't decided he needed to strike out at the vehicle. But he did live a short walk away through the woods. No, he wouldn't do so many things to make himself look guilty.

Jess came back with his jacket, another flashlight and both leather-thong claw necklaces. He examined the claws, but he knew both kinds were spaced too close together to match these scratches. But, as he held up one of each kind of claw against the marred metal surface, it seemed to him the sharp, slanted tip of the badger claw looked about right for the width of the lines. Badger claws, badger fur—it didn't make sense. Why a badger?

Of course, he reasoned, to badger someone meant to harass someone, but that kind of wordplay was too far-fetched, too complex a joke. He couldn't picture anyone around here but Peter Sung thinking that one up. Had his hounds been hunting badgers, since killing bears was illegal in this state? And what did a man care about what was illegal if he'd murdered someone?

The vandal had dared to take his time, making one long track and then the next one, unbroken the entire length of the vehicle. He'd thought he'd heard a noise earlier, a kind of shuffling. If he would not have been so intent on Jess, he might have glanced out and all of this—Mariah's murder, too—would be solved.

"You're thinking," she said, standing back from him and shining her flashlight on the ground as he started to look for tracks, "that those claw marks resemble my mother's cuts. Do you have those photos here too?"

"In a brown envelope between the front seat and the console on the passenger side," he said. Her clear thinking in a crisis surprised him again. "All the photos are there, including ones Tyler took of the sang berries arranged in patterns and the animal head. I showed them to Seth after we returned from the forest, and he didn't bat an eye—again, he denied having anything to do with any of it. Watch where you step, but bring them around, please—Deputy."

At another time they both might have laughed at his calling her that, but she just squeezed his shoulder and walked to get them. One hell of a woman, but then, this was getting to be one hell of a mess. Someone crafty and clever was playing with them, but this wasn't a game.

Yes, footprints were here, but vague. Someone had shuffled along, blurring the size of their feet. Intentionally? He followed the tracks until they went onto the grass toward the forest. He backtracked where Jess was still standing by the vehicle, her hair washed by wan window light. She'd taken the photos out and was keeping off the tracks, bending toward the vehicle to compare the pictures of her dead, disfigured mother. She was brave, too, or else she was still so furious over Mariah's cruel death that nothing was going to scare her off.

"Anything distinctive about the footprints?" she asked.

"It's like the person lumbered along, dragging his feet the entire way."

"Are you sure it's a him?"

"Figure of speech. An educated guess from working with marines and sailors for years, a lot of drunk ones."

"Are you sure it's a person?"

"Jess!" he muttered and took the stack of pictures from her. "I'll admit, because of Tyler's one weird photo, I've nicknamed the figure in it The Thing, but, of course, this vandalism and Mariah's murder were committed by a person. This isn't some Stephen King novel, for heaven's sake. You haven't had some other strange vision, have you?"

"No, Sheriff. Sir, no, sir!"

He thought she'd like to smack him with the flashlight, but again, she directed her beam for him while he compared the pattern of marks on Mariah's cheeks to those on the Cherokee. The perspective and spacing were different, of course. Still, he'd bet a year's salary they were made by the same kind of claws. Badger claws. Could Seth have extra ones, or was someone else involved?

He remembered once betting fifty bucks with another MP in Italy about whether the Kentucky Wildcats or the Wisconsin Badgers would win a tournament basketball game back home. The guy had told him that the badger was such a brave and tough animal that it had been known to drive off a full-grown bear, if it invaded its territory. He'd said Wisconsin was called the Badger State, not because those animals were more common there than other places, but because the early miners were too busy to build homes. During the brutal winters, they were forced to live like badgers in holes they dug with their shovels into hillsides or abandoned mine shafts.

His mind seized on that. They burrowed in with shovels as if they were human claws . . . Had Mariah been hit in the back of the head by a sang spade like Junior Semple's? Drew knew it wasn't Junior who did this, because he was in jail in Highboro. But the numerous local sang diggers or poachers must have hundreds of homemade spades like Junior's.

Vern had some he'd made for sale in his store and had said he had a collection of old, homemade ones in his pride-and-joy museum. The poor guy was always trying to get people to visit it, and they hardly ever did. Like Drew, most locals had never set foot up there, and tourists continued to be minimal—unless Ryan Buford's roads opened things up or word of some feral beast loose in these woods brought in the media and others.

"Let's go inside," he told Jess. "As bold as it was for someone to do this on the side facing your house, when we could have glanced out, I can't do anything else till daybreak. I'm not leaving you alone here tonight. I'll sleep on the sofa."

"You can sleep in my old bed in the back room."

"I want to be where I can look out here, though the damage is done. He's so brazen, he might come back. I'll be fine on the sofa. Let's go in."

On the porch, she waited for him to lock the Cherokee and join her. He lit his way with his flashlight trained on the ground, the steps, then the porch floorboards.

"Drew, look!" she cried and seized his arm, turning her flashlight back on and pointing at some dirt she must have tracked in when he sent her back inside.

"No one's gone in but you, even though the door stood open," he tried to comfort her. Her boldness had disappeared; she'd gone white as a ghost. He watched her play her light along the porch on both sides of the doorstep, then back inside. Faint smudges of tracks were there, women's tracks. Hers, of course, he thought. She was trembling again; her beam actually bounced.

"Jess, trust me on this. No one's gone in, and I'm staying with you."

"Yes. Yes, thanks. I'm just getting spooked by all this, that's all."

He put his arm around her shaking shoulders as they went in, and he shot the bolt behind them.

Jessie couldn't sleep, and this time, it wasn't her poison ivy bothering her. Trying to relax, to find a comfortable position, she kept telling herself that temporary insomnia was natural. She was mourning and frightened and furious. She should feel totally safe since Drew Webb, boy of her childhood dreams, man of her heart—and an armed sheriff to boot—was sleeping just on the other side of that door. She'd heard him get up from time to time and walk around, on guard, on patrol.

But tomorrow she would see her mother's body, publicly begin to face friends and neighbors in what the coroner's wife had called "settin' up with the dead." The dead—that was what was really getting to her, the Chinese customs Peter Sung had told her about the dead.

As Drew had said, those were, no doubt, her own footprints in dirt and dust near the front door. But were her feet that narrow and could she have tracked that much soil in herself? Mr. Sung had said that the Chinese believed that the "spirit of the deceased" returned home about a week after his or her death. The mourning family often sprinkled flour or talcum powder at the front door, so they would know the spirit had come home.

She thrashed her bedcovers again, then sat up and put her head in her hands. A far cry, Mr. Sung had said, from Baptist beliefs, and that was true. Only the Lord could bring someone back from the dead: Himself, of course, and a young girl and His friend Lazarus who had been called out of his tomb after so many days that "he stank." The scent of death had come from her mother, too. For some reason, despite the smells of the ginseng market that day in Hong Kong, she'd thought she had scented something besides the herbs, something fetid and yeasty, almost as sharp as mothballs.

More than once last night, while she and Drew had sifted through the ginseng leaves that had covered her mother, she thought she'd recognized that very smell. "Do you smell something besides sang here?" she'd finally asked him.

"These leaves were near a dead body

for several days. But I didn't bring the ones that were nearest to her."

"So I wouldn't see any blood?"

"I took some of those leaves for evidence the night we found her."

"To have them tested to see if it was only her blood?"

"Yeah. Those leaves are in plastic evidence bags en route to Frankfort for testing. But it will take time, even if they put it on the fast track."

"I know those tests are not done in a couple of hours like on TV forensic shows. Drew, have you ever investigated a murder before?"

He had nodded. "Besides a murder in Highboro I worked on, two in the service, both sailors. One was a guy who was dating an Italian girl whose previous boyfriend took offense and a hammer to him. Another, a knifing, the result of a barroom brawl. You know, as tough as that police work was since we were in a foreign country, turning over every rock in my hometown is one hell of a lot harder."

She'd sympathized, but he wasn't getting her off track. Finally, in the limp sang leaves she'd found some reddish-gray fur that smelled stronger of the scent that was haunting her.

"Smell this," she'd told Drew, putting it in her palm and lifting it toward him.

He'd sniffed, frowned, but nodded. "I must not have the nose you do for it, but Seth says that's badger fur. And the online encyclopedia I used to read about badgers said they have a strong musky odor."

"You and I both know she wasn't killed by the 'attack of a giant badger,' like some horrible Japanese monster movie! Maybe a badger climbed up that other tree where Seth found fur, and it was just a coincidence that Tyler got that weird picture. Then, maybe, by coincidence a badger scratched Mother's face after she was put in the hollow tree."

"Evenly, on both cheeks?" he challenged. "There's no such thing as coincidence in good police work, Deputy." She'd thought he was reaching for the badger fur, but instead he had taken her hand in his. A tingle had shot clear up her arm. "I—maybe we—will find him, sweetheart," he'd whispered. "Promise."

Jessie flopped back in the bed again. Drew had not just been teasing when he'd called her "deputy" last night; he had meant it as a compliment. But when he'd called her "sweetheart," whether it had just been a casual term or he'd really meant it, she had been thrilled. Right in the middle of being obsessed with her mother's murder, she was thrilled.

"Dr. Jessica Lockwood," she muttered, "get hold of yourself."

She was going to look like the living dead if she didn't get some sleep. The wake would go all tomorrow night, although others would sit with her mother's coffin to give her a rest. Still, she would probably be functioning on adrenaline and anger. In the back of the refrigerator she'd seen some of that G-Women power drink, probably given to her mother by Beth Brazzo, because she couldn't picture her mother buying it. The stuff was loaded with caffeine and ginseng. Maybe she'd have one of those for breakfast—if morning ever came.

The next morning, Drew and the Merrimans left Jessie alone with her mother's body in a private back room of the funeral home. When the door closed behind them, she walked over to the open coffin, steeling herself. Gazing at her mother's still upper torso and placid face, gripping the edge of the coffin, she whispered, "I'm so sorry, I'm so sorry, I'm so sorry." She sniffed back a sob. "Sorry that you died—how you died. I always meant to say I was grateful you gave me the world, not just Deep Down. I—I understand why you did it. I'm sorry I was so angry. And I'm so sorry it ended this way, but I'll find out—I'll try—Drew, too—to make it right."

Tears blurred her eyes, making two bland, mute faces of her mother. It didn't really look like her, despite the fact that Etta Merriman had done a reasonably good job with her appearance. Her graying hair was too smooth, her cheeks not smooth enough despite some beige cosmetic putty over the cut marks. The vitality, the very person was gone. No, she would not have an open casket at the wake or the funeral.

But the reality of loss comforted as well as tormented her. In that very second, Jessie decided she would do a sang count, at least a partial tally this year, in her mother's honor. Her current sang notes had obviously been stolen from her backpack, but perhaps Frank Redmond, whom Mariah had reported to in Frankfort, had some sort of records that could be reconstructed so this year's tally would have some basis for comparison. Her determination surprised her. She'd had no intention of actually doing the count until she stood here, so close to her mother's body.

She pressed her stomach and hip bones against the side of the coffin, leaned closer and covered her mother's folded hands with hers. Cool, waxy. She would place a spray of ginseng plants in them tomorrow. But had some speck of thought remained, hovering around the body? It was as if someone had whispered that she must finish the sang count.

"I'll do it," she whispered. "I'll finish your sang count."

Though she felt like a fool, Jessie leaned even closer and closed her eyes, trying to concentrate. She'd had a powerful insight in Hong Kong—the feeling that someone was chasing her, perhaps when her mother was in that very predicament. If only she could envision that again, could she possibly catch a glimpse of who had caused that fear—the fatal attack?

But, no. All she could see with her eyes closed was the picture Tyler Finch took of that strange, shadowy shape in the woods. Only she imagined it moving now, coming closer, snapping tree limbs and shuffling through the leaves . . . with—with something silver in one hand.

She opened her eyes and shook her head to clear the moving image. The picture in her mind had turned from still photo into a movie trailer. She couldn't trust her own thoughts and fears. She had to bury them and face reality—the wake, funeral and burial, and then she must go on.

Jessie figured the word *wake* described the way the mourners stayed with the dead all day and night, as if to keep the deceased company. She was exhausted, so she kept dosing herself with G-Women power drinks or ginseng tea. That kept her alert as she greeted and spoke with a constant stream of neighbors and church members stopping by to express their condolences. As the day dragged on, Vern Tarver had stayed the longest.

"A fine woman," he'd told her more than once, sometimes wiping under his eyes with a handkerchief, though Jessie wasn't sure she'd seen tears. Finally, in a break from talking to others, she went over to where he'd planted himself at the foot of the casket, as if he were the grieving husband.

She took the folding chair next to his.

"I've decided to stay around for a while," she told him. "For one thing, I'm going to finish the sang count for my mother."

"That right?" he asked, stuffing his handkerchief in his back pants pocket. Unlike everyone else, who came in their workday clothes, Vern was more formally attired than the undertaker had been, in suit, tie, shiny shoes. "But she had so much of the count done—that's the impression I got. And some of what she counted could be gone by now if you have to start over."

"Her boss, Mr. Redmond, is going to have to make do with a partial, representative count and extrapolate from there. He's coming to the funeral and church dinner tomorrow, so I'll consult with him then."

"You know, sometimes you still sound like a fancy scientist, Jessie—extrapolate and all that. But that's great. I'm sure you're gonna find the count high enough to tell that Mr. Redmond that Deep Down area sang is not endangered. 'Cause if it was, that'd be a disaster in all kinds of ways," he said with his voice taking a new, sharper edge, as he leaned slightly closer.

If that was a subtle threat, she decided to ignore it. "I'll be doing some lab work here, too," she told him, "but I'm hoping I can take Cassie's job at the Fur and Sang store, at least through your busy autumn season. Seeing what folks bring in to sell will give me an idea of what's out there, too. Cassie's picked up some extra money taking Tyler Finch around for his photography—both for his company and his book."

"Glad to hear that for her. Yeah, Mr. Finch asked to shoot some photos in the store and the museum. Won't that be great to get some extra folks coming in to see the artifacts I have there, the history of Deep Down?"

"That will be great. I'm not sure I've ever seen them, either, but I'd like to."

"You're hired. Don't pay much, but you'll be easy to train since you been around sang all your life—well, mostly."

"It's a deal. Starting . . . ?"

"You just come on in after you get settled, sooner, the better. 'Sides, I can use some help arranging my displays for Finch's photos."

"Excuse me. I see Cassie's here. Pearl's been ill, so I wasn't sure Cassie would be around until tomorrow."

She hurried to the front door and hugged her friend. Jessie could see over her shoulder that Drew was still outside, talking to people, right now Tyler and the Baptist minister, Pastor Wicker.

"Such terrible timing that Pearl would get sick during all this!" Cassie said as they stepped apart but kept their hands linked. "She was throwing up for a while, and now the fever finally broke."

"I'm just praying she's over whatever it was."

"Yes, yes, she is, but she's still not eating worth beans—you know what I mean. Oh, a closed casket."

"I had to, and not just because of the cuts on her face. It just didn't look like her. She's not there."

"Sure, sure, I understand. I'll pay my respects, then me'n Pearl will both be with you for the funeral and the covered-dish dinner tomorrow. But I got to tell you something first. See, Pearl's at her friend Sarah Castor's till Tyler drives me back home. Right now, Tyler's telling Drew something Charity Semple told us, and I figured I'd better let you know 'fore he comes steaming in here. Drew, I mean."

Jessie glanced again over her friend's shoulder. Whatever Tyler had told Drew had upset him for sure. "Tell me before he gets in here."

"Charity says Junior got home yesterday afternoon. Peter Sung paid his bail in trade for a good price on the rest of their sang, which is being dug today. Junior was like to have gone crazy in that cell, and he's still mad as can be 'bout you and Drew putting him there."

17

Jessie sat in the front row of the little church with Cassie and Pearl on one side and Vern, who seemed to have delegated himself as chief mourner, on the other. The slow, sweet sounds of the hymn "This Is My Father's World" washed over her. She amazed herself that she still knew the words by heart. The Creator God had made a lovely world, but someone in it had killed her mother.

In the traditional last viewing of the body before the pallbearers carried the coffin to the front of the sanctuary, with Cassie and Drew at her side, Jessie had placed a spray of ginseng in her mother's hands, then closed the coffin lid so it could be bolted down. Drew, Cassie and little Pearl now seemed the closest thing she had to a family. Cassie had her arm around Jessie's waist. Drew stood close but at attention in full dress uniform—gold braid, brass buttons, striped trousers, sharp pressed jacket—as if he were a marine again and not a small town sheriff. She was especially grateful that Drew was sticking tight because they'd had a big blowup at breakfast, after he'd spent a second nervous night on her sofa.

She wanted to work with Drew, assist him, but he'd lost his temper when she'd told him at breakfast this morning that she'd decided to finish her mother's sang count.

"Are you crazy!" he'd exploded after the mourners who'd stayed all night had left to get ready for the funeral. "Working at Tarver's store is one thing, but I can't let you go out into the forest like she did, where someone can get to you. I can't play bodyguard for all that, much as I'd like to."

"Drew, it's the right thing to do. I've decided."

"Hell, you can just undecide. It's the dangerous thing to do. If someone meant to stop her sang counts, you'd be a magnet for murder, too."

"Obviously, I can only do a partial count this late, maybe a week's worth of representative sites. I hope to get some of her old notes from her boss in Frankfort. I'll get Cassie and Tyler to go along, if they can spare the time. I'll pay for a babysitter for Pearl. I'm sure Tyler would like photos of sang in some of the deep coves for his book."

"No. Absolutely not."

"Drew, I want to cooperate, but I'm not in a witness protection program or something. You're not my keeper or my hus— never mind."

He'd jumped up from the table, stalked to her side of it and bent, stiff-armed down to rant right in her face. "Never mind? Listen, Dr. Lockwood, I'm not staking you out like—like some kind of poor little goat that—"

"Goat?" she'd cried and jumped up so as not to be at a disadvantage to his height, which she still was. Hands on her hips, she'd faced him down.

"Yeah," he had gone on, gesturing wildly, "a scapegoat, waiting for a dinosaur to lunge out of the jungle to devour it like in *Jurassic Park*."

"Oh, for heaven's sake. Dinosaur? I think Tyler's monster photo—which could be fabricated, for all I know about him—is warping your mind."

"Right. You don't know much about Tyler, do you? So you're going to let him play bodyguard for you in the woods? With what? His camera?"

"Look, Sheriff Webb, I'm doing this for my mother and for Deep Down citizens who rely on the sang money. This isn't about your investigation, and it's not in your bailiwick or jurisdiction."

Looking back on their yelling match, she realized now that was their first fight and maybe not their last. Still, he'd stuck by her today, his hand on her elbow from time to time, his eyes watching the mourners.

Her friends from Lexington sat a few rows behind her. Driving two cars, they'd come laden with lab equipment, her clothes and personal items. Her refrigerator contained vials of breast cancer cells now. Though she hadn't been away from her friends for more than two weeks, they seemed almost foreign to her. How long should she stay here in her other, earlier life? Or was this her real life now?

Jessie stared at the polished wood of the coffin with the spray of white roses atop it. She had not wanted to use Peter Sung's flowers, though they were holding up well and still sat on Seth's carved tree trunk at her house. On either side of the coffin, vases of fresh sang plants Seth had cut stood silent sentinel. She had not wanted him to feel ostracized, despite the fact Drew had said people in town were starting to blame the old man for her mother's murder. Trying to keep her mind on the soloist's lovely rendition of "The Lord's Prayer," her gaze drifted to the big arrangement of the exotic birds of paradise that Mariah's boss, Frank Redmond, had brought.

Frank had stood, and was singing away in a good bass voice, just across the aisle from Jessie. Frank was the state's official ginseng controller for the U.S. Fish and Wildlife Service, which, under the Endangered Species Act, determined whether the harvesting of wild ginseng could continue. He'd been thrilled to hear Jessie would do even a partial count. Unlike Drew's reaction, Frank had cried, "You're a godsend!" Arriving at the same time at the church, they had stood by Frank's car as they talked. At forty-something, he was stocky and pale with a balding forehead and eyeglasses with invisible rims that made his eyes seem to pop.

"Since you said her current records are missing," he'd said, "I'll send her notes from the last couple of years to give you an idea of where to look. She included some notations of environs, like cove, hillside, maple cluster. I know this isn't the time, Jessica, but I've got to tell you, the Chinese consulate, as well as scientists and health food corporations, have been hounding me for a couple of days. They're scared to death that if I cross out the word *not* in the report, so it reads that the next harvest *will* be detrimental to the survival of the species, it will halt a multimillion dollar industry and tick off a lot of people. On the other hand, environmental groups, including the Appalachian Ginseng Foundation, are pressing for a low count to protect the future of the herb."

"Mother told me all one hundred and twenty Kentucky counties, except for those with the big urban areas of Lexington and Louisville, have wild ginseng. Could you do without Lowe County's records for one year?"

"No way, I'm afraid. Lowe County is the canary down in the mine, the bellwether for wild Kentucky ginseng. You know," he told her, leaning closer and glancing around as if he were about to share top secret information, "in places where the ginseng economy crashes, some locals are finally letting the hated loggers in just to keep financially afloat. With these stunning, hardwood forests on these hills and mountains, I wouldn't like to see that happen here, so I hope you'll get a decent count."

She thought of the government road surveyor Ryan Buford. Drew had told her he planned road widening, and Seth had said the man "looked at trees with hungry eyes." So who would profit from some logging on wilderness lands around here if the sang market crashed?

She was about to ask Frank's opinion on that, but their conversation was cut short when Beth Brazzo, heading up the church walk, spotted her and hurried over. She didn't wear her usual jogging attire, but a dark-green pantsuit with a plaid scarf pinned to her shoulder.

"Sorry to interrupt," she began, turning to Jessie, "but someone said you're going to continue the ginseng count. That's fabulous, and I'm sure you'll find a healthy crop of it out there!"

Jessie introduced Frank as a friend of her mother's, hoping Beth wouldn't learn who he was and pounce on him. "Vern Tarver must have told you of my decision to do the count," Jessie said to her. After her fight with Drew this morning, she knew he wasn't the one who'd been the messenger. "Yes, in her honor, I want to finish what my mother began."

"A lovely way to think of it," Beth cried, gripping her big hands together as if in prayer. Her huge gold hoop earrings bounced each time she talked. "See, that's the truth of 'deep down satisfaction,' our new advertising motto. Listen, I don't want to hold you up on this sad day, but I just wanted to tell you that I would be happy to go along to help count ginseng in the next few days or so before my ad shoot team gets here—carry your gear, or whatever. Please, just let me know if I can help. I'm staying at Audrey Doyle's B and B. So, Mr. Redmond, you were a friend of Mariah Lockwood's?"

Although Jessie felt she was leaving poor Frank in a lioness's den, she excused herself and went inside. Behind her, she could hear Beth giving the man her hard sell on her ginseng- and caffeine-laced power drinks. No, her first impression of the woman had been right. "Brazzo the brazen" was too assertive and ambitious, and Jessie didn't like or trust her. Despite what a strong physical specimen Beth was, she was not desperate enough to take her out in the woods to help count sang.

Now, with the creaking of the old wooden pews as everyone sat after singing, Pearl, perched between her and Cassie, reached over to take Jessie's hand. The gesture brought tears to her eyes. Kids seemed to get sick and then well so fast. Her bout with the virus had drained the usual vitality from the child but she was still sweet little Pearl.

Pastor Wicker's opening words of comfort and encouragement about her mother's life and the Christian life drew her back to the service. He read from Psalms, her mother's favorite book of the Bible, "'As for man, his days are like grass. As a flower of the field, so he flourishes, for the wind passes over it, and it is gone, and its place remembers it no more.' But many of us here will remember Mariah Lockwood, who moved so gracefully among us and through the forests, who loved the very grasses of the fields, the rich bounty of our woods, which she counted to protect the ginseng. The Lord 'causes the grass to grow . . . and vegetation for the service of man, that He may bring forth food from the earth.' And, in Mariah's case, the precious ginseng vegetation she tended brings forth medicines and supplements to strengthen the bodies of men and women."

Pearl whispered to Jessie, and she bent closer to hear, "I should have some more vegetables, then, and my teddy you gave me should, too, 'cause I think the secret forest food he ate chopped up made him sick."

Jessie nodded and squeezed the little hand tighter as another hymn began. She wasn't sure she'd heard what the child said correctly, because she understood none of the babbling, but out of the mouths of babes . . .

The service slipped past and was over. Everyone stood as the steeple bell began to toll and the six pallbearers, including Vern, carried the coffin out. The pastor followed, then Jessie, Cassie and Pearl. The pews emptied behind them in order.

As she walked slowly out, Jessie noted Charity Semple was sitting partway back, without Junior. Jessie nodded at Seth, who sat on a chair in the far eastern corner, by himself. And why was Emmy Enloe, who had known her mother well, sitting so far back in the shadows by the exit on the west side? Maybe, she thought, it was because she was with Ryan Buford. Drew had said that Audrey Doyle, who was sitting much farther up, probably thought she owned Buford since he was rooming at her B and B. Drew seemed to steer clear of the sexy owner of the Soup to Pie, except to get some meals, and there was little choice about where to eat in Deep

Down. She'd meant to question Drew more about his mentioning Buford and Cassie in the same breath; Cassie, whispering to Pearl, didn't even look Buford's way. Maybe she hadn't seen him.

By the back door, standing at attention, Drew waited as if guarding the entire congregation. Their eyes met, held; they looked away. She felt sad they'd had that argument over her sang count, today of all days. The bell tolled on as the procession turned and started up Cemetery Hill. Everyone seemed to step to its sonorous clang, clang. When she was a kid, youngsters who had memorized Bible verses got to ring that bell on Sunday mornings. It wasn't the piercing tone they'd loved, so much as how, when you were little, the rope almost yanked you off the ground after you'd rung it.

And then Jessie noted Peter Sung was standing outside the fence at the edge of the cemetery, beyond the oldest graves. Since she'd put on her sunglasses, she wasn't certain he saw her staring at him, but he gave a stiff, formal half bow, then walked down the path toward the parked cars and trucks. She wondered if Drew had confronted him yet about springing for Junior Semple's bail. Pulling her gaze away, she wound her way up the center cemetery path amid the tombstones of Deep Down's dead.

Dead . . . her mother was dead. Still, she couldn't believe it. So sudden, so cruel, so unfair. But she'd find justice for her. With or without Drew, she would find the murderer.

She felt bad again about arguing with Drew. She knew he was feeling short-tempered because he hadn't found Junior Semple, despite the fact his wife had claimed he was out in the woods some-where, overseeing Peter's diggers. For all Drew knew, the guy was guilty of more than using poison varmint sticks.

Despite her jumbled emotions over their fight, Jessie believed she'd held up well today. But seeing the new grave gaping open next to her father's headstone, see-ing the pallbearers slide the coffin onto heavy leather straps so it could be lowered—her knees almost buckled.

Drew's hand came hard and sure on her elbow. "Do you want to sit down?" he whispered. "I can get you a chair."

"Thanks. I'm okay."

He nodded. From the pastor, he took the shovel that those closest to the deceased would use to place soil onto the casket once it was lowered. It slowly descended with a winch one of the deacons worked. The straps were pulled up, so the coffin lay below, alone.

Jessie stared at the shovel when Drew handed it to her. Someone had evidently thought it appropriate to use a sang spade. Her hands trembling, she shoved the sharp tool into the pile of loose, reddish soil, lifted and dropped a spray of it onto the coffin. A hollow thud.

Cassie took a turn, then Vern, the pastor, Drew. Seth, too, whom Drew brought forward, however much Vern glared at him. Jessie heard some muttering behind her. The thudding sounds of soil on wood became more muted. Emmy Enloe took a turn; Jessie didn't see Buford anywhere now. Others pressed forward, and then she lost count. Holding Drew's arm, she turned away. She wondered, over the years, if she planted some sang here, would people poach it or let it thrive?

She'd lost Elinor, who'd been cremated,

and now her own mother in just over a year. It was too much.

She jumped when Drew spoke. "I'm going to wait and see that her grave is properly filled," he said. "Do you want to lie down for a few minutes before the church dinner starts?"

"No. I'll be all right."

Walking her back to the church, he turned her slightly to him at the side door. "Jess, I want you to be all right. I'm sorry we argued, especially today. I'll set up some sort of guard for you if I can't go when you count the sang."

"I'm sorry, too. But not sorry that we're back together."

Biting his lower lip, he nodded. As soon as Cassie and Pearl caught up with them, he went back out toward the grave.

"Can I go out and play with the other kids?"

At the head table for the covered-dish dinner, Cassie stopped talking to Jessie and turned to her daughter, who was squirming on her chair.

"No, Miss Pearl Keenan. You've been

sick and can't be running around right now."

Jessie leaned over. "But she sure has cleaned up that third helping of mac and cheese. I'm glad to see the color coming back into her cheeks."

"Well, me, too, but we're not going through a scare like her being sick again. If you're so much better, honey," Cassie said, "I'd like you to eat a few veggies, too, and not just the chocolate cupcakes you still got all over your mouth."

"Pearl told me," Jessie said, "she and that teddy bear both need to eat their vegetables. Now what was the rest of that, Pearl? You've been eating chopped up food that made him sick, too?"

Pearl rolled her eyes and frowned. "It's really fairy food," she said in a whisper.

"What are you two talking about?" Cassie demanded, looking from one to the other. "I can believe Teddy was sick, too, but what chopped up food made him sick?"

"Nothing," Pearl declared, crossing her arms over her chest. Another neighbor had come up to talk to Jessie, who had turned away. "I thought Aunt Jessie would keep my secret," the child said with a pouty, frosting-lined mouth.

Cassie reached over with a paper napkin to wipe her face clean, stood and pulled Pearl by the hand off to the side, then into the cloakroom with its rows of huddled, hanging jackets. "Pearl, have you been eating something you shouldn't?" she asked. "And I don't mean today. I won't be mad, honey, but I got to know, 'cause you were really sick, and we can't have that happen again."

"Teddy ate most of it—in tea I made us," she blurted. "The dried leaves in the treasure box. It's on the shelf in your closet, like in a secret cave."

Cassie gasped. She broke out into a sweat and her stomach cartwheeled. That's where she'd stashed the poison plant parts she'd been hoarding.

She almost collapsed as she knelt next to Pearl and hugged her hard. Why hadn't she locked that toxic stuff up, as well as hid it high? She could have lost Pearl, lost her baby! God must be warning her to get rid of that stuff, reminding her that murder was a foul sin and that vengeance belonged only to the Lord.

She'd flush that stuff down the toilet the minute they got home. She'd rip the rest of it out by its roots and thank the good Lord for giving her a warning and a second chance. But she prayed hard that her and Pearl's deserter and betrayer would some-how die soon anyway. Then he could go face his Maker, who would sure make short work of him!

Jessie waited for Drew when everyone had pretty much gone. He carried his plate and cup over and sat across the narrow table from her to eat a late dinner. He'd been outside for a while, seeing to the grave and even conducting traffic when everyone left the small parking lot almost at once. Imagine, he'd told her, a traffic jam in Deep Down.

She watched him eat Audrey Doyle's fried chicken—only a couple of thighs were left—and what must by now be cold pota-toes and biscuits. Even his coleslaw looked bottom-of-the-barrel, and his coffee strong enough to make a spoon stand up straight. But this man, who'd claimed he liked to do Italian cooking and loved wine, was no doubt used to chow lines from his days as a marine, and leftovers as a poor kid from a big family. In the midst of all her worries, she amazed herself by wishing she were a better cook. Fast food had been her best friend, but when this was all over, here in Deep Down, she'd try to cook the way her mother had taught her years ago.

"So, how soon are you planning to work on the sang count?" he asked.

"Frank Redmond's e-mailing me whatever he has of my mother's previous counts and notes tomorrow, so, I figure, the day after next."

He looked around as if to be certain no one could overhear them. Only the women who had helped serve the dinner still bustled around the buffet tables, so she and Drew were pretty much alone. Vern had finally departed. Cassie had looked so red-faced and watery-eyed when she'd left, Jessie hoped she wasn't coming down with something like Pearl had.

"I know this is sudden, and you probably have a lot to do," Drew said as he buttered a biscuit, "but I'll volunteer to help you get your sunporch lab together if you'll go with me to Lexington tomorrow to talk to Peter Sung."

"Really? While you interrogate him?" she asked, leaning toward him with her elbows on the table.

"I'm going to chat with him—that's all," he said with a lift of his eyebrows that told her he didn't mean it. "I thought, with you along, I'd be even less threatening, that he might be less nervous about it. I think we worked well together confronting Junior—until his little poison gas sticks tripped us up on more ways than one."

"Did you know Mr. Sung was here to-day, hanging around outside?"

"He actually stepped into the service for a few moments when I was standing at the back. He looked really nervous, but I figured he hadn't been to too many Baptist churches, so I didn't put too much stock in that. I told him I'm interested in the Plott hounds he raises, which is true, and that I was hoping to get a hound or two myself, in case we have other missing person's cases, which is *not* true."

"Then why are you interested in his hounds?"

"Because that gets me into his house, where he'll be willing to talk. And because about fifty feet from where we found Mariah,

I stumbled on a dog collar, the kind that has a chip in it so the hound can be traced. I nearly told the guy off today for springing Junior on bail without asking me first, but I want to catch him off guard, so I kept my mouth shut about that."

"Sung's dogs weren't used in the search for her, were they? He said not." His mouth full, Drew shook his head. She went on. "But, with that vague timeline and his being in Highboro, are you thinking Sung was actually in the woods the day my mother went missing? Maybe he tracked her that day with his dogs. But he did tell me he'd run his hounds in those woods at other times, so that could account for the collar."

"It might not even be from his hounds, but I've checked and it's a really expensive, state-of-the-art GPS tracking device collar. If the collar hadn't been trampled by something heavy, it would probably still transmit, and Sung could track it to retrieve it."

"Trampled by something heavy. Did you find a footprint?"

He shook his head and kept eating, switching to a remnant of broken apple pie, talking while he ate. "It was in the dark and under a lot of leaves. Whatever prints had been there—whether dog or something else—were washed out by rain or intentionally blurred, like the ones around my vehicle the night it got clawed."

"Yes, I'll go with you," she told him. "I have a lot of legal work to do over my mother's death, but Peter Sung has a great big motive for murdering her. I was thinking today that Beth Brazzo, maybe even Tyler Finch, do, too. Not to mention our chief mourner, Vern. By the way, Beth's volunteered to go out on my counts with me."

"How nice of her. Either to get you to pad them, or worse. Maybe your challenging me about whether our perp is a 'he' or not makes sense. We should take a closer look at her. She runs the forests daily."

"I think she stopped to see my mother at the house, because there's G-Women drink in the fridge. It's actually not bad stuff. It got me through these two days."

He frowned at her, but didn't comment on that. "I just wish," he went on, "I could have found Junior Semple today. I'll check on him after I get you home."

"The ever-generous Peter Sung's paying Junior's bail was probably just a way to get his hands on all that virtually wild sang, especially if sang harvesting is halted."

He nodded, swallowed and cleared his throat. "Sheriff Akers had to go to Frankfort to testify in a big marijuana case or he never would have let Junior out of jail. But what's really worrying me is the one guy I think is *not* guilty has ugly rumors floating around, making him look bad. Vern's big mouth, I think, or maybe even Junior's, is to blame."

"Seth?"

"Seth. On the surface, everything points to him, but I don't buy it. I think someone's setting Seth up, with the patterns of berries we found in the woods and the damage to my Cherokee." He wiped his mouth with his napkin. He'd eaten in record time. "I'm going to go take one look around outside, then I'll take you home."

"Who around here would consider that kind of clever symbolism—claw the Jeep Cherokee, frame Cherokee Seth?" she asked as she stood, too.

"Not Junior Semple, and I can't see it being Peter Sung's MO. Maybe Vern. I may have to get someone to protect you when you work for him, as well as out in the wilds on that sang count."

He grimaced as he bent back to take a last swig of cold, likely bitter coffee.

"Again," she said, "I don't know what I'd do without you."

"Dr. Lockwood, I'm starting to think that without me, you'd nail a murderer. But you'd still miss me, like you did all these years we've been apart."

"What makes you think I missed you?" she challenged, hoping she didn't look as startled as she felt.

"Because," he said, putting the cup down on the table and winking at her, "however warm Italian women were and however determined Audrey Doyle has been—before Ryan Buford arrived, that is—I was missing you, too. Come on, let's take a last look at the grave, then go home."

Go home, she thought, as she grabbed her clutch purse from the floor and went outside with him. Her girlhood home, her mother's house. The place where she had to get her lab work going again. Yes, for now, at least, especially with Drew at her side, that would be going home.

18

A frantic knocking on her front door made Jessie's pulse pound. Wishing Drew were here, she jumped up from the breakfast table. She hadn't let him spend the night, but she was waiting for him to pick her up so they could drive to see Peter Sung in Lexington.

She raced for the front of the house. Cassie stood there in the morning mist with Pearl at her side and something in her arms. Pearl was still in her robe and slippers, and Cassie looked worse than when she'd seen her last night. Maybe she wasn't the only one not sleeping, Jessie thought as she drew back the dead bolt and pulled the door inward.

"What is it?" she demanded. "Are you sick, too? I'm sorry, I can't keep Pearl today because—"

"You wouldn't want her anyway, after you hear what she's done," Cassie insisted as she came in, toting a square tin box.

"It was only magic and make-believe!" Pearl protested as she followed her mother in.

"What happened?" Jessie asked.

"You just tell her, you tell your aunt Jessie, Miss Pearl Keenan," Cassie cried and collapsed in a chair with the box on her lap.

Jessie stooped, then knelt to Pearl's height. "What was all magic and make-believe, Pearl?" she asked, putting one hand on the girl's shoulder and tipping her chin up with the other.

"The cave where I kept the secret things, the food and magic writing."

"Cassie," Jessie said, turning to her, "just tell me. Drew will be here in a few minutes to pick me up to drive to Lexington, so what happened? What's in the box?" She stood but kept one hand on Pearl's shaking shoulder.

Cassie put her face in her hands, elbows propped on the box. Her voice came out muffled. "She balanced a stool on a chair to reach the top shelf in my clothes closet. She got my metal box, this box, full of strong herbs, off the shelf. She and Teddy had tea from the crushed leaves, just hot tap water, not boiled. Those toxic leaves made her sick and could have— could have . . ."

"Oh, honey," Jessie said to Pearl, "you could have really, really hurt yourself!"

"I already did. But I hid the writing there, too," she said, fidgeting.

Following Pearl's sideways glance, Jessie looked at the box again. She reached for it, sat down in the chair next to Cassie's and lifted the lid.

All that lay inside were a few pieces of lined paper covered with her mother's distinctive handwriting. Jessie gasped as she skimmed the top page and shuffled through the others, seven pages total. "My mother's sang notes!" Some of the pages looked wrinkled and dirty, as if they'd been scuffed in reddish soil. Pearl must have carried them around outside for a while, but she didn't want to get the child in more trouble by questioning her about that. Besides, what did it matter? Like a gift from God, she had some of the sang counts back!

"Mariah stopped by to see us the morning she went missing," Cassie said, her voice calmer now as she leaned back in the chair. "I should have told Drew, but what did it matter? It was just after dawn, and she was showing those to me while we had some oatmeal and toast, talking about how well she thought the count was going—"

"*Well* meaning it was a high count or that she was making good progress?" Jessie asked.

"Making good progress. She never gave a hint about how the count was coming along 'cause then a lot of people would jump on her—you know what I mean. She must have accidentally left or dropped these notes, and Pearl picked them up."

"I pretended they were magic writing," Pearl said. "I put them in the magic cave."

"Which is what, Pearl?" Cassie cried, sounding distraught again. "Now, we been over this before!"

Pearl looked as if she'd burst into tears. "Your closet, where I can't go anymore."

"That's right, 'cause you could have fallen off that rickety perch, and you almost poisoned yourself! Oh, I know I'm to blame, but can't you just behave!"

"It's all right, Pearl," Jessie said and put her arm around her. "Cassie, it's all right. Maybe this was meant to be. Now I have some of her notes—I don't think they're all here—before I start the count. If I can just figure out what she covered so far, I won't have to spend a week tramping through the forests. Maybe I can just spot-check where she's been. These are invaluable to me right now, so I thank both of you. Cassie, are you sure you're not coming down with something? That toxic stuff couldn't have gotten into your own tea or—"

"No, I questioned her about that."

"It was only for children and magic beasts like Big Bear or ogres like in fairy tales, not for grown-ups," Pearl said, hands on hips in a perfect imitation of her mother.

"Cassie," Jessie said, "you know that some of those herbs you use for mordants to set the dye—even foxglove flowers for medicines—are deadly. Pearl's too young to understand all that."

"Yeah," she said as she rose and took Pearl's hand and plodded toward the door, with the metal box under one arm. "We're all too stupid to get things sometimes, till it hits us right in the face."

Her friend sounded so despondent that Jessie rushed to her as she opened the front door. "Until Drew comes, I can fix you something to eat," she volunteered. "I've got breakfast all out. I was just so shook when I saw these papers I wasn't thinking—"

"We can't stay," Cassie interrupted, forcing a smile that didn't match her sad eyes. "Tyler's coming for us later, and I got things to do. I understand about my girl playing make-believe. Lord knows, I done it enough, even grown-up, and no good came of it. I just got so het up 'cause I could have lost her."

Lost her. Those words hung heavy in Jessie's mind as she watched them get in their old truck and head out. She'd lost her mother, but here were some of her notes, a piece of her precious work. Jessie closed and relocked the door, then put her mother's notes in a zip-top plastic bag. She'd keep them in her mother's old denim pack she was using as a purse and look through them as they drove to Lexington.

Leaving the forested mountains near Deep Down and heading toward the rolling green grass of Lexington, Jessie and Drew hashed everything over again. Then she read her mother's sang notes aloud to him in case some clue about who could have wanted to harm her was imbedded in the tightly written pages.

"Once I get her notes from the last couple of years from Frank Redmond," Jessie said, "I'll be able to tell if the numbers are down much this year. I'm hoping this challenge will be much easier than I expected."

"Go on. Keep reading."

"I just don't want you to fall asleep at the wheel. This is not scintillating stuff."

"Police work often isn't."

"Okay. To continue, 'maple wood cove, 44 three-prongers, under S.P.'"

"That could mean under Shrieking Peak," he said. It was obvious that Mariah abbreviated the places she counted, often using natural formations as a guide, though many of her notations hadn't made sense to them.

"Right. She did counts on both sides of the river. The next one says, 'n. rocks w/ golden s. and cohosh under old man—poached but 6 two-prongers.' Goldenseal and cohosh often grow near sang, but 'under old man'? You know, Big Blue does have a rock formation that looks like a hunched old man."

"I'll bet that's it."

"If I can just find one of those places to match what is growing there to these numbers, it may give me something to average out for Frank."

"Is that the end of her notes? That's the last page, isn't it?"

"Just a little more. Oh, this one mentions Seth."

Sucking in a sharp breath, Drew stiffened his arms on the steering wheel, then relaxed them again. "Don't tell me it's something to incriminate him. It's tough as is, keeping the lid on people blaming him."

"It just says, 'poplar stand w/ Seth.'"

"Oh, great, just great! Does that mean he went out to count with her or was going to? He said he never did that. If he's lying, maybe he's outfoxed me. Do you know if he has a stand of poplars on his property?"

"On the far side of his house. I think it's where he cut the fresh sang for the funeral. But Seth hated the idea of the sang count, of her reporting it to the government, so I'm surprised he either helped her or let her count that site."

"Maybe I've been wrong about Seth, and we should head back to Deep Down before he hides out like Junior evidently has."

"But we're almost to Peter's, and you haven't even had a chance to question him yet. We can't turn back now."

"No," he said, reaching out to cup her knee before putting his hand back on the wheel, "we can't turn back now. Finish reading."

"My eyes are about ready to cross. This last one is written up the side of the page, real small, as if it were an afterthought or an addendum," she said, holding it up to catch more light. She glanced out her side window to rest her eyes a moment. Neat white fences blurred by. Sleek horses grazed or ran within many of them; emerald lawns, cut like velvet, surrounded cleanly painted stables, old black tobacco barns, or large, pillared, plantation-style houses. Her life here came flooding back: the town house she'd shared with Elinor, studying on campus, football games and friends and homecoming dances ... homecoming ...

The gently rolling, affluent Lexington region had always calmed her, but not today. Again the differences between this area and the sharply wooded hills of Deep Down struck her. She loved both places, but which was home? It seemed so strange to be here with Drew, who, in her heart, belonged so completely to that other world. She jolted back to reality and squinted at the tiny words again.

"It's hard to read," she told him, "but it says, '24 four-prongers,' and has three exclamation points after that. Twenty-four is a big patch and four-prongers are eight to ten years old, untouched, a real find! But here's the thing. She also wrote very small, 'If beech area is ad site, swear BB to secrecy.'"

"If ad site—*s-i-t-e?*"

"Yes. Beth Brazzo told me she's expecting her ad shoot team soon. My mother's fridge had a lot of G-Women power drink in it. Maybe Beth visited her and convinced her to tell her where she could find a site with a lot of good sang for her ads. Or, since Beth jogs everywhere, maybe she found the site herself. Whichever the case, did Beth tell Tyler about it? He could corroborate some of this. He and Ms. Brazen Brazzo don't seem to hang out together, but they're on the same team."

"Other than the mention of the beech trees, is there any indication where that ad shoot site might be?"

"'I.F.'—*Indian Falls?*"

"At any rate, that means Ms. Brazzo's on the interrogation list, too."

"And Tyler? Maybe if he's too good to believe—for Cassie, for you with that photo of The Thing—he shouldn't be believed. He did happen to show up right about the time Mother disappeared."

"But he would have loved a photo of her doing her sang count, and she probably would have let him. So what's his motive?"

"I don't know. Maybe I'm just paranoid

about everyone. Drew, if that weird photo-graph of his leaks out and a lot of people come pouring in to monster hunt, doesn't that help their ad campaign for their prod-uct?"

"Yeah," he admitted. "It would mean instant media coverage for the area, there-fore for the power drinks."

"It would give Deep Down its fifteen min-utes of fame at a perfect time to boost Brazzo's slogan, 'deep down satisfac-tion.'"

"As I said, I'll have to question her. I don't like it that Cassie didn't tell me she and Pearl were probably the last ones to see Mariah alive—besides her killer—but Beth may have seen her quite late, too. Look, we're here," he told her, leaning for-ward to read a road sign they were almost under. "Check the directions I scribbled down, will you? I think we turn west on Man O' War Boulevard."

"Yes, that's right," she said, looking at his scribbling now instead of her mother's. As he took the ramp and then two other streets to get to the final turnoff, she put the sang papers back in their plastic bag in the bottom of her denim bag. "Drew, if

Peter says something to really implicate himself, you can't just arrest him and haul him back where you have jurisdiction, can you?"

"No. I'd need to get local enforcement assistance and then have him transferred. I've got their number on my speed dial."

"He must know you're upset that he got Junior out of jail, especially since he's evidently jumped bail."

"Don't go weak-kneed on me now. I'm depending on your courage and brains, partner. Remember, we're here to talk about hunting dogs and how the supposedly superior kind he breeds might have helped us locate Mariah the first day she went missing. It's in Sung's best interests to stay on our good side. I'm the law in Deep Down and you—well, to our murderer's way of thinking—you now have, for good or ill, your mother's power over the future of wild ginseng."

Cassie ripped up the last of her poison plants by their roots, chopped them in pieces with her long knife and threw them in a pile to be burned. She'd made Pearl stay in her room today as punishment, however grateful she was that the child's little tea party with Teddy had not hurt her even more. Thank God, Tyler had come into her life. The generous salary he paid her would cover the clinic and pharmacy bill. Cassie just hoped the fact he'd had to postpone their jaunt today didn't spell more bad luck. He'd said he had to meet with Beth Brazzo about picking the exact site for their photo shoot when their actors showed up. More than once he said he thought that Cassie and Pearl would be much more believable in an ad for their client's power drink than whoever Beth had coming in.

"Oh, right," she muttered under her breath as she bent to give the nightshade and ground-cherry branches a last couple of whacks. "A couple of poisoners in a health drink ad."

She sensed someone behind her before she heard a step. She spun and there he stood, daring to come into her holler, onto her land.

"Hello, Cassandra," he said. "I saw you and the girl from a distance at the funeral. Two beauties now instead of one."

He'd been at Mariah's funeral, and she

hadn't seen him? Cassie lifted her long knife in one raised hand. Sweat broke out on her forehead. She started to shake with shock and rage.

"Unless you want to attend another funeral—yours—get quit of here right now," she said, her voice trembling. "When you left, you left for good, and good riddance."

Handsome as ever, he cocked his head slightly; she saw he wore a bulky pack that made him look humpbacked. "Not the welcome I was hoping for. I'll leave, but I'll be seeing you."

She thought of a lot of things to shout at him, but since he'd turned on his booted heel and left, she just stood there, frozen. Finally, when his footsteps had been swallowed by forest sounds, she turned to rush inside. She'd lock the door, she'd call Tyler and tell him to get here as soon as he could.

As she ran toward the house with her knife in her hand, she caught sight of Pearl's pale face pressed to her bedroom window.

Drew didn't turn into Sung's drive but went past it. For once, the immaculate, white fences with bars closer together, probably to keep in dogs instead of horses, and the large, pillared house looked not inviting but foreboding.

"What is it?" Jess cried. "You've changed your mind?"

"No, I just didn't know we'd get here this quickly. I told him eleven-thirty, and I don't want to seem overeager. Besides, I told Emmy she could e-mail me if anything important came up, and that I'd check my laptop before we visited him. We've been so engrossed, I didn't think to stop somewhere."

About a half mile down the road, he pulled off into a side lane by another ubiquitous white fence and reached for his laptop in the backseat. It was a different world out here, he thought. In Deep Down, cell phones seldom worked and never a Wi-Fi laptop.

He booted it up and skimmed his mail. "One thing from her," he said, "something she's forwarding from Tyler."

"Another picture?"

"No, just text with an attachment," he said, skimming her note and then reading the one she'd attached. "Damn. Damn!"

Jess leaned closer. The sweet scent of her hair was distracting. "What?" she asked, trying to read the screen by pressing her chin on his shoulder.

"Emmy says that Tyler stopped by the office this morning—with Beth Brazzo—and left some info for me about Seth," he said, rereading the note she'd attached. "I can see why Tyler wanted me to have it, but it makes Seth look bad again."

"Drew, what does it say?"

"It's pretty strange info on Cherokee lore," he explained, propping the laptop a bit higher against the steering wheel so she could see the screen. "Tyler must be losing his mind, if he believes this or thinks we will. Have you ever heard Seth mention skillies?"

"Skillies? No, what—"

"Okay, listen to this," he said, when he realized she still couldn't see the screen well. "Tyler evidently got this from some Cherokee Web site but also from some blogs on Bigfoot."

"Oh, for heaven's sakes! Bigfoot?"

"Do you want to hear this or not?"

"Shoot."

"According to Cherokee lore, a skilly is a malevolent ghost or bad spirit in the woods, appearing as a large, hairy creature. One particular two-legged skilly supposedly stood over eight feet tall. Skillies can move through the woods like a puff of smoke and sometimes can be spotted by their two, glowing eyes. They usually appear after dark, but have been known to inhabit shadowed forests and mountain coves."

"That's got to be a superstition that developed from seeing deer or raccoon eyes glowing from the dark," she said. He watched her rub her arms with her hands; like him, she had gooseflesh. "I saw eyes like that the day we found my mother's body, but it was just a raccoon. I'm sure of it. I saw one run away. I heard heavy footsteps, but it turned out to be Tyler."

"But you see where he's going with this?"

"You think Tyler Finch believes in skillies?"

"No, I'm thinking he believes Seth might—or might have somehow dressed himself like one and got caught in a picture."

They looked at each other. Her eyes were wide with fear, but she narrowed them, looking as skeptical as she'd sounded.

"Does he say anything else?" she asked, after an awkward silence. She broke their mutual gaze, looking jerkily down at the laptop again, so he did too.

"Just that the basic power of a skilly is fear. That's word for word—'When you come in contact with a skilly, you will be filled with a dark, primal fear, one that you cannot ignore. It will haunt you, even if you escape its claws. The basic power of a skilly is fear.'"

"Claws? Like badger claws, I suppose!" she added, her voice dripping sarcasm again. "Unlike Peter Sung, who seems happy to tell everything about his people's beliefs, Seth's closemouthed. You said he wouldn't talk much about that 'grandfather tree' where my mother was hidden, so he probably won't talk about this. Besides, it's just tradition—superstition."

Drew e-mailed Emmy he had the received message, signed off and shut down the laptop. That reminded him, he wanted to carefully question her about what she really knew about Ryan Buford. But now he had to face Peter Sung and fight an urge to put something as silly as a skilly on his list of suspects for Mariah's murder.

19

Peter Sung came out to greet them with four dark hounds at his heels. The dogs had sleek, black coats brindled with specks of gray, almost smoky-looking. Jessie and Drew could hear other dogs from the kennel beyond the backyard. Compared to the deep howls of most hunt hounds, Jessie noted these Plott hounds had a high-pitched, sharp bark, almost like a woman's shriek.

Smiling, gracious, Peter shook their hands. "We all welcome you," he said with a sweeping gesture at his canine companions. "But do not think the Plotts still in the kennel are baying at *you*. They do not approve that I have only these four with me, but each dog will have his day."

He escorted them into his lovely home. Jessie had expected it to be furnished in Oriental style, but, except for a touch here and there—a painted screen, an ornamental vase—it was tastefully Southern.

"My wife lives in Hong Kong," he told them, proudly displaying a family photograph. "Until our son graduates from his private secondary school there and comes to college in the States, she is best at home."

He had a luncheon table laid out for them, or rather, his young Asian male servant did. Large votive candles with tall, flickering flames served as the centerpiece. Jessie noticed their strange but intoxicating scent, like incense, maybe something exotic like jasmine or frangipani. Come to think of it, the whole house, even Peter himself, smelled faintly of that scent. The day they had spoken outside her house, the fresh air must have muted it, but it was distinctive here.

With the four hounds lying obediently around Peter's chair, the young man served the three of them crab Rangoon, egg rolls, shrimp tempura and fried rice washed down with mint tea. They all ate with chopsticks. The excellence of the food reminded Jessie of her aborted trip to Hong Kong.

"No fortune cookies today," Peter told them. "But despite the tragedy of Mariah's loss, I predict all will be well in Deep Down from now on."

"Which means," Drew said, "I must find a murderer."

"Sadly so. But let us treasure this day you were so kind to visit me and ask about the thing I love third best in this life. First, of course, my family, second my work to bring wild Kentucky *jen-shen,* the root of life, to my people and thirdly, these clever hounds of the hunt. Brilliant, aren't you, boys and girls?" he asked, looking down on the floor where Jessie saw the hounds raise their eager heads.

"I know it's a tiring drive from Deep Down," Peter went on, "so, I thought you might wish to eat and relax before we talk Plotts and tracking collars. Jessica, I'm pleased to see that you are getting away from your cares for a while, though, of course, you carry your loss with you always."

"I am finding ways to honor her," she told Peter. They had decided she should tell him that she was continuing the ginseng count and note his reaction and comments carefully. "I have decided to complete her ginseng work, for which I have her boss Frank Redmond's permission and assistance."

"Ah!" he said with a single clap of his hands. "I am so relieved and so will my sponsors, the Kulong family, be. Am I to understand that Mariah left records of the count she had done so far?"

"A partial, yes."

"I hadn't heard. Vern is kind enough to let me know how things are going in town. Not as a sub-agent, but as a friend. In return, I help to support the museum he so treasures. But, let us speak of the 'sang' again, as Deep Down calls it. A Chinese legend claims *jen-shen* is the child of lightning. Up in heaven, the story goes, water and fire are in an eternal struggle. When those hostile elements battle, they strike the earth with lightning. Where a bolt hits the soil, *jen-shen* springs up, a union of fire and water, darkness and light, yin and yang—eternal opposites. I am not boring you?"

"No, please, go on," Jessie encouraged him. Drew had said the purpose of this visit was to get Peter to talk, to reveal as much of himself and his pursuits as possible.

"Sadly, we Chinese cannot grow the root in our huge country because it takes cool, shady forests and deep soil from centuries of decomposed leaves. Our land is old, played-out, used. Other people value the herb, too, so we get some from them, but not the quality of Kentucky *jen-shen.*"

"Do the other places you buy ginseng have stories of it, too?"

"Indeed. In Korea, a legend says *jen-shen* can talk or even turn itself into another plant to hide."

"I wish that were true," Drew put in. "The sang Mariah was covered in would have a lot to tell."

"Ah—yes. We used to get some from Siberia, too, where the root is highly valued, almost sacred, and was traditionally hunted by a clan of fierce outcasts. From infancy to old age, they dedicated their lives to gathering it. And, it's said some Appalachians—not you, Jessica, I know that—believe the plant can hide itself underground when it believes itself to be in danger."

She heaved an intentionally dramatic sigh. "I wish my mother could have had time to hide when she found herself threatened. But then, perhaps she knew her killer and didn't realize that he or she meant her harm until it was too late."

She noted Peter repeatedly tugged both of his long shirtsleeves down as if he were trying to hide his hands. Body language that meant something, or just a nervous habit?

"I had thought perhaps," Peter said, "she surprised poachers, who just panicked, then they tried to cover up their horrid deed by making someone else look guilty. But, at any rate, pictorial representations for all these *jen-shen* legends can be found in Vern's museum. Sad so few visit it. Not to change the subject, Jessica, but I have something for you—good luck indeed, much better than a hopeful fortune cookie message."

He said, "Stay!" to the hounds, then rose and walked to a massive credenza in the corner of the dining room and opened the glass doors. Jessie turned in her chair and gasped to see what was on the shelves behind her. Tall, clear glass bottles filled with pale amber liquid, in which floated large, perfectly formed ginseng roots, were displayed. Each one, she knew, must be worth thousands of dollars on the Chinese market. These roots were especially precious because each was shaped like a person with the tap root as the torso, then the smaller roots as arms and legs, even to the tiny roots as hands and fingers. Since the plant itself had been lopped off when the root was dug, each body was, of course, headless.

Peter presented one of the bottles to Jessie with a flourish. "The Chinese written characters for *jen-shen* mean 'man-root,'" he told them, "and possessing one of these is very good luck, very good."

"I could use that," she told him, carefully cradling the bottle in both hands. "I don't know if I've ever seen one so perfectly formed, and to think you have an entire array of them. I thank you."

"I meant to give it to your mother when she registered her count this year," he said, "but it is now yours—with the obligations it carries."

She wondered if he meant it as a bribe or a clever, subtle threat. Of course, he intimated that he expected the count to be high enough to keep the ginseng flowing to him and to his country. But she would display this in her lab, and trust Chinese tradition that it would bring good luck to her sang count and her study of cancer.

"My question is," Drew said, "how do you get that big root in that small-necked bottle?"

"Did you never make a ship in a bottle when you were a boy?" Peter asked, smiling. "I cannot give away all my secrets, can I? But I am delighted, Sheriff, that you wish to see my hounds and hear how easy it is for me to track them with the radio transmitting collars. Come outside, please, both of you, and let me give you a thorough demonstration. And, if you approve, I shall keep one pup for you from the next litter. Then I shall train and donate her to find lost souls in Deep Down's forests."

Tyler wanted to go back to the hills and cliffs overlooking Indian Falls, the site they'd visited their first day together. Cassie didn't care where they went. She just plain wanted to get out of the house and off her property, where Pearl could have died from poisoning herself and where the man she had to blame for it all had dared to set foot today.

Pearl sat between her and Tyler in the front seat of the truck, holding tight to Teddy as if she couldn't stand to let him out of her sight. At least she wasn't her usual chatterbox self. Earlier, she'd asked who the man with the big backpack was. When Cassie had told her he was a salesman, she'd only replied, "Did you have to wave your big knife to make him leave?"

"We're going to meet Beth Brazzo here," Tyler told them. "A couple weeks ago, she found a great ginseng site with the falls in the background when she was jogging, and hasn't found a better one since. The ginseng leaves have turned yellow, but we can't wait for next summer for this shoot, so we'll just doctor up the photo to turn them green."

"You can do things like that?" Cassie asked as she pulled into a grassy spot just off the bumpy track that served as a road here. No other vehicle was in sight, so maybe Beth Brazzo had jogged up here. It was only a couple of miles from town, and Tyler had told her the woman ran many miles each day to stay in shape.

"You'd be surprised at my photographic magic," he said. He was happy and excited today, but that made her even more upset than she already was. Once the shoot for their ad was over, surely Tyler as well as Ms. Brazzo would be leaving Deep Down. Cassie knew she was coming to care for him. A mistake, of course, but she couldn't help herself. But it was really riling her right now that he'd mentioned doctoring up a photo. Could he have fixed up that picture with the beast in it, just to get everyone's attention?

Tyler was explaining all the things he could do to make a photo reveal things that were not true. "I can insert clouds in a clear sky," he boasted, "or take them out. I can make someone short look tall, or take a pair of open eyes from one photo and substitute them in the face of someone who had their eyes closed."

"That's really magic!" Pearl finally spoke.

"It's called digital imagery, Pearl. Actually,

amateurs can do that these days, too, but it's my job, so I've been good at it for a long time. The sounds in the ad can be altered, too—as a matter of fact, I told Beth we'll probably have to redub that background whine from Shrieking Peak. Okay, I'll play guide today instead of you, Cassie," he said, getting out his heavy gear, including a silver tripod with a large cupped disk on the end of it. She knew the tripod opened up quite tall, but he had it telescoped right now to one-fourth of its length.

With his free hand, he held hers and squeezed it, then, when she took Pearl's, led them off across the meadow toward the trees with the falls roaring far beyond under the frowning brow of Shrieking Peak.

"Beth said the ginseng's in a stand of beeches and maples just across from the falls," he told them. "You have any idea what beeches look like?"

"So you do need me, after all," Cassie told him. She was amazed at the teasing, flirty tone she'd used. She'd felt so low lately, but Tyler's mere presence perked her up a bit. Is that what love was, not the kind that tore you up but lifted you up?

"Right this way, over here," she said, pointing and tugging him in that direction. "The maples will soon be flaming-red, but the beeches will go gold. Those are beeches over there, see?"

Still holding hands, they looked into each other's eyes. "I'll have to come back to see them when they turn gold. I will come back, to visit my cousin in Highboro, but more importantly, to visit you and Pearl—and Teddy."

"I hope so. I'd like that."

"Deep Down grows on you," he whispered. "I'm kind of glad Beth's late today, because . . ." He leaned forward to kiss her.

Pearl, thank heavens, didn't make a peep. Besides, it was only a peck on the cheek, but it sent her head spinning with possibilities. After he'd set up his equipment and Pearl was picking Queen Anne's lace a few trees away, he kissed her harder on the mouth. She returned his kiss and embrace fervently, surprising herself with the hot rush of need that left her breathless. She'd had no man—wanted no man—trusted no man—this way for years.

When the kiss ended, she peeked at

Pearl. She was getting too close to the steep bank facing the falls. "Pearl, come on back here now," she called, reluctantly moving from Tyler's embrace.

"Bring those flowers, Pearl," Tyler added. "I'd like to take a few photos of you and your mother before Beth gets here."

Pearl turned back to face them but didn't budge. Her pale face had gone even whiter. Cassie's insides lurched. What if she was going to be sick again?

"If she has lots of black hair," the child said, pointing behind her, "I think she's already here. But she's sleeping."

Both frowning, Cassie and Tyler looked at each other, then rushed to where Pearl stood. On a flat stone ledge below, in her jogging sweats and shoes, stretched out with her head twisted at a sharp angle, lay Beth Brazzo.

Drew had to admit that Peter Sung's hounds were amazing. A breed developed by the mountain men of the Plott family over a two-hundred-year period in North Carolina, the muscular, agile dogs were quick and clever, perhaps like their master.

"They can tree anything, including a

bear," Peter boasted. "They're tenacious and fearless. They may drool and slobber a bit, but that's their only weakness. In a home, they're loyal, gentle and good with children, too. But you wanted to see the tracking collars?"

"Yeah. If I had one of these beautiful dogs, I'd sure hate to lose him."

"At over a thousand dollars a pup, I would, too," Peter said, chuckling as if he'd made a joke.

The kennel was immaculate, built like a miniature horse stable. The entire estate looked pristine and new, even the ubiquitous black tobacco-drying barn at the rear of the property. Drew watched closely as Peter opened a wooden cabinet and brought out a collar. Jess came closer, too. The collar looked identical to the one he'd found in the general proximity of Mariah's body!

"It looks like those buckle on tightly," Drew observed. "It would be bad if the dogs lost one. Has that ever happened?"

Peter looked at him instead of the collar. "Not that I recall, but here's how they work. Embedded within is a chip that sends out a radio transmitting signal. Collared dogs are tracked with handheld receivers and antennae mounted on a chase vehicle. I only buy state-of-the-art equipment, a step up from what most locals with other hounds might use. These can even transmit activity and behavior signals. For example, they indicate whether a dog is running or still, even whether his head is pointing upward, as it might be when he were baying at a treed animal."

"Amazing," Jess said, speaking for the first time since they'd come into the kennel. She'd left most of the dog talk to him and Peter. "Could you also keep track of someone—maybe a kid who was out hunting with one of these—if he'd keep it on his person?"

"Do you want to try it?" he asked. "It surely would work, but I think a little demonstration might convince Drew. I don't expect a sheriff to just take my word for things."

That statement hung in the air for a moment. Another challenge or a threat? Drew wondered. Unless he'd fallen victim to the stereotype of the inscrutable Chinese, Peter Sung seemed to speak with a subtext most of the time. Jess agreed to try a demonstration, putting the collar on like a big necklace, then followed Peter's suggestion she walk across the yard to the back porch of the house. She would move and turn while Peter, with his back to her, would read the signals from his equipment and tell Drew, who could see for himself what she was doing.

As Jess walked away, Peter produced a handheld receiver and a long, sturdy-looking silver antenna from his cabinet. The receiver crackled when he turned it on. He adjusted it with a short joystick, from a selection of four of them attached to the small black control box. With his back to Jess, he told Peter, "She's much closer, of course, than a hound would be, but she's moving erratically—weaving."

"True," Drew said with a glance her way. "Does it take much work to learn to read the signals?"

"Some practice. One of these is probably more than a small police department like yours could afford, but I could see myself donating one of these with a hound or two, just to know you are in my corner to keep the ginseng trade going."

The hair on the back of Drew's neck

prickled. A blatant bribe, one that was probably also intended to keep him in Peter's corner should the murder investigation go in a direction he didn't like. Yet they were alone, so he could deny it later, say the new sheriff had misunderstood. How harmless, how generous, the donation of tracker dogs and equipment.

Or worse, was it even a taunt, implying that there was no way a backwoods sheriff could track down Mariah's murderer without help? Could Peter have tried to buy Mariah off with something, and she told him no? Jess was no doubt testing the theory right now that Peter had planted some sort of tracking device on Mariah so he knew exactly where to find her in the random spots she covered.

Drew looked away from Jess's wavering path. She had gone back toward the black barn but was now sitting on a fence on the far side of the driveway near the house. He faced Peter squarely. "It's to everyone's benefit that the sang trade stay strong," Drew told him. "But a sheriff upholds the law, and the government law says, sang count too low, exports no go."

"A poet and you didn't know it." Peter

recovered instantly with a shrug and a smile. "Ah," he said, looking down at the control box and listening to the clicks and static from it, "your Jessica has gone toward the meadow instead of the house, right?"

"That much is right," Drew said. "We appreciate your time and hospitality today. So, when will you be back in Deep Down?"

"Tomorrow, to oversee the packing of Junior Semple's crop at Vern's store."

"I can't find Junior, you know. He's evidently jumped bail."

Peter frowned. "He vowed he would not. Well, when he turns up, you can lock him up longer for that, and his cultivated *jenshen* will help my customers. After all, otherwise some poacher could have stolen it."

The two of them walked back toward the house just as Jess was divesting herself of the collar. Peter's houseboy, butler or whatever he was, came out onto the porch and held out his hand to get it back from Jess. No, that wasn't it. He was holding a mobile phone out toward Peter and speaking to him in Chinese. Drew wondered if it was a call from the Kulong family no one knew much about, and whom Drew had always pictured as a sort of Chinese *Cosa Nostra.*

Peter said, "The call is for you, Drew, from your office manager. Important, she says."

Drew took the phone and put a finger in his other ear to mute the buglelike baying of the Plotts in the kennel. "Emmy, go ahead."

"Tyler, Cassie and Pearl were supposed to meet Beth Brazzo up near Indian Falls. But she must have tripped jogging on the path and broke her neck. Drew, she's dead!"

20

Drew put his portable, magnetic, red flashing light on top of the Cherokee, and they sped back to Deep Down. Drivers quickly slowed or got out of their way. Still, he wished he had *Sheriff* emblazoned on the side of the vehicle instead of those deep scratch marks, ones, he'd noted, Peter Sung had not even blinked an eye at when he greeted them or saw them off. Perhaps the man just didn't notice them in the overcast day. Or maybe he was too polite to pry. Or he figured, if he made a big deal about them, it would look suspicious.

The guy definitely was under suspicion. Possible proximity to Mariah's murder and motive, motive, motive. He had said he'd be back in Deep Down tomorrow, when Jess was determined to start her sang count. Now protecting her would be even harder, since he would have not only Mariah's death to look into, but Beth Brazzo's. Two women dead in little Deep Down in less than two weeks. As far as he recalled, they had never even had two natural deaths in that timeframe. But, of course, Peter Sung had an ironclad alibi that he hadn't hurt Beth Brazzo—if she didn't just stumble while jogging.

Emmy had told him that Tyler would meet him at the place they'd found Beth's body, but he saw Cassie's truck was here, too. Emmy was taking care of Pearl for a while, so Cassie could wait here with Tyler. Both of them walked toward Drew and Jess as they got out. Drew had told Emmy to call the coroner, but he obviously wasn't here yet.

"No one's touched the body or even gone down to it," Tyler told them, "though I did take a couple of photos for you. It's— she's—on a ledge that kept her from falling way down." The man looked distressed, but then he had been Beth's colleague. His hands and voice shook. Drew wondered how well he'd known Beth Brazzo. Had theirs been just a professional relationship or personal, too? Was there friction or harmony between them over Tyler's pet project and his closeness to Cassie? Those questions would have to wait.

"She could have tripped and fallen over the edge—you'll see," Cassie put in, sticking tight to Tyler. "We saw a couple of gnarled roots where she could have caught her foot. It was actually Pearl who spotted her. She said she thought Beth was asleep, but her neck's at a horrible angle."

He and Jess darted a look at each other.

"From the fall, no doubt," Tyler added. "A little puddle of blackish blood is under her head. We shouted and shouted, but she didn't stir. After Pearl pointed her out, we tried not to mess up possible footprints above where she fell."

She fell. Drew noted the words. They were assuming this was an accident, and he should, too, unless evidence proved otherwise. But he'd become so distrustful of everyone since Mariah's death, including fantasy ogres shuffling through the woods.

"You both handled it just right," he assured them. "The coroner's coming with the paramedic recovery team from Highboro, but I'm going to try to get down to her now. I'll take individual statements from each of you after."

He took a coil of rope from the back of his vehicle and slung it over his shoulder. The four of them started toward the edge of the escarpment overlooking the falls and Shrieking Peak. It was a beautiful spot, he thought, despite the perpetual whine of the wind through the distant crags.

"Do you know if she was just out jogging?" he asked Tyler.

"Yes and no. She jogged out to meet us here because this is the spot she'd finally picked for the power drink ad shoot—lots of untouched ginseng. I was going to do some stills to send back to Bailey and Keller so they could okay them. The two actors for the shoot were coming in day after tomorrow."

"Drew," Jess said as she stretched her strides to keep up with him, "a sang site with beech trees with a view of Indian

Falls . . . I'll bet there are twenty-four four-prongers there."

"Yeah. Puzzle pieces are fitting together, but what's the picture?"

"What about this place?" Cassie asked. "Did Beth tell you about it, Jessie?"

When she didn't answer, Tyler said, "Beth told me she'd volunteered to count ginseng with you, but she wasn't sure you were going to take her up on it."

When Jess only nodded, Drew realized she was leaving it up to him whether they explained about this site. "Tell them," he said as they approached the cluster of tall beeches which framed the cloudy sky, distant falls and gray-green Shrieking Peak beyond.

"I think Beth might have been interested in this place for the shoot for over a week at least," Jess told them, "so she must have known it quite well. My mother recorded in her notes, which Cassie and Pearl found, that if Beth was going to use this special sang site for the ad, she wanted to swear her to secrecy about it."

"Secrecy from whom? She was going to share it with Cassie and me, the shoot team and actors," Tyler said. "Not to mention it would be part of a nationally broadcast ad campaign for TV and print media."

"I don't know," Jess admitted. "A lot of things don't make sense yet."

They reached the site and edged out, avoiding the area directly over the ledge in case there were footprints there. Beth lay sprawled below on her side, her legs spread as if she still ran, her arms bent, her head twisted to the side with her raven-black hair fanned around her face. Despite the thick cover of it, Drew realized Tyler was probably right that a puddle of blood had congealed under her head. Drew thought the angle of her head was similar to the way they'd found Mariah, yet these circumstances were night and day from that—weren't they?

"See there?" Cassie said, pointing to the gnarled roots of the beeches that clung clawlike to the edge of the precipice. "She could have tripped on one of these and toppled over."

Drew moved them even farther away from where she must have gone over. He uncoiled the rope and tied one end of it around a tree trunk, one not directly above the body. Yeah, this looked like an accident, but for one thing: the strangely blurred footprints he recognized in the area Tyler had said they'd been careful not to trample. At first glance, they look like the prints he's seen near his clawed Cherokee.

He looped the other end of the rope under his armpits and double-knotted it, then let himself over the edge, slowly, swinging his butt out and walking his way down. His feet missed, then hit the ledge. Not stopping to untie himself, he bent to feel for the carotid artery at the side of Beth's neck. Nothing. She was cold and going stiff. This time, at least, the coroner would be able to estimate time of death.

He lifted a bit of her thick, black hair. She'd usually worn it pulled back in a ponytail. Would she have had it flying free if she was running? Would the fall have been enough to cause it to come loose, or could there have been a struggle? And with whom?

It didn't look as if she'd been struck in the back of the head like Mariah, but he would let the coroner turn her over. Besides, unless someone had leapt out from behind one of these trees when she passed, he couldn't picture anyone catching, murdering, then moving the strong, agile Beth Brazzo the way Mariah had been handled. Two dead women—it had to be coincidence, didn't it? But as he'd told Jess, there was no such thing as a coincidence in police work.

Jessie wasn't saying so, but she'd been convinced from the first that Beth had been chased and murdered, too. She kept quiet about that because she had no proof, but her certainty went deeper than womanly intuition. Gut instinct, yes, but beyond that—she wasn't sure.

"At least," Drew whispered as he walked her toward Cassie's truck for a ride home, "there were no claw marks on Beth's cheeks, and her head trauma could be from the fall. We'll see what Coroner Merriman comes up with. Lately, he's earning his salary around here."

Exhausted and emotionally drained, she nodded. The coroner and the paramedic team—the same people who had carried out her mother's body—had just brought Beth's corpse up from the ledge. Scribbling notes, Drew had questioned Cassie and Tyler separately.

"Anyway," Jessie said, "if this is foul play, we can exonerate Peter. Not only was he miles away but with us. Of course, with his money and local influence, he could have someone who knows this area doing his dirty work."

"Yeah," Drew muttered, "such as Junior Semple. Maybe he already had ties to Peter. Maybe Peter was the one who provided him with those poison gas sticks. The two of them could have made a deal beyond the sang when Peter bailed him out in Highboro. Junior's wife's even saying now that she doesn't know where he is, so he'd need some funds to hide out. I may stake his place out to see if he's sneaking home at night."

"Peter might have viewed Beth as a competitor for Deep Down sang. She didn't only want the ad shot near Deep Down, but the product's slogan was tied to Deep Down sang—*deep down satisfaction.* She was leading the charge to siphon off Peter's near monopoly of wild ginseng."

"We'll talk later," he said, squeezing her upper arm. "This on-site investigation is going to take awhile. By the way, Tyler really doesn't have much of an alibi—says he was on his own this morning before going to Cassie's, taking photos, which he claims will be auto-dated to back him up. But if he can fake photos, maybe he can fake the dates he took them."

"You don't suspect him of anything?"

"I can't afford to overlook anyone. I'll stop by when I can this evening. Until then, keep your doors locked."

By Cassie's truck, she turned to face him. "I will. I'll be planning my route for the count tomorrow. Cassie says she can go along, if she can get someone to watch Pearl. Well, I already have the sang counted here. Amazing a great patch of it like that hasn't been poached."

"Keep safe and phone me or Emmy if anything seems strange. Anything."

They held hands before she turned away to get in Cassie's truck. He closed the door on her side then headed back to the scene, where Beth's plastic-cocooned body was being rolled into the back of the coroner's vehicle. In the rearview mirror, on the other side, Jessie could see Tyler and Cassie huddled, talking, then he hugged her. A miracle, Jessie thought, that from tragedy came something good, not only for her and Drew but Cassie and Tyler—*if* Tyler was to be trusted.

Cassie got in the driver's side and started the old Ford. It shuddered of its own accord and was further bounced by the rutted tire tracks as they headed out.

"I overheard Drew talking to the rescue team—recovery team, I mean," Cassie said.

"And?"

"They don't think she tripped. Those gnarled roots are too far from the edge. Also, Drew said the footprints above the ledge are not from someone jogging. Someone either dragged her body—or they had huge feet, and were kind of shuffling."

Jessie's pulse pounded. She gripped her hands so hard in her lap that her fingers went numb. He must not have told her about the footprints just now because he didn't want her to worry more than she already was.

"But you did say Pearl was picking flowers there. Maybe you and Tyler kind of shuffled to the edge to look down at her."

"I guess," Cassie said with a shrug. "Drew told the rescue guys not to go over the edge right where the tracks were. He wants Tyler to take close-ups of the prints when the slant of setting sun gets just right so the profile and depth of them show up. Jessie? You look really peaked. Are you thinking about that other photo Tyler took? With that large form in it?"

"I don't know how much longer those of us who have seen Tyler's photo are going to be able to keep this—this monster myth quiet. Cassie, you should lock your doors tonight. Drew told me to. I know you never used to but—"

"I have for as long as I've had Pearl. I'm not working the garden anymore in the dark now, no way."

Jessie put her left hand on Cassie's shoulder. She was glad the truck was shaking so her friend didn't know that she was, too.

When they stopped at the sheriff's office to pick up Pearl, Emmy told them, "She's been an angel. I'd love to have a little girl myself, just like her!"

To Jessie's surprise, Cassie, who had

just thanked Emmy profusely and was on her way out the door, rounded on the girl. "I just want to warn you about Ryan Buford," Cassie clipped out. Jessie's jaw dropped.

"Why? What about him?" Emmy asked, wide-eyed from the other side of the counter. She crossed her arms over her full breasts, and thrust out her lower lip.

"I've heard he's also giving Audrey Doyle a lot of attention, and with Audrey, you know what that might mean. That's all."

"I know how she operates, but I trust him," Emmy insisted. "Where else is he going to stay around here? Vern Tarver won't put up anyone but Peter Sung. I know what she's like," Emmy repeated, with a slanted look at Jessie instead of Cassie. "I've seen how she had her claws out for the sheriff since he's been here."

Jessie's eyes got even wider, but she kept quiet. She was fascinated by Cassie's comments about Buford. Her claim that he was romancing Audrey might be reason enough for Cassie to speak out this way about something that was, really, none of her business. But now that she thought of it, Pearl's looks could be a blend of Ryan Buford's and Cassie's.

"Thanks again for watching Pearl with all that's going on," Cassie told Emmy. "Didn't mean to upset you, just a word to the wise." She pulled Pearl outside, muttering, "She's being really stupid, bless her heart."

Back in the truck, heading for her house, Jessie had to bite her tongue to keep from questioning Cassie. Pearl was here; now was not the time. It was getting late. It must be sunset already, for a reddish reflection emanated from the forest as if it mirrored the sinking sun. No, that couldn't be the sun.

"What's that glow in the sky?" she said, craning her neck toward the windshield and pointing. "Could it be a forest fire? It's over to the north a bit, not near my place, but it could spread."

As they turned the corner into Slate Creek Hollow, where they could see that Jessie's house was fine, they both shouted at once, "Seth's!"

Cassie cried, "Let's go back out to the road, then drive down to Seth's from the highway! It'll be faster."

"Not faster than running along the creek. Besides, we've got to get help. You and Pearl go inside—here's the key," she said, digging in her purse for it. "Call Emmy and tell her to get the fire volunteers. Drew will be back at the office soon, so he and some others should be able to come right out."

"Wait! What about you?" Cassie shouted as Jessie got out and slammed the truck door.

"I'm going along the creek to be sure Seth's okay—that he's out of the house. Send help, fast!"

"But Drew told me to be sure you were in your house before I left so . . ." her friend shouted as Jessie tore through her back-yard and along the creek into the darkening forest.

Her things in her purse bounced as she jogged along. Could Seth have accidentally set off a fire with the gasoline he kept around for his chain saw? He heated with gas, but she'd heard no explosion. What really scared her was that someone might have turned mutterings, prejudice and blame against the old man into actions, burning him out. As long as Seth and, years ago, his wife, Anna, had lived here, he'd been a loner who didn't agree with many things. Had someone used the excuse of her mother's murder to drive him out?

Why couldn't she smell smoke? The wind must not be right. The strongest odor in the air was musty, almost like mothballs. Maybe that smell was from fungus in the carpet of wet leaves.

As she ran, she had never been more convinced that Seth had been wronged in this whole thing. He would never have harmed her mother, no matter what the circumstances screamed. Besides, he would have to be crazy to leave evidence that pointed to him, but who could be trying to make him a scapegoat? Tyler was the one who had cleverly come up with that nonsense about Cherokee skillies.

She was surprised it was so dark in the forest, but the thick canopy of leaves blocked the setting sun as well as the red fire glow. If it wasn't put out soon, would it spread to the woods, to her house? Would the poplar stand of Seth's, where she'd wanted to count sang tomorrow morning, burn?

As if she'd passed through a gray curtain, she suddenly saw and smelled smoke. It burned her eyes and bit deep into her lungs. Panting, with a sharp stitch in her side, she made herself slow down a bit.

She was sweating, but a cool breeze snaked shivers up her spine.

Then something cracked close behind her.

As she stretched her strides, she looked back. What had that been? Just a dead limb falling? Someone stepping on a branch? She knew the normal forest sounds and scents, but that heavy smell, fetid and yeasty, seemed to enclose her.

Her brain flashed back to the night they'd found her mother's body, the night she'd run from the glowing eyes and heard the trudge or shuffle of heavy steps . . .

The scrim of blowing smoke made this deeper part of the woods between Seth's property and hers seem even darker, more threatening. Yes, she smelled smoke now. It curled around her, seemed to reach for her . . .

They are like smoke that floats through the woods . . . Drew had read today from Tyler's research on skillies. *Their basic power is one of fear, dark, primal fear.*

She felt it now, felt something near, watching her, stalking her. Terror gnawed at her courage, ready to devour her. Turning her head again, she tried to pierce the narrow, smoke-hazed shafts of sun stabbing almost horizontal between the tree trunks. The vast, dense forest pressed in on her.

Someone was out here close, something waiting to lunge.

She ran faster. Had Beth Brazzo fled like this from a pursuer? Her nostrils flared; hair prickled on the nape of her neck. Fire or not, Seth or not, she should never have come out here alone. She tasted not just floating ash but bitter, raw terror. Her breath rasped in her throat. A roar sounded in her ears. Was it just her memories from the sound of Indian Falls? No high whine intermingled with the sound. This muted roar reminded her of Bear Falls, near where they'd found her mother. It was as if she were near Bear Creek, and she had fallen, lost her pack. She carried that very pack of her mother's, using it for a purse. Footsteps behind her, faster, faster. She remembered that she'd scrambled up and fled again from someone coming, someone swinging a long, silver thing at her head.

Refusing to let the image come closer, she forced the nightmare away. Yet horror filled her, smoky and roiling, suffocating her, trying to possess her.

She burst into Seth's clearing, gasping for breath but only sucked in smoke. Nothing emerged from the forest behind her. She heard only the crackle of flames and her own ragged breathing. Here was real danger as scarlet heat cloaked in gray smoke reached for her.

From her raw throat, she screamed, "Seth! Seth, where are you?"

21

It seemed an eternity that Jessie paced the clearing alone, waiting for help. She shouted for Seth, alternating horrified looks at the flames with glances over her shoulder at the woods. The crackle of flames obscured all other sounds. Nothing leapt at her from the forest. She must have spooked herself.

Seth's truck was parked in the clearing, and that scared her, too, not only because it could be devoured by the fire, but because it could mean he might be home, trapped inside. The blackened roof had partly collapsed; heat had blown the windows out. Fire must have ravaged the interior.

Finally, the ladder truck—the only truck of the Deep Down Volunteer Fire Department, mostly funded by Vern Tarver— rolled down the lane. Four volunteer firefighters jumped out and began pumping water from the truck's tank. Because they wore big boots, heavy coats and helmets, she couldn't tell who they were for sure, except for Vern. She knew Drew was a volunteer, too, but he wasn't here.

Cassie parked down the lane. Holding Pearl's hand, she came to stand beside Jessie with their arms around each other and Pearl pressed between. A small crowd, including Tyler, showed up to gawk. He shot photos from several angles, needing no strobes to light the night.

After parking down the road, Drew arrived. In the dimming light of dancing flames, his eyes met Jessie's. He gave her a quick nod before he hurried to the fire truck, yanked on a coat and helmet and raced to help.

"Where's Seth?" she heard him ask the other volunteers.

"If he's trapped inside, he's gone," one of

the other men shouted. "Been too hot to go in. Ask Mariah's girl—she got here first."

Drew strode over to her.

"I never saw Seth," she told him as he pulled her a short distance away from Cassie and Pearl. Jessie was surprised how raspy her voice sounded, as if it weren't her own. "I shouted for him, but it was an inferno when I got here. It might be a gasoline fire."

"Yeah, but, once again, not an accident. Next to his chain saw, there's a gasoline can, but it's been tipped and emptied. The windows are all blown outward except for the one near the can, where the arsonist evidently threw something in."

"Oh, no!"

"That's just at a first glance. Not a very subtle arson job."

Behind him, a fireman was suiting up in heavier gear, maybe getting ready to search inside now that the flames were under control. Another volunteer trained his light on the front door they had just hacked in.

Jessie grabbed Drew's arm as he turned to head back. "You said *once again* it was not an accident. Do you think Beth's death wasn't, either?"

"Clayton Merriman hasn't had time to rule on it, but he says the blood under her head came from a lateral blow."

"Which could be from her fall onto the rock ledge."

"He thinks it's from a blunt force instrument—weapon. But how did you get here first when Cassie called the fire in from your house?"

"I ran through the forest."

"Alone?" he shouted.

"It wasn't dark yet. I knew it was the fastest way."

"Damn it, Jess. It probably wasn't dark when someone killed your mother or maybe Beth, either! Whoever's doing this is brazen as hell."

"I was worried about Seth."

"Yeah, me, too."

He trudged back to the others. The man in the heavy suit took a light and went in. It seemed he was inside for an eternity. When he came back out, still breathing through his mask with his helmet hiding his face, he shrugged and lifted both hands to indicate he hadn't found Seth.

Jessie sighed in relief. At least he wasn't trapped inside. Since his truck sat here, surely he hadn't literally burned his bridges behind him and left the area because he was guilty of the murder some suspected him of.

Vern continued to spray water on the south side of the house; Drew and two others dragged charred, sodden debris away from the dwelling with long hooks. It began to rain, not hard, but enough to allow Vern to stop pouring water on the embers. Even if it had rained earlier, it would not have been enough to douse fierce flames. The thick tree canopy kept the onlookers dry, and the firemen seemed to welcome the extra water.

But then, as if he'd materialized from the last wisps of smoke, Seth emerged from the forest into the clearing, staring agape at the ruin of his house. The old man's legs buckled; he sank to the ground.

Drew went to him, bent over him. As Drew spoke, Seth kept nodding, nodding, then just sat unmoving, maybe whispering something to Drew. Even from here, Jessie could see that he had another necklace of animal claws around his neck and wore a crude cape made of some sort of animal pelt covering one shoulder and his back. His face was smeared with paint or berry juice.

A strange hush descended as everyone turned and stared at Seth. It was, Jessie thought, like a freeze-frame in a movie. Then Drew straightened and said, "Seth's been out in the woods all day. He's grateful for your help."

Everyone moved again, the firemen walking around to be certain the remnants of the flames were out, the onlookers drifting away but for Cassie, Pearl, Tyler and Jessie. Still Seth sat as if carved from one of the tree stumps that remained in front of the ruins of his home.

Drew spoke to him from time to time, then came back over to Jessie. In his fire gear, he was almost unrecognizable. It wasn't just that the soot on his face made the whites of his eyes seemed to glow in the darkness. The helmet made him look as if he were taller and had a bigger, misshapen head; the coat bulked up his already big silhouette; the long-handled huge hook he carried caught a flash of light as Tyler took another photo. An instinctive shudder wracked her. She was desperate to make herself stop seeing that thing in Tyler's picture everywhere she looked. As she'd run through the trees, it was as if The Thing had been in her memory, in her mind.

"Seth won't leave the site, won't go stay in my apartment, even for the night," Drew told her. He took her arm and pulled her a little ways from Cassie and Pearl. "He says he'll sleep in his truck, but he refuses to take it over to your house. Can you and Cassie drive to your place, get some blankets, water and some food to bring back for him? I'll stay here at least until then."

"Yes, of course."

"It will be a lot later than I'd planned when I get there. I'm going to stake out Junior's house. Maybe Cassie and Pearl can stay with you for the night."

"Tell Seth, if he changes his mind, he's welcome to come over to eat with us. What else did he say? What's with the face paint and animal skin?"

"I'm not sure. I think he's in shock. He did tell me he hasn't been here all day. He went back to Bear Creek to look for more evidence about your mother's murder—despite the fact that Vern Tarver had told him if he didn't keep out of it, something bad might happen to him."

"Are you going to question Vern again?"

"Since I only got him to clam up before, I thought my deputy might do that, when she reports into work for him. Maybe it should take priority over starting your sang count tomorrow. I wish I had a wanted poster to put up in his store, but I'd be laughed out of town if it was the one Tyler took of The Thing. I'm trusting you to finesse something out of Vern that will give me a reason to question him again. Peter said he'd be at Vern's tomorrow, so you could keep an eye on him, too."

"Yes, good. I'd love to do something to really help. I'll bring Seth breakfast and see if he'll let me count sang at his poplar stand first thing tomorrow, then I'll go see Vern."

"Even to count Seth's sang, can you take Cassie along? If not, I'll go with you."

Remembering her panic in the forest to-night, which surely was just because she was so upset about Beth's death and the fire, she nodded. "I promise, I won't count sang alone. But we've got to find out why Seth's wearing that claw necklace and animal fur."

"I can tell it's not badger fur. I think it was a way to honor your mother's spirit. Gotta go. See you either late tonight or tomorrow morning."

He walked over to Cassie, evidently to ask her to stay with Jessie for the night, because her friend glanced at her and nodded. Jessie started for Cassie's truck, thinking how the soot and ash on Drew's face made him look like a coal miner emerging from the depths of a cave. It was only when she glanced at her own face in Cassie's rearview mirror that she realized she looked gray-faced, too. She had not realized that she'd cried, but she had white tear tracks running down her cheeks like pale stripes of paint—or ghostly claw marks.

The next morning, Jessie drove to Seth's with Cassie and Pearl following in their truck. He had accepted the blankets and food last night; today she had a cooler of food and drinks to get him through the day. Drew, exhausted from a long, fruitless stakeout at Junior Semple's, had gone into Highboro to confer with the coroner. When Jessie had phoned Vern this morning, he'd been only too happy to have her come in this morning to "learn the ropes" of grading and buying sang.

It was still raining, but, with Seth's permission, she managed to count his sang back in the poplar stand. Today the woods seemed welcoming, not frightening, alive with leaves dancing from the plop of rain on them. Seth even went along with her, Cassie and Pearl, the three females under umbrellas, Seth ignoring the rain. At least he'd washed the paint from his face. He still wasn't saying much, but, without asking directly, Jessie was trying to get something out of him about her mother's mention of him in her sang count notes.

"Is this where you cut the sang for my mother's funeral vases?" she asked him, after she'd done a thorough count of the plants and recorded her findings.

He nodded.

"I appreciate your letting me count it, because I know you never approved of her doing that for the government."

"In a way, maybe the count will protect the sang. If it's low."

"I saw in her notes that she had written 'poplar stand with Seth.' Were you going to count it with her?"

He nodded. Praying she wasn't pushing her luck with him, she asked, "Were you going to any other sites with her? I don't have her complete notes, so I'm looking for any help I can get."

"No. Just here. Only here."

"I appreciate your returning to the area where she died to look for evidence and honor her yesterday—that's what Drew said."

"He also said you are going to work for Vern Tarver at the Fur and Sang."

"Yes. Most sellers will be bringing in last year's sang as well as this year's, but I thought it might give me an idea of what's out there. In this rain, I'd rather not be out in the woods all day."

"Better there than at the Trader. If the woods are dangerous, I say that place is, too. I thank you for your kindness. Even here in what is called civilization, be careful. More rain with lightning coming," he added so quietly she could hardly hear him as he turned and started away.

Immediately, the wind whipped up. She and Cassie fought their umbrellas as they followed Seth back to the ruins of his house. He'd told Drew he was going to knock it down to its foundations, then build another with his own hands. What else had he told Drew?

Jessie saw Pearl wave to the old man as Cassie pulled out in her truck, heading for home, while Jessie headed for Vern's Fur and Sang Trader with Seth Bearclaws's warning ringing in her ears.

"Bethany Brazzo was killed by a blow to the side of her head," Clayton Merriman told Drew, stripping off his latex gloves as he emerged from the back room of the mortuary that served as his morgue. "And not one from falling on that ledge."

Drew's head jerked up. As tired as he was from his fruitless all-night stakeout at Junior Semple's, his mind and body snapped to attention. A second homicide. He could feel his heartbeat pick up.

"A stellate skull fracture—star shaped," Merriman went on, drawing it in the air. "I'd expect a simply linear fracture from a fall. She was probably beyond help when she went over the cliff. But the blood under her head indicates her heart pumped for a little while after she hit the rock."

As if he recited such horrors on a daily

basis, Merriman shoved the door behind him open with one shoulder and threw his gloves into a waste can. The smell from the room bit deep into Drew's lungs; on an autopsy table in the middle of the room, he glimpsed Beth's form, partly draped by a sheet. His stomach roiled; he fought to keep his focus.

"And the weapon?" he asked. "Was it shaped like whatever smashed Mariah's skull?"

"Not definitive yet," the coroner said as the door swung shut behind him again. "A different pattern could be attributed to a different weapon, or the same one hitting the skull at a different angle. Unlike Mariah Lockwood, Bethany Brazzo had defensive wounds on her hands and arms. I was just going to do fingernail scrapings when you knocked."

"The defensive wounds indicate she fought her attacker? They weren't just wounds she'd get from a fall or a tumble to that ledge?"

"Forearms and wrist bruises on the ulnar side of her arms—the little finger side— where she probably lifted her arms to protect herself. Struck with some sort of long, thin pole or shaft, I'd guess. One bone broken in two places. Also bruised buttocks and a broken coccyx from where she may have fallen down in her flight or struggle."

"And, again, those injuries were not from the fall to the ledge?"

"You find who's doing this, and I'll testify they weren't."

"Time of death?"

"Working on it."

"Tyler says he talked to her on the phone about 9:30 a.m., but I don't just want to go on that, so I'll be anxious to hear what you come up with. Tyler's contacted their office in New York, and they're handling the notification of next of kin. So, could you tell from her position—lividity and all that—if she was pushed over or maybe posed? She looked almost alive, as if she was still running. Damn," he said, pressing his hands to his head as if he could feel a blow there. "A serial killer in Deep Down?"

"No offense, Sheriff, but you look bad. You need some rest. All this is getting to you."

"And not to you? Two dead women with their heads bashed in?"

Merriman shook his head and shrugged. "Served in 'Nam. After the carnage there— not only our guys but enemy corpses, women, kids, too—guess I learned to cope. Sheriff, you want to lie down?" Clayton put a hand to his elbow, then withdrew it.

"No, thanks. I'll be fine." He shook the man's hand and headed out. Admirable. Amazing. Despite Drew's years as a marine, maybe he just couldn't cope with all this, not with Mariah being found like that, and now a healthy, strong woman like Beth Brazzo, beaten, then thrown over the side of a cliff like so much trash.

If anything happened to Jess ... She could have been killed when he took her with him to question Junior Semple. She'd hiked out of the area where her mother had been killed to bring help. She'd plunged into the forest again to help Seth. He'd asked her to help him with Vern, where she'd be facing the lion in his own den, right about now. He'd suggested she keep an eye on Peter, too. He wished he could lock her up until all this was over, but he needed her, needed her in all kinds of ways.

Staring at the prominent scratches on

the side of his vehicle, Drew hunched his shoulders as the rain beat down on him. Lightning cracked; thunder rolled and reverberated. The storm in the mountains echoed the one in his head and heart.

He got in and closed the car door. Gripping the steering wheel, he rested his head on his hands. He was so exhausted he could puke, but he had a lot to do. If he didn't get a little shut-eye he'd be no good to anyone, except to whoever was murdering women in Deep Down.

22

Jessie entered the dim, cavernous Fur and Sang Trader and put her umbrella in an old spittoon. The sweet, earthy smell of sang wrapped itself around her, making her miss her mother even more. Rain beating on the roof sounded like snare drums with the more distant accompaniment of bass drums from the thunder. Despite pools of light from hanging lamps, the gray day made it dark in here.

Vern looked up from dealing with a customer she didn't recognize. "Glad you're here, Jessie. Be with you in a bit," he said and went back to loud dickering on prices.

She nodded, then began to look around. The Tarvers hadn't traded big-time in furs since the 1960's, but Vern had never changed the name of the store, or much else. Though it seemed nearly deserted right now, this was a neighborhood gathering place, the complement to his V & T General Store next door. There, local women congregated; here, it was pretty much a masculine world, but, after all, the vast majority of sang sellers were men. She could hear someone in the back room, which had two pool tables and some video games.

Over the long, wooden sales counter hung a sign she remembered Elinor fretting over. It had attracted her because it was a quote from a Jack London story: "I searched two seasons and found a single root of the wild mountain ginseng, which is esteemed so rare and precious." "There's more to that quote," Elinor, in her best linguistic professor voice, had told Jessie and her mother. "It goes on to say, to paraphrase, 'I could have lived a year from the sale of that one root, but I got arrested trying to hawk it.'" How amazing, Jessie thought, that there had always been those two *yin-yang* aspects of what Peter called *jen-shen,* the great reward and the danger of it, just like with life.

And even more amazing was how she heard Elinor's voice even now, but not the way she'd sensed her mother's voice when she first saw her in her coffin. It was different from the way she had somehow shared her mother's thoughts, her fears, that day she felt threatened in Hong Kong when her mother must have been endangered, maybe even dying.

On the wall between two mounted deer heads, Jessie noted another sign, a typical in-your-face comment from a proud Appalachian who resented being pegged a hillbilly by outsiders: Don't Worry. We Only Shoot Federal Agents and Relatives.

The bearskin rug on the floor was a classic: claws and fangs on display and some backwoods taxidermist's version of a tongue hanging out. The fur itself looked antique and not well-preserved. It would be better off in the museum upstairs, but it did seem to balance the hanging stag and doe heads on the walls. The few times she'd been in here when she was small, she'd always felt a thousand eyes were watching. It was the same feeling she'd had as a kid at Seth's place, only there, everything looked as dead as it was. Here, the living dead had proudly held heads and moist-looking eyes, as if the rest of the animal would step through the wooden walls like in Jean Cocteau's old silent French film *Beauty and the Beast.*

Vern and his customer kept arguing about the price and quality of the sang, which, her mother had said once, was standard procedure around here, part of the game. "You're just lucky I'm willin' to sell you this grade A stuff, Tarver," the seller was saying. "It's the real fine kind. I'd like to grind it up in my sausage mill and drop in some conversation juice, for a pick-me-up tonic with the ladies."

Jessie knew "conversation juice" was moonshine. Vern said, "Marv, all you old sang hunters tell 'bout as many tall tales as a fisherman. Now, the price stands. Least you ain't reamed out the roots and jammed BBs in there like one of your Cut-shin Creek neighbors did last week."

"Now, ain't that a good one," Marv said, slapping the counter. "Okay, sold for seven hundred and thirty dollars then. Hope them

Chinese get a good jolt from it, since I can't now."

Jessie wasn't certain if Peter had arrived yet, but his car wasn't in front. Still, she'd heard he sometimes parked in back, as if he knew his black Cadillac stood out like an ebony-polished fingernail amidst the sore thumbs of the trucks. He could be upstairs in the apartment Vern let him use, next to the two-room museum. She'd always thought that letting the biggest sang dealer in the state stay above this store was like letting the fox into the henhouse.

Vern rang up the sale from his old metal cash register, though she knew his scales were digital and he kept a state-of-the-art safe in the back room. She'd never known him to have a cell phone, but then, they didn't work consistently around here. She'd heard he had a PC but kept it at home. Vern might seem to be clinging to the past, but he did well enough in the present as ginseng middleman. She wondered if the prices for Kentucky sang were still one thousand dollars a pound on the Asian market. It seemed she'd been in Hong Kong ages ago when she'd heard that price, but it had been less than two weeks. An eternity seemed to have passed since then.

She looked around the Trader a bit more. It made her think of a time capsule. The front room seemed untouched with its shelves of candy bars and a soft drink machine. Vern's office shared the back of the building with a storage room and the game room, which boasted twin pool tables and the Nintendo and video games advertised in the front window. She wished she could search his storage and office areas for the rest of her mother's sang notes. Whoever had those also had a lot of questions to answer.

Hearing the click-click of pool balls, she meandered back to glance inside the game room. To her surprise, Ryan Buford bent over one of the tables, playing solo billiards.

"Hey, how you doing?" he asked, evidently recognizing her at once, even in the muted lighting from the fake Tiffany lamp over his table. He straightened with a pool cue in his hand. "I couldn't work in this rain, so I have a little downtime. I'm really sorry about your mother."

"I appreciate that. I saw you at the funeral with Emmy."

"Yeah. I didn't think I should stay for the dinner, though, being an outsider."

"You would have been welcome," she said, walking closer. He was the only one in the room. He'd cleared the table of about half its colored balls. If she played her own game just right, she thought, maybe she could find out if he knew Cassie, especially from the last time he'd been here. She could hardly just demand to know if he'd fathered Pearl and then deserted both of them. She recalled that Seth didn't like this man at all. He'd said something about his killing trees, but deciding what vegetation stayed and what went must be part of a surveyor's job. Maybe she should test the water with Seth first, then come around to Cassie.

"Did you hear about the fire at Seth Bearclaws's place last night?" she asked.

"Yeah. Vern told me. He said it was 'a bear' to put out, but I thought that was a pretty sick joke."

"Vern doesn't think much of Seth."

"Yeah," he said, lowering his voice, "so I gathered. I hear the fire was arson, too.

Makes you wonder who'd want to burn him out, but I've heard some murmurings that he might have had something to do with your mother's loss."

"Did Vern say that, too?"

"No. Maybe it was just something Emmy overheard."

"She's a very nice girl." Jessie leaned her hips against the other table and spun the cue ball across it, where it bounced off the edge and came back. Like Cassie, she suddenly felt protective of Emmy, but she didn't want to scold this man so that he clammed up.

"Yeah, her bright outlook on life keeps me going. But I've been told by her employer and self-appointed guardian, Sheriff Webb, to watch myself with her. He mentioned her trigger-happy father and brothers, but they seem nice enough to me."

If he'd charmed that bunch, Jessie thought, he was even smoother than she thought. "You didn't run into any of the Enloes when you were here last time?" she asked, still trying to get the conversation around to Cassie. He shook his head and hit another shot; the ball he'd targeted bounced off the bumper twice and clunked into the pocket. "Well," Jessie went on, "I guess Emmy herself would have been pretty young then. When was it you were through here last?"

"Five, six years ago," he said. "Camped out and didn't mingle much."

"Didn't you make any friends? You seem to have made them this time."

"I try to get along wherever I'm sent. I move around quite a lot for work. It's not only the military recruits who hear, 'Uncle Sam wants you!' Same goes for us government employees. You know, have government-issued surveying equipment, will travel."

He was as skilled as Peter Sung at shifting topics. "I'm sure it's much nicer at Audrey's B and B," she added, "than wherever you camped out last time."

"Yeah. Good home cooking at the Soup to Pie, too. So, Emmy mentioned you're going to pick up where your mother left off with the ginseng count."

"For a while at least. I'm actually a scientist, working on a breast cancer cure that uses parts of the root to slow the growth of tumors."

Bending low for another shot and squinting down the cue stick as if it were a rifle, he craned his head to look up. "No kidding? I had a friend died of that at home."

"So, where is home?"

"Born in New Jersey but been living in south Florida for years. Man, the Everglades are a far cry from Deep Down. Here, I've been watching out for bears instead of gators or the Ape."

"The Ape? What's that?"

"Just what it sounds like," he said, hitting a ball that missed its mark. He straightened to rechalk the end of his cue stick. The sound of that gave her shivers, as if someone scraped fingernails across a blackboard. "Some locals claim to have seen a big ape with a terrible smell that lives in the swamps."

"Florida's answer to Bigfoot, the Yeti or the Abominable Snowman?"

"Exactly," he said with a smile that flashed perfect teeth. "It can't all be legend, not in so many places."

"I suppose you believe in the Loch Ness Monster, too," she said, but her heart was thudding so hard she was afraid he could hear it. Since he worked in the woods alone, should she tell him about Tyler's photo? She'd better ask Drew first. He obviously didn't trust this man, but was that only because he was protective of Emmy and didn't want new roads for developments here? And Seth detested Buford, so she'd better just keep quiet for now. But what if something terrible happened to him, when she could have warned him?

"You're away from home so much, you must not have a family," she said.

"A rolling stone gathers no moss. Speaking of plants, I only deal with the tall ones that shade your ginseng, but I'll let you know if I spot what looks like a patch you can count. Good luck with all that. With what happened to your mother, I'm sure you'll have protection—a guard or weapon—when you go out there."

He'd made a statement, but she had the strangest feeling he was asking a question: Would she be alone and unarmed? Maybe he was trying to get something out of her as she had him. No, that was her paranoia talking again. She was about to get the subject back to Cassie when Vern poked his head through the door.

"Hey, partner," he called to her. The nickname surprised her; she felt as if he'd been eavesdropping when Drew called her that. "No one else's out front but Peter, who just came in, so let's go over some stuff out here, okay? It's still raining outside, Ryan."

"I can hear it on the roof," he said and cracked another ball off two more and into a pocket. "I'm dying to get back out there, but it's gonna have to wait."

"Now you just mind your manners at Sarah's house today, Pearl," Cassie told her as they pulled up before the Castor family's house two miles farther out of Deep Down than their own. Sarah was the nearest playmate with the closest age to Pearl. They'd be on the same school bus next year, and, hopefully, stay best of friends, just the way she and Jessie had, Cassie thought. "And don't you go telling Sarah or her mommy what made you sick the other day."

"I know," Pearl said, but she was still pouting. "Only Aunt Jessie and Drew can know."

"That's right, 'less I tell you different. You sure you got to cart Teddy along today?" she asked with a frown at the tattered bear. "Won't Sarah think you're too old for that?"

"She has a doll she carries around. It's all right," the child said in such a mature, comforting tone that Cassie knew darn well she'd gotten that from Jessie.

With her old windshield wipers flipping water, Cassie maneuvered as close to the front steps as she could, then leaned over to open the door so Pearl could dash up on the porch without getting too wet. Thelma came out on the porch with Sarah—yep, she was holding a baby doll—and called, "Can't you come in and set a spell, Cassie?"

"Sorry! Maybe when I pick her up. Been staying with Jessie lately and got me too much to do at home."

"Don't I understand!" Thelma called back, wiping her floury hands on her apron. "Those two are going to have to amuse themselves awhile today, but they're two peas in a pod." She waved as Cassie slammed her truck door and drove off. The delicious smell of fresh-baked, yeasty bread that had poured from the house, even through the curtain of rain, now seemed to fill the cab of the truck.

Thelma and Matt had a nice home and a strong marriage. Matt Castor worked way 'round Big Blue in the only coal mine remaining in the area, but he drove home every night rather than staying over in company cabins the way some others did. Thelma loved to do her own sewing and baking, just the way mountain women used to. She sold bread and cookies up-town to both the V & T General Store and the Soup to Pie.

Cassie wished something like that could work out for her and Tyler, though he'd probably try to take them away from here, and her emotional roots ran deep in Deep Down. Yes, Cassie thought, as she made her own daydreams, she wanted a man she could love, not one she just wanted. They'd have other children, too, she'd still do wildcrafting and sell the items to the gift shops and florists, while Tyler commuted to work until his book made so much money he could afford to stay here . . .

Cassie gasped and hit the brakes. The truck skidded on the wet road, but she managed to keep control. Through the mist of gray rain ahead, a dark form darted across the road. For one second she'd thought of that figure in Tyler's photo, but it wasn't that big.

It looked like Junior Semple, but he'd disappeared into the brush as fast as he'd appeared, and she sure wasn't going in there after him. She'd have to rush home and call Drew. Drat, why was it that lately in what used to be boring, quiet Deep Down, she was always calling someone for help?

As Jessie followed Vern back toward the sales counter where Peter Sung sat on a tall stool, she vowed to do a better job of getting things out of Vern and maybe even Peter than she had Ryan Buford. At least he'd admitted that he'd been through here five or six years ago; that made the time-line possible for his being Pearl's father.

But one other thing kept tugging at the thoughts: was it just coincidence Buford had mentioned those beasts of legend like the so-called Swamp Ape?

She'd bet anything that he'd gotten the information about Tyler's strange picture out of Emmy, even though Drew had told her not to tell anyone else. So should she tell Drew that word of The Thing had leaked out, probably from Emmy, but maybe from Tyler, too?

"In only one day, so much tragedy again," Peter said, taking Jessie's hand as if to shake it but then just holding it. "Dreadful about Ms. Brazzo's death and the fire at Mr. Bearclaws's place."

"And Junior's still missing," she said. "You haven't heard anything from him, have you?"

"I have his sang ready to be packed for my drying barn in Lexington, but I've had no word of him or from him," Peter said as she tugged her hand back and walked behind the counter with Vern.

"Is the drying barn that old tobacco barn on your property?" she asked as she sat on the stool next to Vern's.

"Didn't I mention that? We were so busy at the house and with the Plotts, and then you left so suddenly."

Jessie would have liked to have searched that barn and, no doubt, so would Drew. Illegally harvested ginseng could be stored there. Maybe it could somehow be linked to the sang that had been where her mother last counted, or even that she was half-buried in. The sang from what Drew said Seth called "the grandfather tree" was still at Jessie's house in sacks.

"Okay," Vern said, knocking his knuckles on the counter, "here's the quick rundown on handling sang buyers that come in here. We only buy mature roots, at least five years in the ground." From a box on the counter, he picked up a great-looking root and extended it toward her. "You know how to count neck scars?"

She pictured her mother's neck—Beth's, too—bent at a terrible angle from a blow. She fought to concentrate. "Yes, of course. Each annual bud leaves a scar," she said, pointing at the marks on the root. "I use a magnifying glass for that in the lab. I have it in my bag. Actually, I'm carrying my mother's old denim pack, just to have a bit of her with me."

Vern looked teary-eyed; Peter glanced at the bag she'd laid on the counter.

"She would have liked that," Vern said, clearing his throat. "Also, I expect roots to be cleaned of general dirt, maybe lightly brushed with a toothbrush when they bring them in, but not really washed or soaked. Darned if I'm paying for soil or water weight. As for curing, I want them dried, with a white center that will break before it bends," he said, snapping the root. "Now I know you been 'round sang all your life and still work with it, so this is just a reminder."

"I appreciate the review. I didn't have time to ask Cassie about your procedures. Besides, I'd rather hear it from the main man's mouth."

His eyes looked wet again. "Wish I would have been Mariah's main man, Jessie. On both sides, it just didn't work out between us, but at least we parted friends. I thank God for that since she's gone now."

"I understand, really," she assured him, but her pulse pounded. He was still trying to make excuses. All his emotion at the wake, the funeral and now here—could it be guilt over more than a rejection of his offer of marriage? It also interested her that Vern must have shared all that with Peter already, or surely, he would not have brought it up in front of him. How much did the two of them work together on things besides buying ginseng?

"No shrunken roots with the skin wrinkled," Vern went on, "or they dried it wrong, and no way we're paying full price. All roots one-eighth of an inch or smaller should be broken off. They want to sell that as fiber, I'll buy it separate, five bucks a pound.

Last, you know roots absorb moisture on a rainy day, so make a point of that with them if they come in today. We're starting with offers of only six-hundred-fifty dollars a pound today, which gives us a bit of leeway to go up. You okay with all that? I s'pose most of it's old hat to you."

"I understand. I'll be fine."

"Now I'm gonna help Peter pack the almost-wild he bought from Junior Semple, but you need me for anything, I'm in the storage room back by my office. You can't handle somebody's tall tales or sass, just sing out and I'll be right here. You can keep your pack in my office."

"I'll take it back for you," Peter said, swooping it off the counter as he started away.

"Thanks," she said, thinking that would give her an excuse to be in Vern's office later so she could look around, maybe even glance in his desk drawers or whatever files he kept. "Peter, did you hear how Junior was trying to protect that crop you bought?" she asked, still full of questions for both of them. Drew had never figured out where Junior got those poison sticks. Peter turned back, resting one hand on the far end of the wooden counter. She went on, "I don't think Drew and I mentioned he'd planted varmint sticks that spewed poison gas. We almost got zapped by one."

"Varmint sticks? I don't know what those are. Poison gas?"

"I'll explain it to you," Vern said as he rose, too.

Jessie was torn between keeping up the chatter or letting them go. She didn't want to push her luck by grilling them right now, but she might not have a chance later and Drew was depending on her.

"It's lucky," she said to Peter, "you weren't dealing with Junior anywhere but from his jail cell, or you could have been hurt. I'm sure he was glad you bailed him out."

"I believe the man must be claustrophobic—he was desperate to escape his cell—but I didn't know he was deadly dangerous. Poison gas!" he repeated. "Amazing and appalling what desperate measures men go to for *jen-shen.* I suppose what I paid Junior sounded good to him, but virtually wild like his runs only about sixty dollars a pound right now. The farm-grown grade from Wisconsin is barely thirty dollars. All that to say how valuable by comparison is the wild sang. Jessica, I'm glad to see you here helping my friend Vern, but I hope, weather willing, you'll be back out counting soon. From what I've heard passing through here—and I think Vern will agree— the harvest is bountiful and your count, even if you estimate it, will no doubt reflect that."

She knew better than to commit to that or the opposite. "By the way, Vern," she added, "I forgot to say I was really impressed with how well the Deep Down volunteer fire department handled Seth's fire last night."

"Doubly sad," Vern said, frowning, "that the old guy's out a place to live *and* that it was arson. I'm keeping my ears open 'case I pick up anything about who might have done it."

He stared straight into her eyes. He couldn't be lying, couldn't be the one behind that outrage, could he? How could Vern have started the fire, then made it back to town in time to get on the truck and head back to fight it? Unlike with Peter Sung, she couldn't picture Vern hiring anyone else to do his dirty work.

"Thank heavens," she said, forcing a relieved expression, "you were in town when Cassie called the fire in."

"Yep, upstairs, working on getting the displays all set for Tyler Finch. He wants to take photos of them 'fore he leaves for Miss Brazzo's funeral—pictures for his own book he's doing, not for their ads. Wonder if the power drink company will still use Deep Down now at all, 'cause she was the one pushing for that, setting everything up. But I got me the idea Tyler will be back to see Cassie and Pearl, even if the ginseng ads are now off."

Ryan Buford had emerged from the back room so silently that Jessie wondered if he'd been standing in the shadows for a while. If he had any reaction to hearing Cassie or Pearl's names, he didn't show it.

"Hey, Ryan," Vern said, and Peter nodded solemnly to him as if they'd already met.

"Hot soup and sandwich at the Soup to Pie calls," Buford told them, ambling toward the front door. "Anyone want anything brought back? Figured I'd see if Emmy next door wants to go along," he said with a wink at Jessie as he opened the front door.

"Better watch out," Vern called after him. "Audrey might put something in your soup, you drag pretty little Emmy in with you!"

Buford only grinned and went out into the rain.

23

Drew's windshield wipers cleared his view as he pulled onto Seth's property. The rain had blurred the windows of the old man's parked truck, so Drew couldn't tell if he was inside it or not. Surely he wouldn't go off into the forest again in this weather. Drew had stopped here to see how Seth was doing. But beyond that, he wanted another crack at questioning him about what he'd done or found up by Bear Creek yesterday—and why he'd worn what looked like war paint.

Keeping his two-way with him in case Emmy called—Jessie was to go through her to reach him at any time—he got out. Seth rolled his truck window down. The sickening smell of charred wood hung heavy in the air.

"Can I get in?" Drew asked.

"I'm not getting back in yours. This is where I live for now."

Drew got in the passenger side. The windows were so steamed up he couldn't see out. Seth must have heard him coming. Drew saw he'd been eating a sandwich and drinking a G-Women power drink, of all things, but then the food had come from Jess.

"Sandwich?" Seth asked. "She packed plenty."

"Yeah. Don't mind if I do."

The old man reached into the cooler at his feet and came up with a plastic-wrapped sandwich and another G-Women drink. Drew thought about Beth Brazzo, power woman, lying dead in the morgue. He forced his attention back to Seth, who was saying, "Jessie has a note in here to come eat supper with her tonight. A good woman, like her mother."

"Amen to that."

They ate in silence for a moment. Whole

grain bread, cheese, meat, mustard, lettuce, dill pickles. Drew didn't realize he'd been so hungry. Maybe food and the power drink would pick up his strength. The rain seemed to be letting up a bit.

"So, what?" Seth asked, then crunched into an apple.

"I need to know more about what you found—or didn't—yesterday up by Bear Creek."

Seth chewed and swallowed. He took so long Drew thought he would refuse to answer. "I found more badger fur at about a six-foot height on the grandfather tree where Mariah was laid. It wasn't easy to see, so don't beat yourself up for not catching it before."

"The other day, you didn't want to so much as look at that tree, let alone to approach it."

"Old ways die hard."

"Did you bring the fur back so we—I—can match it?"

He nodded, but said nothing else.

"You dressed the way you did and wore the face paint—"

"Blackberry juice with sawdust—"

"—to honor Mariah?"

"To honor the tree. I keep thinking this," he said, shaking his head as his voice became awed. "Did my house burn because I invaded sacred ground, the very place where some of my people once hid to save their lives—and some died?"

"You told me some hid there but not that they died there."

"The government soldiers said to assemble near Bear Creek for the march west. When they were found hiding, some were stabbed or hacked to death with bayonets. I only tell you this because you believe me."

"I do, Seth," he said, turning to face him more squarely. "I'm really sorry. A death tree, not just a grandfather tree. But you don't believe that about the tree cursing you by burning your house? I'm telling you, someone human started it."

"I know," he said, pounding a fist on the steering wheel. "It wasn't a curse any more than some strange creature killed Mariah."

"But you don't sound convinced."

Seth shrugged. "As I said, old ways die hard."

"I need your help again. What the hell are we going to do with badger claw marks on her and badger fur six feet up a tree, in the sang leaves, or anywhere else? I know you don't like to talk about your heritage, but—"

"I like to talk about it with someone who honors it, not someone who does not."

"Okay. What can you tell me about skillies?"

Seth looked even more shocked than when he'd seen his house on fire. His narrow eyes widened; his jaw dropped.

"What?" Drew asked. "Is it some sacred secret?"

"No. But from the first time I saw Tyler Finch's photo, I thought it looked like a skilly."

"You believe in them?"

"My people believed in them years ago, the *kecleh-kudleh,* the hairy savages who came to snatch souls away and spread fear. Now, I believe in them with my heart but not my head."

The nape of Drew's neck felt as if it had been stroked by an icy hand. No wonder Seth had not brought up skillies before. He was already the hated target of rumors and arson, so why tell anyone that The Thing looked like a Cherokee mythical beast?

"Anybody else around here ever mention them?" Drew asked. "Or did you mention them? To Vern? Peter Sung? Junior Semple? Tyler Finch? Anyone?"

"No. Well, maybe I told Mariah, but she didn't pose for that picture or kill herself."

"I just can't accept—in my head *or* heart—that we're dealing with the supernatural. There's no way that—" He jumped when his two-way buzzed. "Gotta take this. If it's nothing, I'll be back. Maybe I'll see you at Jess's for supper."

He got out, slammed the door and ran to his truck. It was Emmy; he steeled himself for bad news.

"Drew, Cassie Keenan spotted Junior Semple crossing the highway between Castors' place and hers. She called me from her house. He was heading east."

"Tell her I need more specific directions— where he crossed. I'm heading there now, so call me back."

He spun his wheels in the mud to get traction, fishtailed, then tore out of Seth's lane.

Jessie was starting to believe that signs from heaven were telling her to search

Vern's storage room and office. He'd just received a call from Widow McGillan up by Crazy Creek, who said that she had a sack of old sang she wanted to sell, but she wanted him to come up and buy it rather than coming in. Peter had driven back to Lexington with boxes of Junior Semple's ginseng in his trunk. But for an occasional seller coming in, she'd been left alone in the store.

She wasn't sure whether Drew would approve of her actually searching Vern's property, but she couldn't miss the opportunity to find something to link him to her mother's stolen sang counts, or something he'd written that might link him to an ongoing disagreement with her mother—anything. Keeping an ear attuned to the front door in case anyone came in, especially since the rain seemed to be letting up, she went down the hall to peek in the storage room and Vern's office.

Both were small rooms without windows. First, she opened the heavy door to the storage room; it had a long table and shelves filled with wooden boxes, obviously stuffed with sang. A small, grated vent high on the outside wall let in air and a tiny shaft of light. She sneezed at the dust from the packing Vern and Peter had done. She noted a bolt lock on the outside of the door, but not the inside. Closing the door behind her, she left it as she'd found it.

She went across the narrow hall to Vern's office. Unsure if it would be locked, she turned the knob and slowly opened the door. Darkness. She felt along the wall and clicked on the light. A small black safe sat in the corner behind a large, neat oak desk and four beige metal filing cabinets. Two chairs were crammed in, one behind the desk, the other, with her mother's denim bag on it which Peter had put there for her—near the door. She stepped inside.

The wall facing the desk was filled with large, framed, black-and-white photos of his parents and grandparents, standing in front of the Trader. A phone sat on the desk, surrounded by tidy stacks of papers. She knew better than to think her mother's notes might be out in the open, but she quickly rifled through the stacks anyway, then tamped them back into crisp piles. It would take forever to really search here. She'd have to snatch time piecemeal when she got the chance.

Besides the hall door she'd come through, the office had two other doors side by side, both closed. She opened the first—a bathroom, toilet and washbasin with a mirror. The next opened to a closet with large, shelved boxes, each neatly labeled in big printing SANG #4. The closet didn't smell like sang. It was more like mothballs, though how could she tell when the entire store was redolent with aromas. After being here awhile, she was probably as nose-dead as someone working in a perfume shop.

"Darn!" she muttered, when she heard the front door open and someone come in. She turned out the office light and hurried down the hall to see who it was.

Despite the fact the rain had stopped and he'd said he had work to do, Ryan Buford was back.

By the time Drew got near the spot where Cassie had seen Junior, Emmy had called back with better directions. Women and directions, he thought. Did Emmy and Cassie think he could find Junior in this overgrown area if their only direction was a two-mile stretch of road?

He shook his head to clear it. He was not only exhausted but feeling desperate and angry. He had to calm down. The fact that it had rained actually helped him find tracks this time, whereas the leaf litter up by Bear Creek had obscured footprints. In ten minutes he'd found fresh boot tracks heading from the spot and in the direction Cassie had said—due east. As far as Drew knew, no one lived out this way anymore. Hunters might come through, but there were no access roads in the area.

With his semiauto pistol in its holster and his 12-gauge shotgun in his hands, he headed deeper into the undergrowth and trees. If Junior was armed—Cassie wasn't sure—it would probably be with his Remington 12-gauge firearm, the deer-hunting weapon of choice around here for years. Drew was pretty sure that Junior hated being locked up so much that he wouldn't hesitate to shoot. Besides, he was in much more trouble than last time, and if he'd had anything to do with Mariah's death, he could be desperate if cornered.

Drew also figured that there could be

more between Peter Sung and Junior than a one-time deal for sang and bail money. Such as free varmint sticks to protect the crop. Such as orders and cash to be sure Mariah Lockwood's ginseng count was good enough to keep the stuff flowing through Peter's pockets to the Kulong family. Or if this year's count would be low, Peter would want to somehow stop her reporting it, until they could find someone else to count who could be bribed.

Occasionally, Drew lost the tracks in leaves or grass, but managed to pick them up again. Where in hell was the guy going? If he'd been hiding out, wouldn't he have stuck to an area closer to home he knew better and where he could sneak in to see his wife?

He was careful not just to keep his head down, but to look ahead too, in case Junior had stopped or sensed pursuit. Mountain men had been known to "get the notion" that tipped them off to someone else nearby in the woods.

Drew wondered again about Jess's vision of her mother's death, the old mountain sixth sense. It wasn't exactly a psychic ability and seemed to come to the person in random fashion, as if they could not control it, but—

A sharp sound! The crack of a limb? He jumped behind a tree. In a small clearing up ahead, smoke—or was that just a drifting wisp of mountain fog?

Holding his shotgun ready, he moved closer, going from tree to tree, not coming directly in, but edging around the small clearing. He watched where he stepped, even tried to make his breathing more shallow. Not since basic training had he stalked someone like this. Stalked someone—was that what The Thing was doing in the forest the day Tyler took that picture? And who was it stalking then? Another woman to murder? Even Cassie or Pearl?

"I saw Vern and Peter leave while I was sitting in the restaurant," Ryan told Jessie as he came in, closed the door and leaned against it. He looked really nervous. Though her instinct was to retreat, she walked closer to him so they could both be seen through the front windows. She wished she wasn't so on edge, so paranoid. Had he come to admit he had fathered Pearl?

"I just wanted to tell you something,"

Ryan said, "without them hearing me. I know you're close to Sheriff Webb. I don't want to get in the middle of any of this, but he should know Vern's been really bad-mouthing Seth, even stirring up feelings against him over your mother's murder."

"I knew it! I got that idea from what you told me about Vern's sick joke over the fire being a bear to put out."

"Yeah. The guy seems prejudiced against Seth."

Or jealous of how her mother had admired Seth, she thought. Knowing full well that Seth didn't like Ryan, she asked, "Have you had the chance to get to know Seth? I appreciate your standing up for him."

"Tell you the truth, last time I was here he cussed me out for planning more roads around here, mostly, I think, because it would cause trees to be cut down. Government red tape halted my work then, but I'm back now to pick up the assignment. The old guy should accept that progress is necessary."

So, Ryan was an honest man, or at least was willing to admit that Seth didn't like him. "So why are you standing up for Seth?"

He stood up straighter, not leaning against the door. "Basic human decency. Down where I've lived for years, the Seminole tribe interests me, too. They've got big casinos raking in a fortune and a couple of reservations, but years ago they were driven off their land, just like the Cherokees up here. It just wasn't fair, and still isn't."

"I'll let the sheriff know what you said. You should tell Seth you admire the Seminoles and Cherokees."

"I hate to admit it, but I'm a little afraid of him. He has a terrible temper he hides under that supposedly stoic nature. One other thing." He shifted his feet as if he needed to get going. "I don't want to get Emmy in trouble, either, but I told her she needs to let the sheriff know she did tell me about that weird photo the New York photographer took—just today at lunch. She was worried about me since I need to go back into the general area where she thought it was taken."

"I wanted to tell you about that, especially when you mentioned all those Bigfoot-type-legends, but we don't want rumors getting out."

"Mum's the word with me. I don't really

believe in the Florida Swamp Ape, either, or we'd have photos or bones. The thing is, I think I have proof Vern could be behind that photo—be *in* that photo. Have you taken a look at his upstairs museum recently?" he asked, with a roll of his eyes.

"No, but I'm supposed to help get it ready for Tyler Finch to take pictures there."

"I know it's kind of a joke around here, but just for the heck of it, I went through it last time I was here. He's got a mannequin wearing a costume from some kind of Siberian ginseng hunter. It looks a lot like what Emmy described in the photo. It's a big, fierce-looking thing."

"A Siberian ginseng hunter?" Hadn't Peter mentioned something about that yesterday, she thought.

"I know it sounds far-fetched, but maybe there's some connection, like Vern wore the costume to scare off poachers or got caught by your mother in it—I don't know. Listen, I got to get back to work."

"Ryan, thanks."

"Sure. But I'd appreciate it if you don't get me in trouble with Vern. He's big man about town around here, so I hesitated to say anything. Got to go."

The minute the door closed, Jessie decided to go see that display in the museum. How could a man who had deserted his daughter be as decent as Ryan Buford seemed? She'd outright ask him next time, but her mother's murder investigation took precedence over Pearl's paternity right now.

Jessie wasn't sure whether to lock the front door or not. She could always tell Vern that business was slow and she decided to take a look at the museum.

But the door opened again, and two of Emmy Enloe's brothers came in, though she wasn't certain of their first names. Taking a look at something as far out as a Siberian ginseng hunter costume would have to wait.

24

Drew surveyed the irregularly shaped clearing that was obviously Junior's hide-out. No wonder he'd bivouacked here. Not only was there a fairly heavy tree canopy for protection from the elements, but a deer hunter's blind huddled in some berry bushes, making an even better shelter from the wind, rain or cold.

But on second glance, it was obvious from Junior's wet sleeping bag that he was not using the small, square, roofed canvas shelter. Sheriff Akers had said Junior had almost gone nuts when they put him in his cell. If he was claustrophobic, was it so bad that he'd choose to stay out in the open despite all the rain they'd had?

And where was he?

His skin crawled as if he were being watched. Slowly, carefully, looking all around, his shotgun cocked and locked, Drew held his ground. Junior's rifle leaned against the hunter's blind. Had he heard him coming and laid a trap, so that if Drew went into the clearing to get the gun, Junior would shoot him with another?

But, no, Junior walked out from behind the trees, hiking up and zipping his jeans. Nature's call, that's all. But before Junior got to that gun, it was now or never.

About thirty feet away, Drew stepped into full view, racked his shotgun and commanded, "Police! Don't move!"

Mouth and eyes wide, Junior raised his hands as if to give up, then shouted, "You're gonna have to shoot me in the back, boy. Then you just explain that, 'cause I ain't goin' in again, no way."

"Don't move!" Drew repeated, keeping the shotgun trained on him and coming closer.

Damn the man, he spun away and ran.

Pointing his shotgun up instead of at

Junior, Drew vaulted into the clearing and pursued. Once they were past the hunting blind, the terrain got rough and uneven, and the wily bastard obviously knew it better than he did. But he was in much better shape than the older guy, and maybe just as desperate. Something had to break to lead him to Mariah and Beth Brazzo's killer.

As Junior darted down a small incline toward where Drew could hear a stream, he dropped his shotgun and leaped off the elevated terrain. He hit hard into Junior. They went down, rolled, clipped one tree—Junior took the brunt of that—then slid into a thicket.

The thorns scratched and dropped rainwater so thick at first Drew almost couldn't see. Junior flailed away, landed one good blow on his jaw, but he had him now. Amazed at Junior's strength, Drew straddled him, pinned him and flipped him facedown, as he had the last time they'd fought. Would the guy never learn? Damn, Junior was desperate. Drew yanked his prisoner's hands behind his back and cuffed him.

Drew crawled out of the thicket backward, scratched and snagged, dragging

Junior behind him. Ignoring the babbling and curses, he patted him down and relieved him of a jackknife, a cigarette lighter, a can opener and set of keys. As Drew stuffed the items in his own jacket pockets, he gasped in deep breaths while Junior whined and hyperventilated.

"Just let me drown in that stream, Sheriff—don't take me back, don't lock me up."

"Then tell me what I need to know." Drew stood, retrieved his shotgun, hauled Junior to his feet and shoved him up the incline toward his camp. He held on to Junior with one hand and his shotgun with the other. "For starters, where did you get those varmint sticks you had around your sang patch?"

"Bought them from a cat'logue."

"Looks like I'm gonna have to question your wife to back that up. Besides, you've obviously had an accomplice to stay on the run like this."

"Leave her be!"

"Let's try this question before I haul you into my nice little jail in Deep Down—smaller jail, smaller cells than Highboro. Is Peter Sung paying you for more than just sang? You two have some other deal going?"

"Leave me be. Can't you just leave me be?"

"Get real, Junior. At the least, you've endangered lives, including mine. You've jumped bail. Now we've got two unsolved homicides and an arson in town, and you could have committed all three."

"What? Who else but Mariah's dead? I ain't got nothing to do with murders or arson!"

"Then we can make some sort of deal, reduced cell time for information. What's the name of the company you bought the varmint sticks from? I'll check on that, for starters, then trace—"

To Drew's surprise, Junior dropped to his knees, pulling him off balance. Though his hands were tied behind his back, he rolled toward his hunting rifle still on the ground.

"Just let me shoot myself!" he shouted as Drew stepped on the rifle and dragged him away from it. "Rolled me in a rug till I couldn't breathe! Can't do that no more!"

"Who did that?" Drew gritted out as he hauled him to his feet again.

"My brothers, when I was little. Over and over when Ma wasn't looking. I can't—can't—breathe!"

Once he assured himself that Junior wasn't having a heart attack, and half hating himself for what he was about to do, Drew shoved the berserk man toward the small, enclosed canvas blind. "I'm in a big hurry to get back to town, but I think you're almost in the mood to answer my questions."

"Don't put me in there!" he shouted, bucking backward.

"We'll just call this our little interrogation room," Drew said, yanking open the back flap and shoving the cuffed man into the small space. He saw a pile of dry clothes and some cans of food and soda pop inside, a storage room that could have made a cozy bedroom in the wilds. He pushed Junior to his knees, then tied his ankles together with the sleeves of a sweatshirt. Drew kicked the cans and piles of clothes outside, then tied Junior's hands and feet to the opposite poles that held the canvas sides erect. He'd blindfold him if he had to, but he didn't think it would be necessary to get the guy to talk.

"I've got things to do in town, Junior, so I'm only going to be outside here for a few minutes before I leave you. You answer my questions, I drive you into Highboro, get you help in dealing with your problems—both the legal ones and the claustrophobia. You don't answer my questions, I'll be back to get you tomorrow, or whenever. Nice of you to pick a place so deserted."

He slapped the flap back down, then checked through Junior's stash of food and clothing while the old man cursed and shouted. Nothing unusual in the clothes or cans, except that the shirts looked pressed and the cache of food wasn't meant to last for long before it was replenished. The guy must have been back and forth to his house, only he hadn't visited during Drew's stake-out. Nothing was working out in this investigation. He just needed one little break—and breaking Junior might be it.

"Pearl, let's go in now!" Cassie yelled.

The child had been playing quietly in the garden with Teddy and a doll her friend Sarah had loaned her while Cassie squeezed rainwater out of her moss on the line, just like she was wringing out clothes. If they hadn't spent last night with Jessie, she'd have been here to get these inside before they got all soaked. No way the florists in Highboro or Lexington wanted sopping wet moss.

"Pearl!"

No answer. The girl had been real stand-offish since she'd been sick, but then she'd been scolded bad for taking those herbs that had made her sick. Magic caves and magic writing, baloney! Sure, little girls had to have some fancies growing up, but one thing Cassie intended her daughter to learn was that the world was not the place you might wish it to be. But then again, she thought, recalling Tyler's sweet words and kisses, maybe there were some happy-ever-after endings.

Wiping her muddy hands on her apron, Cassie rounded the corner where Pearl had been playing. No Pearl. She must have gone into the house to the bathroom or to get something to eat.

Cassie went inside. "Pearl? You in there? You sing out now. If this is a game, it's not a bit funny, so you get right out here, my girl!"

No answer, no sound.

Cassie tore through the house, even looking in the forbidden closet. One thing Pearl never did was wander off. Not into the woods or out of the holler. But after that unwelcome visitor yesterday, she should have had another chat with her about not talking to strangers. She shouldn't have passed the child's father off as a salesman. She should have told Pearl there might be some sort of bear—a beast—loose in the forest, though she still wasn't sure she believed Tyler's scary photo one bit.

Cassie ran outside, shading her eyes from the midafternoon sun. "Pearl! Pearl!"

Panic made her heart thump harder than her exertions did. She ran this way, then that, all the way around the house. She looked in the cab and bed of the parked truck. She looked under the truck. "Pearl! Pear-r-r-l-l!"

She almost collapsed with relief when she saw her, coming out of the forest, the doll and Teddy still in her arms. Cassie's first instinct was to shake her and scream at her for scaring her to death, but the child had the strangest look on her face. Dazzled? Puzzled?

Breathless, Cassie ran to her and simply asked, "What?"

"I heard you calling, but . . . but that salesman was back. He whispered to me, but I told him to go away for you. I knew you were busy so I listened to him."

Cassie's strength gave out; she fell to her knees, hugging Pearl hard. "What did he say—do?"

"He said he's not a salesman, that you were wrong. That he's my friend, and he's got a big surprise coming for me and you, too—Paris visits."

"What?" Cassie cried, setting Pearl back and gripping her shoulders so hard the child flinched.

"He says tell you he's going to get Paris visits to Florida for me where Disneyland is. But is Florida close to Paris?"

Cassie glared at the forest, then stood and dragged Pearl so fast into the house that her feet almost left the ground. Inside, she bolted the door, then knelt before Pearl again. "He didn't hurt you, did he?" she asked.

"No—he's really nice. Handsome, too, like a prince. He said I should ask you his name and who he really is."

The liar was so good at seduction, Cassie thought. Women, even little girls. So why did she have the icy-cold feeling he really hated women rather than loved them?

She stood and ran into the back room, opened the old trunk, and dug under Big Bear for something else she'd locked up there. Her Daddy's hunting rifle and—oh, yeah—a box of cartridges. Would this old thing even shoot? It smelled of mothballs as bad as the bearskin.

"You call Sarah and ask her if you can come over for a while," Cassie shouted to Pearl. "You remember her number. Hurry up now."

"But who is he?" she called from the other room. "He said he's not magic and not an ogre or troll that lives in the forest."

Cassie whispered to herself, "He's the big, bad wolf. Oh, Pearl, I've done such a bad job with you." Then she said louder, "I'll tell you later, honey. You just call Sarah's house right now."

Whatever that traitor's game was, Cassie thought as she shoved Big Bear back in place, at least she could translate his message Pearl had garbled. He might not have told the child he was her father in so many words, but he'd promised he was going to get "parent's visits." There was no way she'd allow that. He was deliberately tormenting her and threatening her. He'd tempted her when he was here last time, and she'd willingly given in. Now he was daring her to stop him at any cost. She'd had to give up a plan to poison him, but no way was he going to poison Pearl with his sweet-talking ways.

Cassie wrapped the rifle and cartridges in an old hook rug and slammed the trunk on Big Bear's wide-eyed stare.

As soon as Jessie had concluded her first deal to buy Deep Down sang from Emmy's brothers, Clint and Amos, and they trekked out the door and drove off, she flipped the front window Open sign over to Closed. The Enloe brothers had said they liked Ryan Buford well enough, even though he was more worldly than their "little" sister. She'd gotten that endorsement out of them as well as a fair price, she thought. Since the Enloe boys thought Ryan was, as they'd put it, a straight shooter, that meant what he'd told her about Vern was probably the truth. Besides, she'd had the feeling from the first that Vern had lied about not arguing with her mother over her rejecting his marriage proposal. The way he'd looked so emotional at the wake and funeral might suggest a guilty soul.

As she hurried up the narrow wooden stairs under the Deep Down Museum sign, she realized she should have visited Vern's displays long ago. But she knew people who had lived within sight of the Statue of Liberty who had never taken the ferry out to see it or Ellis Island, either.

The stairs creaked. She hoped Vern was taking his time buying sang from the Widow McGillan. Crazy Creek was a ways out of town, on twisting, washboard roads, but she'd still have to hurry.

She passed the closed door to what must be Peter Sung's room when he stayed here, no doubt a huge step down from his Lexington home. Maybe she'd have time to search there, too, but only after checking with Drew. She was tempted to try the door to see if it was locked, but she wanted to check out the Siberian sang hunting costume Ryan had mentioned.

The museum door stood open. She turned on the only power switch; the lights clicked on loudly in sequence, from nearest to farthest. The two rooms were quite bright, a good thing, because most items had typed cards with information about the displays. Although the glass cases and wooden floorboards looked clean, she sneezed twice. The place smelled of sang, maybe mold, age—and, somehow, danger.

Jessie walked quickly through the first room about the history of the town itself. Pioneer artifacts, rifles, mannequins dressed in calicos, buckskins and coonskin hats. Vern seemed to favor lifelike tableaus. She noted one small corner area focused on the early Cherokees. Vern must have studied their customs. Could he have used some of his knowledge to make Seth look guilty? She'd have to look at that display later.

The second larger room had a sign over

the doorway, The History of Sang, Here and Beyond. A rather grand title for so small and crowded a space. She entered and scanned the room. Nearest to the entry were lots of sang samples in glassed-in cases and displays of various sang-digging tools. Drew had once said it would be impossible to compare the size and pattern of Mariah's head wound to all the poachers' spades, but maybe he could start with these.

As in the other room, glassed-in mannequins in various garb on slightly elevated platforms stared down at her. In the first display case, a stunning, crimson silk Chinese costume Peter might have donated dominated the case with cards telling about Imperial *jen-shen*. When she didn't see a display with the "big, fierce-looking thing" Ryan had described, she went to the fourth display, an empty case that had only a very tall, sheet-draped male mannequin.

She skimmed the series of printed cards for Display #4. Yes, this was where the "Siberian Ginseng Hunter" had been, but the costume was gone. Perhaps Vern had been using it lately.

Leaning close, she read the explanation and description as carefully and quickly as she could. Her pulse pounded; her knees began to shake.

The wild ginseng hunters of Siberia roamed the forests of Northeast Asia until at least the 1930s. With their characteristic oversized height and girth, they were dedicated to their task from infancy to old age, walking hundreds of miles through trackless wilds. To mark their passage, they left broken branches, so their "brothers" would know the area had already been explored.

They lived wild and solitary lives, carried a long stick to part leaves and grass, and wore the distinctive clothing seen in this display: a leather apron to protect themselves from dew, a head covering of birch bark, which made their head look large and misshapen, and shoes of tarred animal skins. Badger skins sewn together hung behind them on a belt, which let them sit on wet ground, and they slung badger fur with dangling claws over their shoulders to protect themselves from rain.

They viewed ginseng as sacred, the source of universal energy and invisible life, possessing a supernatural force. If anyone dared to steal it, the thief would be found dead with huge, blurred tracks and dead ginseng leaves around him. Although no murderer was ever caught, it's believed the forest hunters smashed their victims' skulls with their bone spades, and sometimes made ritual incisions on their faces with long, flexible knives they carried to cut roots from the ground or with the badger claws attached to their garb.

Jessie realized she was on her knees before the case with her hands raised on the glass, as if she worshipped at some strange shrine. She had slid down as she'd read the cards and left sweaty, smeared handprints on the glass. She'd been holding her breath; now she gasped in air, panting like a trapped animal.

Staring, horrified, at her own distorted reflection in the glass, she knew her mother's murderer had to be Vern. He'd taken the idea and the costume from this case. He had been furious with her mother, stalked her, planned to kill her, but couldn't face her, couldn't bear to let her know it was him, so he'd worn the costume. Later, maybe when he was stalking Cassie because she'd seen her mother before her death and feared Mariah had told Cassie that Vern was angry with her, Tyler had caught him in a photo frame.

But even before that, almost at her moment of death—maybe when her mother had seen the beast Vern had become in more ways than one—Jessie had psychically glimpsed him, too, somehow through her mother's eyes. She had to get to Drew, tell him all this, tell him the costume was still missing.

But as she scrambled to her feet, she realized where Vern might be keeping it. This was the fourth tableau—Display #4. Vern had those big boxes in his office closet labeled Sang #4.

She tore out of the museum, thudded downstairs, into Vern's office. She dragged over the closest chair so she could manage the big boxes. Badger fur hadn't made sense before, but it did now. Vern had tried to put the blame on Seth by using animal claw marks instead of a sang-digging knife. He figured no one would realize it was badger claw marks instead of a bear's. He'd tried to turn the town against Seth and someone—maybe even Vern, if he was quick enough—had burned down Seth's house.

The top box was heavier than she expected. She almost went off balance but managed to heft it onto Vern's desk. It displaced air that blew his neat paper stacks awry, but she didn't stop to rearrange them. As she lifted the big box lid, she gasped to see within distinctive grayish-reddish fur. The badger skin—no, a series of skins sewn together—were folded next to a long, double-edged knife. Worse, badger claws were still attached by the paws, just as with a bear rug.

Evidence! Proof that Vern Tarver was a murderer! And the smell from the skins: it was so reminiscent of the strange scent she'd encountered in the Hong Kong ginseng market, which must actually have emanated from her nightmare of her mother's death. She had to let herself remember all that again, because maybe the vision went even further. Instead of thrusting it away, she should let it come and maybe glimpse Vern in that costume.

She lifted down and opened the next box: thick-soled shoes wrapped in some kind of oilskin and a hump-shaped hat made of tree bark, though it wasn't birch. No wonder the creature seemed so tall and left blurred footprints. No doubt the other boxes held some sort of bodysuit and mask, maybe even the sang spade that had smashed her mother's skull— perhaps Beth Brazzo's, too. Surely, Vern had some motive for wanting to eliminate the power drink woman, too, but right now, they had to get him for her mother's murder.

Jessie was desperate to put these boxes in the trunk of her car before Vern returned, then get out of here to find Drew. Or should she put them back in place, then call Emmy to have her track Drew to get him to arrest Vern here with the proof on his property? No, she couldn't stand to be near him now that she knew the truth.

She gasped when she heard the front door—which she'd locked—open and close. Vern called out, "Jessie, I'm back.

You okay? Why's the door locked and the Closed sign out?"

When she rushed to get the heavy boxes back up on the shelf, she dropped the top one. The badger skins spilled out on the floor as his footsteps crossed the front room and headed down the hall.

25

Jessie ran out of Vern's office to meet him in the hall. Trying to look calm, she stood in the middle of it to block him from going directly into his office, where he'd see the box open, the spilled badger skins and his once neatly stacked papers in disarray on his desk.

"Oh, Vern, glad you're back. I bought some sang from the Enloe brothers," she said, forcing a smile, "but I got such a roaring headache I needed to take some aspirin and sit down for a couple of minutes, and my purse was in your office so—"

"Sure, that's fine. Wait till you see the grade A stuff I got from Addie McGillan," he told her, giving a big wooden box a shake. It sounded loaded with roots. "She's been hoarding them for her old age, as if it were a retirement fund in a bank. Man, Peter will want a couple of these babies for his precious root-in-a-bottle collection."

He took a step toward his office; her mind raced. It took everything she had not to scream at him that he murdered her mother, but he might attack her. She had to get the evidence to Drew, get Vern locked up.

Then it hit her. She could lock him in the sang storeroom right behind him. "How about you put it in here, so I can take a look at it?" she suggested. "I saw how neat your desk is, and I'll bet that sang's dusty." She unbolted and opened the storeroom door for him. With a nod, he carried the box in. Feeling both horrified and justified by what she had to do, Jessie slammed the door and shot the bolt.

His voice came as muffled as it was mad. She hoped the single, small vent would not let him be heard outside. He pounded on the door, shouting her name. "What the hell's wrong with you?" she made out as she threw her bag—her mother's bag—over her shoulder, shoved the badger fur garment back into the open box, and carried it to her car.

She put it in her trunk and went back for the other boxes. Again flipping the Closed sign to the outside, she looked up and down the street and sauntered to her car, though she wanted to run to its protection. She not only had the proof who killed her mother, but she had the murderer locked up! She had to get to Drew, bring him here, let him take over before someone let Vern out. Thank God, it was only a short distance to the sheriff's office. Even if he wasn't there, Emmy could call him on his two-way.

She was behind the wheel of her car before she saw a small, folded piece of paper jammed under her windshield wiper. Not Drew's handwriting, she thought, so whose? She unlocked the door, leaned out and pulled the paper inside. Slamming the door, she locked herself inside before she unfolded the note. In large print, it read,

Jessie: Sheriff and me are heading to the tree where we found Mariah's body. I found more proof there of who killed her. He said that you should meet us at the old logging road. We'll go in together. —Seth

At least she knew where Drew was now. With her proof and whatever Seth must have found, they'd have an airtight case. She just hoped Vern would keep until she told Drew. Once Drew saw the costume in her trunk, he might even want to head back to town to arrest Vern right away.

Trying not to speed the way she wanted to, thankful she didn't pass any other cars on the road, Jessie headed for the old logging road entrance under Snow Knob.

Cassie saw Drew's police vehicle parked beside the road as she drove to drop off Pearl at Sarah's house. It was still there on her way back into town. So he'd gone after Junior Semple, but evidently hadn't found him yet. At least she knew he wouldn't see her speeding. She was in a big hurry, only slowing down when she hit the Deep Down limits.

She parked in front of the police station and rushed in. Emmy Enloe was there, but not Ryan. Why she'd thought he'd run right to Emmy after talking to Pearl, she wasn't sure. Maybe she'd been afraid that his idea of parental visits would mean he'd be settling down with a new wife who could help him take care of a visiting child, that's all. Pearl had sure enjoyed the time when Emmy had taken care of her yesterday.

"Cassie," Emmy said, rising from behind the counter and her computer screen. "You look all het up. What is it?"

"It's truth *and* consequences time, I guess," she told the younger woman as she leaned against the counter to keep her legs from shaking. Evidently unsure what was coming, Emmy stood her ground behind her desk. "The reason I warned you about Ryan Buford the other day—it's 'cause last time he was here in Deep Down, he took me for a real ride." Cassie bit her lower lip and pressed her fists on the countertop. Her car key bit into her palm. "We were lovers, but he deserted me the minute he found out I was pregnant. He was real bitter—blamed me, said I was trying to trap him when he was the one who trapped me. Into wanting him. Into being really stupid to think he'd stay with me or take me with him."

"Ryan is Pearl's daddy?" Emmy gasped, then, wide-eyed, covered her mouth with both hands.

"I swear to God. You're the first one I've told, including Jessie and Drew—and Pearl. I know you'll be thinking you can change him, but who knows that he doesn't have a girl in every port—you know what I mean."

Emmy looked like she'd puke. "Has he—been to see you this time, too?" she asked.

"Only skulking around and today talking to Pearl about 'parent visits.' I told her he was a salesman the other day, but I'm gonna tell her the truth, after I tell him to keep away from us again. You know where he is?"

"I—yes, kind of," she said, finally coming around her desk toward the counter. "He was going to go back to the Fur and Sang Trader, for another quick game or two of billiards, he said. He planned to pick up his gear at Audrey's, then maybe go out to work at the old logging road under Snow Knob. I told him about that photo your friend Tyler Finch took, warned him something weird was in the area, but he said it must just be someone fooling around."

"I s'pose you're upset with me bursting your bubble about him," Cassie said as she took a couple of steps toward the door, then turned back. She was relieved that Emmy was not screaming at her to get out of here. "It's not just sour grapes, I swear it," she told the teary-eyed girl. "It's just he can be like day and night, like the way he was so sweet and then turned on me. I found out too late he thinks Deep Downers are pretty dumb, 'a few cards short of a full deck,' as he put it. Well, I gotta go. I'll try all three places. I realize you'll tell Drew what I said, and that's fine. I should of told him long ago for sticking with me like a good friend."

"Yeah—he's great. Gave me this job, let me make a mess of things while I learned. He's out looking for Junior Semple, thanks to you."

"I saw his Cherokee way down by Castors' place. Thanks for not killing the messenger of bad news, Emmy."

"I admit I kind of picked up on how Ryan thinks most of us are a bunch of hillbillies, but I been lying to myself—lying with him, too, the rat. Guess you protected him too long, but I won't make the same mistake. I think he's fixing to move on real soon anyway." She shook her head. Tears spilled down her cheeks; she looked hopping mad. "And here, I was hoping he'd come back if they started to build the roads and properties he's laid out, after the Sunrise Mountain area's cleared."

"Cleared? Of trees? Logged? You mean just a few strips of it, for the single road and a few properties."

Emmy shrugged. Tears dripped off her chin, but she didn't bother to wipe them away. Even with the counter and Ryan separating them, Cassie felt so close to the girl she could have hugged her. But she had something big to do.

"See you later," she said and went outside. She walked right down to Vern's Trader. The window sign said Closed. Where was Jessie, on her first day of working here?

She climbed back in her truck, so she'd have it if she needed to make a fast getaway after facing down Ryan at Audrey's B and B. It was about to be prime time at the Soup to Pie now.

Though she knew it was right where she hid it under the seat, she leaned down and touched the rifle and box of cartridges before she pulled out.

Drew's stomach churned as he listened to Junior's diatribe. He cursed a lot of people, including him. Peter Sung's name was in the disjointed hysteria, too. Drew could not believe an independent mountain man like Junior Semple would crack like this, but he knew damn well that people's childhoods could damage them for good—or bad. He had to get Junior out of here, get him help. He'd have to go at this another way.

He drew back the flap of the hunter's blind and started to untie his feet. It took him a minute to realize that Junior was finally making a confession, but it was so clearly under duress, he wondered if any of it would be admissible in court. Maybe he'd gone too far, but for Jessie and Mariah, he guess he might even go farther.

He strained to hear what Junior was saying. "Peter, he promised to buy the sang, gave me the sticks, see? Promised me a hunt dog—keep the sticks away from dogs, 'cept the ones steal sang. Year of work, poachers get them, take it all . . ."

Drew loosed the man's hands from the other pole but left him cuffed. He sat him up. "You're saying Peter Sung got you those varmint sticks?"

"Yeah—to protect the sang he'd promised to buy. Wants all the sang he can get, at any price."

"What else did he want from you in return for the sang money, bail money and the hound?"

Finally, the man's eyes seemed to focus. "'Nother crop of virtual wild, soon as possible."

"Did he ask you to keep an eye on Mariah's sang count?"

"She came to count mine, that's all."

"I need more, Junior!"

"I told him I thought her numbers weren't so good this year."

That might have panicked him, Drew thought. Maybe he'd tried to buy Mariah off, and she'd refused, or even threatened to go to her superiors. But if Junior wasn't Sung's lackey, would the rich, elegant businessman stoop to getting his own hands dirty with murder? With arson, and trying to pin the blame on Seth? Of course, Beth Brazzo would be in his way, too, with her grandiose, competitive plans to buy lots of local sang.

"But nothing else?" he asked, his face close to Junior's. "You didn't follow Mariah to see what else she counted?"

"I didn't hurt her!"

"Did you tell Peter Sung where she said she was going next?"

"He asked me. Yeah, guess I did." He looked dazed. Was he only telling him what he wanted to hear, or was it finally the truth? "Didn't think nothing of it," Junior went on, his voice rising again. "Listen, I need a head doctor, not a jail cell. Told you all I know. If Peter did more, it wasn't with me. I can't go back to jail!"

Drew helped him to his feet and wiped one of his folded shirts across his sweaty face. His eyes and nose were running, but Drew had no intention of uncuffing him. As if he'd escaped from the gates of hell, Junior hoofed it back to the road, suddenly the model prisoner. The only thing was, if Junior had to testify in open court, would he tell the same story he'd revealed in a closed box?

Jessie was surprised to see that the old logging road entrance to the forest under Snow Knob was closed off to cars. Bright orange plastic tape stretched across the entry where a No Vehicles sign hung. So where had Drew and Seth parked? She did see Ryan Buford's truck and what looked like surveying gear laid out on the ground. He evidently heard her car, because he appeared from behind his truck to wave and walk toward her.

"Sorry about the barrier today!" he called as he approached. He wore a white hard hat and a bright orange jacket that matched the tape. "You might know the day I decide to do this final positioning, it's Grand Central Station here."

"I'm supposed to meet Sheriff Webb," she said as he leaned down to talk in her window.

"That's what I mean. The sheriff and Seth Bearclaws drove in a little bit ago—separately. I asked them both to park out of my way in the brush farther back, just for the day," he explained, pointing toward the north. "By the way, I took your advice and told Seth that I admired the Seminoles and Cherokees. He didn't say much, but he nodded."

"That sounds like him. But where are they?" she asked, looking far past him.

"They just walked into the forest, not more than—" he glanced at his watch "—six, maybe seven minutes ago. I figured it was you driving in, because they said if you came quick enough, you should follow them. I think they were really eager to retrieve something."

"Can I leave my car right here? I'm sure I can catch up with them."

"Sure. I'll bet you can because Seth wasn't moving too fast and they had some stuff with them. A camera, backpacks, not sure what else."

She turned off the ignition and unlocked the door. Ryan opened it for her. She considered getting the badger skin out of the box in the trunk to show Drew and Seth when she caught up to them, but decided not to risk something happening to it or having to explain it to Ryan. She'd thank him later for giving her the tip about Vern having that Siberian ginseng hunter costume. Maybe he'd even have to testify against Vern. Right now, she needed to make tracks. At least she knew exactly where they were going.

Pulling her mother's denim bag over her shoulder and locking her car, she thanked Ryan and sprinted for the forest path she knew all too well.

Drew took Junior to the office to book him before taking him into Highboro. Emmy looked up from squinting at the computer screen. "Oh, you got him!" she cried.

"Yep, and he'll be our guest until he writes out a statement for me. Junior, I have to put you in the cell for a few minutes, but you can just look straight out down the hall through the bars, not at the other three walls. I'm going to phone Highboro and make sure you'll have a lawyer and a doctor when we get there. You'll write down everything you told me about Peter, right?"

"Ain't got no choice now."

"As soon as you do, you can call your wife, and we'll get her in to see you."

He walked Junior down the hall and, though he felt him tense up as if he'd balk, he put him in the larger of the two cells and locked him in. Like in some cartoon, the man stood with his hands gripping two bars and his face pressed between them, staring out.

"Drew!" Emmy called to him and motioned before he could even stop in the john.

"What?" he asked, following her down the hall toward her workstation. Although they were the only two in the room, she kept whispering.

"Cassie was here, and she said something you should know."

"Tell me. Hey, have you been crying, or are those red eyes from staring at the PC screen?"

"She said I could tell you that Ryan Buford is Pearl's father. He's been harassing her, talking to Pearl. He— She wanted me to know before I got in too deep with him."

"Damn him! I'm sorry, Em," he said, putting his hands on her shoulders and giving her one gentle shake. "For her and you. Well, one mystery solved. So she wants to file a complaint or get a restraining order, or have me talk to him? Actually, I'd like to put my fist to that handsome jaw—maybe once for her, once for Pearl and once for you. Where is she now? I can phone her before I take Junior to Highboro for safer keeping this time."

"I told her some places he might be. I don't really know where she went. But something else," she said, tugging him toward her desk. "I decided to use Google to find Rat Ryan through the Department of Transportation that he said he works for—but he doesn't. Look."

He leaned over her shoulder to see what she had on her screen. He studied the crowded Web site page for a minute. "But that's a list of operatives for the logging industry—their on-the-field lobbyists and information brokers," he said.

"Yes, but see, his name is listed here as the senior aide to the Lumber Logging Lobbyists, the LLL. I can't find him listed as an employee or aide or anything for Transportation. In south Florida—at least *that* wasn't a lie—he oversaw the clearing of large tracts of forest to make way for resorts, condos and golf courses. You know, I overheard him on the phone once laughing about some motto—'Cut out and get out.' But I had no idea he meant trees."

Drew felt as if he'd been sucker punched in the gut. Just a few driveways and retirement cabins, my foot! Timber theft or tree poaching was small potatoes compared to what Buford's cronies must have in mind for the Deep Down area. Wouldn't that mean that Buford had a vested interest in keeping the sang count low? If the government slapped a moratorium on digging and exporting sang, locals would be more likely to want to sell land and the timber on it. Maybe he saw Mariah as someone who would lead a campaign against any serious logging.

"Get Jessie on the line over at Vern's Trader," Drew told her. "Then try to track Cassie down somehow. Try her home phone, too. Tell them both to stay put, and patch them both through to me."

"Drew, if Ryan lied about who he worked for, I can see why. People would have hated him, maybe hunted him down around here. You—you don't think he hurt Mariah?"

"I'm not sure. I still think Peter Sung hurt Mariah, so I'm going to call the Lexington police from my office. If Peter's home, they can take him in for questioning. Get on the phone, because I want to bring Jessie up to speed and keep Cassie from facing down Buford alone. Same for you with him—keep clear for now. You understand?"

She nodded grimly as she reached for the phone. "When I heard what he'd done to her and Pearl, I knew my dream with him was over. Truth is, I'd like to kill him with my bare hands, but I don't think I'll have to once word gets out what he's really doing and who he really is."

26

The muted chiming of keys and coins inside her mother's denim bag accompanied Jessie's steps as she jogged the path Drew and Seth had taken. She figured she'd catch up with them before she came to the clearing along Bear Creek. She wished they would have waited for her, but they were obviously on to something big, maybe evidence that could degrade or be taken by someone else. She couldn't wait to tell Drew what she'd learned about Vern.

The headache she'd lied about to Vern clamped her forehead like a metal band. Even as she ran, she fumbled for her bottled water and plastic bottle of aspirin in her mother's bag. Having something her mother valued and carried with her on her last day was comforting. Besides, now they had answers. Thank God, the man who had killed her—no doubt while wearing that terrifying costume—was locked up and would soon enough be locked away for good. Solving her mother's murder had eased the guilt she'd felt over never quite forgiving her for sending her away with Elinor. She understood it, yes, was even grateful for it, but deep down forgiving was something diff—

What was this in her bag? Her hand seized on something long and leathery. She shuddered. It felt so much like a stiff snake that at first she gasped and stopped to open the bag and look inside.

A dog tracking collar! She was carrying one of Peter Sung's dog tracking collars!

She glanced all around but saw nothing, no one. When could he have put this here? Oh, yes, he'd been so eager a couple of hours ago to carry her bag into Vern's office for her. But was it just a gift for her or Drew, or was it secreted here so he could stalk her?

She could not take the chance. If it was a harmless gift, she'd retrieve it later. She dug it out of her bag and wedged it in the crotch of a maple tree just off the path. A large rock marked the tree, so they could retrieve the collar on their way out. It would be something else to tell Drew. Let him decide what its purpose had been.

Her next thought shocked her so that she almost stopped running. Could Peter be guilty of her mother's death, too? Vern and Peter were obviously close friends. If they were in collusion for Mariah's murder, maybe they were responsible for Beth's, too. Peter, of course, had the perfect alibi for the second murder, since she and Drew were with him at the time in Lexington, but he'd been in the general area the day her mother was killed. As for Beth—Jessie had not had a shadow of doubt that Beth had been murdered, too, and by her mother's killer.

Anxious that she'd fallen farther behind the men now, Jessie pushed herself even harder. Ryan had said Seth wasn't walking too fast, though she knew he was usually quite sprightly, even for his age. Maybe his losses had really gotten to him.

Despite the sporadic sunlight bleeding through the trees, even with the bird sounds, Jessie suddenly felt alone and afraid. Her heart pounded, echoing her footsteps through the rustling leaf litter. At least, she told herself, when she got to the clearing and the creek, she'd be able to spot the men. She could hear the creek and the muted roar of the more distant falls already. She was almost there.

Sprinting out of the forest into the clearing, she looked in the direction the men must have gone. No one. Behind her, not a soul in sight. But she couldn't see as far as the ancient tree that had cradled her mother's body, so she pushed on.

The wind chilled her perspiring skin, as if looming Snow Knob breathed down on her. For the first time in her headlong rush to tell Drew about Vern and to be a part of his and Seth's discovery of another piece of proof, she began to shake. Surely Ryan had not been mistaken about the way Drew and Seth had gone. Besides, Seth's note had backed up what Ryan said. But with Drew's concern about keeping her safe, wouldn't he have waited for her?

Maybe they were on the other side of

the tree up ahead. "Drew! Seth!" she shouted, then switched to screaming. "Sheriff! Sher—iiif!"

Something was very wrong. She could feel it, taste and smell it. She was getting out of here. Ryan had misunderstood.

As she shaded her eyes with one hand to scan the area, she realized she was close to the spot where she and Drew had seen the sang patch with the spade's slash marks and the strange berry designs that were echoed in the cuts on her mother's face.

Hair prickled on the nape of her neck, and gooseflesh iced her skin. The headache she'd meant to treat got worse. The boulders being gnawed on by the waters of Bear Creek, swollen by the rain, seemed to waver before her eyes. Had she run so hard that her brain was oxygen-deprived? She'd never fainted in her life, but she felt woozy now. Too little sleep, too much exertion, pressure, grief and fear.

And that smell! Out here in the fresh air, could she have carried the scent of that badger fur on her hands? She lifted them for a deep sniff. The stench seemed the same even when her nose was right up to her palms.

She spun around into the wind, heading back toward the path she'd taken coming in. But ahead, blocking her way, stood The Thing that had haunted her from Tyler's picture.

She gasped and froze. Shook her head and blinked. No, she wasn't hallucinating again. But—but Vern was locked in his storeroom, and she had the Siberian sang hunter's costume locked in her trunk! Or could Peter have had an outfit like that, too?

It lumbered toward her, surely a human beast, not a feral one. She wondered if she could be dreaming, but this was pure nightmare. Staring wide-eyed at it, she felt she was seeing double, the vision both here before her and in the unrolling thoughts of her mind's eye. She knew she must find the courage to let the vision of her mother's death reveal itself, but not now. Now, she shoved the vision away and faced the reality of The Thing in front of her.

Think! she screamed silently at herself.

It wants fear and panic to devour you. That's why he—but who was he?—had gone to all this risk and trouble. Think!

If only she hadn't exhausted herself running in. If only she could get back to the creek, maybe scramble over the boulders to the other side. The creature, with its size and bulk, would find it hard to follow. But she could be trapped against the rocky sides and pounding water of the falls.

It came closer, stiff-legged on those big feet—yes, skin wrapped and tied around raised shoes. That and the headgear made it seem gigantic. It was a monster meant for the midnight hours, but the fact it dared to appear in the slanted shadows of daylight made it more real.

This must be about the same time of day it attacked her mother. The sun was in her eyes but she edged along the creek, trying to get a good angle to flee into the forest a different way from the path it blocked. The beast must have emerged from near the spot Tyler had taken the picture of it.

When it came closer, still without a word or a sound beyond heavy breathing—only its distinctive smell preceded it—she saw it carried a long, silver knife in one fur-gloved hand and a crude sang-digging spade, maybe of wood tied to bone, in the other. The murder weapon!

Under the huge hat, its face was covered with a dark hood of fur cut with four holes, two for eyes, one each for the nose and the mouth. The leather apron, which hid its body, and the cape of badger fur and claws swung from side to side as it—he—came closer. It's a person, she told herself, not some mythic beast! And yet it *was* a beast, maybe more horrifying because it was a human being under all that, a human being doing this. He must be demented, but who had she met in Deep Down that was this much of a Dr. Jekyll and Mr. Hyde?

Her mother had fled from this, and that tough, tenacious Beth Brazzo must have fought it. The results of both had been fatal. Somehow, she had to outwit him. She had to survive.

Despite Junior's pleas to Drew to not leave him in the cell, Drew tore out of his office to the Fur and Sang Trader. The window sign said Closed, but he banged on the door to be sure. No wonder no one had answered the phone. He frowned at the finality of the word Closed. Damn, he wished his murder cases were solved and closed.

Fists clenched, he stalked back toward his office. Bringing Jess up to date and helping Cassie keep Ryan Buford off her property and out of her life should be secondary to arresting Peter Sung. He hadn't even had time to phone the Lexington police when Emmy said she couldn't locate either Jess or Cassie. Neither had answered the phone at her house. Where were those two? Man, he was in a black mood. Maybe he wasn't meant to be sheriff here, because the things he should do right now—get Junior's statement, run him into Highboro and arrange for Peter to be picked up and questioned—were going to have to wait.

Maybe Cassie had come to the Trader to find Buford but had only found Jess, who had agreed to go with Cassie to face him down. Yeah, that was a likely scenario. Emmy said the women weren't at Audrey's B and B, so could they have gone out to the other place Emmy had told Cassie to look for Buford—the old logging road under Snow Knob?

He didn't even go back into his office. He'd call Emmy on his two-way. Maybe Seth hated Buford not only because he wanted change around here, but because the wily old guy had guessed he was the one who had deserted Cassie and Pearl. At any rate, he hoped he found Buford before the women did.

Jessie continued to edge along the creek, trying to watch her footing on the stony bank but unable to look away from what Drew had called The Thing. She forced herself to reason out who this must be. Dear God, she must have been wrong about Vern! But was this Peter Sung or Junior Semple? Why that tracking collar in her purse, if this wasn't Peter?

Could it even be Ryan Buford? No, he could never have raced here in time from where she left him and have put on that outfit. It must have taken her almost fifteen minutes to run back here; he'd have to drive to beat that. Still, Drew and Seth must not have come out here at all, so Buford had lied. She'd trusted him, just as Emmy had and maybe Cassie, too. But if it was him, what was his motive? Peter and Vern, even Junior, had reasons to worry about a possible low sang count and the commercial promotion of sang by Beth Brazzo. But Ryan Buford? Still, why would he lie to her but to set her up for this? Somehow this wasn't Peter's style, and Junior wasn't this clever.

She decided then to risk who it must be. You're a smart girl, she urged herself on. Take your best guess and best shot. Try to sound rational, calm, in control.

"Ryan, stop it!" she dared in a loud voice. "The Halloween garb, your combination of Siberian sang hunter and Swamp Ape costume, is ridiculous! You don't think I really trusted you enough to come back here alone, do you? Once I got in the forest, I called Drew on a two-way radio. He and Seth are right behind me!"

The Thing stopped, shook its furry head—in denial or rejection?—and growled, the sound so real it shocked her. Then it stalked her again, now only about fifteen feet away. Had she guessed wrong? She'd been praying her strong approach could buy her some time, even some conversation so she could try to reason with him.

She dropped her bag to free her arms. Her mother must have done that when she fled for her life, for they'd found it abandoned and ransacked near here. Jessie bent to grab a tree limb as thick as her wrist and a stone, not a big one, but one she could grasp in one hand.

The Thing charged her. She leapt out on two small rocks in the water, then made a stand on the large one, which her mother had called her and Daddy's island. She prayed it would protect her, but she soon saw she was wrong again.

Lifting both the knife and the spade, The Thing waded into the stream after her.

Her instinct was to flee, to plunge into the water, even to run toward the falls. But that might be his plan. He'd tried to make it look like Beth had fallen. Maybe he wanted it to seem that his third victim slipped and drowned or fell over Bear Falls.

Wait! she told herself. Hold your ground for another second. Do not do what it expects.

At least The Thing looked unsteady in the water. Its big shoes must have filled.

Maybe the leather apron and badger cloak would get waterlogged. Steady, she told herself. Don't run yet. She felt her mother's common sense and Elinor's cleverness pour through her. Draw it out into deeper, swifter water. Even if it somehow outran and overcame Beth Brazzo, conserve your strength. Wait until it's almost here but not in range to swing that spade.

Ten feet away, as it went slightly off balance clambering onto a mossy rock, she heaved her stone at its head. She hit its cheek, knocking its headgear awry. It halted, then lunged toward her, splashing, swinging the spade she countered with her stick. The tree limb stopped the impact, but her limb cracked, splintered.

Jessie jumped off the rock, as furious as she was frightened. Her feet slipped on the next rock; she splashed knee-deep into the cold current but managed to scramble up the bank. She could hear it coming after her, sloshing through the water, breathing deep and hard. Dreading the next swing of that spade against her skull, she lifted one arm above her head.

The weight of the swing was strong; she heard her left ulna crack, even before she felt it. Red pain knifed through her, but she tried to concentrate, to keep going. If that thing jumped her, she'd never get it off.

With her good hand, she held her broken arm to her chest, despite the pain that caused her to scream through gritted teeth. Keep moving. Run zigzag. Take the trail toward the car. She stumbled back toward the logging road, then decided The Thing might have a harder time going in the thicker woods.

She darted off the path. But in a splotch of sun, a massive shadow loomed over her, covered her. No way was this monster going to cut her, kill her! Avoiding tree trunks, bouncing off saplings, she kept putting foot before foot, but she was weakening now.

Oh, she saw her mother again—no, she *was* her mother. She'd fallen over a tree root and scrambled up, on hands and knees at first, then running, running. It was coming after her in wide strides at a jogging pace, breaking tree limbs, hitting the bone spade against tree trunks. She was sweating but shivering. Stark fear shredded her stamina, her courage. But she knew at the last moment that her mother had been proud of her. She'd regretted giving her away, sending her away . . . yes, she heard her mother whisper that to her even now.

Jessie saw the shadow of the spade in the air. It whirred at her again, catching her on her good shoulder. Trying to break her fall, she screamed as she hit the leafy turf faceup to keep the ground from crushing her arm. Huge feet pressed against her hips as The Thing towered over her. Then it sat on her, pressing her down under its weight, putting the long wooden handle of the crude bone spade across her throat, pressing just enough to keep her immobile and nearly breathless.

What in hell was all this tape blocking off the old logging road? Drew wondered. At least, Jess's car was here. But there was no sign of Buford.

He drove right through the tape barrier, yanking it all down behind the Cherokee. Cursing the fact he couldn't drive all the way into the forest, he actually wished the road had been extended here. Then, off to the right, like a gift from God, he saw the entry to a new, narrow service road

Buford must have cut through the trees. How deep into the woods did it go? And, if he took it, would he miss Jess and Cassie, since they'd probably taken the usual hiking path in?

Two roads, two ways, always choices. Please, God, let it be the right choice, in case Jess and Cassie were in danger. At least they were together. Safety in numbers. Mariah and Beth had to face their murderer alone.

27

Waves of pain ripped through Jessie's arm and her entire body. With the weight of The Thing on her, she gasped for air, but it was polluted by his smell. He had brown eyes. It could be Peter or even Seth, but she still thought it was Ryan, however he'd managed to get out here so fast. Her head spun; her captor and clouds above her rotated faster, faster.

"Finally, you've stopped fighting me," The Thing said, in a muffled voice as his horrid visage leaned close to her. "And you can stop lying to me. My two-way radio doesn't carry from here, so yours doesn't, either—if you even have one on you. So I don't think you have rescuers coming, unless someone else read my note. Compared to the other two—even the power woman—" he said with a snicker "—you've put up a good fight."

My note! Seth? No, it couldn't be Seth.

The stench of him was not just from the badger fur; he'd deliberately doused himself with something else—mothballs? "I've got to hand it to you, before we end all this," he went on, still out of breath. "I admire your cleverness and courage. Wish I'd stumbled on to you instead of Cassandra, because you and I would have made one hell of a team." It—he—Ryan—snickered again. "You might even have known about birth control."

She tried to follow his words. Some way—there must be some way out of this. But he'd forged that note from Seth, so no one else knew she was here.

His tone went from taunting to irate. "But how did you know it was me?" he demanded.

It was Ryan Buford! Her head cleared. She knew his voice now, no longer a growl, no longer disguised. Which, meant, of course, he intended to kill her, as if there had been any doubt about that.

"I just guessed at the lowest of the low," she gritted out.

"I thought you went for everything I said," he insisted with a slight shake of his head. "Want to know my deep, dark motive before it's lights out? You're a bright lady—I owe you that. I do regret the fact the world is going to lose a cancer researcher. My grandmother died of breast cancer, and she's the only one who really gave a damn about me in my entire family."

"Oh, yeah," she dared, more furious than afraid again. She couldn't help herself. She was absolutely outraged that this smug moron had killed her mother. "Being hurt as a kid's a perfect reason to become a serial killer."

"Shut up! That's not why!" he shouted, ripping off his huge hat and hood. Ryan Buford in the flesh, red-faced, sweating. If this monster was Pearl's father, how could she be so sweet? "It's because this stupid 'sang' is ruining everything I've worked for," he raged, his face contorted with fury. "Some very important people in D.C. had to pull me from getting this area logged once because of your sang—a stupid root stupid people think has power. A hillbilly plant that the commie Chinese venerate! How about good old American wood being the big crop here?"

"Oh, I see. You're a patriot," she choked out, her voice dripping sarcasm.

"I said, *shut up.* I just want you to know you didn't outsmart me, even with your big deal education hiding your ties here. Maybe I can save Pearl if I get her out of here in time, away from Cassandra and Deep Down. I'll be sitting pretty when we close this deal. Cut and get out, that's my motto. With this area stripped of trees—which people will accept, with a low ginseng count—at least for this year with your mother and you gone—"

"And Beth Brazzo," she wheezed and started a coughing fit.

"Yeah, Ms. Promote-ginseng-to-the-entire-country Brazzo."

"Why the outfit?"

"You know, I thought it would cause general chaos, detract from how much I was surveying. But the sheriff sat on the picture I managed to pose for. Even the photographer did."

"As if a series of murdered women wouldn't cause chaos, too!"

"Let people think there's a curse on people harvesting wild things in the woods!"

"It may take awhile, but the sheriff will find you."

"I tried to set up Cherokee Seth, but when that fell through, I fingered Vern. As for this outfit, I've used a Swamp Ape suit down south for some laughs, too. Besides, you know about costume parties, don't you?" he said, bending so close to her face that she could smell his breath—mint—mingled with mothballs. "People in a mask do things they might not do otherwise, and . . ."

He kept rambling, but she couldn't follow him. Leaning forward against her stomach, he was cutting off her air again. Excruciating pain wracked both shoulders, her broken arm—and her hopes for rescue.

Drew jumped out of his vehicle. He'd scratched it up even more by careening down the crude, narrow service road evidently meant for Buford's truck. That vehicle was parked just ahead near Bear Creek, a natural dead end. Dead end, he thought. Dead end.

He got out, grabbed his shotgun and tore along the creek. He could see no one was up ahead at the grandfather tree. Damn, no one in sight anywhere! Why had he been so certain the women would have come after Buford here? If they were back somewhere in the forest, he might have made a fatal error driving in, especially if Buford turned dangerous when Cassie confronted him.

Just as surely as Jess had her visions of her mother's fear and flight, facing down her killer, he felt certain Jess was in danger now. Maybe not from Buford, but where was Vern? And Peter might not be in Lexington at all.

Should he get back in his vehicle or run the path into the forest back the other way? Holding his shotgun before him, he ran.

Jessie knew she was going to pass out. But before she did and this murderer finished her the way he had her mother, she tried to shut out his words . . . tried to hold on to the very best things of her life, like memories to take with her.

Mother and Dad, the beauty of Deep Down. Drew, dear Drew, so young and lost when she first reached out to him and loved him and then they were torn apart. Now they'd found a second chance but too much . . . too much went wrong . . .

Cassie, so different, but so special. Pearl, sweet, elfin Pearl, had come from this fiend who was ranting about being rich and taking his child to live in the very heart of their nation, the very heart. . . .

Jessie struggled to shut him out again, his words, his face. Elinor, her second mother, was reading her poems . . . *"Two roads diverged in a yellow wood . . . Of the forest primeval, the murmuring . . . the murmuring"* . . . of Deep Down life slipping away, leaving forever . . . Poor Drew when he found her body. Dear Drew, it wasn't your fault . . .

She felt the crushing weight of being buried in the churchyard, but then it left her. She sucked in a breath and partly came to, but she knew it was too late. Through tear-filled eyes, she saw the nightmare of a man stand and lift his bone spade, not to dig a root but to smash her skull.

Jessie closed her eyes but tried to shift away. He dripped water in her face. It brought her back when she wanted to drift away. Caught, her hips caught still between his sopping wet feet to hold her here.

Then she heard her skull crack. No, a gunshot. The Thing that was a man still swung his spade, but missed her as he crashed headlong across her, a bright crimson flower blooming in the middle of his head. Lying close to her, he made a gurgling sound, then didn't move.

Startled, Jessie stared up at the patch of sky where he had towered over her. Someone scrambling closer. Dizzy, still breathless, she tried to turn her head.

Cassie! Cassie stood over her with an old gun in her hands. Then, ignoring the dead man, her friend fell to her knees and hugged her. The pain was staggering, but that didn't matter now.

The sound of a single gunshot crazed Drew, but at least he knew where someone else was now. He cut off the path into the trees, running hard, trying to protect his eyes from twigs and limbs.

None of the murders had been by a gun. It could be some local hunter or poacher. It had sounded like an old hunting rifle.

Cassie hated guns, and he didn't think Jess had one. Most women around here could shoot, but guns were pretty much a man's world.

He burst into a small clearing. His entire life flashed before his eyes as if he were dying. Jess on the ground; Cassie hovering. And, from the looks of the man in a monster suit—Ryan Buford, deader than dead.

Cassie cried out until she saw who he was. "Jessie, Drew's here," she said, as he knelt over Jess next to Cassie, trying to assess if she was hurt. Cassie looked dazed and Jessie like she was in shock, white as a ghost, shivering, obviously in pain.

"Drew's always here," Jess whispered, not looking at him, but beyond at the sky. "Here in my heart, even if his father throws him out again."

"She's out of her head," Cassie whispered. "I killed him, Drew. He was going to smash her head, and I—"

"It's all going to be all right. I know it's going to hurt her, but I'm going to carry her to the Cherokee and drive her to Highboro instead of waiting to get a squad way out here. He'll keep. Bring both guns. Come on."

"I think she fainted."

He felt for her pulse. Rhythmic but weak. It wasn't until he blinked and tears flew that he realized he was crying.

While the emergency room doctor and a nurse set her arm and put her shoulder in an elastic wrap connected to a sling, Drew never left her side. At least she thought so, but she was so doped up, so out-of-it that she had even thought she'd seen him crying.

When she woke in a hospital bed, he was still there, pacing the small room. Cassie sat on a chair at the foot of her bed. When they saw she was awake, they both jumped up to hover over her.

"Did all that happen?" she asked. Her voice was a raspy whisper. She tried to clear her throat.

"Damaged larynx," Cassie explained, "but they said it will heal. We've all got to heal."

"How did you know where I was?" she

asked them, despite her raw throat. It helped to whisper. Maybe she'd just talk like this the rest of her days—it sounded sexy, but her shoulder-to-wrist cast and other wrappings made her look like a mummy from a horror show. A horror show—was the nightmare of murders over now?

Cassie was talking. Jessie tried to focus on the words. "I wasn't trying to find you, but him."

"She saved your life, Jess," Drew said, bending over the bed and gently stroking her left cheek with the back of his fingers. At least, Jessie thought, Buford didn't have time to cut her the way he had her mother—at least not that cheek. But what about the other? She was suddenly afraid to ask. "When I saw Vern's store was closed, I came looking for both of you," Drew explained. "But I would have been too late."

"Never too late," she whispered. "We are getting a late start but not too late."

He nodded as Cassie said, "I think that's my cue to take a little walk to the waiting room. Tyler's there with Pearl, but he's got to fly out to Beth's funeral. I'll go tell them you're doing fine—and about to be finer. Is—is it okay if I go, Drew?"

"Sure. I'm not worried about you skipping bail."

Cassie bent to kiss Jessie's forehead and, with a little wave, went out.

"Don't talk if it hurts," Drew insisted.

"Nothing hurts anymore. But—Cassie isn't under arrest, is she?"

"No, but I imagine there will be a grand jury convened to consider an indictment for her shooting her former lover."

"But she did it to save me. Otherwise, she never would have . . ." She stopped talking, not only because her throat hurt, but because she remembered those poison herbs Cassie grew and stored. She'd admitted she'd gone looking for Ryan, and she just happened to have a gun with her, although she hated guns. "Are you sure she'll be all right?" she choked out, then took a sip from the water glass Drew held to her lips.

"With both of us testifying for her and the fact she feared for her life in those woods—which is where we'll use Tyler's photo and testimony—I'd bet on it."

"Drew, I thought the murderer was Vern. That's why I locked him in his storeroom. I hope he'll forgive me."

"A customer finally heard him shouting and got his manager from the store next door to let him out. With that costume he had in his closet—which he said he needed to take to Highboro to get dry-cleaned before Tyler took his photos—he says he understands. But I'd try working for him for free for a while, if I were you. He admitted he lied about how he parted from your mother, too. It's been eating at him. Besides, the illustrious sheriff of the county was convinced that Peter Sung was to blame. I came that close," he said, holding his thumb and finger an inch apart, "to having him arrested in Lexington, and I don't think he would have been quite as forgiving as Vern."

"If you'd known he'd put one of those tracker dog collars in my purse, you would have nabbed him for sure."

"Did he? I'm tempted to report his attempted bribes. But that's small potatoes next to the big lumber industry lobbying scandal that's about to hit the fan. Still, it will be worth it to get rid of the 'cut and get out' scheme Buford had set up, with him getting a huge cut of their profits."

"A huge cut," she echoed, again trying

to put her right hand up to be sure her face wasn't cut, but she was tethered to IVs.

"Your face is beautiful—and uncut," he added, as if he could read her mind. "I see Mariah in you. Listen, Cassie's going to finish the sang count you had planned. Depending on your other professional plans, you can get your ginseng leaf lab going in Deep Down, and she can do the counts in the future—or maybe both of you together—*if* we can convince you to stay. I know you'd be giving up a lot, but—"

"But, deep down, it's where I want to be. I'll see if I can get a grant, commute once in a while to the university."

"Then, how 'bout I start really sweethearting you, as they used to say in the old days?" He leaned down to kiss her check, then, when she turned her head slightly, her mouth. The kiss lingered, both yearning and promising so much more.

"It's about time," she whispered, though she wanted to shout. "Too much of two separate lives have passed since we both tried to get things started and were rudely interrupted."

"We'll make up for all we've lost, I swear it, my love. My partner."

Though she was exhausted, sore and so doped up she could hardly move, she could have flown.

On an early summer day, the thirteenth anniversary of the day they'd been parted in Deep Down and the six-month anniversary of their marriage, Jessie and Drew made a sort of pilgrimage. They stopped at the spot where they'd been found making love so long ago. In the middle of the day, in the sun on the grass, they made love.

"To seal the deal," he'd told her breathlessly when they finally sat up and reached for their clothes.

"I'll say," she said with a sated smile. "We'll show them who should be together! You know, I think we should meet here on a weekly basis."

"Too close to the nosy Miss Pearl Keenan and her herb-hunting mother," he said, with a grin. "Besides, although I wouldn't mind a photo of us together here, I wouldn't trust Tyler not to put it in his next *Wildlife in Appalachia* book."

As Drew had predicted, the grand jury had not indicted Cassie for her former lover's death. She and Tyler were closer than ever and were talking about a Christmas wedding. Tyler still went back and forth to New York, twice taking "his girls" with him. When he was in town, he lived above the sheriff's office in Drew's old rooms.

Holding hands the entire duration of their long hike, Drew and Jessie walked through the forest to the grandfather tree and laid a spray of roses there from the bush in what had once been Mariah's garden. Seth kept the hollow tree filled with dry ginseng leaves in the winter, but a neat row of new sang plants sprouted all around it now, also courtesy of the old Cherokee.

"Life sprouts anew," Drew said.

"It does indeed," she agreed, and tugged him away toward the creek. "There's one more spot here I want to visit before we head back." They were going to a community cook-out tonight, a sort of housewarming for Seth's new cabin. Deep Down citizens who had murmured against him last year had even provided some of the wood—timber that would probably have been cut and trucked out if Ryan Buford had had his way—and they were bringing gifts for the inside of the new place today. Seth's building was done so quickly that he had helped Jessie remodel her sun porch into a cozy, useful lab where sang leaves were proving to provide as strong ginsenosides as the more rare and precious roots had.

"Your parents' little island, where you made your stand against Buford?" Drew asked as she stepped across the stone to the big rock and he followed.

"I felt their love and protection that day here, even though The Thing still stalked me. I'm not afraid anymore when I sense my mother's presence, and think I hear her voice."

On the rock, he nodded, and they held hands. "I thought about giving you your engagement ring here," he admitted, "but I figured it might hold bad memories for you."

"Which I banish this very minute," she told him, smiling through her tears, "by telling you here that, as you said, life sprouts anew. Drew, I'm pregnant."

He looked startled, then he whooped and picked her up and swung her, moss-edged rock or not. "I'm so happy—so happy!" he told her with tears in his eyes, too. Somehow, in this special place, she felt her baby's grandmother Mariah was happy, too.

Author's Note

As a lover of ginseng tea, I've been saving articles on ginseng for years, thinking I might make it "the hook for a book" someday. Ohio, where I live, has some good ginseng areas, but my love of Appalachia made me decide to set this book in eastern Kentucky. Also, as a history buff, I was fascinated by the background of ginseng. It was of interest to such diverse people as George Washington and Daniel Boone, and, in China, to the emperors who guarded their precious Imperial ginseng under threat of death. All this added to my desire to make ginseng a main character in this book. When I read about the outcast race of Siberian ginseng hunters, I couldn't resist using their unusual costume in the novel.

Two books I relied on heavily (among many others) in my research are the following, both of which make good reading: *Ginseng Dreams: The Secret World of America's Most Valuable Plant* by Kristin Johannsen, The University Press of Kentucky. Although I had other research on how ginseng is being used in the battle against cancer, this far-ranging book has an excellent section on this. Also *Ginseng, The Divine Root: The Curious History of the Plant That Captivated the World* by David A. Taylor, is very intriguing. Additional information on ginseng is available on the Web site of the Appalachian Ginseng Foundation: *www.a-spi.org/AGF/faq.htm.*

As for Beth Brazzo's power drinks, much of my research was done by visiting supermarket shelves as well as by noting numerous TV ads and newspaper articles, which promote such products as Diet Pepsi Max and Danone's new energy drink Volvic Revive, which contains ginseng and guarana. Ginseng's botanic name, *Panax,* is the root word for our term *panacea,* so even in the plant's name lies a hint about many cultures' beliefs in its curative powers.

The price of ginseng fluctuates, as do the protective measures each state and the U.S. government set forth to protect the crop. But in December of 2007, as I began this book, "brokers were selling the highly prized Kentucky root for as much as $1000 a pound on Asian markets" and "Diggers who harvest the tiny roots by hand [were] demanding up to $800/pound." (From the *USA TODAY* article, "States Seek to get Grip on Wild Ginseng Market," by Donna Leinwand, December 2, 2007.)

As for the practice of the logging industry (and logging lobbyists in Washington) making it easier to build roads and cut trees, I've seen numerous articles on this contested practice, including, "Forest Official Makes No Apologies for Cut-first Timber Policies," by Matthew Daly, Associated Press, *Naples Daily News,* Feb. 24, 2008.

Thanks for advice on Appalachian speech to Patty Taylor, who lives in Appalachia; to Jeanie Snell for the supply of "sang" tea; to Heather Kurtz for advice on advertising firm campaigns; and, of course, to Don for jaunts through Appalachia as well as for proofreading and putting up with an obsessed author. As ever, to my editor Miranda Indrigo and the great Mira support team, and to my dynamic duo of agents, Meg Ruley and Annelise Robey.

Karen Harper

August 2008